HER FIRST KISS

The cold began to seep into Callie's bones, and she shivered. Jace fished in his coat pocket and pulled something out. ''Here,'' he said. ''This might help.''

She scowled at the silver flask. ''*Whiskey!*''

''Please, Miss Callie. Take a sip.''

She glared at him. ''I'm temperance,'' she said.

''But you're also cold.''

The first timid sip brought tears to her eyes, but the second one burned its way down her throat and into her belly with a soothing warmth. ''That does feel good,'' she said.

''And to make you even warmer,'' he said, ''if you wouldn't think it too presumptuous of me . . .'' He reached out and pulled her close to him.

She was beginning to feel light-headed and giddy. She wriggled closer to him. ''I'm still cold.''

He brought his other arm around her and held her closer. And then she felt his lips on her neck. Mesmerized, she watched as he moved his lips closer to hers. She felt the gentle warmth of his breath on her mouth. *Now may I be confined to the fires of Hell*, she thought, and closed her eyes to receive his kiss.

Her first kiss.

To Erika —

GOLD AS THE MORNING SUN

One of these days

Sylvia Halliday

we will actually meet!

love,

Zebra Books
Kensington Publishing Corp.
http://www.zebrabooks.com

ZEBRA BOOKS are published by

Kensington Publishing Corp.
850 Third Avenue
New York, NY 10022

First Printing: October, 1997
10 9 8 7 6 5 4 3 2 1

Printed in the United States of America

Chapter One

Colorado Territory 1870

It was the prettiest wedding gown that had ever come out of Mrs. Beasley's Bridal Emporium in Boston. Full-skirted white satin, trimmed with yards of lace—an exquisite copy of the very gown Queen Victoria had worn at her wedding. It had belonged to Callie Southgate's mother. She hated it.

"Callie, what in tarnation are you doing all this time?"

Callie hastily reached for the tissue paper to cover the billows of silk and turned to give her little sister Beth a stiff smile. She felt as guilty as a schoolgirl caught fibbing at a ladies' seminary. "Nothing!" she exclaimed—too quickly, too brightly. She shifted on her knees and made a great show of rummaging through the brass-bound trunk before her. "That is . . . I thought I might find a pretty doily in this old trunk. The dresser in the spare room has a scratch that's most unsightly."

Beth bounded into the room, her best crinoline swaying like a bell beneath her skirts and revealing the merest glimpse of her lace-trimmed drawers. She plopped herself down on the foot of Poppy's oversize bed, grinned at Callie, and peered over the heavily carved footboard into the trunk. "That's Mummy's wedding dress! I haven't seen it in ages. I was afraid Poppy had left it behind in Boston."

"Bosh. He'd never." Callie reached up to tickle the freckles on Beth's uptilted nose. "When you can't wait to grow up and be a bride? This gown is just sitting here, waiting for you."

Beth tossed her blond braids in pleasure and grinned again. The gaps from her missing baby teeth made her look like a mischievous jack-o'-lantern. "And you? You've been wearing your hair up forever, and I don't hear any talk of beaux around the supper table. You're almost an old maid!"

Callie touched her red-gold chignon self-consciously. "Stuff and nonsense. Plenty of women are unmarried at twenty-one."

Beth snickered. "Only your ladies' circle back in Boston, wearing the bloomer. They looked silly. And sounded it, too. All that talk of emancipation."

"I was proud to number 'women's righters' among my friends. Heaven knows I won't find any of their quality in this godforsaken territory."

Beth wrinkled her nose. "You sound like a prig when you talk like that. I *like* Colorado. I'll be jiggered if I don't!"

Callie compressed her lips in a thin line. "You mustn't use slang. It's not ladylike."

"Oh, botheration! The man I marry someday won't mind. He'll be one of those miners who goes out in the creek and dips his pan and comes up with more gold than he knows what to do with! And proper talk be hanged."

Callie's mouth curled in disgust. "And tramps into the house with his hobnail boots that scratch the floor, and pounds on the table for his supper."

Beth laughed, a joyful giggle. "That's just the ticket for *me.*" She giggled again, her blue eyes twinkling merrily in her eight-year-old face. "But maybe *you* should marry Mr. Perkins when he gets here. Just your sort. He sounds like a silk-hat mollycoddle from his letters. A regular daffy-down-dilly. A first-class twiddlepoop!''

Callie rolled her eyes. ''Mercy! Where do you get such language? I'm sorry we left Boston. I swan, the words out of your mouth these past three months have fairly blistered my ears!''

''I've heard lots worse at Poppy's store. Dang my buttons, but those prospectors can jaw! You should come down more often.''

''*You* should stay home more often, and apply yourself to becoming a lady,'' said Callie primly. ''And Mummy in her grave little more than a year. You'd turn her hair gray, I can tell you, if she heard such talk.''

The twinkle vanished. Beth fidgeted on the bed and traced a pattern on the quilt with one stubby finger.

Callie felt a pang of remorse. It didn't seem fair to raise Mummy's ghost merely to keep her boisterous little sister in line. But this wild young Colorado Territory seemed to have infected all the Southgate children. Sissy, a formerly placid three-year-old, was developing a temper. And Weedy, tall and muscular for fifteen, had begun to swagger and come in late from town, smelling of Demon Rum.

Poppy didn't seem to notice or mind. He was too excited about their ''great Western adventure''—the spanking-new store, the raw land, the rowdy town of Dark Creek, nestled in the Rockies. This crude house, so newly built that the pine boards still oozed pitch. Callie sighed. She felt like a fish out of water.

''*Will* you marry Mr. Perkins?'' Beth ventured at last, her normally bubbling voice subdued.

Callie chucked her under the chin to show her they were still friends. ''We haven't even met him yet,'' she said gently. ''And he's only coming to help Poppy with the store.'' A lie, of course, though she had begged Poppy to keep the secret from the others. She didn't want to face the truth. Not yet.

But what had dragged her—unwilling, hesitant, reluctant—

to Poppy's room today to look at Mummy's wedding gown? What, if not that unwelcome truth?

Beth bounced up and down on the bed, her exuberance returning. "Mrs. Horace Perkins, Mrs. Horace Perkins," she said in singsong. "Oh, don't it sound capital?"

Callie held up a warning finger. "Hold your tongue. I don't want Mr. Perkins bedeviled by a pigtailed matchmaker. What will happen, will happen. I won't have a single word about marriage passing your lips. Nary a word."

Beth nodded and turned an imaginary key on her mouth. "Tick tock, double-lock."

"Thunderation! Why are you girls dawdling in here?" Big Jim Southgate filled the doorway, his massive shoulders and wide-legged stance blocking the view of the corridor beyond. His shock of snow-white hair, untamed by oil or pomade, nearly touched the lintel of the door; it framed large but fine features— piercing gray eyes, an aristocratic nose, a wide mouth that was accustomed to smiling. Despite his size and bulk, his black frock coat fitted him to a tee, giving him a distinguished appearance. He seemed like a great lord, larger than life, graciously stooping to mingle with mere common folk.

"Callie? Beth?" he said in his booming voice, pitched just one step below a jovial roar. "Is the house slicked up already?"

Callie stared, awed—as always—by his imposing presence. "Neat as a pin, Poppy," she murmured.

Beth scrambled from the bed, raced to the door, and threw herself into her father's arms. He lifted her up and swung her once around. "And I made the biscuits, Poppy!" she said, breathless with excitement. "All by myself! Mrs. Ackland allowed as how they were the most amazin' light biscuits she ever laid her peepers on!"

Callie winced as the slang words grated on her ears. Another month in this territory, and Beth would be swearing like the bummers who congregated around the saloons on Front Street! She fished in the trunk and came up with a linen runner, frosted with embroidery. "Here, Beth. See how this looks on Mr. Perkins's bureau."

Beth reluctantly slid from her father's arms and pulled the runner out of Callie's outstretched hand. "Botheration," she grumbled. "All this fixing-up! If he wasn't such a namby-pamby, he could stay in the storeroom behind the shop. Then we wouldn't have to hire a watchman to keep things safe. Or spend all day fussing over his room."

Big Jim kissed Beth on the top of her head, then sent her scampering to the stairs with a firm hand to her bottom. "Do as your sister says, pet. Mr. Perkins doesn't sound like the kind of fellow who's used to roughing it." He turned to Callie and chuckled. "That outhouse takes getting used to on a cold mountain morning!"

Callie blushed at her father's indelicate words and busied herself with putting away Mummy's gown. Then she reached for her cane and struggled to her feet. "I'm sure it will seem like a palace to Mr. Perkins," she said stiffly. "Beggars can't be choosers."

"Now, Mousekin, that's not fair. The war left him destitute. Without funds or living kin. Like many another man. And I'll allow as how he's roamed about since then, never lighting on anything permanent. But he comes from good Baltimore stock. And my friend Cooper vouched for him before he died. Poor as Job's turkey, he said, but honest. And as genteel as you could hope for."

"But Mr. Cooper only knew him from before the war, and scarcely saw him after. And we don't have so much as a photographic likeness. Only a few letters." She hobbled past her father into the hallway, her mouth curved in a bitter line. "All I know is, Mr. Perkins jumped at your offer of travel money. And agreed to marry me without a meeting first. I'm only surprised he's coming in on the stage, and not a freight wagon, like a piece of machinery or a parlor chair. Bought and paid for. My mail-order groom."

"Now hold on just a minute, girl! You come right back here!"

Big Jim's bellow stopped Callie dead in her tracks. She turned and limped back into the room, avoiding her father's eyes.

He closed the door behind her with a loud bang. "This business isn't set, not by a long shot! And Mr. Perkins knows it. He's here to manage the store. If he looks sharp and proves his worth, I might make him my junior partner. But there'll be no wedding until *you* agree to it. He knows that, too. And if you don't take a fancy to him, I'll send him packing and look for another prospect back East. Do you understand? I'm not pushing you into anything, am I?"

She crumbled before the onslaught of his words, his domineering presence. Had there ever been a time when she hadn't given in to him? "Of course not, Poppy," she said, barely above a whisper, "but . . ." A spark of rebellion flared unexpectedly in her breast. "Why must you send for a husband at all?"

"Because you're too finicky and citified for the men here!" he roared. Callie flinched. Big Jim's hard expression softened; he patted her shoulder with a gentle hand. "I want what's best for you, Mousekin. The happiness of home and husband and children. But I don't know why you have to settle for a whey-faced city boy. I've seen a heap of good-looking prospects since we came out here. *Real* men."

"Who? Miners and ruffians? Ranchers who smell of sheep-dip? Or maybe one of the saloon keepers or gamblers," she said in disgust. At least the unknown Mr. Perkins had some refinement, according to Mr. Cooper.

"What about Ralph Driscoll, the new banker? Say the word, sweetie, and I'll approach him."

"He didn't catch my fancy," she said, tossing her head as though Ralph Driscoll were beneath her slightest discourse. In truth, she'd found him the most attractive man in Dark Creek— older, roughly handsome, with a great deal more polish than the other rowdies in town. But he had watched her hobble down the street one day, leaning heavily on her cane, then quickly averted his gaze, his face a mask of condescending pity.

Big Jim riveted her with his searching eyes. "Not catch your fancy?" he boomed. "Why the devil not?"

She had never been able to lie to Big Jim. "Well, even if he had," she said defensively, "I surely didn't catch *his* eye. He passes me by as though I were invisible."

"Speak up, then! Don't be a mouse. Say howdy-do to the man!"

She felt her face growing warm with shame. "Oh, Poppy, how could I? With . . . this?" She placed a tentative hand on the hip that had never quite been right, despite years of exercises and dozens of trips to doctors and bone specialists. "Why would he want a . . . a cripple?"

"I don't know why that should make you shy. And don't call yourself that ridiculous name! You have an imperfection. Nothing more! A slight *imperfection,* that's all. And you've a pretty face and a good mind. All that book learning. A man should be proud to be seen with you. I surely am!"

Somehow, his faith in her always made her feel worse, not better. If the world didn't treat her as Poppy expected her to be treated, it could only be because she was less the woman than he thought. But how could she make him understand? "It's only that I . . ."

He brushed aside her stumbling words with a wave of his hand. "Mrs. Ackland said you plan to stay here when we go to town to meet the stage," he growled.

She gulped nervously. She hadn't wanted him to know in advance. "Yes. A few last-minute chores."

His brow darkened. "*No,* by jingo! Mr. Perkins deserves a welcome from the whole family. Especially you."

"But . . . but, Poppy," she stammered, "you know I'm . . . uncomfortable in town."

"Dag nab it, I'll not tolerate a mouse for a daughter much longer!" he thundered, storming to the door and throwing it open. "There's no call for it. You're too fine a woman for that. Your *mother,* God bless her, wasn't shy!"

How would you know? she thought sadly. Mummy had never been anything but reserved and meek around Poppy. A frail woman next to a big bear of a man. Completely overpowered. Like a feather in the midst of a nor'easter. She sighed. But she herself would be obedient to Poppy's wishes—because she knew no other way. And because she loved him so much.

"When shall we go into town?" she murmured.

"That's my good girl," he said gruffly. "Weedy will hitch up the horse and wagon at two. Wear your best bonnet." He gave her a loving smile that warmed her heart and left the room.

But when the sound of his heavy footsteps had receded down the stairs and vanished into silence, she surrendered to her despair. She closed the trunk on Mummy's gown, then limped to the window to stare out at the mountains that crowded in on the large house.

The high peaks were still covered with snow, though it was the middle of June. Below the timberline, the dark green of the lodgepole pine was somber, even in the sun, and the aspens quivered helplessly in the sharp, unceasing wind. A solitary hawk wheeled and turned, black against the cold blue sky. A lonely, empty vista, so different from the warm bustle of Boston. But no more empty than her heart.

"Oh, Poppy," she whispered to the silent room, "what if I don't *want* a husband?"

Chapter Two

For as long as Jace Greer could remember, he had been hungry. For food, warmth, money. For the comfort of family. A vague ache that filled his days, twisted his guts, disturbed his nights. A longing that was never satisfied, no matter what he did.

Not that he couldn't take care of himself, of course. He'd knocked around so much in his twenty-seven years that there wasn't a damn thing that could rattle him. He'd starved and frozen, stolen and cheated. He'd had money, and he'd gone begging. He'd shivered with fever and dysentery in a Reb prison camp and still got up whistling his defiance every morning. Life was like that. You licked it, or it licked you.

But still the hunger persisted—a quiet gnawing in his vitals that he'd tried to ignore. Oh, these last five years, since the end of the war, had been pretty good, sure enough. Champagne and oysters at Delmonico's in New York, the best damn whores Baltimore's brothels could supply, the luck of the Irish at hundreds of gambling tables from Philadelphia to New Orleans.

And a smooth confidence game, now and again, to fill his pockets with fresh gold.

But it wasn't enough. It would never be enough.

He sighed and rubbed at the bulge beneath his vest. He could feel the money belt under his shirt, thick with the wads of greenbacks from that little bank outside of St. Louis. Five thousand dollars. His future. His grubstake for a chance at a silver mine in Colorado. Or a vein of gold, just waiting for him.

He'd covered his tracks well. Damned if he hadn't. Shaved his whiskers and mustache when the railroad train reached Cheyenne, given a false name when he'd booked the stage for Denver. Mr. Johnson. Bland and anonymous. The Pinkertons wouldn't be able to track him. And he'd left those murdering bastards, the Wagstaff brothers, sleeping off a drunk in Chicago. It had probably taken them two days before they realized he was gone.

Then why did he feel so edgy? So heavy with discontent that he wanted to jump out of his skin? *Christ!* he thought with disgust. *Am I beginning to develop a conscience?*

He swore softly as the careening stagecoach hit a rocky patch in the road and jolted him to the other side of the hard, horsehair-stuffed seat. He was getting damn sick of being jounced around. Scarcely a letup since they'd left Denver and hit the Front Range of the Rockies—except for a brief stop for a greasy meal and a fresh team of mules. And these last two hours, as the road had latticed back and forth across the rock-strewn bed of Clear Creek, had shaken the very teeth in his head.

He glanced across at his fellow passenger: A lanky fellow with an innocent face and the eyes of a frightened deer. A city boy, used to nothing but soft living. His skin had turned the color of ashes when the coach had hit this particular stretch of steep, narrow road, rattling and swaying up the gulch. His delicate, womanish hands curled desperately around the window frame, clinging like lichen to a rock.

Jace felt a perverse sense of satisfaction and pleasure at the man's terror. At least it had shut him up for a while—a blessed relief after nearly three days of unending chatter. He reckoned he'd heard every detail of the man's life twice over.

The man gave Jace a wan smile and laughed nervously. "Oh, my stars, Mr. Johnson. I never anticipated a ride like this."

Jace settled himself back against his seat and shrugged. "The stagedriver figures we'll reach Dark Creek in about an hour, Mr. Perkins. And he said the last stretch is along the creek bed. Not too much twisting and bumping. You'll arrive at your destination in style. Not a hair out of place."

Perkins smoothed his slicked-back hair, then grimaced prissily at the mixture of Macassar oil and thick road dust on his palm. "And you, sir?"

"I'm going over the Continental Divide, toward Blue River valley. I may have to get me a ride with a freight wagon for the last leg of my journey. Only oxen can make it over those high mountains, they say."

"Can it be any worse than this? Cheese in crackers, I fear my innards will never be the same again!"

Jace stretched a hand out the window and slapped the outside of the bright red coach. "It's these big Concord stages. With their leather thoroughbraces, they need the ballast of a full load. Nine, ten souls, to keep everyone from tossing all over the place. I've taken journeys that were a damn sight more comfortable than this, squashed in with fellow passengers. But you'll survive," he added dryly. "By tomorrow at this time, you should be behind the counter of your new employer's store, charming the good citizens of Dark Creek."

Perkins plucked at the sleeve of his linen duster and made a face. "But I must look a fright." He gestured toward the rice-straw hat on the seat beside him. One side of the crown was crushed. "And look at that. My chip hat is all-to-smash! What will the Southgate family think of me?"

Jace suppressed a smile. If the man's correspondence was anything like his conversation or manner, the unknown Southgates knew *exactly* what they were getting in Mr. Horace Perkins. He surveyed the sorry figure opposite him. When they'd left Cheyenne three days ago, the man had looked like he was going to a cotillion—starched, cuffed, and collared, his white cloth ankle spats spotless. Now his linen was wilted, his collar was stained with sweat, and his spats were soiled from tramping through muddy gulches.

Son of a gun, thought Jace. Only a prissy fool would dress for a big city when he was going to a mining town. Still, he thought, there must be brains behind that vapid young face, if Southgate could hire him merely on the strength of his letters and the word of an old friend. As manager of his store, no less! Perkins had even hinted at a junior partnership down the road. "They can scarcely expect you to look fresh after this trip, Mr. Perkins," he drawled.

"Oh, drat. I did so want to make a good first impression. If they weren't meeting me in town, I could find a hotel and change." Perkins gave a doubtful smile. "You don't suppose the driver would stop, do you?"

The coach hit a rut, sending up a thick puff of acrid dust that filled the interior. *Son of a bitch,* thought Jace, coughing and waving away the gritty cloud. He'd just about been ready to pull out a good cigar. But between the dust and the jolting around, it would be more trial than pleasure. Unless . . . He smiled at the sudden thought. "I don't see why the driver shouldn't stop for you, Mr. Perkins. I think I can arrange it."

Perkins's face lit up. "That would be splendid, Mr. Johnson."

Jace pulled off his battered felt hat and leaned his head out of the coach window. The sound of clacking wheels and creaking springs was intensified. He raised his voice and shouted up to the stagedriver. "Halloo! Mr. Perkins wishes to stop, sir!"

The driver swore at his mules and cracked his whip over their haunches to keep them at their steady ten-mile-an-hour pace. Without turning around, he made an obscene gesture with one gloved hand.

"Son of a whore," muttered Jace, pulling in his head and

brushing back his tousled black hair. He really had a hankering for that cigar now. But it would do no good to shout curses at the driver. The man could ignore him till kingdom come. There had to be a better way.

"Your pardon for a minute, Mr. Perkins," he said, standing up in the speeding coach. He stuck out his head and arms, turned around, hooked his hands onto the outside doorframe, and hauled himself out of the window.

He heard Perkins cry, "Heavens to Betsy!" before the whining wind swept the words away.

He grinned, took his bearings, then began the precarious climb to the roof of the coach, using the windowsills for footholds and grasping the top railing with a firm grip. He stopped for a moment, swaying and clinging, while the carriage jolted across a series of deep ruts, then resumed his ascent. He swung one long leg over the railing, hoisted himself up, and came to rest on the stack of baggage and deliveries from Denver lashed to the roof.

He paused to admire the view. They were in a steep-sided gully of golden rock and earth; it was dotted with trees and gray granite boulders that seemed to have been carefully placed by a giant hand. Craggy peaks, covered with snow, rose in the distance, crisp and blinding white in the sun. Beside the road flowed the creek, its depths roiled by stones, its foam-flecked surface reflecting back the clear blue of the sky—like sapphire chips resting on snowflakes.

This land is beautiful! he thought. He wondered why he'd never come this far west before. It made him feel free, as the crowded, dirty cities never had. They'd always reminded him of the Reb camp, the cold orphanage, the chain gangs he'd seen plodding along red Georgia roads. Filled with hollow-eyed captives who had lost hope. The openness and majesty of this territory took his breath away. How could a man leave it, once he'd seen it?

He remembered his cigar, waiting for him in his coat pocket. A good cigar was almost as great a pleasure as a bad woman.

Though he wouldn't mind a whore right now, either, he thought wryly. He scrambled across the roof of the bouncing coach and plunked himself down on the box next to the driver. He grinned at the man's startled expression. "About that stop, sir," he said cheerfully, raising his voice above the wind.

The driver stared, his jaw hanging open. "Are you plumb crazy?"

"Not at all. But Mr. Perkins wants a fresh change of clothes before we reach Dark Creek."

"Mr. Perkins can go to hell! And you, too. I got me a timetable to follow."

Jace gave him his most disarming smile. "Ten minutes. What's the harm? It would take you longer than that to rehitch the team. That is, if someone should happen to leap down onto the mules and cut the lines."

"Jesus, Mary, and Joseph." The driver glared at him from beneath his broad hat and slapped the shotgun beside him. "Now, what feller would be damn fool enough to do that?"

Jace nonchalantly pulled back his coat to reveal the small, pearl-handled derringer in its shoulder holster. "Not I, I can assure you, sir. Derring-do is not in my line."

"You ornery snake," muttered the driver. "You want your head blown off?" His lip curled in a savage snarl, but his eyes flickered with apprehension.

Jace continued to smile. The man wouldn't risk a shoot-out, despite his brave words. "I have no wish to quarrel, sir. Let my words persuade you. Mr. Perkins is about to meet his new employer. He wants to look his best. Mr. James Southgate. I hear he's an important man in Dark Creek."

The coachman whistled. "Jesus! Big Jim Southgate? He's got the biggest damn mercantile store in town!"

"Do tell!"

"He's only been there a few months, but he's rakin' in the greenbacks, hell-for-leather."

Jace clicked his tongue. "That important? I'll be damned! I'll bet he could be the mayor one of these days."

"I never thunk of it. But I reckon so, when the town's big enough to need one."

"Such an important man. A pillar of the community! Now wouldn't it do you proud, sir, to know you'd done a favor for the new manager of his store? If *I* were Big Jim, I'd be mighty grateful."

"You reckon so?" The man was clearly weakening.

Jace could almost taste that cigar. "I myself will put in a good word with Southgate."

"That's damn decent of you. Just ten minutes?" He frowned. "Naw. I can't do it. Too much fussin'. If that greenhorn wants a change, I'll have to untie the whole kit and caboodle to pull down his luggage."

"I'll help you retie it when we start up again."

"Well . . . I don't know . . ." The driver jerked his thumb in the direction of the baggage. "I got me a payroll for a mining camp back there. They get mighty itchy if I'm late."

"Hell's bells, man. Ten minutes!"

The driver hesitated, then pointed with his whip to a small clearing up ahead, a grassy meadow beside the road that backed up to a stand of trees. "I'll stop there." He looked at Jace, shaking his head in bewilderment. "I must be cracked! Jesus, man, you could talk the feathers off a chicken!"

Yes, I know, thought Jace. Had the talent ever failed him? "Not at all, sir," he said expansively. "You're simply the reasonable man I took you for." And a loaded gun didn't hurt.

The cigar—Denver's best—was even better than he'd anticipated. Rich, expensive tobacco filtered through the crisp mountain air. Worth every bit of that madcap climb to the coach roof. He leaned against a rock, puffing in contentment, and watched a grateful Perkins rummage in his carpetbag. After a moment, the man came up with a natty checked suit; then he pulled a stiff round bowler hat from his leather hatbox.

Fine for New York, thought Jace, *but ridiculous out here.* And about as prissy an outfit as a man could wear, East *or* West. He glanced at his own slightly shabby frock coat and trousers. He and the Wagstaffs had been down on their luck before that bank job, and there'd been no time to buy a fresh outfit before he'd lit out from Chicago. His own battered valise held a spare flannel undersuit, a couple of shirts, and not much else besides his double-action Colt revolver and the fancy holster he'd treated himself to after he'd fleeced that pigeon in Omaha. But, what the hell. He didn't need a new suit. He'd buy himself a good horse and some work clothes before he went out prospecting. And a pair of hobnail boots to replace his worn shoes. He patted the thick roll of bills at his belly. He could afford it now.

Perkins held up the suit and smiled sheepishly. "Handsome, isn't it? Mr. Southgate was very generous when he sent me money for my trip. I wanted him to see I used it to advantage."

Jace nodded. "You'll cut a dash in Dark Creek, that's for certain," he said dryly. Every ragamuffin in town would be after that hat with a snowball, come winter.

Perkins peeled off his duster and frock coat, then paused nervously as he put his hands to his galluses. "Mr. Johnson, I . . ."

Christ! thought Jace. Was he waiting for them to turn their backs, like a shy virgin in a melodrama?

"May I . . ." Perkins cleared his throat. "May I take advantage of your friendship to show you something?"

That piqued Jace's curiosity. Something new? He figured after three days he knew everything there was to know about this fellow. "Of course, sir."

Perkins bent to his carpetbag, pulled out a small photograph, and held it out to Jace. "The Southgate family," he said, blushing.

Jace eyed the picture with interest, studying the carefully posed figures. Big Jim Southgate surely lived up to his name— a mountain of a man, with a strong, handsome face and a generous sweep to his brow. Despite his white hair, he looked young and vigorous, with a gleam in his eye that appealed to

Jace. *He must have been a ripsnorter as a young man,* he thought.

But it was the woman standing next to him who caught Jace's eye. A soft-eyed beauty with a figure that made his mouth water—full breasts tapering to a hand-span waist. She looked lusty, but oddly virginal. He sighed. It had been a long time since he'd seduced a virgin. Whores were more his style. "Mrs. Southgate?" he asked.

"*Miss* Southgate. California Southgate. Big Jim's daughter."

"She looks charming." *And ripe,* he thought. "I reckon Big Jim thinks mighty highly of you—advancing funds for your trip, and all. Could it be he's measuring you for a son-in-law?" He chuckled and winked at Perkins.

The other man tugged at his collar while his cheeks turned a darker shade of pink. "Yes, well ... I'm not at liberty to speak freely. But I have hopes."

Jace tapped at the picture. "And this strapping lad here, between the two little girls. Big Jim's son?"

Perkins nodded. "Weedy, I think they call him."

"Why doesn't the old man get *him* to run the store?"

"He's young, I gather. And turning to wild ways." Perkins's nose twitched in distaste. "Mr. Southgate made it *very* clear he wants a genteel man for his manager. It was one of the points he emphasized in his letters."

"Well, I'm sure he'll be quite pleased with you," said Jace, struggling to keep the mockery from his voice.

"Jesus! Hurry it up, man!" called the driver, pacing nervously beside the coach. He pulled out his watch and scowled at it. "I'll have to cut dirt to get there on time. Them miners'll have my scalp!" He frowned up at a drifting patch of clouds. "And if it rains ..."

His words were cut short by the deafening crack of gunfire, a loud report that rolled across the meadow and bounced off the sides of the gulch. The driver uttered a sharp cry and pitched forward onto the grass, a large red blotch staining the back of his coat.

Jace spun toward the stand of trees and reached for his derringer. Three masked riders were bearing down on them, pistols blazing. He heard the whine of bullets beside his head, then a scream from Perkins behind him. He managed to get off a shot at the first rider, but the bullet missed him. He was just raising his pistol for another shot when something exploded in his head.

He went down groaning, his left temple throbbing with pain. He was dimly aware that the riders had dismounted and were heading for the coach. He still had his pistol clenched in his fist, but he wasn't about to use it again. Even in his groggy state, he hadn't lost his instinct for survival. Better to play possum than hero. He lay quietly, feeling the blood oozing from his head, and wondered how badly he'd been hit.

One of the gunmen scrambled to the top of the coach. Ignoring the baggage and supplies, he untied the bindings from a small iron chest and handed it down to his two confederates. While one of the men strapped it to his horse's flanks, the other rolled the coachman onto his back with his booted foot and began to rifle his pockets.

"Hellfire!" said the man on the coach. His voice was muffled by the bandanna tied tightly around his nose and mouth. "What are you doin'? We got what we come fer."

"Go to hell and pump thunder!" With a shout of triumph, the scavenger lifted the coachman's large gold watch and dropped it into his pocket. Then he turned and moved toward Jace.

Jace stiffened in alarm. He'd be damned if the bastard would get his grubstake! He watched out of half-closed eyes as the man swaggered toward him, holstered his pistol, and dropped down beside him. The man had cold slits for eyes above his bandanna, and the hand that reached for Jace's coat was marred by an odd, zigzag scar.

Jace waited, holding his breath, until the gunman leaned in close. Then he lifted his pistol to the man's chest and pulled the trigger. The man gasped and collapsed against him. Jace pushed away his heavy body and scrambled to his knees. If he was quick enough, he might be able to get the other two before they could react.

But it was too late. He heard a loud shout from behind him—"Son of a bitch!''—felt the crunch of a boot against his ribs, and went down in a hail of kicks. The sky seemed to fill with stars that faded into nothingness. And then, silence.

The shadows were creeping along the steep canyon walls when he opened his eyes at last. The gulch was growing dim, and a sharp wind had sprung up. His head felt ready to burst, and his ribs ached front to back. He sat up, took a deep breath, and winced in pain. It would be a blasted miracle if he didn't have a few broken bones.

He touched his temple with tentative fingers. From the slight indentation and ragged flesh, he reckoned that the ball had just creased his skull. "As usual, Jace, old man," he muttered, "you're a lucky son of a whore." But maybe he ought to wrap his head with a handkerchief until he could get it patched. He reached toward his vest pocket.

"Damn!" he swore. "Those cross-eyed bastards!" His vest was torn open. And his shirt. And that nice, thick wad—that had warmed his belly all the way from Chicago—was gone. He bent his head in frustration and pounded on the grass beside him. Then he looked up at the blue sky and laughed—a dark laugh born of weariness and dashed hopes. "Lord, you *do* find ways to try me."

Well, he'd pulled himself together before. He could do it again. He found his handkerchief and tied it as tightly around his forehead as he could; it eased the pain. His derringer lay near at hand, overlooked by the gunmen. He slipped it into its holster and struggled to his feet.

The man he'd shot was gone; his partners must have taken his body with them. But Perkins lay a short distance away, half his face shot off. The poor bastard. His arms were spread out on the grass in a gesture of wonder and surprise, as though he had scarcely believed the bullet that had ended his life. His pockets were turned inside out. Picked clean.

Jace swore softly. Not even a plugged nickel to buy a beer, if he should manage to get to town. He limped over to where the stagedriver lay beside his coach. He was dead, all right; the bullet had gone clean through him and left a gaping hole in his chest.

Jace sank to his knees, overcome by a wave of dizziness. He'd better decide what he was going to do before he passed out again. Already the turkey vultures were beginning to circle overhead.

The coach looked intact, and the mules fidgeted in their traces, stamping and pawing the earth. He was less than an hour from Dark Creek, he reckoned. Impossible to walk, in his condition, but . . .

His mind was awhirl; he blinked and forced himself to focus on a plan. It wasn't as difficult as he'd thought, with his limited choices. Those thieving bastards had seen to that. And it was a godsend, when he came right down to it. He'd come West for a new life, hadn't he?

He struggled to the coach and climbed up onto the driver's seat, grunting with the exertion. He pulled off his coat and vest and trousers, wincing at every movement that strained his bruised ribs. He shivered. His flannel drawers and thin shirt were not much protection from the wind. He crawled across the top of the coach and found his valise, digging toward the bottom until he located his revolver and holster. He threw it to the ground along with his derringer, tossed his clothes into the valise, then refastened the ropes that held the luggage.

Getting down was easier than climbing up. He crouched on the driver's box, wrapped his arms tightly around his ribs to keep them from jolting, and jumped to the ground. He carried his guns to Perkins's carpetbag and stowed them on the bottom beneath a stack of shirts, then picked up the checked suit. It still smelled fresh and new from the store.

He was grateful that Perkins had been so tall and rangy: the trousers and jacket cuffs were short on him, but not by very much. And his own shirt cuffs, falling below the jacket sleeves, took up the slack. He guessed that he looked like a man who didn't know how to buy clothes, rather than a man who was wearing someone else's suit.

He closed up the carpetbag and carried it and the hatbox to the coach, then tossed them onto one of the seats. His ribs were aching, and he was beginning to sweat and feel light-headed. He remembered that the driver had kept a bottle of rotgut whiskey under his box; a couple of healthy swigs gave him the strength to go on.

Getting the dead bodies into the coach was an agony of dragging and lifting; his body protested the strain he put on it, shooting him through with painful spasms that left him breathless. He closed the door and sagged against the frame, fighting the waves of exhaustion and nausea that swept him.

"Oh, hell," he muttered, frowning down at the smears of blood on the checked coat. He chuckled at a sudden, absurd thought. Perkins would have said, "Heavens to Betsy!"

He took another swig of whiskey, then crossed the meadow one last time. A gentleman couldn't be seen without his bowler hat. Despite the handkerchief around his brow, he managed to anchor the hat firmly on his head.

He was about to return to the coach when he saw the photograph of the Southgate family, where Perkins had dropped it as he fell. He scooped it up and studied it while he made his way back to the carriage.

He hoisted himself painfully onto the box and picked up the reins. He looked at the picture once more, running his finger over the woman's lush body as though he could almost feel her curves.

"California, darlin'," he said with a wry laugh, "you're about to meet Horace Perkins."

Chapter Three

"Beth, come and sit by me." Callie put down her book and frowned at her sister.

On the other side of the dusty street, Beth leaned against the hitching post in front of the saloon, watching in openmouthed wonder as a woman emerged and lit a cigarette. The woman smiled and waggled her fingers at the little girl.

Callie pursed her lips at the sight of the painted hussy. Her scarlet dress was cut shamelessly low across her bosom, and her bustled skirt was so short that Callie could almost see the creature's knees. With the exception of the stolid, plodding miners' wives, there seemed to be no other sorts of women in this town besides these "sporting gals."

"Beth!" she said again, louder and more sharply. "It's too hot in the sun." Several passersby turned to look at her. Embarrassed at having drawn attention to herself, she stared down at her fingers.

Beth shuffled across Front Street, kicking at pebbles in the dirt, and flounced into the hard wooden chair beside Callie. The two chairs were set on the planked sidewalk, shaded by the small, pitched canopy of the deputy sheriff's office. "It's not too hot anymore," the little girl said sulkily. "It's after five." She bounced up and down on the chair. "And I'm tired of sitting."

"You should have brought a book, as I did."

Beth pointed toward the end of the street, where a sign over a large, raw-timbered building proclaimed: GENERAL MERCHANDISE AND DRY GOODS. "Why can't I go to Poppy's store?"

"Don't point," said Callie. "It's not ladylike. You can't go to the store because I don't want you disturbing the clerk at his work."

Beth pouted. "I *like* Billy Dee."

"So do I—when he's sober." She couldn't understand why Big Jim would hire an old, broken-down drunkard as a part-time clerk and watchman. All the employees of the Boston store had been well-bred and genteel. But Big Jim had a soft spot for derelicts and stray dogs.

"And he gives me horehound candies for helping him," Beth added. She tugged at her straw hat with two pudgy fists, pulling it down over her face until only her petulant mouth was visible.

"Candies will spoil your supper. And don't do that to your hat."

"Oh, botheration," Beth grumbled, pushing back her hat. "Poppy's been in the saloon for hours. I bet he's spoiling *his* supper! I don't see why we can't go into the saloon, too."

"I swan! Where do you get your notions? Saloons are not for ladies. And if you were 'temperance'—as I am," she added primly, "you'd pray that Poppy sees the error of his ways and gives up the vice."

"Well, I don't know why we have to sit here for hours. Not when there's heaps to see all over town."

"Hmph! I dare say." Callie looked up and down the long street with contempt. Dark Creek was a typical mining town, like the half dozen or so they'd passed on their way from

Denver. The bumpy, unpaved road with its cluster of ramshackle buildings, the meandering creek, the mountains that surrounded the high, narrow valley—climbing ever upward toward the western peaks.

It might have been beautiful once, when the first prospectors came by, searching in the sandbars and loose shale of the creek bed for "color"—that flash of gold that could make a man a tycoon overnight. But most of the placer gold—on the surface and waiting for the taking—had pinched out long since. A great many of the claims now belonged to Eastern companies, almost the only ones wealthy enough to carve out mines to search for the more resistant gold. Picks and shovels and prospecting pans had given way to dynamite and stamp mills. Belching smoke from squat brick chimneys, the mills crushed and ground the ore-bearing rocks into a rubble that was carted away to smelting factories near Denver.

The serene, rustic setting had been destroyed; slag piles rising up beside the noisy mills, trampled grass, barren gulches hacked by a thousand picks. The nearby hills had been stripped of their trees, and mine shafts dotted their slopes. A lonely string of telegraph poles followed the creek, like a lifeline to civilization.

There were still a few old-time sluices in the creek outside of town—the work of independent, dogged prospectors, sustained by an occasional gold find and buoyed by their hopes. Their primitive cabins clung shakily to the steep hillsides, or crowded the narrow side streets of the town.

Most of the rest of the raw-pine buildings catered to the needs of a rough, male-dominated society—one that had not yet moved beyond the basic necessities of a new town. There was a sawmill on the creek, a doctor's office, a livery stable. Painted signs, their elaborate lettering in odd contrast to the plain stores behind them, announced their offerings: Prescriptions, Dentist, Blacksmith, Undertaker. Besides Big Jim's large general store, there were two other merchandise shops; in spite of their modest size, their signs proclaimed grandly "Gentleman's Clothier" and "Hauptmann's Fine Emporium." There was a single hotel with a small restaurant, and half a dozen shabby boardinghouses.

And, of course, there were the dozens of saloons, variety halls, sporting palaces, and brothels—the blue lanterns above those last establishments indicating the shameless trade within. Behind the nondescript fronts of the others, Callie knew, all manner of vice was practiced. Gambling, drinking, immoral musical performances by indecently clad females.

And other practices that Callie didn't even like to dwell on. She was familiar enough with the trade of the brothels— Mummy had been uncharacteristically frank on that score. Moreover, Callie had awakened often enough in a Boston night to hear the coarse sounds and utterances coming from her parents' bedroom. It had always seemed as though Mummy was suffering—enduring the lusty appetites of her husband with patient fortitude.

But in Boston, at least, the lewd establishments had been invisible and far from the view of decent folk—tucked into the less-fashionable quarters of the city, where a body didn't have to be assaulted every day by the sight of crude, lickerish-eyed patrons, gamblers, drunken bummers, and women who had sunk to the lowest level. In *Boston,* at least, people put such behaviors in their proper place—an occasional lapse in judgment, not a way of life.

The men Callie encountered on Front Street ran the gamut from French-speaking trappers—descendants of the early voy-agers—to vigorous German freighters, to barely civilized min-ers. There were penniless transients—still wearing the ragged, threadbare blue or gray serge of their old regiments—their eyes haunted by horrors they couldn't forget, their restless feet carrying them on a weary quest for a peace that always eluded them. There were slick adventurers, sharpers and cheats, whose fortunes rose and fell on the turn of a card or the roll of a die. Even the men who managed the mines were only a cut above the common laborers. The remote Eastern companies disdained to send university-trained engineers, importing instead Cornish miners who were used to working in dark, murky tunnels.

Callie even saw an occasional Indian in town—Arapaho or Cheyenne—though the Sand Creek Massacre of 1864 had created new distrust between the red men and the white. Callie passed them by in silence, as embarrassed by their presence as they, no doubt, were by hers.

She sighed and gazed at the large canvas tent at one end of the street, a small cross painted on its entrance flap. It was the only church Dark Creek had ever known. Its presence testified to the crudeness and barbarity of this territory. The stamp mills roared with activity twenty-four hours a day, even on Sundays. And the brothels and boisterous saloons did the same. But the men who could squander a fortune in gold on a night's revelry could never find enough in their pockets to build a proper church.

Callie sighed again. It surely wasn't like Boston. She straightened the ruffle on Beth's pinafore and wondered how her sister could see this place with such unquestioning eyes. "Where's Weedy?" she asked.

Beth shrugged. "Wandering, I reckon."

"How are my girls doing?" Big Jim strode across the street from the saloon, a broad smile on his face. "Losing patience?"

"Well, I'm glad we left Sissy with Mrs. Ackland," said Callie.

Big Jim raised his already booming voice and roared toward the door of the deputy sheriff's office. "Hepworth! Where the devil is that stage?"

After a moment, Mr. Hepworth came out of his office, scratching his ear. He still looked like the ranch hand he had been—despite the brand-new, shiny deputy's badge on his plaid shirt. Dark Creek was such a small town that it wasn't entitled to a full sheriff.

"Wal, I don't rightly know, Big Jim," he drawled cheerfully. "Zeke ain't never been late afore. You can bet your bedrock dollar them miners'll be hollerin' fer their pay purty dang soon.''

''But it's more than two hours late, man. Shouldn't you be concerned?''

Hepworth tipped back his large hat with one sun-darkened thumb. ''I reckon I could ride out a ways and see what's up. We ain't had no rain, so the road couldn't be flooded. But mebbe . . .''

He was interrupted by a shout from the end of the street. The huge red Concord stagecoach came careening down the incline leading to town. Cracking his whip with a wild swing of his arm, the driver swayed precariously on his box. The mules, covered in sweat, looked like they were about to drop, and the vehicle seemed almost out of control.

''What in the Sam Hill!'' cried Big Jim, running into the road.

He was followed by Hepworth. ''Holy Jumpin' Jehoshaphat! That ain't Zeke!''

Alarmed, Callie rose from her chair, took up her cane, and hobbled to the edge of the sidewalk. She grabbed Beth's shoulder to keep her from following the men into the street.

As the carriage neared them, Hepworth waved his arms frantically over his head, signaling to the driver. In response, the man pulled back on the reins, and the coach ground to a standstill in a cloud of dust.

Callie studied the driver with curiosity. He was a young man with a handsome face, a slender hawknose, and keen eyes. But the bowler hat he had pulled low on his forehead looked absurd, and his checked suit—too short, too snug across the shoulders—was an abomination. She would have taken him for a reckless fool and a silly prig, and nothing more—except for the great quantities of blood on his face and collar, and the red smears on his coat front.

He flashed a grin that was a grimace of pain as well, nodded to Big Jim, and held up a photograph. ''You'll be Mr. Southgate,'' he said in a hoarse voice, and pitched forward, nearly toppling from his seat.

Big Jim and Mr. Hepworth scrambled to the box to help him down. He groaned as they half carried him to the plank sidewalk and set him in one of the chairs. He lifted a quivering hand and pulled off his bowler. His head was wrapped in a bloody handkerchief.

''Mercy!'' Callie bent to him in concern, her normal shyness forgotten in the face of his distress. ''Beth, run upstreet to the hotel and fetch a glass of water.''

The man looked up at her. His eyes were a clear blue, warm and friendly. But Callie thought she saw a devilish twinkle in their depths. He snorted. *''Water?''*

She stared in shocked surprise. ''What could you possibly want instead, sir?'' she asked through tight lips.

There was no twinkle. She surely had been mistaken. He looked aside, evading her eyes, and tugged nervously at his coat cuff. ''B-bless my whiskers, ma'am,'' he stammered in a voice that was so high-pitched it set Callie's teeth on edge. ''Forgive me. But if it won't upset your sensibilities too much ... that is ... Oh, cheese in crackers! There's a bottle of whiskey under the coach box.'' He brought his eyes back to hers. They were soft and helpless. ''Just this once. For medicinal purposes, you understand.''

Big Jim gave Beth a gentle nudge. ''See to it, pet. Mr. Perkins looks mighty peaked.'' He cocked an eyebrow at the young man. ''It *is* Mr. Perkins, isn't it?''

The man responded with a shy ''Yes.'' He rubbed his hand across his eyes. ''I'd hoped to meet under more auspicious circumstances, sir. Oh, my stars, I never thought I'd make it to town at all.''

''Where's Zeke?'' demanded Hepworth, frowning.

Beth came running up and handed Mr. Perkins the whiskey. He took a tentative swallow, his little finger crooked in a gesture of ostentatious refinement, then choked on the mouthful. ''Dear me, it's so strong!'' He managed another large gulp, then turned to Hepworth. "If you mean the driver, Sheriff,"—he cast pious eyes to heaven—"that poor soul has gone to meet his Maker. He's in the coach. We were ambushed in a meadow. A half hour back, I should reckon. By masked road agents."

Mr. Hepworth swore violently. "Those bristle-headed, back-shootin', low-lived cowards! Zeke were a friend of mine. Was you forced off the road?"

"No. We were an easy mark. My fellow passenger wished to disembark and refresh himself in the creek. Zeke was kind enough to oblige him. While we were resting, the miscreants caught us unawares. I think they were after the payroll Zeke told us about. They took nothing else except the change from our pockets."

"Sounds like a put-up job to me," growled Big Jim. "A prearranged ambush."

"I would be inclined to doubt it, sir. We stopped quite by chance. And the other passenger is in the coach as well. Quite dead, alas. A Mr. Johnson. May he rest in peace," he added fervently. "We boarded together at Cheyenne."

"And how come *you* escaped with your skin, young feller?" There was a sudden note of suspicion in Hepworth's voice.

"Only through God's good graces," murmured Perkins, touching his head. "They shot me, and I played possum. Then when one of them came to . . . when the scoundrel saw that I was still alive, he and his confederates kicked me into insensibility. I have no doubt they thought I was dead."

"And you never saw their faces?"

"No. They were wearing bandannas." He took another healthy swallow of the whiskey. Callie noted that he didn't choke this time.

By now, the road had filled with curious townspeople, crowding in to hear every detail of Perkins's story. There were muttering and grumblings, and more than a few curses for the loss of the payroll and Zeke, who had been well liked.

Hepworth gestured toward the crowd. "You fellers. Don't stand around gawkin'. Fetch out them bodies and git 'em over to the undertaker. The town'll pay fer the burials. Zeke ain't got no kin.''

Mr. Perkins turned to Callie. ''Best avert your eyes, Miss Southgate. Mr. Johnson is not properly dressed. And his wound is dreadful. My stars, I thought I'd *swoon!*'' He brought a fluttery hand to his breast. One of the bystanders snickered.

Callie chewed at her lip in consternation. If this was what passed for genteel in Baltimore, they were surely raising a generation of timid milksops. It offended her that Big Jim had spent so much money to import this poor excuse for a man.

''I've seen blood before, Mr. Perkins,'' she said crisply. ''And unless the man is entirely unclothed, I'll not be distressed.''

He gave her a smile of awed admiration. ''Oh my, ma'am, what a refined generosity of spirit you have.''

She stirred in discomfort. Was he mocking her? She wished she could flee the town, the crowd, his strangely unsettling eyes—so at odds with the priggish words that fell from his lips.

He seemed not to notice her unease. He turned to Hepworth. ''Mr. Johnson took off his coat and duster. I'm afraid I left them in the meadow when I carried the bodies to the coach. But the poor soul should be decently buried.''

Hepworth pointed to a grizzled miner. ''Rufus, you go fetch 'em. Take my horse.''

The old man nodded. ''Yup.''

Big Jim scowled at Mr. Perkins. ''How badly are you hurt, Horace?''

Mr. Perkins cleared his throat. ''If I'm not being too presumptuous, Mr. Southgate,'' he said hesitantly, ''I have always disliked the name of Horace. My . . . middle name is Jason. Friends call me Jace. As for my wounds, I think the bullet only grazed my head. But my ribs are all-to-smash, where they kicked me. I'm sure several bones are broken.''

''Have I missed all the excitement?'' A tall, awkward youth

elbowed his way through the crowd, wobbling slightly. His eyes had a glazed look, and he smelled of alcohol.

Callie frowned at her brother, Weedy. "You might have stayed to keep Beth company."

Weedy grinned. "I had better things to do."

"I dare say." *Oh, why can't Poppy see what is happening to his son in this wild land?*

Big Jim motioned to Weedy. "Come on, son. Help me get Mr. Perkins to the doctor."

Between them, they lifted Perkins to his feet and supported him from both sides. Callie was surprised to see that the man seemed even taller than Big Jim, though he was stooped with his injuries, and it was difficult to tell.

He took a tentative step, clenched his teeth in pain, and muttered something under his breath. When he saw that Callie was watching him, he smiled sheepishly. "Oh, fudge, Miss Southgate. I'm such a trial to your family. And I did so want to make the proper first impression."

You did, she thought in disgust. *Mr. Cooper must have been senile before he died.*

Big Jim chuckled, his booming laugh rolling across the street. "If you hauled the bodies back to the coach in your condition, sir, and then managed to drive to town . . . Well, you sure as hell impressed *me,* Mr. Perkins!"

"Mercy me, what else could I do?" he squeaked. "I couldn't leave those poor men for the buzzards."

His simpering modesty was enough to make Callie want to bring up her midday dinner. She looked uneasily at the faces around them. Surely the whole town must suspect that Poppy had summoned this mincing fool to be her groom. She wanted to die of shame.

"Mousekin, take Beth and the wagon and go home," said Big Jim. "I'll get someone to drive us out when Jace, here, is patched up. And fix up your room for him."

Callie clenched her jaw, resentment boiling in her breast. He was already "Jace" to Big Jim. As familiar and welcome as that! And she was expected to give up her room for this . . . this namby-pamby? Except for Poppy's room, hers was the most elegant in the house, filled with all her favorite things from Boston. "But Poppy . . ." she protested, finding her courage.

"Don't quarrel with me, girl!" he bellowed.

She cringed. Were they all laughing at Big Jim's crippled daughter now? Weak in spirit as well as body?

Perkins's eyes had gone soft. With sympathy? Or pity? "I wouldn't dream of putting you out of your room, Miss South-gate," he said. He sounded almost sincere, and his prissy voice had deepened to a rich baritone.

She didn't need pity. Especially not *his!* She wrapped herself in her tattered pride and swallowed her resentment against Big Jim. He meant it kindly, though his requests always came out like roaring commands. "Nonsense, Mr. Perkins," she snapped. "You need a comfortable setting in which to recuperate."

"In that case, Miss Southgate, I can't think of anything I'd rather do than sleep in your bed." He smiled, and the sly twinkle appeared in his eyes—a sparkle of blue that made him look like a devil.

Her head snapped up at his suggestive words. "I beg your pardon, Mr. Perkins!"

Even as she watched in disbelief, he seemed to shrink between her father and her brother. "Oh, mercy me," he said with a moan, "how my head hurts. Please, gentlemen, lead me to the doctor upon the instant. I *must* have a headache powder."

She watched their slow progress down the street, her thoughts spinning. Had she only imagined that twinkle? Read a hidden meaning into his words—a meaning that only her foolish fancies had conjured up?

Shaken to the very depths of her soul, she took Beth's hand and limped to the wagon.

Chapter Four

Callie paused at the entrance to her bedroom and set down her pitcher of warm water. She glanced over to the bed and rolled her eyes. Why had she allowed Big Jim to intimidate her into this ridiculous situation?

Horace Perkins lay sprawled on her bed, snoring gently. The man even *snored* like a . . . a daffy-down-dilly, as Beth had called him. A soft, feminine-sounding snort, high-pitched and grating. The thought of spending the rest of her life listening to that sound made her cringe.

But Big Jim had praised the man lavishly at supper tonight, going on forever about "Jace's" strength and fortitude in the doctor's office. Two broken ribs, a dozen stitches to his head, numerous welts and bruises, and a concussion that would have disabled a lesser man. It was clear that Big Jim had already decided Mr. Perkins would make a fine husband; whether or not Callie agreed seemed to be beside the point to her father.

She sighed. Despite the puppy-dog whimpers coming from the bed, she was grateful that Mr. Perkins was asleep. She had no wish to attempt a conversation with him. It would only take her a minute to fetch the book she'd forgotten on her night table. Then she could climb the stairs to the spare room, wash for bed, and settle in for an hour or so with Mr. Emerson's essays. The book had been a farewell gift from her ladies' circle—she'd been promising herself for days to write to them with her critical appraisal.

The room was dim, lit by a single kerosene lamp on a low flame; it cast a golden glow on the walls and sparkled on the window glass, seeming like a firefly against the night sky beyond. Callie tiptoed across the room, painfully conscious of the click of her cane on the floor—a sound that was magnified by her own unease and embarrassment. A lady didn't belong in a room where a man was sleeping.

Certainly not such a young and handsome man. She tried not to look at him as she reached the night table, but she couldn't stop herself. She had never seen so much exposed male flesh before, and the sight of him gave her a shiver that was oddly pleasant. She was reminded of the time she and her friends had discovered a forbidden volume of Michelangelo's drawings, tucked away in a corner of the library; they had pored over the pictures and giggled like excited schoolgirls.

Arms thrown wide, Perkins lay with the quilt folded down to his waist; only a narrow bandage, wrapped tightly around his ribs, covered his naked torso. He was extraordinarily muscular, and the thick patches of black hair on his chest and arms and armpits made him look like a wild animal. Callie gulped at the raw power in every line and sinew. His manner might be overrefined and prissy, but his body was primitive, savage, brutish. The one disgusted her; the other filled her with fearful apprehension. If she married him, would those strong arms close possessively around her, crushing her into helpless submission?

She found it easier to look at his face, especially in repose. The sharp angle of his long, thin nose was softened by the glowing lamp, and the strong jaw seemed less challenging. And though his eyebrows still peaked in devil's arches, she felt less threatened when his eyes were closed. There was something in the way he looked at her that made her want to run and hide.

The doctor had put a plaster on his head wound and had washed away some of the blood from his face, but traces still remained. Rusty streaks that stained his high, sharp cheekbones and spoiled the perfection of his wide mouth—a thin, bowed upper lip and a full lower lip that held the hint of a pout. Parted slightly, his lips quivered with each soft snore, intensifying their seductive appeal. His tousled black hair gleamed like a raven's wing in the firelight.

I swan! Callie thought, dragging her eyes away from his face at last. A body would think she'd never seen a man before, the way she was gawking at him!

She reached for her book, then stopped, her hand frozen in midair. The snoring had ceased abruptly. Trembling in embarrassment, she turned and scurried for the door.

"Please," he croaked, "may I have a drink of water?"

Reluctantly, she limped back to the bed. A glass and a small carafe of water sat on the night table. She poured out a small quantity and held the glass to his lips.

He lifted his head, took a tentative sip, then fell back against the pillow. "How kind you are, Miss Southgate," he said primly. But there was something less than genteel in the way his blue eyes appraised her face and body. He lifted his hand and ran his finger along the side of her cheek. "You're even prettier than your picture."

She jerked her head away, alarmed by his searching eyes, his sensuous touch. Surely he hadn't meant it as a caress! "Mr. Perkins!"

At once, he lowered his gaze. "Oh, mercy me," he said, giving her a simpering smile. "Do forgive my boldness, ma'am. I wasn't myself. I was dreaming of angels just now. And here you are." He glanced down at himself and gasped, seeming aware of his nakedness all at once. "Heavens to Betsy!" he squeaked, scrambling to pull the quilt up to his neck. "What you must think of me!"

"Don't disturb yourself, Mr. Perkins," she said in disgust. In truth, she was beginning to think he would be as useless in Big Jim's store as he would be as a husband. The rough miners would eat him alive if he behaved like a timid girl in their presence. "How do you feel?" she managed at last.

"It's difficult to breathe."

"You have two broken ribs, Poppy says. And the thin mountain air takes getting used to. Do you want supper? We've eaten already, but Mrs. Ackland, our housekeeper, left something in the pantry for you before she went home to her husband."

He closed his eyes for a moment and put a delicate hand to his forehead. "No. I'm still a trifle dizzy." He gave her a shy smile. "But I expect to be peckish by morning. I hope she's a good cook. I surely do like to eat."

She couldn't imagine him doing *anything* with gusto. "I have no doubt you'll be more than satisfied. Western cooks are accustomed to he-man appetites." She could scarcely keep the contempt from her voice.

He looked bewildered at her sharp tone and turned his head aside. "Oh, cheese in crackers!" he exclaimed. "Look at the pillowcase. Is that my blood that has stained it so dreadfully?"

"The doctor only cleaned your face enough to stitch your wound. We don't have the niceties of nursemaids out here," she added with sarcasm.

He didn't seem to be aware of the insult. He rubbed his fingers across his cheeks. Despite his prissy movements, Callie noted that his hands looked strong—long-fingered and dexterous. "My face feels like leather," he said in a whining voice. "All that dust, and now the blood . . ."

She limped to the door and picked up her pitcher. "You can wash. Here's hot water." She brought it to the night table, then fetched a basin and a towel from the washstand. The knowledge that he watched her awkward, hobbling progress back and forth in the room only made her more self-conscious. All she wanted to do was flee his presence—as quickly as possible. "Here," she said, waving her hand impatiently in the direction of the pitcher. "I'll leave you to your ablutions."

Grimacing in pain, he struggled to sit up. Callie nearly laughed aloud, watching his clumsy movements as he tried to rise and protect his modesty with the quilt at the same time. He was all fumbling hands and shy titters. At last he sighed and collapsed helplessly against the pillow. "Oh, fudge, Miss Southgate. I can't do it. Would you . . . ?" He chewed at his lip. "May I . . . prevail upon your kindness once more and ask you to bathe my face for me?"

She felt herself blushing at the thought of such an intimate chore. Then common sense returned. Why should she feel shy or uneasy in front of this milksop? He wasn't manly enough to be frightening. For heaven's sake, her emancipated women friends in Boston had more backbone than *he* did!

She pulled a chair up to the bed, sat down, and rested her cane against the table. It clattered to the floor. At once, her eyes flew to his face, dreading to see his reaction. He smiled in understanding; she felt her humiliation melt away. He might be less than a man, but he seemed to have a kind heart.

She poured the water into the basin, dipped a corner of the towel, and began to wash away the blood. "Poppy says they'll bury Zeke and Mr. Johnson tomorrow," she said. Small talk would help her forget his disturbing nearness. "After the coach was unloaded, Poppy said they found an extra valise. It must have belonged to poor Mr. Johnson."

He stiffened. "You didn't open *my* case, did you?" he asked sharply. His voice had suddenly deepened in alarm.

She wondered what a man like this could possibly have to hide. "No. Of course not." She indicated a corner of the room, where his carpetbag and hatbox sat. "There they are."

He relaxed and gave a nervous laugh, high-pitched and prissy. "It's only that . . . a man's personal effects are far too intimate for the scrutiny of a delicate woman. I'll unpack for myself when I'm stronger."

Mercy sakes, she'd seen a razor before! "Of course," she

said dryly, suddenly wishing that the man's spirit was as virile as the face she was tending. "They looked through Mr. Johnson's valise, hoping to find personal effects," she went on. "They even telegraphed Cheyenne, Poppy said. But there's no way to discover if he had family. Or even who he was."

"From what he told me, I think he was alone in the world." Perkins gave a heavy sigh. "As I am."

Good grief! Was he going to turn maudlin now? "Poppy says if Mr. Johnson's clothes fit you, you might as well keep them," she said quickly. "Mrs. Ackland and I can wash and mend and iron them. She managed to get the smudges of blood off your suit, but I'm afraid your shirt is ruined." Big Jim and Weedy had helped Mr. Perkins undress for bed—suit, shirt, and shoes. And drawers. Callie tried not to think of what lay on the bed so near to her, modestly concealed by the quilt.

"You're all so kind and generous to me," he simpered. His sickly-sweet voice grated on her ears.

"Poppy has invested a great deal of money in you," she said through clenched teeth. "He's far too thrifty to see it go to waste." She finished washing his face in silence, dried it, then reached across his head to the pillow on the other side of the bed. "I'll just give you a fresh pillow, and then you can sleep again. Lift your head and shoulders."

He complied with her directions, grunting and screwing up his face in pain all the while. But after she had switched the pillows, he suddenly clutched at her shoulder to steady himself as he eased his head back onto the pillow. She tried to pull away, but his grip was firm—hot and intimate through the thin cashmere of her dress.

She gulped. Had it been deliberate? "You really must sleep now, Mr. Perkins," she said, conscious that her voice quivered.

His hand slid down her sleeve to rest on her bare fingers. "I'm not tired yet," he said. "Please stay. Mr. Johnson was poor company for three days." His blue eyes were as warm as a pool in a sunny meadow. She felt as though she were drowning in them.

She shook off his hand and drew herself up with righteous indignation. "It isn't proper, Mr. Perkins! A lady in a man's bedroom."

He grinned unexpectedly. He had a dimple in one cheek. "But it's *your* room, Miss Southgate. And I'm injured, and helpless. You're not afraid of me, are you?"

She wavered. Was that the devil she saw again, peeping from his laughing eyes?

The devilish grin—if it had ever been there—became a sheepish smirk. "Cheese in crackers, ma'am. I couldn't hurt a fly."

She felt cornered, trapped by her own irrational fears. "Well, perhaps a few minutes . . ."

He looked around the dim room. "This is a pleasant room. And handsomely furnished. That's a Chippendale bureau, isn't it? And the chairs, as well. Your father must be quite prosperous."

"You have a shrewd eye, Mr. Perkins. You like expensive things, I see." *But then why else would he have accepted Poppy's generous offer?* "It isn't like my room in Boston," she added bitterly. "I've never lived in such a crude house."

"You have no faith in the future. I feel sure your father will soon turn this into the showplace of Dark Creek."

She snorted. Would anything ever replace the gracious house on Beacon Street?

"Is there no room for hope or optimism in your life, Miss Southgate?" he asked gently.

She looked down at her hands and twisted her fingers together. She had never known what to say to people, even in casual conversation. More personal discourse left her uncomfortable, wishing she could just hide herself in her books. She wondered if it wouldn't be too insulting to leave him now.

He cleared his throat in the awkward silence. "Do you suffer from an injury, Miss Southgate?"

Her eyes shot to his face. It told her nothing. "I beg your pardon?"

"Your cane. A fall, perhaps?"

"I . . . I was born this way. The doctors have never been able to discover the cause." What in God's name had prompted her to be so frank with a virtual stranger?

"All your life? What a pity." His voice had deepened in that strange way, as though another person dwelt within him. "You must have been lonely as a child."

How dare he presume to probe her soul? "I had as many friends as I wanted!" she snapped.

"Is that why your father calls you Mousekin?"

She gasped in outrage. "Mr. Perkins, you go too far!" She reached for her cane. She wouldn't stay another moment with this man!

He gave a squeak of dismay. "Oh, dear me! You're quite right to chide me, ma'am." He lifted a fluttering hand to his bandage. "I can only blame my lapse in good manners on my injury. A feeble excuse, but I beg you to accept my humblest apologies for my presumption."

He seemed genuinely contrite. "Well, I suppose . . ." she began.

"Oh, good! You're awake!" Beth stood in the doorway, clapping her hands for joy.

Callie clicked her tongue. "Beth! Why aren't you in bed already?"

Beth skipped across the room and plopped down on the bed beside Perkins. "I wanted to see Horace first."

Callie rolled her eyes. *"Mr. Perkins."*

He grinned at Beth. "Jace. It will do quite nicely."

Beth giggled. "Poppy says you're an all-fired hero. And, dang my eyes, I think so, too!"

"All I did was survive," he said dryly.

"Criminy! That's good enough for me. I think you're some pumpkins!"

"Beth! Such common language. And in front of our guest. What must he think of you?" Callie sighed in exasperation.

"You'll grow up into the kind of lady that nobody wants to associate with."

Perkins laughed. "Oh, I don't know. I think Beth will be a charmer. And a beauty. All the men will fight over her."

Beth beamed. "Will you? And wait for me?"

"I might."

Beth giggled again, slid off the bed, and danced around the room, stopping at the bureau upon which rested Perkins's bowler hat. She popped it onto her head and preened before the mirror. "I like your hat."

"Do you? Then you can wear it whenever I'm not wearing it. Matter of fact, you can have it. I think I might get one of those Western-style hats instead. To look like one of the fellows. You know," he added shyly, "rough-and-ready."

Callie nearly choked at his words. The mincing fool! She couldn't imagine him being ready for anything. And as for *rough . . . !*

But Beth seemed delighted at the thought. "Oh, you'll look capital!" she exclaimed.

"Thank you, Beth." He frowned. "Beth. What does it stand for?"

"Elizabeth."

"A pretty name. And Weedy?"

"He's named James, after Poppy. But they call Poppy Big Jim. So Weedy became 'Jim's son.' You know, like the weed. Jimson."

"And then 'Weedy'?"

"Yes. I think it's an amazin' good name, but Weedy doesn't much cotton to it."

"And do you like to be called Beth?"

"Do you have a better name?"

"I think I'll call you Princess."

Beth laughed and hid her face in her hands. "Oh, Jace."

He returned her laugh. "Oh, Princess."

Listening to their lighthearted banter, Callie felt a pang of envy. It was so easy for Beth to be comfortable around people.

And so difficult for her. But of course Beth was a child, and impressionable. All it took was a bowler hat and a flattering nickname, and Perkins already had her eating out of his hand. "It's time for bed, Beth," she said sharply.

Perkins gave her a warm smile, as though he were aware of her feeling of isolation. "Miss Southgate. California. Where did *that* come from?"

"Not that it's your business to know a lady's age," she said stiffly, "but I was born in '48. The year of the gold strikes in California. Poppy always longed for adventure. I think he would have been on the first stage West, if I hadn't been born."

"But now you're here."

"Yes," she answered bitterly. "We were scarcely out of mourning for our mother before he uprooted us and brought us to this godforsaken land."

"You prefer the city?"

She stood up and leaned on her cane. "I prefer the civility of Eastern folk and Eastern ways."

"Bless my whiskers, then you and I will get on famously." He smiled again, while his eyes traveled the length of her, from the tips of her shoes to the top of her upswept, red-gold hair.

She shivered at the sudden possessive look in his eyes. Was he already imagining them married?

She hobbled to the door, sick at heart. She dreaded the next few months.

Chapter Five

Jace slipped his arms into the checked coat and winced. Every muscle ached, and his chest felt like a faro table was sitting on it. Thank God his head had stopped pounding, though the wound had swelled painfully under its plaster. He was tempted to rip the damn thing off, and to hell with the doctor and his instructions.

He probably shouldn't have gotten up so soon. But after two days of lying in bed, with no one but Mrs. Ackland for company, he was getting restless. He would have welcomed a visit from Beth—she was a sweet kid—but she seemed to have been forbidden to disturb him. By California, he reckoned.

He looked around the spare room. Not as large, or as well furnished as California's room. And the sloping sides of the attic ceiling were so damned low he banged his head against the pine boards every time he moved out of the center of the room. He'd even have to stoop down to climb into bed. But he'd known worse, by a long shot. And the housekeeper could cook up a meal that had him drooling for the next one. He figured he'd landed on his feet pretty damn good this time.

He glanced out of the dormer window to the grassy meadow behind the house. California was still there with Beth, notebooks spread out on a table before them. He was glad he'd charmed Mrs. Ackland into changing his room this morning, while they were busy at Beth's lessons. He felt enough like a jackass playing Horace's role; he didn't have to get caught scooting upstairs in his drawers.

He frowned into the mirror above the bureau and ran his hand over his slicked-back hair. He was half-tempted to stick his head into his washbasin and scrub away Horace's aromatic hair oil. And his throat was beginning to scratch from keeping his voice pitched so high. He was sorry he'd shaved off his whiskers. At least he might have *looked* more like a man, if not sounded it.

But, what the hell. If they wanted genteel, by God they would get genteel! Even if it killed him.

Horace's suit was another matter. He wasn't sure how much longer he could wear it. It looked ridiculous and felt like hell. Tight and itchy. But Big Jim had stopped off this morning, while he was having breakfast in bed, and handed him a twenty-dollar gold piece—an advance on his first month's wages. As he'd done with the bowler hat, he reckoned he could make up a story about wanting to "look Western," and buy himself a new suit lickety-split. And he'd have "Mr. Johnson's" clothes to augment his wardrobe.

All in all, he was feeling mighty pleased with the way things were going. A bang-up place to live, a steady job, enough gambling halls in town so he could run up his pay into a grubstake in no time. He'd have to be careful, of course, and not forget he was "Horace Perkins." But that might work to his advantage. No one would expect an Eastern greenhorn to be a slick card player. Certainly not anyone as spineless as "Horace Perkins." And by the time the town got wise, he'd be long gone over the mountains.

And, in the meantime, like a bonus, there was the woman. She was a looker! Hair the color of copper threads dipped in gold, silvery green eyes that darkened and changed like a stormy sea. And a body that made his hands itch to touch her. She was painfully shy and skittish, and too straitlaced by half. But there was a spark that seemed to glow within her—deep and fierce. He wondered if she was even aware of it.

But he sure as hell was! If her glances and her words had been matches, he'd be burnt to a crisp by now. He'd felt it from the first moment—that hidden anger and hostility. Directed at him. Or Horace, as the case might be.

But what had he done? Surely she hadn't expected to become Big Jim's partner in the store, and resented him taking her place. Mrs. Ackland had made it clear that California almost never went to town, let alone to the store. She seemed to spend her days buried in books.

He shook his head. She was a puzzle, that was for damn sure. But he'd solve it. He'd never yet lost a woman he'd set his sights on. He reckoned it would take him a month or so to get into her drawers. He was in no hurry. The game made the final victory all the sweeter.

And what a game! He chuckled aloud. Three days with that snipper-snapper Perkins had given him a ready-made persona, like a playactor being handed a script, with all the dialogue complete. Oh, he'd slipped a couple of times; that was natural enough until he got used to the role. But only California had reacted with suspicion. And he wasn't at all certain that she wouldn't have mistrusted the *real* Horace.

He'd had all he could do to keep from laughing the other night, when she'd come into his room. Snoring like a Miss Nancy while he watched her out of slitted eyes. And then, when he'd sweet-talked her into washing his face and leaning in close . . He'd almost lost it. He'd come as close as a whisker to pulling her mouth down to his, tasting it to find out if it was as sweet as it looked.

He glanced out of the window once more. The meadow was now empty. It must be close to dinnertime. He frowned at Horace's carpetbag. He could unpack it after dinner, but he probably ought to stash his guns before he left the room. Mrs. Ackland had the kind of eyes that marked her as a busybody.

There was a tall linen cupboard near the window, with boxes and hampers stacked on top. He stowed his guns and holsters in Horace's hatbox, then reached for a chair to use as a ladder. He wasn't about to strain his ribs by stretching. He steadied the chair and climbed up.

"What are you doing?"

"Damn," he muttered, startled by the voice in the doorway. He slammed the incriminating hatbox onto the cupboard, pasted a smile on his face, and turned to Beth. "Hello, Princess."

She was wearing his bowler hat. She pointed up to the hatbox. "Dash it all, why are you putting that away? I thought maybe you'd let me have it, too. Since I have the hat."

"Well, now," he said, stepping down from the chair, "I'll need something for *my* new hat when I buy it. In case the posse's after me and I have to skip town in a hurry."

She giggled. "You're funning me."

He looked solemn. "Not a bit of it." He pointed to her hat. "I saw you out the window. Why weren't you wearing your hat then?"

"Callie said don't wear it during lessons. It's too frivolous."

"Callie's a regular 'Miss Don't,' isn't she?"

"Dang my britches, she never stops!"

He pursed his lips in mock dismay. "You're using unladylike slang again. Shall I tell 'Miss Don't'?"

She gave him a crafty look. "If you do, I'll tell her you just cussed like a trooper!"

He chuckled. "Princess, I'll keep your secret if you'll keep mine."

She put her fingers to her lips. "Tick tock, double-lock."

He copied her gesture and words, then held out his hand. "Shall we go down to dinner?"

She placed her small hand in his. It was warm and soft. "Oh, Jace," she said, her blue eyes shining, "I'm so glad you're here!"

He smiled back. One sovereign state conquered, and with so little effort it astonished him. Now, if he could just stake a claim in California . . .

He had to duck to come through the doorway into the dining room. Callie watched in disgust as he minced across the room and held out Beth's chair for her. With an exaggerated flourish, he helped the little girl tuck her napkin under her chin. Callie's stomach lurched. How did such a big, strapping man come to the ways of a silly fop? She could smell his Macassar oil clear across the table; he must have poured half a bottle of the stuff on his head! She'd be scrubbing pillowcases all her married life.

He nodded to Weedy, took the chair to Big Jim's right, and acknowledged Callie with a warm smile.

She lifted her head and looked down her nose at him. Beth might behave like an adoring puppy dog, but she had more sense than an eight-year-old. "Don't wear that hat at the table, Beth," she said sharply.

Beth and Perkins exchanged grins, as though they shared a secret.

"No, *don't,* Beth," he said.

The little girl took off the bowler and dissolved into a giggle.

"Good to see you up and around, Jace," boomed Big Jim.

Perkins tried to look self-effacing, but his smugness showed through. "Deary me, I'm not used to doing nothing. Idle hands are the devil's workshop, as they say. And I was beginning to miss your company." He beamed at Callie. "Especially yours, Miss California. Why haven't you visited me?"

All eyes turned to her. She hated being the center of attention. She looked down at her lap and fidgeted with her napkin.

"Not visited?" said Big Jim, giving her a meaningful look. "That wasn't very friendly of you, Mousekin. Under the circumstances."

Every fiber of her being wanted to scream out: I don't *want* a husband. Especially not this one! Instead, she turned to Perkins with a thin smile. "You seemed to need time to recuperate, *Mr.* Perkins. And I prefer to be called Callie, not California. Even better, you can call me Miss Southgate."

"Listen to me, girl!" Big Jim bellowed. "He'll call you Callie, and you'll call him Jace! Do you understand? He's practically family, now that he's living under our roof."

"B-but, Poppy . . ."

His voice softened. "I know what's best for you, sweetie. You'll do as you're told. Like a good girl." His smile was warm and loving, but there was no crossing Big Jim.

She crumbled. "Of course," she said in a timid voice. The air was heavy with her humiliation.

"I'm feeling tip-top this afternoon, sir," said Perkins quickly. "I thought I should like to visit your mercantile establishment today. Go back with you after dinner, if it wouldn't be too much trouble."

Big Jim leaned back in his chair and tapped his fingers together in satisfaction. "Splendid. Splendid! It's not too soon to begin learning the ropes." He gestured expansively toward the platter of elk steak and fixings that Mrs. Ackland was setting on the table. "Help yourself, Jace."

Callie couldn't help but notice that Perkins, for all his priggish manners, was quite generous to himself, heaping his plate with food as though there were no one else at the table. And when he picked up his fork, he curled his other arm around the plate in a possessive gesture that seemed almost primitive and defensive. *Good grief!* she thought, *does he think we're going to steal his food?*

Weedy had sat, mute and sullen, since Perkins had come into the room. Now he banged down his coffee cup and glared at Big Jim. "Why can't *I* come down to the store?"

Big Jim smacked his palm on the table. The dishes rattled. "What in the Sam Hill! Do we have to go through this all again? And in front of Jace? Because you're going to have a better life than I did, by jingo! That's why! As soon as we hear

rom Harvard College or Yale, you'll go back East. It's what
our mother wanted for you."

"You did all right without an education," grumbled Weedy.
'And what am I supposed to do all summer?"

Perkins put down his fork. "A proper education is a fine
hing to have," he said, his voice unexpectedly deep and
houghtful. "A man is set for life with a well-trained mind.
've often regretted . . ." He shook off the somber moment and
miled fussily. "Heavens to Betsy," he said, his voice rising
n octave. "How I do run on! I'm sure you'll enjoy your
chooling, Weedy. I envy you. I truly do! But, in the mean-
ime . . ." he smoothed his greasy hair, ". . . do you hunt?"

Weedy scowled and shook his head. "No," he grumbled.

Callie stared. "*Hunting* is one of your amusements, Mr.
erkins?" She looked uneasily at her father. "Jace," she
mended.

Perkins threw up his hands. "Bless my whiskers, Miss Callie,
'm not very good at it. But I should be happy to instruct Weedy
n the finer points sometime." He bobbed his head in Big Jim's
lirection. "With your permission, Mr. Southgate."

Big Jim nodded. "Splendid! Do the boy good."

Callie hadn't seen such a hopeful smile on Weedy's face
ince they'd come to Colorado. Perkins was like a parasite,
vorming his way into everyone's good graces. *Well, not mine,
ou . . . twiddlepoop!* she thought. She'd never indulged in
lang before, but it was the only word that suited him.

"I haven't hunted since I was a boy," said Big Jim.

"In Boston?" asked Perkins. "I think your letters mentioned
ou had a store in Boston."

Big Jim laughed. "Hell, no! I was raised in the north woods.
Maine. Cut lumber till I was Weedy's age. Hard work. But . . ."
e shrugged. "You know how it is. The feet get itchy. I came
o Boston and met the prettiest little gal in the world. And
retty gals need pretty things. So I started the business."

"And you were successful at once?"

Big Jim beamed in pleasure. "You're right! And when the

war came . . . By jingo, I had enough to open a small arms
factory, besides. Sold it in '66.''

Perkins leaned forward in his chair, his eyes bright with
interest. "Do tell. You must be well fixed."

"Well, we're not starving. And I have plans for this house.
One of these days, I'll put a water tank on the roof and run
some pipes. Hire a few workmen from back East to paper and
panel these walls. That sort of thing."

"Bless my stars, that takes a great deal of money!"

"Oh, Poppy can afford it!" Beth piped up. "Mummy used
to say everything he touched turned to gold."

Callie bit her lip. *I wish Beth hadn't said that. Perkins is
entirely too interested in the state of Poppy's finances, for all
his seeming nonchalance.*

"Mercy me!" Perkins laughed, a high, silly titter, and Callie
wondered why she'd been suspicious, even for a moment.
Poppy was adventurous, ambitious, willing to grab life by the
throat. His enthusiasm might have landed them here, in this
awful place, but his exuberance was a part of his nature, his
open personality. Perkins didn't seem to have the gumption
even to cross the street without permission.

Perkins laughed again. "With your talent for finding gold
in the most unlikely places, Mr. Southgate, I wonder you don't
go prospecting here in Colorado. It's here for the taking, they
say."

"I can do better selling pans to the prospectors than panning
for gold myself. Besides, there's not much ready gold left. Dark
Creek was pretty well pinched out and dying until they figured
out how to smelt the resistant ore. Some Professor Hill, from
Brown University. He worked it out."

Perkins beamed at Weedy. "Ah! You see? There's a use for
an education." He turned back to Big Jim. "But if you have
so much capital to invest, why don't you get into it anyway,
sir?"

"Not much adventure in owning a mine or a mill. Not like

finding it with your bare hands. You want to get rich quick, go over the Divide and look for silver. *That's* the future here.''

''Cheese in crackers.'' Perkins clutched at his breast. ''That's too rough for my taste. But surely there's still *some* ready gold left here for the offhand prospector.''

Big Jim snorted. ''I reckon so. If a fellow wants to waste his days rooting around in these hills.'' He pushed away his empty plate and waved his arm at Mrs. Ackland. ''I'm ready for some whiskey. Will you join me, Jace?''

Perkins glanced at Callie's disapproving face, then shook his head. ''Oh, my, no! It goes straight to my head. And I'm a simple man. Used to quiet ways.''

''But you've knocked around since the war, Cooper said. A man's entitled to a bit of wildness. Sow his oats, so to speak.'' Big Jim tossed back his glass of whiskey and called for another.

Perkins hung his head in embarrassment. ''While I must confess that I've been . . . unable to find a prospect that suited me, my positions have always been those of humble clerks.'' He sighed, clearly inviting their sympathy.

''So you said in your letters.''

''And the family farm, near . . .'' he hesitated. ''Fredericksburg,'' he said at last. ''It was so trampled during the fighting that it was impossible to grow a single crop. I was forced to sell it for almost nothing to pay my late father's bills.''

''Why didn't you stay in the army?'' asked Callie sharply. It might have made a man of him.

He shook his head. His blue eyes had grown dark and troubled. ''After that Reb prison camp,'' he growled, ''I wanted to be as far away from the army as possible.''

Callie stared in surprise. ''Prison camp? But your letters said you served as an orderly to an officer and never even saw battle!''

It was his turn to look startled. ''Did they?'' he squeaked. ''Well, I . . . that is . . .'' he tugged at his collar. ''Oh, fudge! The truth of the matter is that I . . . was captured while on an errand for my superior. My stupidity entirely. Completely avoidable.'' He gave a nervous laugh. ''One doesn't like to talk about such an error in judgment.''

''You must have a heap of stories about the war,'' said Weedy in awe. ''Tell us.''

''Yes, *do!*'' cried Beth. ''I've heard some amazin' wild tales at the store.''

Perkins was looking more and more uncomfortable. ''I should prefer . . .'' He turned with a relieved smile as Mrs. Ackland ushered Sissy through the door. ''But here's the only Southgate I haven't met!'' he exclaimed. He rose from his chair and knelt before the little girl. ''Hello, Sissy. What a pretty little thing you are!'' He wrapped one of her honey curls around his finger.

Callie twisted her lip in disgust. He fairly oozed oily charm, as though he were confident of making one more Southgate conquest.

Sissy stood on solid, pudgy legs, her hands curled into fists, a look of distrust on her three-year-old face. She tugged her hair away from his grasp, measuring him with a cold stare. Then she raised a chubby finger and poked at the bandage on his forehead. He flinched and drew back. Sissy turned to Mrs. Ackland and wrapped her arms around the woman's legs.

''Want my nap and my blankee,'' she said with a pout. She turned and gave Perkins one more malevolent glare before she allowed Mrs. Ackland to carry her from the room.

Callie could have crowed for joy. Perkins seemed stunned, as though no one had ever rebuffed him before. *So much for you, Mister Namby-pamby,* she thought. At least she wasn't the only one not charmed by his sickly-sweet manner and fawning ways.

Big Jim finished his whiskey and stood up. ''Time we were getting down to the store, Jace. I don't like to keep it locked more than an hour or so for dinner.'' Without waiting for a response, he strode from the room—the king in command of his domain.

Beth jumped from her chair, retrieved her hat, and squashed it over her curls. "Can I go, Callie?"

"Only if you stay out of mischief," said Callie firmly. "Don't pester Billy Dee. Or Mr. Perk . . . Jace. And *don't* go wandering up and down the streets alone." She was mystified again by the look that passed between Perkins and Beth.

Perkins came around to her chair. "Allow me to help you, Miss Callie." He slid back the chair and put out his hand for her to grasp. She took it with reluctance; his grip was stronger than she would have imagined. She reached for her cane at the same moment she stepped away from the table.

He reached for it at the same time. "Please. Allow me. Oh, drat!" he cried, as the cane slipped from his fingers and crashed to the floor. He lunged wildly toward it.

Left with no support but his one hand, and shaken by his sudden movement, Callie grabbed for his shoulder to steady herself. The feel of his hard muscles under his coat brought back the unwelcome memory of his bare chest. "If you'll just guide me back to the table," she said, strangely out of breath, "I'll be fine. I'm not totally helpless," she added. She didn't want him to think she depended on him, just because her hand was in intimate contact with his person.

"Cheese in crackers," he said, grimacing at her grip. He released her hand and fumbled to wrap his arms around her waist. A firm embrace that brought his chest close to her breasts. He grunted in pain. "I'm more helpless than you are, Miss Callie. With my wounds and all. Perhaps we should stand here for a few minutes, until we both recover our equilibrium."

She trembled in alarm, the perspiration of embarrassment forming on her upper lip. His arms were warm and solid around her, and there almost seemed to be laughter in the depths of his blue eyes. "Beth," she said in a shaking voice, "please hand me my cane before Mr. Perkins thinks that I enjoy this."

The laughter was gone. The silly prig had vanished. "I'm not such a fool that *I* don't," he murmured.

At her shocked gasp, he seemed to shrink into himself. Stammering foolishly, he eased them both toward the table, releasing her as soon as her fingers grasped the edge. "H-h-heavens to Betsy," he stuttered. "Mr. Southgate will be waiting for me."

She sank into a chair. Her waist still burned from his arms, his intimate touch. *Lord save me,* she thought. How could such an excuse for a man make her feel so weak?

Chapter Six

All he needed was a good cigar to make the day perfect.

Jace jounced along in the back of the wagon, his arms behind his head, and grinned from ear to ear. Callie would be easier than he thought. He'd felt her lush body trembling in his arms, even through her corsets. And her eyes had glowed with a dark light, confused yet hungry. And though she might interpret her reaction as fear or outrage, he knew it was something else. He'd seduced enough women in his time to know when they were interested.

It was devilishly hard, of course, to seduce her as "Horace." He had to keep pulling back, retreating into simpering helplessness, lest she take a fright or get suspicious. But it merely upped the stakes, increased the challenge.

He'd nearly slipped when they'd talked about the war. Horace had only spoken briefly about his service in the army. He'd assumed the man had seen battle. But he should have realized that a goody-goody fellow like Horace would have managed a safe job. No Pennsylvania Volunteers for him. No bloody Shiloh.

He swore softly. It had been stupid of him—to bring up the Reb camp. But the talk of the war had touched a nerve in him, and he'd spoken without thinking. He'd have to be a lot more careful, at least until he was solidly fixed in their midst.

He thought he could make a friend of Weedy—the poor kid was so squashed by Big Jim he didn't know which way to turn. Mostly to the saloons, Jace reckoned. Weedy had been tanglefooted drunk that first day. But it would be a novel role for him—after the life *he'd* led—to play Dutch uncle to the boy, put him on the straight.

Not that Big Jim was a monster. Far from it. Jace had liked him at once. Open, friendly, filled with infectious enthusiasm. But he was just so damn ... well, *big*, in every way. And overpowering. His children esteemed him highly, that was clear. But they lived in his shadow. And he was such a bull of a man, so filled with swaggering self-confidence, that he didn't see what he was doing to his family.

Well, it wasn't his problem. He had enough on his mind trying to fight his own damn conscience. He kept seeing that poor bastard Perkins with his face blown away. And Zeke. Maybe if he hadn't talked Zeke into stopping, they might be alive today. If they'd been ambushed in a moving stage, they'd have had a fighting chance. "Aw, hell," he said aloud, shaking off the pangs of guilt. "You're getting soft, Jace, old man."

The wagon bumped to a stop. He glanced up at the seat. Beth was scrambling over the top, guided by Big Jim's strong hand. She landed by Jace in a flurry of skirts.

She laughed and wriggled up against him, anchoring the bowler more firmly on her head. "I told Poppy I wanted to sit with you for a spell."

"I welcome your company, Princess," he said, as the wagon started up again. "But 'Miss Don't' would have a conniption fit, to see you back here like a hired hand."

She tossed her blond braids. "Oh, Callie's an old foo-foo. If that's what being grown-up means, I don't want a bit of it!"

She glanced up at him, her eyes filled with adoration. " 'Cept for you, of course."

He smiled back. He liked being with Beth. He didn't have to be so careful, so all-fired "Horace-like." "Callie will come 'round," he said, "if she can stop being so shy. Has she always needed her cane?"

"Pshaw! The doctors told her years ago to throw it away and get used to walking without it. But she swears she'll fall. So Poppy stopped pestering her about it."

The wagon was coming down the last slope into Dark Creek. Beth pointed to the first ramshackle buildings as they passed. "What do you think of our town?"

He tugged at her braid. "I haven't seen it yet."

"Did too. The first day you came."

"The only thing I remember about that day is the doctor's office." He tugged her pigtail again. "And a whippersnapper who brought me whiskey."

She eyed him shrewdly. "I don't think you hate it as much as you let on."

He rolled his eyes and pitched his voice higher. "Mercy sakes! How can you say that?"

She giggled. "Well, just don't let Callie see you. She's 'temperance.' It would just rile her up."

He shook his head. "Course I won't." In truth, the thought of Callie riled up, full of passion and fire, was enough to set his pulse to racing.

Beth scrambled to her knees. "We're coming to Poppy's store now," she said excitedly.

Jace sat up straighter in the wagon and let his glance run the length of the main street. Except for the towering mountains that crowded in, Dark Creek looked like many another new town he'd seen on the prairies—rough, raw, bursting with energy. But there was more. Perhaps it was the whiff of gold in the air that gave it a jangling recklessness, a sense of living on the edge. The tinny piano tunes coming from the saloons and variety halls were more strident, the rowdies who swaggered up and down the boardwalks were more raucous and menacing, the heavy freight wagons that rumbled along the street seemed impatient to get to their destinations. Jace felt ignited by the excitement in the air, buoyed by the sense that he'd found his place at last.

Big Jim's store was all that he'd hoped it would be. Large, rambling, crammed with goods to satisfy every customer. And he could own a piece of it someday, if he played his cards right. He'd worked behind a counter more than once, when he'd needed a little cash, and he had a good head for figures. This might turn out to be his gold mine, without the need to go digging in the hills.

"This is a first-rate establishment, Mr. Southgate," he said after Big Jim had shown him around the shop and the storeroom in back—Beth trailing them like a shadow all the while. "I only hope I can live up to your expectations."

Big Jim measured him up and down with a searching look. They stood almost eye to eye, though Jace had an inch or two on the older man. "Don't worry," said Southgate with a sly chuckle. "I have no fear you'll fill the bill." He winked. "In every way, if you catch my meaning."

Jace didn't—but he wasn't about to ask. "Where shall I begin, sir?"

The other man smiled broadly. "You can begin by calling me Big Jim!" he said in a cheerful roar. "None of your mincing 'Mr. Southgate' or 'sir.' This is the West, not a tea party."

"Oh, look who's here," said Beth, pointing toward an elderly man who had just shuffled through the door. She ran to him and greeted him warmly, receiving a friendly pat on top of her bowler in return.

Big Jim motioned the man forward with a wave of his large hand. "Jace, I want you to meet Billy Dee, who'll help you out when I'm not around. Billy Dee, this is Horace Perkins, my new manager."

Billy Dee was a grizzled old coot with a weather-beaten face, rheumy eyes, and a red, bulbous nose that attested to a fondness for drink. At Big Jim's introduction, he held out his hand to Jace, eyed his dandified suit with disgust, then scrubbed his hand across his work shirt before holding it out again.

"Howdy-do," he muttered, glaring at Jace from beneath shaggy brows.

Jace shook his hand warmly. "I do very well, Billy." *And so do you,* he thought. Forty-rod lightning, or he missed his guess. A drink that could kill a man at that distance.

"They calls me Billy Dee, young feller," he grumbled. "And I ain't about to change my name fer a no-account dude like you."

Jace smiled primly. "Of course not, my good man." He wondered how many customers the lop-eared son of a bitch had chased away with his belligerence. Well, things would change, now that he was here.

Big Jim looked at Jace as though he were disappointed he hadn't protested the insult. "No call to be ornery, Billy Dee. Did you finish taking stock before you went to lunch?"

"Yup."

"And . . . ?"

"Two sides o' bacon and a sack o' beans. And one o' them galvanized coffeepots."

"Dammit, man, you're the watchman! How the hell could those things vanish last night? That's the third time in two weeks! How many new locks do I have to put in? Weren't you in the storeroom?"

Billy Dee shifted his eyes from one side of the room to the other. "I was sleepin' like a baby. Innocent as they come."

"And sober?" asked Jace quietly.

Billy Dee doubled his fists and advanced on Jace. "Why you toad-hoppin', chicken-bred galoot . . . !"

Jace simpered at Southgate. "If you'll excuse us, Big Jim," he said. He reached out and took Billy Dee by the shoulder. It seemed a casual gesture, but his fingers were tight enough to make the old man wince. He steered Billy Dee to a corner of the store and fixed him with a tight-jawed smile.

"Listen to me, you son of a whore," he said in a low, pleasant voice. "I've known rummies like you all my life. If I find out you had anything to do with the thefts from this store, I'll shoot you down dog-dead in the street."

Billy Dee's jaw dropped wide. "No need to get tetchy, young feller," he stammered. "It were just a few things. Some prospector prob'ly run out o' cash."

"Then we'll give him credit at the front door. Not let him come sneaking in the back. Do you understand?" He tightened his grip ominously. He could feel the fragile bones beneath the man's thin shirt.

Billy Dee gritted his teeth in pain. "Whatever you say, young feller."

"Good!" he exclaimed, releasing the man's shoulder. "Shall we rejoin our employer?" He led the old man back and beamed at Southgate. "Everything is settled, Big Jim. Billy Dee has pledged to be more punctilious in his duties as night watchman. I trust we've seen the last of the thefts." He smiled at Billy Dee. "Isn't that so, old-timer?"

The old man nodded vigorously. "Yessir, Mr. Perkins."

"Glad to hear it!" said Big Jim, giving Jace a thump on the back that jolted his broken ribs. "Why don't we . . ." He stopped as several people came into the store. "Well, my boy, you seem to have won over Billy Dee. Let's see how you do with the customers."

For the next several hours, Jace was kept hopping. Not that it was difficult for him. Big Jim was there to tell him the prices of everything, and Billy Dee did all the reaching and lifting, so he didn't have to strain his injured body. He even roped in Beth, who was delighted to tie the strings around every package he wrapped.

And of course his charm didn't fail him. Even playing Horace's role, with a great deal of mincing and simpering, he was able to talk a miner's wife into an extra yard of calico, and convince a new saloon owner that the glassware in Big Jim's store was better than anything he'd find west of the Mississippi.

He even managed to settle a quarrel between two whores who were fighting over a single pair of fancy boots. "Ma'am," he said to one of them, holding up a scarlet flannel petticoat, "your feet are not your best feature, I'm sure. You should show off your exquisite limbs instead. A little flash of red when you lift your skirts will draw a gentleman's eyes to exactly the right spot. Let your sister have the boots. It would be my pleasure to sell this garment to a woman who can do it justice." After assuring the other whore that she had the daintiest feet it had ever been his pleasure to see, he watched them leave arm in arm, happily cradling their purchases.

He yawned and stretched gingerly. Hell's bells, but he was getting tired. And his head was beginning to pound, his chest to ache. He shouldn't have made such a big show out of feeling up to snuff. Not while his body was still healing.

Big Jim nonchalantly pulled his watch from his pocket. "I think we'll go home early tonight," he said. "I'm plumb tuckered out."

Jace smiled his gratitude. "If you think so, Big Jim." He saw a figure through the front window of the shop, hand reaching for the door. "Let me just help this last customer."

Southgate looked toward the door and chuckled. "That one? That's your rival. Ralph Driscoll. I think Callie's sweet on him."

My rival? thought Jace in bewilderment. Was he expected to spark Callie? And, more to the point, was it *her* idea, or Big Jim's? This "Horace" business was more complicated than he'd thought.

The man who stepped into the store was compact but strong-looking, with pomaded brown hair—graying at the temples— a broad nose and piercing black eyes set in a craggy face. He was clearly a man of substance: his frock coat and striped trousers were finely tailored, and he wore a silk hat and carried a pair of yellow doeskin gloves. He seemed to be about forty.

He was followed by a man who looked like a ranch hand from his rough shirt, leather leggings, and the large pistol strapped to his hip. He wore a sweat-stained felt hat and dusty boots.

The gentleman doffed his silk hat and nodded at Big Jim. "Afternoon, Southgate."

Big Jim returned his salute. "Afternoon, Driscoll. What brings you here? Closed up the bank early?"

"I heard you had a new clerk. I thought I'd come round to meet him, like a good neighbor." He indicated the man behind him. "And Carl, here, my ranch foreman, says we could use new machinery for the well. It was a slow day and, well . . . with this, that, and the other thing, I thought I'd mosey over, too, and see if you have something in a catalog."

"Sure enough." Big Jim jerked his thumb in Jace's direction. "This is Jace Perkins, my new manager."

Jace smiled and held out his hand as though he were afraid of getting it crushed. "Mr. Driscoll, sir," he said primly.

Driscoll took his hand and squeezed. Hard. A vicious, bone-crunching grip at odds with his smiling face. "Glad to meet you, Perkins. You'll go far, clerking for Southgate here."

Jace recognized his words and his handshake as deliberate challenges. It was all he could do to keep from smashing his other hand against the man's slick smile. But if he wanted to maintain this charade, he couldn't be as open as he'd been with Billy Dee. Though no one would believe the ravings of a rummy, one false move now might unmask him in front of Big Jim.

"Oh, my stars, Mr. Driscoll. I'm a *manager,* not a clerk," he said with a shy smile, and squeezed back. It gave him a deal of satisfaction to see Driscoll wince and pull his hand away.

"I understand you were the only one to survive the stage holdup," said Driscoll. "The story's all over town."

Jace touched the plaster on his temple. "Yes, sir. It was a close shave."

Driscoll's eyes narrowed with suspicion. "Sounds mighty queer to me. A convenient stop. An ambush."

"They were lying in wait, that's for sure. They would have stopped us on that stretch of road, no matter what we'd done."

"And no one even got off a shot?" asked Driscoll sharply.

Jace hesitated. The bastard was clearly fishing for a conspiracy, measuring his neck for a rope. And there was always a chance that the truth would come out. Gossip had a way of spreading. Best to be as honest as he could. "As a matter of fact, I think I killed one of them."

Big Jim looked startled. "You? Do you carry a gun?"

He retreated into stumbling foolishness. "Dear me, *no*. I only . . . Mr. Johnson had kindly allowed me to hold his pistol while he refreshed himself. The scoundrels shot me. And then, when they came to see if I was truly dead, I . . . took the opportunity to fire." He shuddered. "I think I killed the villain, but his partners in crime took away his body." He shuddered again. "It was dreadful. Dreadful! I shall never forget it."

Carl snickered and put his hand over his pistol. "You're a reg'lar desperado. I wonder how you'd do in a showdown."

Jace fixed the man with a bland stare. "I can't say I like the way you've got of introducing yourself, stranger. I learned to shoot in the army. I don't suppose *you* served. But I reckon I could take you on in a gentleman's challenge." He brushed an imaginary speck from his coat. "That is, if you're a gentleman."

Carl growled, pulled his pistol from his holster, and leaped toward Jace. Holding the gun to Jace's head, he cocked the weapon.

Jace held his ground. He'd played enough poker to know a bluff when he saw it. His only homage to "Horace" was to pretend to look startled.

"Hold on, Carl!" cried Driscoll. "Don't be a hothead. Put up your gun."

Carl wavered, fear dancing in his eyes at Driscoll's scowl, then replaced his weapon with a muttered curse.

Driscoll turned to Jace. "I must apologize for my foreman,

Perkins," he said smoothly. "He gets a little riled when someone talks about the war. He had a bit of trouble with the army."

Jace clenched his teeth in rage. The man had probably been a deserter, or a damned bounty jumper—taking a cash bounty to join a regiment and then deserting. The scum of the earth. He was tempted to throttle him on the spot.

But Big Jim was watching him, an odd look on his face. And Beth, whose cheeks had gone pale when Carl pulled his gun, was tense with fright. Jace forced his anger to cool. "Oh, fudge," he said with a dainty wave of his hand. "I have no quarrel with the man. Let him go his way."

"Good. Good." Driscoll smiled his relief and turned to Beth. "And how are you today, missy?"

She gave a little curtsy, the color returning to her face. "Very well, sir."

He tapped the top of her bowler. "Don't you know ladies don't wear hats like that?" he teased.

Carl found his courage and his voice at the same time. "Yup. A reg'lar tomboy."

Beth stamped her foot. "Am not!"

"Am too, you little ragamuffin. You'll be wearin' britches next."

Beth gaped, her soft lip quivering, her eyes brimming with tears. Big Jim made a growling sound in his throat.

Jace's seething anger boiled over, heedless of common sense. He grabbed Carl by his neckerchief and gave it a savage twist. "You owe the little girl an apology."

"Now, now," said Driscoll quickly, separating the two men. "Perkins is right, Carl. Say you're sorry to the kid, then get out of here."

Carl glared at his boss, mumbled an apology, and swaggered to the door, hat pulled low over his forehead.

Driscoll cleared his throat. "Sorry about this, Southgate," he said. "But with this, that, and the other thing, Carl hasn't been himself lately." He marched to the jars of candy sitting on the counter. "What say I treat your little girl to a sweet or two?"

Big Jim pulled Beth into his safe, warm embrace. "What say you keep that lout out of my store from now on?" he said in an icy voice.

Driscoll gave him a rigid smile, then replaced his silk hat. "Just so. I can look at that catalog another time." He turned on his heel and strode from the store.

Big Jim shook his head. "Driscoll's a decent fellow. Why does he keep a lowlife like that in his employ?" He patted Beth on the shoulder. "Help yourself to a candy, pet. But don't tell Callie."

Decent fellow or not, thought Jace, there was something about Driscoll he didn't like. And Beth felt it, too. He'd seen it on her face when Driscoll had greeted her. "Are you ready to close up, Big Jim?"

Southgate rubbed his chin. "In point of fact, I could use a good whiskey right about now. What say you and I go over to the El Dorado for a spell?"

A drink sounded fine to him. It would ease the soreness in his ribs. But he didn't want to seem too eager. "Well, perhaps *one*," he said doubtfully. "But what about Beth?"

"Beth can stay here with Billy Dee. We'll pick her up on the way home."

Beth pouted. "What'll I do while you're gone?"

Jace knelt before her. "Well, Princess, see that pile of bandannas? That last mule skinner made an all-fired mess of them. Do you reckon you could fold them all nice and neat for me?" At her enthusiastic nod, he stood up and turned to Southgate. "I'm ready, sir."

Big Jim cast a chagrined eye over Jace's checked suit and shook his head. "We've got to do something about your Eastern rig pretty damn soon. You can pick out a suit from the stock tomorrow. Something that *fits*, for goodness sake! And whatever else you need to outfit yourself. In the meantime ..." He pointed to a shelf. "Mr. Stetson makes a damn fine hat. Try one on."

The hat was black felt and broad-brimmed. Creased and tilted at a natty angle, it made Jace feel a little less citified and prissy. He'd dreaded going into the saloon in Horace's suit, a target for every sniggering roughneck.

"I'll reimburse you for my clothing, Big Jim," he said as they made their way down the street in the glow of the setting sun.

"Like hell you will."

Yes, by God, he thought, feeling an unfamiliar surge of moral rectitude. He didn't usually bother with such niceties. But he'd earn whatever he got from Big Jim. Damned if he wouldn't. "I must insist, sir."

"You'll do as I tell you, no ifs or buts!" Southgate boomed. It wasn't an angry command—merely a statement by someone who was used to being obeyed.

Jace stopped in the middle of the street. "Do you still want me to keep your books, Big Jim?"

Southgate stopped in his turn, staring in surprise. "Why the hell not?"

"In that case, I'll see that the store is reimbursed from my pocket," he said firmly. "You'll have to hire a bookkeeper to have it any different."

"What the Sam Hill?" growled Big Jim. They stood toe-to-toe for a moment, measuring one another with their eyes. Then Southgate laughed. "I'll tell you one thing, Jace. You're up to snuff, and a pinch above it."

"Thank you, Big Jim."

Southgate reached into his coat pocket. "I reckon you'd like a smoke with that whiskey." He pulled out two thick cigars and held one out to Jace.

Jace hesitated, then took the cigar. Hell, even *Horace* was allowed to have a vice or two, wasn't he? He pulled a match from his pocket, struck it on his shoe, and took a deep draw on the tobacco. "That's a mighty fine cigar, Big Jim," he said as they resumed their way toward the saloon.

Southgate was silent, an odd frown creasing his brow. At last he spoke in a low and thoughtful voice. "I don't know who the hell you are, Jace. But you're not the man you're supposed to be."

He felt a finger of alarm tickle his guts. "Cheese in crackers," he squeaked. "Whatever do you mean?"

Southgate gave a dry laugh. "Save that for Callie. Whoever the man Timothy Cooper knew, the war must have changed you. And all to the good."

He exhaled with relief. At least he could temper *some* of Horace's prissy mannerisms when he was with Southgate. He dropped his voice to a more natural pitch. "The war changed all of us. A man would have to be a blithering idiot to remain untouched." He tried to keep the bitterness from creeping into his tone.

"All I know is, I'm damned glad you're here, son."

Jace stumbled on a rock in the road, gulping to control the sudden thickness in his throat.

Son. He'd never heard that word before—not in his whole miserable life.

Chapter Seven

"Don't let Beth stay up too late, Mrs. Ackland." Callie placed her cane in the wagon, then hoisted herself up onto the driver's seat, using her good leg for support.

Mrs. Ackland shielded her eyes with one large, raw-knuckled hand and scowled toward the west. The sun hung low, scraping the tops of the mountains. " 'Tain't right for you to go at this hour, Miss Callie. The sun'll be just about gone when you get to town. And you'll come home in the pitch dark." She clicked her tongue. "And your father off in Denver on business. My land! What'll he say when he finds out you been gallivantin' around Dark Creek in the dead of night? And all by yourself!"

Callie pursed her lips in annoyance. "He doesn't have to find out."

The housekeeper tried to look reasonable. "What say I scoot on home and fetch my man? It's just a spell up the road."

"For heaven's sake, I'll be perfectly safe! And I won't be coming home alone. I'll have Weedy with me. I'm sure there's a good reason he didn't come home for supper, as he promised."

Mrs. Ackland jammed her fists on her wide hips. "I'll be blamed, that scamp is gettin' wilder and wilder."

Callie smoothed on her leather gloves and picked up the reins. "Don't wait up for us."

"Hmph!" The housekeeper shook her head, turned, and marched back into the house.

Callie was grateful that Mrs. Ackland had agreed to stay overnight—bunked on a cot in Sissy's room—during the time Big Jim was in Denver. Her father had insisted on it, for propriety's sake, so there'd be no gossip in town about her and Perkins. But she was glad she'd had the older woman to turn to when Weedy hadn't appeared this evening. She never would have been able to leave Sissy and Beth alone. And she was worried about Weedy. He had never been so irresponsible in Boston.

None of this would have been necessary, of course, if Perkins hadn't virtually abandoned them every evening since Big Jim had been gone. "Working late," he always said, though Callie couldn't imagine anyone wanting to go shopping at all hours of the night.

He certainly had kept reasonable hours—punctual and conscientious—in the nearly two weeks he'd been working at the store. Up at dawn, breakfasted and out on his horse long before Big Jim was ready to leave. He stayed in town for dinner, as well, so Big Jim didn't have to close up when he came home for his midday meal. And in the evenings, he and Big Jim would come in promptly for supper, laughing and chatting about their day in the store. Her father couldn't stop extolling his abilities as a clerk and manager—though Callie couldn't imagine he had the gumption for it.

But in the last few days, since Big Jim had been gone, she hadn't heard Perkins's horse come up the road until almost midnight. While the cat's away . . . ?

She jiggled the reins and made a clicking noise, and the horse trotted obediently through the gate and onto the narrow dirt road. *Well,* she thought, making an effort to be generous, *perhaps Perkins is taking inventory.* There had been several more thefts from the storeroom in the past two weeks. Nothing of great importance, Big Jim had said. But it riled him nonetheless. Maybe Perkins thought to ingratiate himself with his employer by taking a careful count of all the goods while Big Jim was away.

She snorted in disgust. Not that Big Jim needed to be won over! The two men were already as close as Siamese twins. What her father saw in Perkins was beyond her. He minced around the house, simpering and tittering, deferring to her as though he feared she'd bite off his head. Had such a spineless creature ever existed in this world before *he* was born? She gave a bitter laugh and poked at her windblown curls. Was she any different? "Wear your hair down, girl," Big Jim had said. "You'll be more winsome. We don't want Jace to think you're an old spinster, do we?" And she had meekly obeyed.

She shivered and looked around her. The road was already in shadow, hidden from the sun by the mountains, and the air had turned cool. She would never get used to this weather. The end of June already. And the nights still descended with a heavy chill that sent her to bed under thick quilts.

She sighed. She shouldn't have been so proud and stubborn when Mrs. Ackland had urged her to take a shawl. But she'd felt the need to show a *little* spunk. A spark of independence to hide the fact that she had willingly allowed Big Jim to lay out her future for her.

Marriage to Jace Perkins. They hadn't talked of it yet, but she knew it was inevitable. She remembered something she'd read from Abigail Adams's correspondence. "All men will be tyrants, if they are allowed." And, Lord save her, she had allowed with Poppy—as Mummy had allowed. She had watched her mother gradually lose every aspect of her personality under the strong-willed—if kindly—domination of her husband. Would *she* be any different, even with Jace Perkins? Or would "Mousekin" become an atomy, a gnat to be squashed under his foot?

What is it in the affairs of men and women, she thought sadly, *that causes women to be so docile?*

And yet, and yet . . . Jace Perkins didn't seem to be strong enough to dominate anyone. So why should the thought of marriage to him unsettle her so?

Maybe it was the look in his eyes, that strange gleam that appeared when he thought she wasn't watching him. Maybe it was the way his voice darkened unexpectedly, sending shivers up her spine. Maybe it was the sight of his manly form, so overwhelming, so at odds with his manner. And maybe it was the heat that radiated from his flesh every time he touched her—and the fact that he took every opportunity to touch her. A hand to her elbow to steady her, the brush of his shoulder as they passed through a doorway together, the firm clasp of his fingers on hers to emphasize the sincerity of his words. At those moments, she always experienced a thrill of fear, feeling herself in the presence of a stranger.

And then there was the prissy Jace, the man who revolted her. So effeminate in his ways, so weak and useless. She had wanted someone genteel, to be sure. But not a man who was so helpless that she couldn't look up to him.

"Callie," she said aloud, "you don't know *what* you want, you foolish creature." Not a strong husband, surely, who would reduce her to a shell of a woman. But she didn't want a namby-pamby either.

Her ladies' circle in Boston had understood the dilemma. They had made a secret pledge never to give themselves to the opposite sex. The institution of marriage simply made a mockery of a woman's claims to emancipation.

She sighed again, filled with confusion. She only knew that the next few months loomed like a death sentence. And she was the powerless victim, awaiting the jerk of the rope around her neck. So inevitable. So dreaded.

She had reached Dark Creek at last. She guided the horse down Front Street to Big Jim's store. Perkins was just locking up. Callie wrinkled her brow in surprise. If he was closing at the usual time, why had he said he would be home late?

He turned and smiled as she brought the wagon to a stop. "Miss Callie!" he exclaimed. "What brings you to town?"

She chided herself for noticing how handsome he looked in his new suit, the rakish tilt of his hat that gave him a dangerous air. "Weedy never came home for supper," she said sharply, annoyed at the unexpected jolt of his masculine presence. He reached up and lifted her from the wagon, setting her on her feet with such slowness that she wondered if it was deliberate. She steadied herself against the wagon with one hand and glared at him. "You may release me, now," she said in a tight voice, "and give me my cane. *I,* for one, don't wish to make a show of familiarity for the passersby."

"Of course, ma'am," he simpered. "Heavens to Betsy, did you think that I . . . ?"

She cut him off with an impatient wave of her hand. "Where do you think Weedy could be?"

He tugged uneasily at his collar. "Well, Miss Callie, if his recent behavior is any indication, I fear he is in one of the saloons. Why don't you wait inside the shop while I look for him?"

"Stuff and nonsense. I'll go with you."

He frowned. "I scarcely think that's wise. The low establishments in this town are not the place for a gentlewoman."

The thought of a twiddlepoop like this warning her against saloons made her want to laugh. "Do you think I'm helpless? Or completely naive? We shall go together."

He sighed. "Very well. If you must." He pointed down the street. "The Golden Bough is a likely place to start. I've seen Weedy go inside from time to time."

"And never stopped him, I suppose!" she snapped.

"Miss Callie, it's not my place. Besides, a young lad needs to flirt with manhood once in a while."

"Did you?" she said with a sneer.

He stared at her for a moment, his blue eyes filled with

unreadable thoughts. Then he tittered. "Cheese in crackers. I had my share of scrapes as a boy. Candlewax on the neighbors' windows at Halloween. And an occasional theft of candy when the clerk wasn't looking."

"Oh, my," she said in a sarcastic tone. "How very dangerous."

He looked bewildered. "I think you're twitting me, Miss Callie. But this doesn't help us find Weedy. Come along, if you please."

The Golden Bough was even more wild and libertine than Callie had expected. Crowds of shaggy-haired miners and ranchers cursed at one another beneath a thick blue haze of tobacco smoke. They gathered at gaming tables, congregated around the pianist who plunked out a steady stream of raucous tunes, leaned up against the bar with its garish display of glasses and bottles.

As for the women in their shameless gowns, bright with spangles and feathers . . . Callie shuddered. How could God's creatures allow themselves to sink so low?

Perkins took her elbow. "Perhaps the barkeep can tell us where Weedy is." He steered her across the floor, his hand firm and warm on her arm.

The music stopped. Every eye in the place seemed to be fastened on them as Callie's cane tapped a clumsy rhythm across the floor. She felt faint, burning with embarrassment. Why had she been so stubborn and foolish? She stumbled and would have fallen; only Perkins's strong grip supported her.

It seemed an eternity until they reached the bar. Perkins glared at the men on either side until they smiled sheepishly and drifted away.

The barkeep hurried over. "Evening, Jace."

Perkins nodded. "Evening, Clem."

Clem grinned with a mouthful of rotting teeth. "You want to try your luck again tonight? You skunked them bullwhackers real good last night, damned if you didn't!"

"Watch your language in front of a lady," growled Perkins,

much to Callie's surprise. She hadn't expected him to defend her with such manly vigor. "This is Miss Southgate," he went on. "Big Jim's daughter. She's looking for her brother Weedy."

"Hell, ma'am . . ." Clem reddened under his tan. "That is . . . shucks, ma'am. I ain't seen him all night."

"Thank you, my good man," she said barely above a whisper, conscious of the eyes and ears turned in their direction.

Perkins offered her his arm. "Shall we go then, Miss Southgate?"

The retreat from the saloon was even more humiliating than their entrance. Callie could hear whispers as they passed, mocking giggles from the saloon girls. And, as they reached the street, the place exploded with loud guffaws. She leaned against the hitching post, trembling. She was grateful that night had begun to fall; the darkness hid the blush that burned her cheeks.

"We can try the saloon across the street," said Perkins.

She hesitated, not sure whether she could endure another scene like that.

"Would you prefer to wait outside, Miss Callie?" His voice held the gentleness of sympathy.

As though I were a poor, pitiable creature—the crippled Miss Southgate, she thought, mortified. "No," she said, fighting to keep the tremor from her voice.

She thought he would respond with understanding. Instead, his voice deepened to a low, angry rumble. "Then hold your head up with pride," he commanded. "You're a woman of refinement. Better than anybody in that place."

She stared in surprise. Who would have thought he could show such authority? But perhaps it was only because he considered her the weaker sex in this situation. Still, encouraged by his faith in her, and bolstered by his strong hand, she managed to sail into the next saloon with more confidence than she would have imagined. Only the painting above the bar—a crude portrait of a partially clothed woman—gave her a moment's unease. But she reminded herself that she had seen more than

one nude in the museums of Boston, and managed to keep her
eyes averted from the picture without seeming to be a prude.

The conversation with the barkeep was repeated. This time,
the man nodded vigorously. "Sure enough, Jace. Weedy's over
to the Red Bull."

"Where's the Red Bull?" asked Callie when they had
returned to the street.

"Down the road a piece," he said. "But you'll wait outside."

She banged her cane on the boardwalk in exasperation. He
was taking his authority too far! "Must we have this quarrel
again?"

"Mercy me!" he said, retreating. "The last thing I want is
to quarrel with you. But the Red Bull is a . . . oh, fudge! A
sporting palace, ma'am."

She gaped. "And Weedy is in *there?*"

"You may not have noticed it," he said delicately, "but
he's not a little boy anymore." He led her down the street, set
her on a bench outside the door of the Red Bull, and went
inside. The night air was shrill with the sound of female laughter
and the clink of glasses.

Callie shuddered at the sound. Had Weedy sunk so low into
depravity that there was no saving him? She wondered what
Big Jim would think.

"Howdy, little lady. Waitin' fer a feller?"

She looked up in alarm. A large, rawboned cowboy stood
before her, grinning and scratching his stubbly chin. His face
was a sickly yellow in the light streaming from the windows
of the sporting palace.

"I . . . beg your pardon?" she said.

"You look like you could give a feller a good time. A lusty
handful. Whatta ya say?"

She gasped her outrage. "How dare you speak to a lady like
that, sir?"

He backed away from her. "No need to get techy, ma'am."
He tipped his hat, turned, and swaggered down the street. "But

if you ain't no whore," he shot back, "you ain't got no call to be sittin' outside a whorehouse."

She watched his retreating back with an odd mixture of anger and pride. Even an emancipated woman could feel flattered that a man found her attractive. There had been very few masculine overtures in Boston. It made her wonder about Perkins. Did *he* see her as a woman? The thought gave her a strange shiver of pleasure.

After a few minutes, Perkins emerged with Weedy. Callie was dismayed to see that her brother was swaying slightly. His clothing was rumpled and disheveled, and his eyes burned with rebellion.

"Damn it, Jace," he growled, "who do you think you are?"

Perkins took him firmly by his shirtfront. "You can ruin your life, if you want to. And rot your guts with liquor. No one can stop you. But you'll not frighten your sister like this again. Or you'll have to deal with me."

Weedy doubled his fists and thrust out his jaw. "And who the hell are you?"

Perkins scowled, raised his hand, and smacked Weedy across the side of his face. "Watch your mouth in front of Callie. Now apologize to her for making her worry about you."

Weedy glared at Jace, rubbing his sore cheek; then his glance wavered. "I'm sorry, Callie," he muttered.

Jace patted him on the shoulder. "I know you didn't mean to be thoughtless. Now, if you can sober up, maybe we can go hunting tomorrow afternoon. I'll close the store early, or let Billy Dee take over."

Weedy nodded, breaking into a grateful smile. "I reckon that sounds good enough."

"Good. Fetch your horse from the livery stable and tie it to the wagon. And take Callie home."

"Wait a moment," said Callie, rising from the bench. "Aren't you coming, too?"

"No. I have some business to attend to."

"Gambling?" She curled her lip in disgust. "That *was* what

Clem was referring to, wasn't it?'' She had scarcely believed the barkeep's words. It seemed so out of character for Perkins. But perhaps her instinct had been right, when he'd talked to Big Jim about his financial state. ''Are you more money-hungry than you let on, Mr. Perkins?'' she asked sharply.

He frowned as though her words had discomposed him, then turned his head away in a shy gesture. ''Oh, mercy me, Miss Callie. Can you forgive my momentary weakness? It's a harmless indulgence that I allow myself. To try my luck at cards once in a while. I certainly don't intend to gamble tonight.''

''Then what keeps you in town?'' She glanced uneasily at the sporting palace.

''Heavens to Betsy! Not *that*. But I've been camping out at night near the storeroom, hoping to find out who is stealing from your father.''

For all its embarrassments, tonight had been an adventure, a heady mixture of excitement and novelty that had fired her blood. She didn't want it to end so soon. ''I'll watch with you,'' she announced.

He shook his head. ''No. It will be a long, cold vigil. And nothing might happen. I've watched in vain these past three nights.''

''Mr. Perkins!'' she said, her voice rising in anger. ''Why do you always treat me like a helpless ninny? I insist on staying with you.''

He conceded with a weak smile, then turned to Weedy. ''Go on home. If Mrs. Ackland is worried, tell her we'll be home . . .'' He pulled out his pocket watch and frowned at it. ''Eleven, at the latest.'' As Weedy opened his mouth to protest, Perkins raised a warning finger. ''And don't beg to stay with your sister and me. A drunkard is of no use at all if there's going to be trouble.''

Weedy sighed in resignation, then shuffled down a side alley to the livery stable, wobbling as he went.

Chapter Eight

Callie stared at Perkins in awe and disbelief. "I haven't seen Weedy so obedient since we came out here. You acted just like a stern parent. The way you talked to him."

He hung his head and shuffled his boot on the boardwalk. "Forgive me, Miss Callie. It will never happen again. It's not my natural inclination. I just tried to remember how my dear papa behaved. And Weedy seemed to need a bit of severity, for the moment. To set him on the track to righteousness."

"Yes, of course." Why did his prim speech fill her with disappointment?

He gave a shy laugh. "Now to our 'detective' work, if you will."

"What do you intend?"

"Well, Billy Dee has already gone to sleep in the storeroom. I've begun to suspect that he sneaks out at night and leaves the place unprotected. I propose that we take up our vigil across the street. There's a small shop with an overhang. It will keep us in shadow even if someone comes along with a lantern. I'll put your wagon into the livery stable before we begin our . . ."

he giggled again," . . . our adventure. I don't want it to be seen outside your father's store."

The alley next to the storeroom door was surprisingly well lit: several saloons dotted the street, their windows and open doors casting a golden glow into the road. But the loud noises coming from within those establishments made it unnecessary for them to speak in whispers.

Perkins indicated the planked boardwalk next to the shop. "I wish I had a cushion. But you'll find it more comfortable to sit, even on the hard board, than stand for hours." He sat down and leaned his back against the wall to protect himself from the wind, which had begun to rise. His legs were so long that his low boots caught the light; laughing nervously, he drew up his knees.

Callie followed his lead, tucking her knees demurely to one side and arranging her skirts to cover her ankles. "I swan, it's cold," she said. "It was foolish of me not to bring a shawl."

"I hate to be cold," he said in a strange, faraway voice. "It always seemed to be cold in the . . ." He stopped abruptly and turned his head aside.

"In Baltimore? But it's a warm climate, I've heard. And you had a comfortable childhood, you said in your letters."

He tittered. "Yes. Of course. But in the prison camp, with no blankets . . . Oh, fudge. You don't want to hear this."

"Why not?"

"It's not fit for your delicate ears."

She laughed at his prissiness. "At the moment, my delicate ears are getting very cold."

"Then that's the second reason I'm glad you're wearing your hair down."

"And the first?"

He leaned in close, his voice soft and intimate at her ear. "Because your hair is the most beautiful I've ever seen. Like spun gold when the light hits it." He inhaled sharply. "And you wash it with lavender soap. Very enticing." His hand played with a curl at her cheek.

She had been basking in the warm flattery of his compliments. But there were limits to how far a gentleman could go! "Mr. Perkins, you presume too much," she snapped, jerking her head away. She waited for his stumbling apology.

Instead, he sighed mournfully. "I *presumed* that you'd call me Jace, since your father wanted it that way. But when he's around, you don't use my name at all. And when he's gone, you call me **Mr.** Perkins."

She felt humiliated that he'd noticed her deliberate snub. "There are times when what I want, and what my father wants, are not the same," she said with more venom than she'd intended.

"But what if I were to say it would bring me great joy to hear you call me Jace? Could I persuade you?"

She lifted her chin proudly and looked him full in the face. He wasn't about to cajole *her*. "Not in the slightest degree."

"You will, someday." He smiled oddly and lapsed into silence.

Oh, the scoundrel! Was he so certain of their marriage? She was determined not to say another word to him tonight. She sat quietly, her eyes on the storeroom door across the street.

But after a while the cold began to seep into her bones and she shivered. "Why does it get so cold at night here?" she said.

"They say it's the mountain air. It's thin, and can't hold the day's warmth." He fished in his coat pocket and pulled something out. "Here. This might help."

She scowled at the silver flask. *"Whiskey?* Since when have you begun to travel with potent spirits?"

He smiled sheepishly. "Those long rides home are mighty cold. The night air, you know. Surely you'll forgive a man a few minor vices."

She snorted. "You seem to have taken on all the wild ways of this territory. And in an extremely short time."

"Dear me. I trust that I shall never go so far that I displease you." He pressed the flask into her fingers, unscrewing the top. "Please, Miss Callie. Take a sip."

She glared at him. "Mr. Perkins, I'm 'temperance'!"

"A worthy goal, to be sure. But you're also cold. And it won't harm you. In fact, it's quite beneficial in moderation. And it will take the chill from your bones. I wouldn't dream of suggesting it for any other reason."

She wavered, then wiped the top of the flask with her gloved fingers and held it to her lips. The first timid sip brought tears to her eyes, but the second one burned its way down her throat and into her belly with a soothing warmth. "That does feel good," she said shyly.

He beamed and helped himself to a generous mouthful. He insisted she take one more sip, then he closed the flask and put it away. "And to make you even warmer," he said, "if you wouldn't think it too presumptuous of me . . ." He reached out with his arm and pulled her close to him.

She knew she should object, but his arm was too comfortable and snug. And the whiskey had given her a cozy glow that warmed her to her toes. *Good gracious,* she thought. She had never known alcohol could be so soothing.

He slid his hand up and down her sleeve—a long, slow glide. "Such a thin dress. You must be frozen."

She shivered, but not from the cold. His sensuous touch made her heart pound and her mouth go dry. She knew he was only being kind and thoughtful. How could he suspect that his touch felt like a caress, his friendly hug a lover's embrace? He was too civilized to court her in an unseemly fashion. She cursed her own foolishness, her overwrought emotions. She gulped. "My throat is so dry. Do you suppose . . . ?"

At once, he held out the flask. "Mercy sakes, are you sure it won't go to your head?"

His words struck her like a challenge. She hated to feel like a weak female. "Of course not," she said with bravado. "I have indulged in wine on festive occasions. And felt no ill effects afterward." She drank more than she had intended, but she wasn't about to back down. "And if it's beneficial, as you say . . ."

He helped himself to another swallow. "Oh, most certainly. I've always found that a little whiskey accomplishes what I want it to."

She was beginning to feel light-headed and giddy. She wriggled closer to him. "I'm still cold."

"Perhaps two arms . . . ?" He brought his other arm in front of her; his elbow pressed against her breast, and his hand held firmly to her waist.

She felt warm and safe, encircled by his embrace, her back against his solid chest. When he wasn't being priggish, he could be downright pleasant. She wondered why she had always viewed men with such trepidation.

And then she felt his lips on her neck.

She gave a start of alarm. "Please release me, Mr. Perkins." Her voice trembled.

"But you'll be cold," he murmured. His tone was low and seductive. He ran his lips up her neck to catch her earlobe between his teeth.

She moaned in surprise and pleasure. What in heaven's name was happening to her? She could scarcely speak. "P-please, Mr. Perkins," she stammered.

He gave a soft chuckle and blew against the shell of her ear. She shivered. "That's not my name," he said.

This was madness, and she knew it in that part of her brain that could still function. "In the name of pity," she whispered, "let me go. Jace."

"Not until you look at me."

She turned in his arms, fearful to see the look on his face. Was he mocking her? But he smiled so warmly, the dimple marking his cheek, that she felt her insides turn to jelly. She wanted nothing so much as to stay in his arms forever.

"Now say my name again," he said.

"Jace." It was a soft croak rather than a spoken word.

"And do you promise *never* to call me Mr. Perkins again?"

"Y-yes."

"Yes, *who?*"

"Yes, Jace."

"Sweet Callie, you deserve a reward for that."

Mesmerized, she watched his head lower to hers, felt the gentle warmth of his breath on her mouth. *Now may I be consigned to the fires of Hell,* she thought, and closed her eyes to receive his kiss. Her first kiss.

She felt his body stiffen, and then he pushed her away. "Damn," he muttered.

Her eyes flew open. A ragged prospector was creeping down the street toward the storehouse. He held a crowbar in one grimy fist. He lifted his hand and knocked softly on the door.

Jace released her, scrambled to his feet, and held a silencing finger to his mouth.

The storehouse door opened. Billy Dee appeared, his body rigid with tension. He looked warily around the alley, then crept outside. Callie could see the gleam of a key in his hand. He locked the door, then turned to the prospector. The man fished in his tattered coat and pulled out a bottle.

Billy Dee snatched it from his hand, pulled the cork, and took a long swig. He rubbed his sleeve against his mouth and nodded his approval. "Don't start till I skedaddles out o' here," he said, turning to go up the alley.

Jace reached down and pulled a small pistol from his boot top. He stepped off the boardwalk into the light of the street. "Neither one of you will 'skedaddle,' gentlemen, if you know what's good for you."

The prospector froze. Billy Dee turned and swore softly.

"Now," said Jace, coming closer and pointing his pistol at the level of their heads, "would you care to tell me what this is all about?"

Filled with curiosity, Callie hobbled from the sidewalk to join the men.

The prospector began to babble. "Well, sir . . . that is, ma'am . . . I'll be danged, sir . . ." He took a deep breath. His face was lined, and his shoulders curved in a dejected posture. "It's like this, sir. It's got down to the hardpan, and dollars are skurce. I reckoned I'd get me a little sowbelly and hardtack. Nothin' fancy, you understand. Not more'n army rations is what I had in mind."

Jace reached out and pulled the bottle from Billy Dee's hand, scowling at the crude label. "And all for the price of cheap rotgut," he said in disgust.

"It don't matter much to you," the prospector whined, "but I gotta have food to work my claim. And I ain't the only one. Lots of fellers had their deals with Billy Dee."

Jace pointed to the crowbar. "And did any of you factor in the cost to Mr. Southgate of a broken door and lock?"

"Jeez, sir, are you gonna send me to jail for that? Have a heart. I never done this afore."

Jace hesitated, scanning the man's sorry appearance. "Come around to the store tomorrow," he said at last. "I'll give you supplies on credit."

The prospector sighed in relief. "Christ, man, you're the salt o' the earth."

Jace snorted. "I doubt that. And I'll want the mortgage on your claim, in case you can't make good." He gestured with his pistol. "Now get out of here."

Billy Dee cleared his throat. "Well, ever'thing's safe. I'll just mosey on back, Mr. Perkins."

Jace took a menacing step forward, the pistol steady in his hand. "You'll just stay where you are, or I'll blow your head off." He brandished the bottle of whiskey. "I ought to crown you with this. Who else but Big Jim would have given a rummy like you a chance?" He took another step forward and raised the bottle. His jaw was clenched in fury.

Billy Dee gave a terrified squeak and threw up a quaking arm to protect his head.

Callie felt his fright. She hadn't thought Jace was capable of such contained rage. "Jace, no! You mustn't!" she cried.

He turned to look at her. In a moment, the anger in his face had turned to chagrin, like a child's toy that changes faces at the tug of a string. "Oh, fudge, Miss Callie," he said, lowering the bottle. "I wouldn't really hurt the man, no matter what he's done. Not when Beth is so fond of him." He managed a smile in Billy Dee's direction. "Tell you what, old-timer. I'll supply you with two bottles of good Taos Lightning a week, and a big keg of lager once a month from the Rocky Mountain Brewery in Denver. And an occasional bottle of Old Crow, if you look sharp. You limit yourself to that, and nothing more. Agreed?"

Billy Dee ran his tongue around his leathery lips and gulped. "That's right decent o' you, sir. Them's mighty fine drinks."

"They come with a price, however. You do your job, and guard that storeroom. Otherwise, I'll find me a good sharp knife, and lop off one of your fingers every time there's a theft. Do you understand?"

Billy Dee gulped again. "Y-yessir."

"Good." Jace uncorked the bottle and poured its contents onto the ground. "And when you *do* drink, I'll expect you to drink inside. And sleep off your drunk—if you should be foolish enough to overindulge—*inside.*" He jerked his chin in the direction of the storeroom. "Now, get going."

Billy Dee looked wistfully at the puddle of liquor, then scurried off, counting his fingers.

Callie turned to Jace in indignation. "Cut off his fingers? Are you a savage?"

He shrugged sheepishly. "Cheese in crackers. I would never do such a thing. I only wanted to frighten him. Dear me, those thefts were playing havoc with my bookkeeping!" He stowed his pistol and held out his arm. "Shall we get the wagon and my horse, and go home?"

She was silent as he tied his horse to the back of the wagon, lit the lanterns, and took the seat beside her. But when they were on the road out of town, she turned to him. "Gambling and drinking. And now a gun? I'm beginning to wonder if you're the man Mr. Cooper said you were."

He seemed genuinely disconcerted. "I . . . that is . . . Mr. Cooper knew me before the war. Times change. Men change. I confess I do drink a spot of whiskey, from time to time. It's good for the blood, I've been told. As for the gambling, I . . . learned to play cards in the Reb camp. It was all we had to pass the time. And I'm occasionally lucky. A head for numbers, I suppose. So I indulge." He put his hand on hers. "Will that make you hate me, Miss. Callie?"

A humble apology, but she wasn't about to ease his conscience so soon. She pulled her hand away. "And the pistol?"

"I only procured it when I knew I'd be keeping watch for the thief. It seemed a prudent course. Now that everything is settled, I'll return it to its shelf in the store."

"Humph!" She tossed her head.

"Don't be peevish, Miss Callie. Not when the night is so beautiful." He pointed to the top of a mountain, where the moon sat like a shining globe, suspended in inky blackness. "It never looked so close before. Pure silver."

She eyed him sharply. "Has prospecting fever struck you, then?"

He looked horrified. "Mercy sakes, no! When I have such a fine, steady job?"

"Most men come out here just to get rich by digging for ore."

"That isn't so. What about your father? And Mr. Driscoll? Good businessmen who saw an opportunity and took it." He stared up at the moon and sighed. "Your father says you're sweet on Mr. Driscoll."

She felt her face burning. "I'm no such thing!"

He turned and smiled at her. His eyes sparkled in the moonlight. "I'm glad. I don't like that man. He's far too slick for my taste."

"Oh, don't be absurd! Everybody in town likes him," she snapped. She chewed on her lip. Had she been too quick to defend Mr. Driscoll? Surely Jace would read it as a sign of her secret interest in the banker. "I'm sure you're just jealous of his success," she said sourly. "He's the most properous man in town."

"And as slick as a confidence man."

"How would *you* know?" she sneered.

He laughed, an odd, secret laugh that he seemed to share only with himself. "Well, as they say out here, I wasn't born in the woods to be scared by an owl. And that man's a caution."

"I don't like unkind gossip," she said primly. "I don't think we should talk about Mr. Driscoll anymore."

He smiled and scanned her face and form. "Shall we talk about how pretty you are in the moonlight?"

She gasped. "Certainly not!"

"You didn't mind it in town."

"In town, Mr. Perkins, we . . ." She stopped and twisted her fingers together. Now that the effects of the whiskey had worn off, she could think clearly. She had let him embrace her, would even have allowed his kiss. But now that she was sober again, she really ought to put a stop to any improper ideas he might be harboring. She began once more. "In town, Mr. Perkins, we behaved most shamefully. I confess that I am equally to blame. And I have no doubt that our imprudence was brought on by the unseemly quantities of drink that we consumed. I don't intend for it to happen again. Please put aside any thoughts you might have of taking liberties."

He grunted, but said nothing. But when they had reached the house and he lifted her down from the wagon, he held her close in his arms for a moment. "You promised to call me Jace," he growled. "Is that also to be put aside?"

She gulped at the nearness of him, his handsome face sharp and angular in the moonlight. He was holding her in a very ungentlemanly way. Perhaps he had been drinking earlier, before she had come to the shop, and was still feeling the effects of the liquor. Filled with false courage. How else to explain his immodest embrace, the odd look on his face? And he certainly had been out of character in his behavior toward Weedy and Billy Dee.

There was only one way to escape his presence—sober or not. "I suppose a promise is a promise, *Jace,*" she said reluctantly. "No matter the circumstances. Now please let me go."

He grinned and released her. "I'll just put the horses away, *Callie.* Good-night."

If only they hadn't been drinking, she thought, as she pulled off her gloves and began to undress in her room. None of this would have happened. They wouldn't now be sharing the embarrassing memory of an indiscreet moment. *She* had certainly learned her lesson on the evils of drink! But had he?

As she put on her flannel nightgown, she remembered a temperance book she had. *Friendship's Offering.* She pulled it from its shelf and scanned the pages. It was filled with poems and little moral tales on the dangers of overindulgence. It was meant for one friend to give another, as a gentle hint. Maybe he could profit by it.

It wasn't too late. He had probably just come in from bedding down the horses. She threw a wrapper over her nightdress, picked up the book and her cane, and clumped up the stairs to his attic room.

"Come in," he said at her knock.

She hobbled in and froze. The book dropped from her hand. She felt her heart begin to pound in an alarming way.

He had taken off his shirt, and stood in the center of the room, stripped to the waist. The clean white bandage around his ribs only accentuated the black hairiness of his torso. "Oh . . . oh, my," she stammered. "Pardon me. I only wanted . . ."

She turned to flee. The tip of her cane caught on a protruding nail in the floor and jerked out of her hand. She teetered for a moment, trying to keep her balance, then crashed in a bone-jarring fall. She trembled with embarrassment, her pride aching more than her body.

At once, he was by her side, kneeling in concern. "Are you hurt, Callie?"

She struggled to sit up, fighting tears of shame. Crippled Callie. She shook her head. She couldn't even look into his eyes. "Just hand me my cane. Please," she said in a choked voice.

"Nonsense. You can't possibly walk after such a fall." He slipped one arm under her knees, and the other beneath her shoulders, and stood up.

She could feel the warmth of his body through her thin nightclothes. She knew she was blushing. "Please put me down," she whispered.

"No." He started for the door.

"But you can't . . . your ribs . . ."

"They're nearly healed. And you're as light as a feather." Ignoring her continued protests, he carried her down the stairs and laid her gently across her bed. But instead of leaving the room, he lay down beside her and leaned up on one elbow.

"Mr. Perkins, you must go!" she said in alarm. She tried to rise, but he held her down with one hand to her shoulder. She put her hands against his hairy chest and pushed. He felt as soft and as hard as goose-down covering a bar of iron. And impossible to move. "What do you want?" she croaked.

He smoothed the curls at her temple, then traced the curve of her cheek. His eyes were so blue they blinded her. "Pretty little darlin'," he murmured. "I should have kissed you before, and the devil with Billy Dee."

"You have no right . . ."

"I know that." His seductive voice was like a tantalizing finger tickling up and down her spine. "But will you take pity on me, and grant me a kiss now?"

Her refusal stuck in her throat. Before she had the chance to say "No," his lips covered hers. She moaned at the feathery contact of his mouth, every muscle of her body relaxing into helpless passivity. She had dreamed of kisses, envying the lovers on the Boston Common. But nothing had prepared her for the exquisite thrill of a man's lips. He stroked his mouth gently across hers—a kiss of sweet devotion—sending her into a realm of delight that took her breath away.

At last he lifted his head. His eyes were bright with wonder.

"My God, you're like a precious rose," he whispered, "unfolding for me petal by petal. I never imagined . . ."

He might be delighted, but she felt an odd disappointment. The kiss—sweet as it was—had been nothing more than gentle and respectful. It left her hungering for more, feeling a shameful urge she could scarcely understand. She ached to pull his head down to hers again.

Then her proper upbringing reasserted itself. *You're a fool, Callie!* she thought. *A weak-willed fool.* And she was playing with fire. To let him invade her bedroom, kiss her, fill her ears with honeyed words. Land sakes, they were both practically *naked!*

She struggled to sit up. "Go at once!" she ordered, pointing to the door. "How dare you take such liberties? Leave my room, or Poppy will hear what happened."

He seemed to consider her words; then he stood up and modestly crossed his arms against his chest. "Cheese in crackers. I beg your forgiveness. What could I have been thinking? You were so pretty in the moonlight. And now, all in white like an angel . . ." He smiled sheepishly. "A man has a right to dream, hasn't he?"

She pursed her lips. "I think I'm the one to decide when, and *if,* that dream becomes a reality. Now go away."

He hung his head and crept from her room.

But when he'd gone, and she had doused the lamps and curled up under her quilts, she found herself unable to sleep. Her mind was in turmoil, reliving the whole scene.

His kiss had really been quite unsatisfying, the more she stopped to think about it. So brief, so passive. A mere bird peck! She had no other kiss to compare it with, of course, but still . . .

"There must be more to it than that, for heaven's sake," she muttered aloud, her anger growing. She flipped onto her face, thrust her arms around her pillow, and kissed it with savage intensity, wriggling against the mattress with her breasts and hips. It wasn't quite the same as kissing a person, but the wild passion, the unchecked vigor of her movements was infinitely more pleasurable.

That was the kind of kiss she wanted. Not a polite, timid kiss from a . . . a twiddlepoop!

Chapter Nine

"That's the ticket, Weedy! Follow the bird with your body. Swing out as though the gun were just a part of your arm. Like I showed you the other day." Jace lifted his shotgun to his shoulder, pulled the trigger, and picked a Canada goose out of the sky.

"Hell!" said Weedy, as he fired and missed.

"Try again. There's one more, coming from those trees. Quick, now! You can do it."

This time, Weedy's shot was true. With a triumphant shout, he brandished his shotgun in the air as the bird fell to the ground.

"Come on," said Jace, tramping toward the aspen that dotted the hillside. "Mrs. Ackland can welcome your father home with roast goose."

They searched for the birds among the trees; all the while, Weedy crowed about his first kill, alternately bragging and thanking Jace for his advice. When they finally found the geese, resting close together on a bed of rose-colored hawkweed, Jace made a point of praising him lavishly.

"Damned if your bird isn't bigger than mine," he said, and watched the smile spread across the boy's face.

"Shucks," said Weedy modestly, "it was just beginner's luck."

"Not at all. You're a good shot. And in the fall, when the elk are rutting, we can try our hand at them. In the meantime, what say we come out next week and hunt for rabbits?"

Weedy beamed. "I'd surely like that."

"It's a lot more fun than getting screwed on rotgut every day, isn't it?"

"What's one have to do with the other?" Weedy growled.

Jace frowned. What the devil was it about young men that they had to drink to prove their manhood? He himself would be in his grave by now, but for old Sam Trimble.

He put a fatherly arm around the boy's shoulders as they made their way back to their tethered horses. "Look," he said, "I've seen a heap of men kill themselves with drink and whoring. Why ruin your life before it's even begun? The world is waiting for you. You've got a future. A pa who can afford to send you to a good school. Son of a gun, I wish *I'd* had that."

Weedy's lip curled in bitterness. "Big Jim doesn't even know I'm alive. And what the hell does the world care? I'm just Weedy. Jim's son."

Jace snorted and swung up into his saddle. "Beth told me you hate your name. But hell, man! Do you want to be called *Little* Jim?" He eyed the lanky boy as he mounted his own horse. "Christ! You'll be taller than me, one of these days."

Weedy straightened in the saddle, pride radiating from his face. "You think so?" He laughed. "Well, maybe 'Little Jim' would be comical. I reckon 'Weedy' isn't so bad."

They rode back to the house in companionable silence, the geese hooked like trophies around Weedy's pommel. Jace stirred in his saddle, feeling the soothing warmth of the early-afternoon sun on his back. He had never known such contentment. The dogs of restlessness that had nipped at his heels for years seemed to be sleeping, at least for the time being. He had a solid job, a comfortable home. Even a secret occupation to satisfy his adventurous streak.

The prospectors who came into the store were uncommonly frank about their finds. And easy to charm out of information regarding a likely strike. After all, why would a shop clerk care about searching for gold? Jace had gone out twice now. Once on a Sunday. Once on a slow afternoon, leaving Billy Dee to mind the store. He'd found a few nuggets in the mountain streams—enough to fire his blood and keep him interested. He wasn't about to file a claim. Not yet. He didn't need the South-gates to know what he was up to.

The Southgates. He'd done all right for himself in that depart-ment, too. Beth worshiped him, and Weedy looked up to him with brotherly admiration. As for Big Jim, who gave him trust and respect . . . He reckoned he'd come as close as he'd ever come to knowing what a father was like.

Oh, yes. He'd played his cards right. And the hand was still going in his favor. It might be a stolen life, but he wondered if Horace would have appreciated it half so much as he did.

He lifted his hat, ran his fingers through his clean hair and smiled to himself. He'd finally felt comfortable enough in the family's midst to throw out Horace's stinking hair oil. Too ''Eastern-style,'' he'd told them. He'd even begun to gradually lower his voice to its natural pitch—no one seemed to have noticed. Or perhaps they accepted him so well as Horace that he didn't need to depend on that particular affectation anymore.

He was definitely feeling smug and self-satisfied. Only Callie was left to conquer, and she was weakening, he could tell. He'd had to use every ounce of self-control to keep from kissing her as he'd really wanted to, the other night. But as that pert-nosed fancy woman from Savannah used to say, always leave 'em panting for more.

Sissy was another matter, of course. Hostile and suspicious from the first. But he'd find the key to her stubborn little three-year-old soul, damned if he wouldn't. He wasn't used to failure.

Damn, he thought, shaking away the uncomfortable memory of her pouting scowls. What did he care? She was just a kid.

Beth was sitting on the veranda, rocking, as they rode up to the house. She jumped up and ran out to greet them. "What's up, pards?" She pointed to the birds on Weedy's saddle. "Shoot me by the clock, if those don't beat all!" She anchored her bowler more firmly on her head and smiled up at Jace—a warm, shy smile. "Howdy, Jace," she murmured, then ducked her head.

He threw back his head and roared with laughter. "Princess, you really ought to stop listening to those miners at the store. Callie will take a fit!"

She stuck out her lower lip. "Are you going to be *Mister* Don't?"

He hitched his leg over the saddle and slid to the ground. "Of course not. I promise never to say 'don't.' But I want you to try and watch your language when Callie's around." He held out his pinky finger in a gesture that had become one of their private games. "Deal?"

She hooked her little finger in his and recited the childish doggerel in a solemn singsong. " 'Pinky, pinky, bow-bell, Whoever tells a lie, Will sink down to the bad place, And never rise up again.' " Her eyes twinkled with sudden mischief. "But it's a deal only if you agree to play cards with me tonight. And let me win."

"Little scamp," he said, and tweaked her nose. He turned to Weedy and smacked his lips. "I wonder if I can get Mrs. Ackland to do something delicious with those birds for tonight? Why don't you stable the horses in the meantime." He chuckled. "And don't worry. I'll have Mrs. Ackland carve a 'W' on the breast of the big one, so everyone knows it's yours."

He took the geese from a beaming Weedy, held out his hand to Beth, and led her to the door. "Come on, Princess. Let's go see Mrs. Ackland. And then we can find out what 'Miss Don't' thinks of this fine day."

The rambling house was festive in anticipation of Big Jim's

return from Denver. Large pots of pink geranium and blue flax decorated the parlor, and the scent of freshly baked cherry pies filled every corner of the downstairs. A crisp, starched cloth covered the dining-room table, and the windows were sparkling clean.

Mrs. Ackland stood at the kitchen table, rolling out biscuits, while Sissy sat on a hobbyhorse nearby and rocked placidly. Jace tossed the geese onto the table and grinned. "There you are, Mrs. A. Didn't I promise you birds for supper?"

She wiped her flour-covered hands on her apron and held up one of the geese. "So you did, Mr. Perkins. And these are splendiferous."

"The fat one's Weedy's. He's kind of proud of it. Do you suppose you could mark it in some way?"

She gave a hearty laugh. "How 'bout I put a wreath of laurel leaves around the drumsticks?"

"Excellent. Oh, and Mrs. A.," he said, sidling up to her and putting an arm around her ample waist, "I'm mighty partial to sausage and dried-apple stuffing with my goose."

She snorted and pushed him away, leaving a floury handprint on his vest. "You sly devil. You could make a stone squirt lemonade."

"And you can cook to cheer the angels. You need never fear the fires of Hell, Mrs. A. God will want you up there in his very own kitchen."

"Hmph. Enough of your bunkum. You'll get your stuffin'. Now skedaddle out of here so's I can finish these biscuits."

He stole a piece of raw dough from the edge of one biscuit, downed it with relish, then stole another to hand to Beth. "Just let me say howdy to Sissy first." He turned to the little girl, knelt, and pasted a jolly smile on his face. "Well, Sissy. Riding your horse to town today?"

She gave him a withering look and punched him in the chest.

Son of a gun, he thought, rocking back on his heels. What did the perverse imp want of him? He tried again. "Shall we play bo-peep?'' he asked. He covered his face with his hands, then opened them quickly and cried "Bo!"

Sissy jumped in alarm and began to wail.

"Glory be!" exclaimed Mrs. Ackland, hurrying to soothe the child. "Stop pesterin' the mite. You want supper before midnight, you just scoot outta here and leave me and Sissy in peace.''

Shaken more than he cared to admit by Sissy's rebuff, Jace picked up a willing Beth and carried her from the room. *Son of a bitch!* he thought. He could split a bullet on a nickel edge at twenty feet and amaze a whole barroom full of roughnecks. So why couldn't he win over one little girl?

"Here we go, Princess," he said, putting Beth on his shoulders and prancing like a horse. "Let's go find Callie."

While Beth whooped in mock fear and squeezed his neck with her knees, he galloped wildly up the stairs. Callie's door was ajar. He knocked once with his boot, stooped low, and trotted through the door, coming to a halt with a loud whinny.

Callie sat on a chair near the windows, reading a book. She looked up in surprise. Glory, but she was a magnificent woman! Her dress clung to the lush curves of her breasts, a swelling fullness that produced an equal reaction in his own body. And her long, loose curls, gilded by the sunlight, dazzled his eyes.

She reached for her cane and stood up, frowning. He suddenly wanted to kiss the funny little crease between her brows. "Oh, Beth!" she said, "Look at you. Your skirts are up to your knees!" She glared at Jace. "I don't know why *you* have to undo all my training."

He managed to look shamefaced, and set Beth on her feet, brushing down her skirts to a modest level. "Heavens to Betsy, Miss Callie. We didn't mean to rile you." He winked at Beth. "Did we?"

She smothered a giggle and pointed to his vest. "You still have flour. You better get slicked up before Poppy comes home." She broke into a wide grin. "I'm monstrous glad he's coming home. Aren't you?"

Callie rolled her eyes. It made her look adorable. "Don't point," she said. "And *don't* use slang."

He exchanged a secret look with Beth, cautioning her silence with his eyes. But it was too late. She burst into a merry laugh and covered her face with her hands.

Callie looked bewildered and uncomfortable. "What is it?" she demanded.

"It's nothing," he said solemnly. "Beth just has the giggles today." He turned to Beth, a stern expression on his face. "Didn't Mrs. Ackland want you to help her shell peas?"

"I didn't hear . . ."

He interrupted her protest. "Of course she did." He waved his hand toward the door. "Shoo!"

"But, Jace . . ." she whined.

"Go. Or I won't dance with you at the Fourth of July picnic next week."

"Will too," she said, edging toward the door.

"Will not," he said, and laughed.

"Will too." She tossed her curls and scooted out of the room. "You just want to be alone with Callie."

When she had gone, Callie looked uneasily around the room. "You shouldn't be here."

He moved closer, wondering if there was some way to touch her without making her skittish. "No, I reckon not. But it's such a beautiful day. And I knew you'd be up here, hiding away in your room."

She frowned again. "I wasn't 'hiding.' I like to read."

"But there's more to life than books." *There's a man and a woman, darlin',* he thought. He decided on a bold approach. "Can't you stand without your cane?" Before she had time to protest, he took one of her hands in his, then dislodged her cane and took the other hand at the same time.

"Mercy sakes!" she said in alarm. "What are you doing?" She teetered for a moment, then clutched him by the elbows.

He put his hands around her waist to steady her. She felt

good, even through her armor. "Why do you wear a corset? I've noticed lots of the women out here don't bother."

She glared at him, but the body beneath his hands had begun to tremble. "The subject of a woman's undergarments is not a fit one for a man. Not a gentleman, certainly! And, as you can see, I need my cane." She glanced nervously behind her, clearly trying to see if she was close enough to her chair to escape him. "I thought I made it clear, the other night, that you were never to come into my room again."

"Oh, deary me," he said, lapsing into his "Horace" voice. "Perhaps I misunderstood. Perhaps it's wrong of me to come every night, after you're asleep, just to look at you." An intriguing idea; pity he hadn't thought of it until now.

She gasped, her cheeks turning pink. "You don't!"

She was enchanting when she blushed. His blooming rose. He didn't want the color to fade too quickly. "Perhaps I do," he teased.

"Oh, you're just funning me," she snapped, and twisted out of his arms to grab for the chair. She sat down in an awkward flurry of skirts, blushing even more furiously. "You *and* Beth. Do you have some secret joke between you?"

He scratched his ear. "I think we've both decided you're too serious. You don't laugh enough. Are you so afraid the world is mocking you?"

He instantly regretted his words. Tears sprang to her eyes. "What do you know?" she said bitterly.

He knelt before her and put his hands on her knees. A gesture of friendship and comfort. He must be getting soft, he thought. The old Jace would have reached up under her skirts first. But she was so vulnerable, so isolated by her shyness. It didn't seem right to take advantage. "I know that you're a beautiful, desirable woman who shouldn't be so afraid of life and laughter. Shall I tell you what our joke is? Beth and I? We call you 'Miss Don't.' Do you know how often you say the word to her?"

"M-Miss Don't'?" she stammered.

"It's not meant to be cruel. But Beth knows how to see the fun in life."

She bit her lip, then managed a shy smile. "I suppose it is amusing, from a child's perspective."

"Why don't you try saying 'don't' a little less often?"

"Perhaps I shall." She looked down at his hands on her knees, seeming to notice them for the first time. She glanced up at him, the beginnings of alarm clouding the silvery depths of her eyes. "Mr. Perkins . . ."

"Jace." He wondered if he should attempt a kiss.

His decision was made for him by the loud crash of the front door downstairs, followed by the heavy clump of footsteps across the vestibule. "Cheese in crackers!" he exclaimed, jumping to his feet. "Is that Big Jim already?"

He retrieved her cane, and together they made their way down the stairs. Beth was already in her father's arms. Big Jim kissed her on the forehead, set her on her feet, and clapped Jace on the back. "Good to see you, my boy. Everything going well at the store?"

"Just capital, Big Jim. And your trip to Denver?"

"Splendid!" boomed Southgate. "Found me a new line of shotguns that should put the rest of our stock in the shade. Billy Dee is already unloading them. And I picked up some more hardware and tinware. And put in an order for a case of Havanas and some real French wine. And this slick salesman from Chicago had . . ."

"Yes, of course, sir," he interrupted. Damn the man. Why was he ignoring his other daughter? "But Miss Callie here is waiting to greet you. Can't we talk about the new stock down at the store tomorrow?"

Big Jim turned to Callie with a wide grin. "Did you think I'd forgotten you, Mousekin?"

She tried to smile. "Of course not, Poppy."

"I was waiting for Weedy and the men to bring in my surprise." He strode to the door and threw it open. A large wagon stood before the house. Several men from town swarmed over it, struggling to lift down a heavy piano.

"Oh, Poppy!" Callie gasped, and covered her mouth with her hand. Her eyes sparkled with tears.

Big Jim turned to Jace. "The one in the Boston house was too fragile to make it over the mountains," he explained.

It took a great deal of straining and puffing, but at last the piano was ensconced in a place of honor in the parlor. Callie smiled all the while, her face radiant with happiness. Big Jim thanked the men and sent them back to town with a bottle of his best whiskey.

"Well now, sweetie," he said to his daughter, "I haven't heard you play in a long time. Will you favor us?"

Jace watched in wonder as Callie sat gracefully at the piano, flexed her fingers, and began to play. All her shyness melted away when she lost herself in the music. It wasn't anything Jace had heard before—high-toned music that was played in homes that had been barred to him. But she was entrancing, sure and skilled, bringing forth sounds he had never heard from the instrument.

When she was finished, he led the applause. "By golly," he said, "if that isn't the finest playing I've ever heard, Miss Callie."

Big Jim beamed. "She's some pumpkins, isn't she, Jace?"

Callie dropped her hands to her lap and turned red. "Oh, Poppy," she said, barely above a whisper.

Southgate barreled through her murmured protest. "No, by jingo, I want to hear what Jace thinks of you. Maybe if you hear it from someone else, you'll stop fretting about your slight imperfection."

Her eyes clouded with pain. She gulped and reached for the cane that leaned against the piano. "I should see if Mrs. Ackland needs help," she said, breathless with embarrassment.

At once, Jace hurried across the room and sat beside her on the bench, preventing her from rising. He put his hand over hers. "I haven't found any imperfections, sir," he said softly.

It gave him an odd sense of pleasure to see Callie's smile of gratitude.

In the awkward silence that followed, Beth skipped to the piano and plunked several keys with her finger. "I like the sound. Do you play, Jace?"

"Not like Callie does. But, yes." He'd thumped the ivories in many a brothel in his time. "How about a Stephen Foster tune?" He gave Callie a gentle nudge with his elbow. "If you'll give me a bit of room, ma'am." He glanced at her face, still pink with shame from her father's thoughtless words. He wondered if he should provoke her further.

Aw, hell, he thought, making up his mind. *Let's see what she's made of.* He stretched his long fingers and then began to play, singing softly so only she could hear. " 'Sweetly she sleeps, my Alice fair, Her cheek on the pillow pressed, Sweetly she sleeps while her Saxon hair, Like sunlight, streams o'er her breast.' "

He heard her outraged intake of breath, and finished the song without looking at her. Clearly, she remembered his supposed nocturnal visits to her room.

"I know a Foster song, too," she said, when he had played the last note. Her voice sounded strong and assured, filled with unexpected fire. "Perhaps you know it, Jace? 'Comrades, fill no glass for me.' "

I'll be damned! he thought in surprise and delight. *She's got spunk.* He cleared his throat, trying to look remorseful. "Indeed, ma'am, I do, to my mortification. I think it was in a temperance book someone gave me recently. Oh, fudge! Is there anything worse than the evils of drink? A creature is lured into doing all sorts of wicked things—under the influence."

She pursed her lips. "You needn't grovel," she said in disgust. She lifted her hands to the keyboard and attacked the song with vigor.

He felt his blood stir with a desire that astonished him. He could scarcely sit next to her without wanting to crush her in his arms. There was fire deep within her. And passion untapped.

He'd seen a glimmer of it, from the first, and wondered how to bring it out. And now it was crystal clear.

Somehow, "Horace" the softling touched a chord in her soul. But not in the way he had at first supposed. She had *seemed* to want a genteel man, but the more he simpered, the more the silver-green sparks shot from her eyes. And that was the key. He'd tease her with Horace's prissy ways, torment her with sickly-sweet kindness until she was ready to explode and leap into his arms.

He put a fluttering hand to his breast. "Heavens to Betsy, Miss Callie," he said, his eyes wide and innocent, "if you surely aren't some pumpkins!"

The full-lipped scowl she threw his way almost drove him to distraction. If it was the last thing he did, he'd bed her, by God!

Chapter Ten

"That's a mighty fetching hat, Miss Callie."

Callie self-consciously touched the pink ribbons of her straw hat and blushed. "Thank you, Jace."

He pulled back on the reins as the wagon rumbled down a steep incline in the gulch, then clicked to the horse as they reached the bottom and sped up again. He grinned up at the clear blue of the sky. "Sure is a fine day for a parade." He turned and smiled at her. His eyes were as blue as the sky. "And bless my whiskers! Wait till you see the store. Billy Dee and I were up on ladders all day yesterday, hanging the bunting."

She frowned. "I don't know why Poppy wanted me there so early. The parade doesn't begin until ten. I could have come with Mrs. Ackland and the girls in the other wagon, when they bring the picnic fixings."

He tugged at his freshly starched collar. "Truth to tell, *I* wanted you there," he said, casting her a sidelong glance. "I just didn't have the gumption to say so. You haven't seen the store since I've begun working there. And with the new shelves and woodwork . . .'' He smiled shyly. ''I won't think it's fine until you tell me so.''

She stared at him in disbelief. He was *courting* her, for heaven's sake! *No doubt about it,* she thought, recalling the subtle changes in his manner these past few days. The compliments at the piano, the sweet attentions and humble deference all this week. And now this subterfuge to get her to the store early, by pretending it was what Big Jim wanted. Perhaps the timid kiss in her bedroom had started him to thinking, and wondering when they were going to talk about marriage. And he'd decided to hurry things along.

But she was in no hurry. Not by a long shot. She liked his attentions, of course, liked feeling admired and flattered. Beautiful, he'd called her. Desirable and *perfect.* As though her crippled leg meant nothing to him. It was all so new to her—to have a man she could think of as a beau. But still . . .

Though he'd proved to be less prissy than he'd first appeared, his fastidious ways still offended her. Whatever else Big Jim had been to her mother, he had been her rock and her strength. She couldn't imagine turning to Jace for more than polite conversation and the latest word on the new fashions in the catalogs.

''I'm sure you've done a wonderful job in the store,'' she said. ''But why should my opinion matter?'' It was bold of her to ask him outright, but she was enjoying this newfound feeling of being wanted as a woman.

He pulled the horse to a standstill. ''If you have to ask that,'' he said softly, ''you're not as clever as I think you are.''

How did women play these games? Her Boston friends— militant in their private discourse but hesitant in the world around them—had been as ignorant of courtship as she. ''Perhaps I'm not so clever,'' she said, trying to sound coy. ''You'll have to explain yourself.''

He took her hand in his and gently squeezed her fingers. ''I esteem you above all women, Miss Callie. This past month has brought me great joy, merely being in your presence.''

She felt a pang of disappointment. If this was his idea of

courtship, it was as lackluster as his manner toward her. "Is that all?"

"It's all I dare to say now," he said. "But . . . would you think me too forward if I were to ask for a kiss?"

She looked around the deserted countryside. The morning sun beat down on the dust of the road, and chickadees chattered among the pine trees. Not very romantic, but perhaps isolated enough to be dangerous. She stirred uneasily. It might be wise to refuse him.

Oh, bosh, she thought a moment later, her common sense coming to the fore. There was nothing dangerous about the man! And wagons would be passing by all morning; the local folk were eager to get to town for the festivities. Besides—if she admitted it to herself—she was curious to see if his second kiss would be better than his first. She turned her face to him. "Just one," she said primly.

He took off his broad hat, tipped up her chin, and planted his lips on hers.

This time, she could almost taste her discontent. The kiss in her bedroom, at least, had had the novelty of a first kiss to lend it magic. Now all she felt was an aching frustration. His mouth was soft and undemanding, as though the mere contact of her lips was enough to satisfy him. She wanted to scream aloud. Impatiently, she threw her arms around his neck, hoping to draw him closer.

He jerked away with a squeak of alarm, his eyes opening wide. "Heavens to Betsy!" he said. "That's enough of that, or I might forget myself."

"I can scarcely imagine that, Mr. Perkins," she said sourly, shaken by his abrupt end to the kiss. "Not unless you have your flask of whiskey to fortify yourself."

He frowned. "Oh, cheese in crackers, are you angry at me?"

It was absurd, of course. She was only angry at herself for expecting more. "No," she snapped. "Of course not. But shouldn't we get going again?"

For the rest of the ride, she couldn't shake her feeling of

discontent, a gnawing irritation that teetered on the edge of fury. It was little comfort to her that he was smiling—and rather smugly, she imagined.

The main street of Dark Creek was already filling with crowds when they arrived in town: ranchers with their wives and children, miners in their Sunday best waving small flags, gamblers and saloon girls and tradesmen. On a side street, the volunteer firemen were polishing the ornamental brass on their hose carts and draping them with red, white, and blue bunting. Half a dozen brass bands, their numbers made up of miners, practiced their tunes and unfurled the banners of their respective companies, while several wives bustled around them, stitching a loose button or tacking a piece of braid on colorful uniforms.

In the middle of Front Street, carpenters were hammering the final nails into the grandstands, where the day's speeches would be given. An open field on the edge of town had been filled with benches and makeshift trestle tables to accommodate the afternoon picnickers; in the evening, it would be cleared in the center for dancing.

Callie had never seen so many national flags and so much bunting in all her life—on storefronts and saloons and variety halls. Not even Boston, with its connections to the early Republic, had shown such patriotic fervor on the Fourth.

Poppy's store was the most splendid of the lot. Swags of bunting hung from the roof edge, a brass eagle sat above the door, and large rosettes of red, white, and blue perched over the windows. A large flag had been raised on the roof, and it snapped and danced in the morning breeze.

Jace helped her down from the wagon. "Doesn't it just give you gooseflesh, all this excitement?"

The joy in his eyes was infectious. It was foolish to be angry with him. He was what he was. A twiddlepoop. Kindhearted, to be sure, and well-meaning. But a hopeless specimen of a man. She returned his smile. "You and Billy Dee should be proud of yourselves. Poppy's decorations are beautiful."

He beamed and led her inside the store. Big Jim was standing behind the counter, stacking boxes of cigars. He looked up as they came in.

"Glad you're here, Jace!" he boomed. "Thought we'd open the store an hour or two this morning, before the parade. Never know when folks'll need something at the last minute." He jerked his thumb toward the boxes of tobacco. "Clem, over to the Golden Bough, figures there'll be a heap of smoking and chewing to go along with all the whiskey he's planning to sell."

Jace put his hat behind the counter. "Do you want me to get Billy Dee to take the order over to him?"

"Hell, no! That man sees the inside of a barroom before noon, and he'll be blind drunk for days!" Big Jim shook his white mane. "Though I don't know what the Sam Hill's gotten into him. He's been pretty sober all this week."

Jace gave Callie a knowing smile. "Maybe he's learned to do his drinking only at night."

"I'll take the cigars," said Big Jim. "You pull down a couple of sacks of flour for Mrs. Watts. I ran into her in front of her boardinghouse this morning. She'll be in to pick them up."

When he had gone, Jace escorted Callie around the store, proudly pointing out the new shelves piled with bolts of calico, tools, and cooking utensils. "I've persuaded Big Jim to order some fine silverware from back East," he announced, opening a large cabinet that was already fitted with sectioned drawers. "We'll keep it here. It won't be long before the ladies of Dark Creek will be hankering to set as fine a table as their Eastern cousins."

Callie snorted. "I haven't seen many 'ladies' in Dark Creek. Unless those painted creatures have begun to take on airs."

His eyes glittered with a sudden cold light. "Now, Miss Callie, you're not a snob, are you?" There was an odd intensity to his voice.

"Of course not!" she said indignantly. "I believe in women's rights. And a woman is entitled to do what she wishes."

She sniffed in disdain. "Though such occupations are certainly not *my* preference. But I have yet to find anyone here who can equal the friends I had back in Boston."

"Maybe you haven't looked hard enough." His expression was tight and disapproving.

She stirred uncomfortably beneath his gaze. "Are you criticizing me, Mr. Perkins?"

He hesitated, then relaxed into a sheepish smile. "Heavens to Betsy, no. I'm only saying I've met a number of fine folk in Dark Creek. You should come down to the store more often. Work a spell behind the counter."

The thought terrified her. "Oh, I couldn't do that!"

"Because you're self-conscious about your limp?"

She felt herself blushing. "Jace, please."

He cupped his hand under her chin and tipped up her face, forcing her to look into his eyes. "Lots of folks are as scared of people as you. But they don't go running to their rooms and hiding behind books."

She opened her mouth to protest his unjust charge, but he silenced her with a finger to her mouth. "Tell you what," he said, running his finger seductively back and forth across her lips, "you wait on the first customer to come into the store, and I'll give you a reward."

She shivered at his sensuous touch, her knees going weak. "A reward?" she croaked. Would she finally get the kiss she dreamed of?

He gave her a self-satisfied grin. "I'll sit with you when they have the fireworks tonight. The whole time!"

"Oh!" The impossible milksop! She shook her head free of his touch and clumped across the room toward the door. "I think I'll wait outside until Mrs. Ackland and the girls arrive." If this was courting, she wanted no part of it.

Just then, the door opened and a small, plain woman came into the store. She wore a faded calico gown and clutched a threadbare shawl about her thin shoulders. "Good morning, Mr. Perkins," she said in a soft voice.

He nodded his head in salute. "Mrs. Watts."

"I've just come for . . ." She faltered on her words, then stopped.

He held out his hand and indicated Callie. "Miss Southgate would be happy to wait on you, Mrs. Watts."

Callie shot him a glance filled with equal parts panic and rage. How could he do this to her? She felt a cold trickle of perspiration run down her spine at the thought of waiting on a customer. A stranger. Then she saw the look on Mrs. Watts's face. Bleak and frightened.

She took off her straw hat, limped to the counter, and moved behind it, turning to give the woman a reassuring smile. "What can I do for you, ma'am?"

"I've baked so many pies for today there's not a smidgen of flour left in the pantry for tomorrow's breakfast biscuits. And . . . could you spare some lard?"

Jace was already pulling the items from the shelves. "Two sacks of flour, I think Big Jim said. Right?"

The woman nodded without looking at him or Callie. "I'm mighty low on coffee," she murmured.

Callie's heart went out to her. She looked like she wanted to sink into the floor and die. She patted Mrs. Watts's hand. It was dry and chapped from hard work. "What are biscuits without coffee?" she said kindly. "Will you need sugar?"

"I'd better not. The . . . the fact of the matter is, Miss Southgate . . ." Two bright spots of color appeared on the woman's sallow cheeks, and she gulped. "May I . . . may I pay you on Saturday? It's when my boarders' rents are due."

Callie suddenly remembered what Big Jim had said many a time in Boston: Goodwill is worth more than the price of all the goods in the store. She smiled at Mrs. Watts. "I don't see why not," she said. She turned to Jace. "You'll arrange that, if you please, Mr. Perkins. And add a sack of sugar to Mrs. Watts's order. As a holiday present from the Southgate establishment."

When Mrs. Watts, carrying her purchases and murmuring

her thanks, had finally left the store, Jace turned to Callie and grinned. "We'll make a shopkeeper of you yet, Miss Southgate. Danged if we won't."

She felt absurdly pleased with herself. "I never thought it would be so easy to do."

"The world isn't made up of monsters. Only folk who carry their own burdens—and have little time or care for yours."

"I always feel as though everyone is *looking* at me."

He laughed. "And so they are." His eyes scanned her form. "But not for the reasons you might think."

His glance seemed a trifle less than innocent. Perhaps she could tease him into a more ardent courtship. "Jace, that sounds almost wicked," she said, putting a coquettish note into her voice.

He pursed his lips. "Oh, mercy me. I meant no disrespect."

She sighed. "No. I'm sure you didn't." She heard a footstep on the boardwalk outside the shop. "I'll wait on the next customer," she said boldly, and turned to face the door.

She regretted her hasty words almost at once. Ralph Driscoll came striding into the store, filling it with his commanding presence. She felt her courage evaporate. She glanced at Jace. He had an odd smile on his face. Was he daring her to back down?

She took a steadying breath. "May I help you, Mr. Driscoll?"

"Miss Southgate," he said smoothly. "How charming you look today." He stole a glance at her cane, then smiled in understanding. "But you shouldn't be on your feet, little lady. What with this, that, and the other thing, it must be a trial for you." He snapped his fingers in Jace's direction. "Perkins! Bring Miss Southgate a chair."

She wanted to die of mortification. She would have preferred him to ignore her, rather than to endure his condescending pity.

And why did he have to be so dangerously attractive? The wings of gray at his temples, the deep-set black eyes, the firm, strong mouth. No doubt, *he* knew how to kiss a woman!

He scowled. "Dash it all, Perkins. That chair!"

Jace scurried to fetch a chair from the end of the counter and set it behind Callie. "Here you are, ma'am," he said solemnly.

She turned away from Driscoll and rolled her eyes at Jace. "Oh, for heaven's sake," she hissed, "I'm not helpless, and you know it." She turned back to Driscoll with a smile, her chin held at a proud angle. "I thank you for your concern, Mr. Driscoll. But I'm here to serve you in Big Jim's stead."

He looked doubtful. "Well . . . Truth is, I've made a healthy profit at the bank recently. I thought my ranch could use some good furnishings. Do you have some catalogs?"

Catalogs? She looked helplessly at Jace, feeling as though she were drowning in a sea of inexperience.

Jace cleared his throat. "I can show you some catalogs, sir."

Driscoll eyed him with contempt. "You? Selling petticoats to the ladies is more your style, isn't it?"

Callie could hear the crunch of Jace's jaw, but he managed a simpering smile. "Heavens to Betsy, Mr. Driscoll. I know a Chippendale table from a Belter. Though I think something with less refined lines would be more to your taste."

Driscoll's eyes narrowed. "Do you, you little squirt? Well, I'd rather do business with Big Jim. Is he around?"

The smile was now frozen on Jace's face. "He should return in a minute."

"Do you know where he is?"

"Of course."

Driscoll smoothed his slicked-back hair. "Then fetch him. I don't think Big Jim would appreciate it if I took my business elsewhere, because of you."

Callie held her breath. Driscoll was deliberately challenging Jace. *Show a little spunk, for heaven's sake!* she thought.

He glanced at her and seemed to make up his mind. "Cheese in crackers, sir. No need to get yourself all riled up. I just don't like to leave Miss Callie alone."

Driscoll doubled his fists and advanced on Jace. "Get going."

She could read the anger in Jace's eyes. Again he looked at her, scanning her face. Then he ducked his head and put one hand to his ribs. "You don't mean to harm a man who's still recovering from his injuries, do you?" he asked with a nervous laugh.

"I only want to see Big Jim."

Jace edged toward the door. "If you can assure me that Miss Southgate will be safe with you . . ."

"Get out of here, I said!"

Jace sighed in resignation and disappeared.

Driscoll turned to Callie with a patronizing smile. "If you'll allow my frankness, Miss Southgate, I think Perkins has a sneaking notion for you. A timid affection that he's afraid to reveal."

She was drowning in humiliation. Why couldn't he have stood up to Driscoll? "That's none of your concern, Mr. Driscoll," she said, fighting to keep the tremor from her voice.

He gave her an indulgent pat on the shoulder. "Never mind, little lady. I'm sure he's a welcome prospect."

For a cripple? she thought bitterly. That's what he'd meant. "The air is close in here this morning, Mr. Driscoll. If you don't mind, I think I'll step outside. I'm sure my father will be here in a moment." She grabbed her hat and retreated from the room like a beaten soldier, conscious of the betraying click of her cane on the floor.

She leaned against the outside of the store, fighting her tears and shame. How had she imagined she could deal with customers when a self-confident man like Driscoll left her feeling helpless and tongue-tied? There were more Ralph Driscolls than Mrs. Wattses in this world. And she certainly couldn't look to Jace for support.

She bent her head and gave way to her misery. She would *never* set foot in the store again.

Chapter Eleven

"Hang me for a woodchopper! Where in tarnation is that Jace?" Beth jumped up and down, trying to see over the heads of the crowd on the edge of the open field. "He promised me the very first dance!" She pointed to where men were moving the last of the picnic tables and benches from the center of the field to the sides. Two bewhiskered old fiddlers, their white beards shining like gold in the setting sun, were already tuning up their instruments, while a group of miners piled logs for a bonfire to brighten the coming night. Beth smacked her hand petulantly on the top of her bowler. "They're going to start soon, dang it."

Callie glanced around the field in vexation, too upset to remind Beth to speak and act in a more ladylike way. *Where is Jace? For that matter, where are Poppy and Weedy?* They seemed to have lost all of their men in the course of the day.

Weedy had been the first to go, after the parade.

It had been more splendid and stirring than Callie would have imagined. Perhaps it was the clean air, the backdrop of the snow-covered peaks, that had lent the modest procession an air of majesty and pomp. Rows of laughing people crowded together on the boardwalk, small children perched on their fathers' shoulders, breathless with anticipation. The blare of horns ringing through the gulch, the rat-a-tat of drums, as the brass bands stepped grandly down the street. The brightly colored Stars and Stripes, carried proudly by veterans in uniform, bringing a patriotic tear to many an eye.

The townsfolk had cheered themselves hoarse, then cheered again as the volunteer firemen appeared. Grinning and waving, they had strutted beside their hose carts, stopping now and again to squirt water at the knots of gaping children. Some of the town dignitaries—the doctor, the pharmacist, the undertaker—had followed in gaily decorated carriages. There had even been half a dozen prancing dogs in the procession, dressed in Uncle Sam costumes.

The ceremonial speakers had followed. They had taken their turns on the bunting-draped grandstand to exhort the crowd to give thanks for the bounty of this glorious land; to remind them of the blessings of liberty; to pray for fallen comrades of the late war; to send a message to faraway Washington that the Territory of Colorado yearned for statehood.

The Reverend Maples had given the invocation and begged his listeners to support the building of a church. Ralph Driscoll, as the town banker, had spoken at great length, dazzling Callie with his brilliant oratory; he had been followed by Deputy Sheriff Hepworth, awkward and stumbling over his words. The self-styled town "judge"—a disbarred lawyer—and the manager of one of the stamp mills had nearly put their listeners to sleep. Representing the town merchants, Big Jim had spoken last—a speech full of buoyant goodwill and optimism that had roused the flagging crowd to wild applause and brought a blush of pride to Callie's cheeks.

Someone had shouted out that Big Jim should be named mayor of Dark Creek one of these days, and Weedy—proud, for a change, to be Big Jim's son—had waded into the conversation, going off at last with a group of young men about his own age. Callie hoped their ultimate destination wasn't one of the wilder establishments in town.

The picnic had come next. While the women had unpacked their baskets of food on the trestle tables, the children had raced around the field, playing tag and snap-the-whip. Mrs. Ackland had brought cold fried chicken and corn bread and all the fixings; Jace, always interested in his food, had declared himself "as savage as a meat ax" and dug in with a will.

Callie had been glad of his preoccupation with the meal; it made it easier to ignore him. Between his tame kiss and his namby-pamby behavior in front of Driscoll, she wasn't feeling particularly friendly toward him today.

The afternoon had been filled with races and contests of all sorts, and that's when they'd lost Big Jim. A wager with a group of men over the outcome of a hose-cart race among the firemen had led Big Jim to a heated discussion on the relative merits of a man's arms as against his legs. Declaring that strong biceps were more valuable than speedy limbs, he had trooped off with the men to pitch horseshoes behind the livery stable.

Callie stifled a yawn and rubbed the small of her back. She still felt stiff from the nap she'd taken on the hard ground. She looked down at a pouting Beth. "Didn't you see where Jace went while I was sleeping?"

Beth shook her head. "No. I fell asleep, too."

"Oh, botheration." Who could tell them where Jace had vanished to? Mrs. Ackland had taken the remains of the picnic and gone home hours ago, when Sissy had begun to fuss and fidget.

Beth pointed to a tent that had been set up as a beer garden just beyond the clearing. "Maybe he's there."

Callie stared in horror. "Drinking? At this hour of the day?"

"Oh, Callie, don't be an old foo-foo. It's almost night! And I reckon there ain't nothing but beer in the place. Even Poppy drinks whiskey at dinnertime."

"Well . . ." She chewed at her thumbnail. The thought of going into a rowdy place like that alone . . . But Beth was nearly jumping out of her skin in impatience, watching the fiddlers with anxious eyes as they were joined by a trumpet player and a flutist.

Callie indicated the bench that she and Beth had saved for themselves. "You stay here," she said, and grasped her cane more firmly to give herself courage.

The beer garden was filled with knots of men gathered around small tables, drinking and puffing on cigars and cigarettes. Their laughter rose with the smoke to the top of the tent, where unlit lanterns waited for the night. Callie waved away the thick cloud and peered into the gloom. At least in this light she wasn't so conspicuous.

She spied Jace at last, seated at a corner table with several men. He lounged in his chair, his hat set cockily on the back of his head, and chomped on a fat cigar. In his hand, he clasped a fan of cards, resting it against his vest front. The table in front of him held a neat stack of coins and a mug of beer, close to his elbow. His expression was innocent and bland.

There seemed to be only one player left against him—a slick gambler, from the look of his fancy coat and vest. After searching Jace's face, the man scowled and tossed his cards onto the heap of gold and silver coins in the center of the table. "You son of a bitch, Perkins," he said loudly, his voice carrying above the clamor. "You're too much for me. I fold. What've you got?"

Jace took a long, deliberate puff of his cigar and grinned through the exhaled smoke. He looked like a cat licking cream. Then he glanced up and saw Callie, nearing the table; at once his expression changed. He shuffled his cards, frowned, laughed nervously, and spread the cards face up on the table before him. "Oh, my stars, what do you make of that? I *thought* I had a pair of kings."

The gambler stared, slack-jawed, then jumped to his feet. "You goddamned bluffer! You got me to fold for nothing?"

Jace took off his hat, swept the coins into its upside-down crown, and stood up. He towered over the gambler, oddly menacing. "I wouldn't call this nothing." He smiled primly. "And please don't swear in front of the lady."

The gambler growled and went for the pistol at his hip, but something in Jace's eyes seemed to stop him.

While Callie gasped in alarm, Jace merely smiled. "Heavens to Betsy, I don't like violence. Do you?"

One of the other players put a restraining hand on the gambler's arm. "Let it go, pard. He won fair and square."

"Gentlemen." Jace nodded in dismissal, transferred the coins from his hat to his coat pockets, and moved around the table to take Callie by the arm. "I reckon Beth is wondering where I am, Miss Callie. But I haven't forgotten my promise." Smiling as though nothing untoward had happened, he steered her out of the tent.

But when they stood in the fresh air again, she shook off his grasp. "You seem to have forgotten everything else!" she snapped.

He hooked his thumb in the direction of the tent. "What do you mean? That? I told you I play cards some, ma'am."

She snorted. "Like a regular Sam Slick, I'll be bound. It was a disgusting display!"

"Would you feel better about it if I lost?" he muttered, scratching his head. "Like some sort of atonement?"

"Oh!" She waved him away with an angry sweep of her hand. "Go away and dance with Beth. The music is starting." She watched him shrug in bewilderment and amble off to find his dancing partner. She felt like a fool. Of course she didn't want him to lose! So why had she made such a fuss? Because of the beer, the cigar? But he had told her of those weaknesses in his character, and they hadn't disturbed her before. Land sakes, Big Jim drank and smoked and played cards, and it didn't diminish *him* in her eyes.

Then why was she so upset? Perhaps it was because of something darker, vague and mysterious—that strange aura she'd seen about him, in the moments before he'd caught sight of her. An undercurrent of danger, a sense of a different man—

a man she wasn't sure she wanted to know. It gave her a shiver of unease.

By the time she got back to their bench, Jace and Beth were already dancing—a slow waltz that they managed by Beth taking large steps and Jace deliberately taking small ones. But when the tempo of the music changed and quickened, he picked up the little girl, held her close to him, and spun her in dizzying circles. At the end of the dance, he set her on her feet and they returned to the bench, laughing and breathless.

He grinned at Callie. "Cheese in crackers, ma'am, but *you* should learn to dance."

Was he mocking her, the scoundrel? "Don't be absurd!" she said in a shrill voice, then cringed as several women turned and stared at her. She took a calming breath. "Dancing is quite out of the question for me, Mr. Perkins," she said coldly. "Or hadn't you noticed?"

"I know you can keep your balance one-handed, holding on to your cane. If we dance, you can put both your hands on my shoulders." He raised a questioning eyebrow. "Are you afraid to try?"

She'd already made a fool of herself once today, because of his challenge in the store. She wasn't going to repeat the humiliation. "I'm not about to be a public spectacle," she said firmly, and planted herself on the bench.

The field was beginning to crowd with dancers. Those few miners whose wives had been hardy enough to follow them to the goldfields proudly stepped forth with their partners. The rest had to content themselves with dancing the woman's part with other men, tying handkerchiefs around their sleeves to indicate their altered sex. And when they lined up for a reel, it was almost comical to see their exaggerated, dainty poses as they curtsied and skipped up the line.

Jace bowed solemnly to Beth. "Princess, will you favor me with another dance?"

Beth made a face. "I'm getting tired. Maybe I'll sleep till

the fireworks.'' She sat down on the bench beside Callie, took off her bowler, and put her head in her sister's lap.

Callie smirked up at Jace. ''Mercy sakes. Now who will you dance with? Would you like to borrow my handkerchief?'' she added with an edge of malice. She was pleased to see a flicker of annoyance in his eyes.

''You've a sharp tongue, Miss Callie,'' he said in a tight voice. ''When you forget to be shy. But I can find my own partner.'' He gave her a curt bow and strode off into the crowd.

He was gone for such a long time that Callie began to regret her unkind words. And her unkind behavior to him all day. When he'd acted like a perfect gentleman, polite and self-effacing, she'd snapped at him, wishing he were more manly. But when she'd found him at the beer garden, engaged in manly pursuits, she'd treated him like a brute who disgusted her. How could he hope to please her if *she* didn't know what she wanted?

And then he appeared at the edge of the clearing, shepherding a dozen of the sporting women from town. And her remorse died in her breast. While the more proper ladies turned their heads away in disdain, he distributed the hussies among the grateful men still searching for dancing partners.

He swaggered over to Callie, a self-satisfied grin on his face. ''Is my Princess still asleep?''

Callie smoothed a lock of blond hair at Beth's forehead. ''Alas, yes,'' she said with a curl to her lip. ''You're back where you started. Without a partner.''

''Hardly that. Those charming damsels are indebted to me. They'll oblige me with a dance or two.''

''How did you contrive to arrange that?''

''I bought their services for the evening. With my ill-gotten gains. Since you seemed to feel that it was already tainted money, I thought I could scarcely soil it further by buying a few dancing partners.'' He grinned again.

''I find you beneath contempt, Mr. Perkins,'' she sniffed. ''What on earth has gotten into you? Whiskey?''

"I'm perfectly sober. And you haven't called me Jace for hours."

"Nor do I intend to!" She felt her anger growing by leaps and bounds. He should be begging her forgiveness for his scandalous behavior. Instead, he was flaunting those . . . those creatures to her face. And enjoying her discomfort! "Go away," she said. "You're a dreadful man."

He looked alarmed at that. His voice became a high-pitched simper. "My stars! Have I displeased you today, Miss Callie? Beyond all redemption?" He sighed. "Well, we'll be friends again when we watch the fireworks together. I recollect I promised to sit with you."

"I would be most pleased if you'd absent yourself from my company for the rest of the evening," she snapped.

He hung his head. "As you wish."

He moved off toward the dancers, scanned the field for a moment, then tapped the shoulder of a miner who was waltzing with a saloon girl. They exchanged a few words; then the creature smiled, held out her hand, and melted into Jace's arms.

Callie watched them together, her insides churning with unfamiliar emotions. The creature was so beautiful, full-bosomed and seductive in a lavender blue gown covered with spangles. And he held her so tightly, his dimpled smile filled with warm admiration. She hated the painted hussy.

Oh, for heaven's sake! she thought a moment later. She was just jealous because she wanted to dance herself, and knew she couldn't. And he was merely smiling to be polite. Why should she care?

But she watched in an agony of fascination as night fell and the bonfire was lit and he danced with one girl and then another. He was so graceful, so strong and masculine in the firelight. She sighed. It wasn't fair—that a mincing fool should be encased in such a manly form. And she would probably spend the rest of her life as Mrs. Horace Perkins, wishing that Ralph Driscoll would look her way.

The dancing was over. Beth awakened, refreshed and eager

for the fireworks. Big Jim had returned as the fiddlers were putting away their instruments. Now he plunked Beth onto his lap and smiled while he recounted his successes at the horseshoe pitch.

A stillness fell over the crowd. Everyone was hushed, waiting breathlessly for the first bright rocket. The sky above was an inky vastness, lit only by the sliver of a waning moon. The sound of a tinny piano from a distant saloon drifted on the still night air and a solitary dog barked high up in the hills.

Shivering in anticipation, Beth reached out and squeezed Callie's arm. "Oh, golly! Why don't they start?" she whispered.

There was a faint sputtering sound from somewhere beyond the field, and then the sky exploded in a great starburst of white light. A collective "Ahh!" rose from the crowd, followed by squeals of joy as another rocket blossomed into a giant flower that seemed to cover the heavens.

Callie looked around her at the upturned faces, wide-eyed with wonder. She had always loved fireworks, had often gone down to the Charles River in Boston to watch the pyrotechnic displays on Independence Day, gaping and marveling like everyone else. But tonight she was strangely unmoved.

She hadn't seen Jace since the dancing ended. She wondered who he was enjoying the fireworks with. *I should have been more civil to him,* she thought, remembering his tentative courtship of the morning. Would it have been so difficult to encourage him? Instead, she'd been a complete prig all day, finding fault and chiding him for every lapse. He was probably as uncomfortable with their situation as she was. More so, perhaps, since he was the one under consideration—like a piece of furniture bought on approval and brought home to see if it fit into the parlor.

She stirred restlessly on the bench and stood up at last. She couldn't sit for another minute. And the whistle of the rockets and the boom of the firebursts were beginning to make her head pound. She yearned for solitude and shelter.

She spied the beer-garden tent. It was probably deserted by now, all the patrons having rushed out to watch the fireworks, no doubt. She limped toward it and peered through the opening. Her heart sank. There were still half a dozen hardy souls inside, impervious to the dazzling nightime display, their mugs of beer more valued than a handful of gunpowder and a few colored salts.

She put one hand over her ear. The pyrotechnics were building to a crescendo, a grand finale of glittering light and sound. It might be quieter behind the tent, sheltered from the full force of the blasts. She hobbled around to the back, and then stopped, her hand going to her breast.

A couple stood beneath a tree, locked in a passionate kiss. The woman was pressed up against the man's body, her arms entwined about his neck. The man's hands clutched at her skirt, which seemed to be pulled up to her thighs. Callie could see the gleam of pale flesh as the woman wriggled and undulated against him. Repelled and fascinated all at the same time, Callie backed up to flee the intimate scene.

Just then, the sky exploded in a final dazzling display of light. It shone like a beacon, illuminating the tableau before her. In the brightness, Callie saw the flash of lavender blue spangles.

And Jace.

Chapter Twelve

"Come on, Milkweed, don't lose heart. We'll find you something to drink." Callie gazed out at the lush mountain meadow and urged her horse forward.

Now that she'd begun to ride out once in a while, she had to admit to herself that this country was truly beautiful. The heavily mined areas around Dark Creek and the nearby gulches had been despoiled by greed and the shortsightedness of man. There was neither pristine beauty nor the reasoned, orderly stamp of civility that made Boston so charming.

But the wild, untouched parts of this land looked as pure as if God had just created the scene, using a brand-new paint box. The grassy meadow—a brilliant emerald—was dotted with wildflowers of dazzling yellow and purple and vibrant pink. It stretched out before her in gentle waves of green, rising gradually to a dense stand of dark, spiky evergreens, and from thence to the highest peaks, which thrust steel gray fingers into the blinding blue of the sky.

The breeze was pungent with the fragrance of pine, and the silvery gray bark of the spruce gave off a warm aroma that was as heady as incense. The thin air at this altitude seemed to intensify the warmth of the sun, so that Callie felt surrounded, enveloped in a golden aura.

And, of course, there was the splendid horse beneath her. Big Jim had bought half a dozen animals as soon as he'd come out to Colorado; the stable behind their house had been built almost before the house was finished.

Callie had ignored Milkweed at first, though the spirited roan mare with its white forelock had been chosen especially for her. She had resented being torn from the safe haven of the house on Beacon Street, had missed the docile filly that had taken her out to the Concord woods and the farms around Lexington.

But after a while, her stubborn resistance had seemed foolish and childish, and she had succumbed to Milkweed's charms. Though it took most of her energies to put the new house in order, she'd managed to ride a few times, taking day long outings into the hills around Dark Creek.

She'd always loved it—riding free and independent through the countryside, the wind in her hair. As a child, envying her schoolmates who could run and jump, she had soon learned that she was their equal on a horse. And in one of her few moments of rebellion, she had insisted on learning to ride astride so she wouldn't be hampered by the constraints of the sidesaddle. It had always scandalized her dressmaker—to fashion a riding habit with split, overlapping skirts and sturdy, masculine-style trousers beneath, rather than the thin flannel drawers favored by the Boston matrons.

She glanced down at the ground. The grass-covered earth beneath Milkweed's hooves seemed to be growing spongy; surely they were nearing a pond. She guided the horse toward a few scrubby pine trees and a graceful willow and saw the shine of water. A small pond spread out before her, buzzing with insects and filmed with pale green algae. Masses of delicate blue columbine ringed its banks, and tiny hummingbirds hovered above the blossoms, probing their depths for nectar.

Callie frowned. Though the setting was enchanting, the stillness of the pond troubled her. The water might be too stagnant or alkaline to drink safely. Milkweed seemed to agree. She lowered her muzzle to the edge of the pond, shook her mane, and backed away. Callie remembered once seeing a creek nestled among the pines and junipers up ahead; its crystalline waters trickled and flowed freely over granite pebbles.

She tightened the cord on her broad-brimmed hat—her one concession to Western-style riding. "Come on, girl," she said, giving the horse a firm prod with her boot heels. "Let's see how fast we can find that creek." Milkweed responded at once, breaking into a smooth gallop.

They flew across the flower-filled meadow, horse and rider as one. But could they ever go fast enough for Callie to outrun her thoughts?

She had been in a turmoil all this week, reliving the horror of that moment when she'd seen Jace with the saloon girl. Surely that hadn't been the same man who had kissed her so timorously! The man who stammered and simpered in her presence. She had crept away, unseen, that night, and never spoken of it to him. But she'd studied him all this week, while her confusion grew—recalling all the facets of his personality that had revealed themselves in the month since he'd been with them. It was like trying to mold a statue out of too-soft clay: the moment you thought you had the shape defined, it softened and shifted into something else.

Who are you, Jace Perkins? she thought.

She slowed Milkweed to a gentle gait as they reached the trees, and guided the animal into the cool shadiness of green boughs and overhanging branches. The carpet of pine needles gave off a muted whisper as they moved among the trees, and the woods were alive with mysterious creature-sounds. A chipmunk with a striped faced looked up, startled, as they passed, and a dusty red grosbeak took flight, its wings whirring softly.

And still the woods echoed with her silent question: *Who are you, Jace?*

She was glad he'd gone out early this morning. She'd done her best to be reserved and distant since the Fourth, and had dreaded his unescapable proximity on this Sunday. Yet her suspicions gnawed at her. Was he spending the Lord's day in town, at one of those disgusting establishments? With a beautiful girl in a lavender gown—a girl who could stand on her own two feet and dance with him? And kiss him so shamelessly?

She sighed, trying to ignore the pangs of envy. Perhaps he only found his manly courage with women like that.

She heard the gurgle of water as they emerged from the trees to a spit of sand. The broad creek bubbled past her, so clear she could see the pebbles and shale on the bottom, so lively that the sunlight flitted like butterflies on its surface.

She reined in Milkweed and dismounted, reaching for her cane in its special sling on the saddle. She limped to the edge of the creek and knelt by the water, pushing her hat off her head to rest between her shoulder blades. While Milkweed bent to the water, she pulled off her riding gloves, made a cup with her hand, and drank greedily. The water was cold and fresh, with a sharp tang that tasted of the snowcapped mountains whence it had come.

She lifted her head and watched the meandering course of the creek. The bank seemed to go on for some distance—a natural path. It might be fun to explore for half a mile or so. She remounted Milkweed and turned the animal's head upstream; the sandy spit looked wider in that direction.

She felt at peace—at least for a little while. She could lose herself in the contemplation of nature in all its glory. Mrs. Ackland had named for her many of the wildflowers, trees, and birds of the Rockies, and several travelers' guides had added to her knowledge. She found herself recognizing birds and small animals, shrubs and flowers. White mountain parsley and purple fairy slippers; sooty lark buntings and bleating pikas.

And when she saw the glint of fish in the creek, she was able
to name them as well.

"Mercy sakes!" she said in surprise, as her eye was caught
by something in the fast-flowing current. *A man's hat!* It looked
so incongruous in this pastoral setting, bobbing along on top
of the water, that she nearly laughed aloud.

Then she frowned. It wasn't waterlogged as though it had
been drifting for a long time. Whoever lost it must be upstream,
just around the next bend or so. Some poor cowboy, no doubt.
She wondered if he knew he'd lost his hat, if he was in trouble.

The hat snagged on a branch protruding into the creek. Callie
hesitated, then dismounted and retrieved it, hooking it on her
saddle horn before she climbed back onto Milkweed. She felt
rather noble as she continued upstream: the hat looked quite
new, and the cowboy would be grateful to have it back.

But the longer she rode, the more her unease grew. This was
still a wild land, after all, and the hat might belong to a desperado. Hadn't Jace's coach been ambushed almost on the edge
of town? And then again, though the territory was at peace
with the Indians, there could be a renegade up to no good. She
examined the hat more carefully and was relieved to find no
apparent blood on it.

Still, it wouldn't hurt to be cautious. She slowed Milkweed
to a gentle walk, and approached each twist and turn in the
creek with trepidation.

She heard his voice before she saw him. "Goddamned son
of a bitch!"

She stifled a gasp. *Jace?*

She heard the splash of water and a metallic clang. She
ducked under a low-hanging willow tree and came around the
bend just in time to see Jace, knee-deep in the creek, hurl a
broken pick onto the sandy bank. The violent gesture made his
biceps bulge menacingly below his rolled-up sleeves. His body
was taut, his face twisted in fury.

Near him in the water was a large granite boulder upon
which rested a heavy sledgehammer and a prospecting pan. He

skimmed the pan angrily onto the bank, slung the sledge over one shoulder as though it were a toothpick, and stomped to shore, sending up sprays of water from his heavy boots.

Staring in disbelief, Callie nudged Milkweed forward. "Jace?" The word came out as a soft croak.

His head snapped up in surprise and alarm, eyes going wide. At once he dropped the sledgehammer to the ground and sheepishly rubbed the back of his neck. "Oh, my stars, Miss Callie! You gave me a start." He reached for the coat that lay across his horse's saddle, rolled down his shirtsleeves, and shrugged into his coat. He smiled up at her, his dimple showing, and slicked back his tousled black hair. "I didn't know you like to ride. You sit a horse well. You surely do."

She knew that smile. It was the one he used when he wanted to soft-soap a person. Well, she wasn't about to tolerate his pious dodge. Not *this* time. She'd heard the foul words from his mouth, even if he thought she hadn't. And she had a pretty fair idea of what had brought him to the creek. She gestured toward the prospecting pan. "What are you doing here?" she demanded.

He tried to look embarrassed, digging the toe of his wet boot into the sand. "Well, everybody in town talks about panning for gold and . . . oh, cheese in crackers. I thought I'd try my hand." With a disconsolate sigh, he pointed to his pick. "And now my tool is all-to-smash."

She had no patience with his namby-pamby excuses today. She drew her mouth into a tight line of disapproval. "You've been very careful to hide it, Mr. Perkins, but I've begun to think you're nothing but a contemptible money-grubber. Nosing around Poppy's business affairs, gambling with more skill than you let on. And now this. A lust for gold. Perhaps Poppy ought to look at those books you've been keeping so carefully."

His eyes narrowed. "If I'd wanted to steal from Big Jim, I could have done it the first week," he growled. "And been out of here so fast you'd still be eating my dust. I don't steal from friends."

"And who *do* you steal from?" she said with a sneer.

He inhaled a deep breath through clenched teeth. He seemed to be fighting to control himself, his hands knotted into tight fists. "Just what is it about me that sticks in your craw, Miss Southgate?" he said at last. "That I like money? That I like having it?"

"Do you deny it?" she sniffed.

He spun away from her and stared into the darkness of the trees behind them. She could see the heave of his shoulders, the tension in the set of his head. And when he spoke, it was with a different voice—low and deep and filled with bitterness. "How self-righteous you are. Did the war touch you at all? You sat in your fine house in Boston while your father wallowed in money from his arms factory. And maybe when they posted the lists of the dead and wounded, you allowed yourself a sympathetic tear or two. And went on with your comfortable life."

He had touched too close to the truth. She felt the need to defend herself. "Th-that's not so," she stammered. "There were family acquaintances ... employees ... They paid the final price for the Union. And we all did our part."

He turned slowly and glared at her. His eyes were like blue crystals, cold and hard and glittering. "I've always admired your refined sensibilities, Miss Southgate," he said with sarcasm. "You make a great show of moral rectitude, defending a cause with passion. Your temperance crusade, for example."

She glared back indignantly. "If I have the strength of my convictions . . ."

He gave a mocking laugh. "You're very careful to choose convictions that don't truly touch you. Some of us, however, didn't have that luxury when it came to the war. We had to live our convictions. I saw men die beside me in the field. They had as many hopes and dreams as I did. But their lives were cut short, in the flower of their youth. When I came out of the Reb camp, after three years of hell, I didn't have a plugged nickel to my name. Not even a pair of shoes or a shirt without holes in it. And I envied my fallen comrades."

She was beginning to feel uncomfortable. "I'm sure it was dreadful, but . . ."

He cut her off with a wave of his hand. "I knew sanctimonious women like you. They look upon me and my kind as the 'noble poor'. Deserving of their pitty and charity. But the milk of human kindness is a bitter dish when you're the one who has to drink it." He thrust out a defiant chin. "I make no apologies for wanting money, Miss Southgate. But that doesn't make me a thief, willing to steal from your father."

She felt ashamed of her cruel accusations. Painfully aware of the narrowness of her own experience, she edged Milkweed closer to him and put a hand on his sleeve. "I'm truly sorry, Mr. Perkins. *Jace*. I judged you harshly. And unfairly. Can you forgive me?"

He took a steadying breath; then his face relaxed into a thin smile. "Miss Callie, I can forgive anything when you look at me with those eyes." He held out his arms to her. "Come down from there and give your animal a rest."

She smiled shyly in return and allowed him to help her down from her horse. Milkweed immediately trotted over to a tuft of grass and began to feed.

Jace pulled out his watch and squinted at it. "A clever horse. It's well past noon. Are you hungry, Miss Callie? I brought some chicken from Mrs. Ackland's larder. I'd be pleased to share it with you."

She gestured toward her saddle. "I have some corn bread there, myself. And your hat. I found it downstream."

"I think we can dine very agreeably."

They ate their impromptu picnic in a small, grassy clearing among the trees. It was a quiet meal—he was still resentful of her sharp words, no doubt. And Callie burned with remorse at her thoughtlessness. He hadn't told them before that he had seen battle. She'd treated him like a man with no substance, seeing nothing beyond his prissy ways. But clearly there was a depth to him she hadn't perceived before, a darkness forged by suffering.

She gave him a sidelong glance. "I'm sorry for the dreadful things I said."

He shrugged. "It's not the first time." He looked away, as though he were embarrassed to meet her gaze. "Why are you always vexed with me?"

She chewed at her lip. How could he ask such a question, when Big Jim's plans had forced them into this impossible situation—a marriage they were bound to honor, willy-nilly. "Doesn't it trouble *you* that . . . ?" She couldn't go on. It was too intimate a topic.

"What?"

She shook her head. "Nothing."

"Are you so unhappy with your life here that I must bear the brunt of your discontent?"

"I miss my friends in Boston," she said in her own defense.

He snorted. "Ah, yes. Beth told me. And did *you* ever wear the bloomer?"

"I . . . I didn't think Poppy would approve."

"And so you played at emancipation while you allowed your father to dictate your life."

"That's not so at all!" she said heatedly. "We were very independent, my friends and I. We read all the women's rights journals and discussed them at length."

"In the safety of your parlors, of course. Just you and your books, hidden away."

She felt her anger growing. "Why do you consider the reading of books to be . . ." She sputtered over her words and couldn't continue.

"An escape from life? Isn't it?"

"Not at all!" She leaned on her cane and rose to her feet, drawing herself up with outraged pride. "We conducted many symposia on the evils of drink. And lectured on the need for women to be independent in this century."

He uncurled himself from the ground in a lazy, graceful

movement and stood up in his turn. As always, Callie was startled by how tall he was next to her. "And did you yourself ever take the lectern?" he asked.

She took a stumbling step backward. "That's not fair, Jace. You know I couldn't."

"Why? Because you limp?"

She gulped, fighting the painful memories. "Do you know what it was like to be teased as a child?" she whispered.

He gave a dry laugh. "I can imagine it. But if it happened to me, I wouldn't hide behind my cane."

"Hide behind . . . ? Don't be absurd! I *need* my cane."

"And I say you don't." Before she had a chance to stop him, he had reached out and pulled the cane from her grasp.

"Oh!" She tottered on unsteady legs, waved her arms wildly in the air, and managed to throw them around his neck just in time to keep from falling. She felt his arm go around her waist to steady her and pull her close. Breathless with shock, she looked up; her heart seemed to catch in her throat.

His face was so near she could see the faint stubble on his strong jaw. Feel the breath from his tempting mouth. "Mr. Perkins . . ." she began, her voice quivering.

"Jace." Was that a smile of triumph, lurking in the corners of his lips?

Devil take the man! It was just like him, with his cowardly ways. He didn't have the gumption to declare himself openly. He had to play games, wait until they were isolated, before he remembered he was a man! She twisted in his embrace, reaching for the cane he still held in his free hand.

She was filled with scorn, recalling and magnifying all her grievances against him. "I see you do a bit of reading yourself, Mr. Perkins. Dime novels, no doubt. Isn't this the way of those books? A man who can't stand up to other men, but who hopes to win the heroine's favors nonetheless. So he plies her with drink, or sneaks into her room, or contrives an 'accident' that throws her into his arms. Just to take liberties with her. To steal a kiss he's afraid to ask for." She uttered a sound of contempt, deep in her throat. "Isn't that his way? Most especially if he's a . . . a spineless *twiddlepoop!*"

She grabbed her cane and broke free of him, turning back toward the creek and her horse. "I wish you good fortune with your prospecting," she said haughtily.

She heard a low growl behind her. And then she was caught, spun around, slammed hard against his chest. The cane flew from her fingers.

His eyes burned like blue fire, and he bared his teeth in a scowl. "If I want a kiss, lady, I don't need an 'accident.' And I don't have to ask for it, either. I simply take it. Like this."

His mouth ground down on hers in a hard, demanding kiss. Her lips were crushed beneath his, captured by the savage intensity of his fiery mouth. His kiss was a flame that raced through her, burning its way to her pounding heart, igniting her vitals, sending tongues of fire to the most intimate, forbidden parts of her body.

She moaned and slapped weakly at his shoulders. Surely it was wrong to feel what she was feeling: more light-headed and intoxicated than if she'd been drinking the strongest wine. She tried to wrest her mouth away, but he tangled his fingers in her hair and held her head firmly to his. At the same time, the hand around her waist slid down to cup her bottom in a shameless embrace, pulling her hips against the hardness of his loins.

She felt nerveless and weak, overpowered by his will, caught in a dizzying spiral of fear and delight. She felt his mouth open over hers, felt the hot, sensual stroke of his tongue along the line of her lips. She gave a helpless squeak as a shiver ran down her spine; her lips parted of their own volition.

At once, his tongue was within her mouth, gliding along the edge of her teeth and reaching farther inward to torment the moist cavity with pulsating spasms. Her knees went weak. Her arms ceased their flailing to clasp his shoulders tightly, lest she fall to the ground.

Just as she thought she'd faint from breathlessness and ecstasy, he released her mouth and head, though his arm still held her close. Gasping, her whole body aquiver, she stared up into his face and felt all her certainties melting away.

His eyes were unreadable, dark with secrets. But the face was the face of the stranger she'd dimly perceived for weeks. The man whose voice could deepen to a commanding growl. The man who could sit at a card table as though he owned it. The man who could embrace a whore and lift her skirts and . . . She trembled at the frightening, tantalizing thought.

Who are you, Jace? she thought, anguished.

Then he smiled—with such smugness that her blood, already heated by his passionate assault, boiled over. She scrubbed her fist across her tingling lips as if she could wipe away the lingering effects of his brutish kiss. Curse the man! She wanted nothing more than to wipe that self-confident smirk from his face.

She leaned back in his arm, raised her hand, and slapped him across the face as hard as she could. He gave a start of surprise and dropped his arm. Caught off-balance, she wobbled for a moment, then tumbled to the grass.

He was on his knees beside her at once. "Oh, my stars, Miss Callie, I'm sorry. Sometimes I . . . forget myself when I get riled up." He groped for her cane in the grass and held it out to her. "And you're so pretty, and I did so want to kiss you, and I . . . oh, fudge! Are you vexed with me again?"

Vexation was scarcely the emotion she was feeling! She burned with shame—for having succumbed to his kiss, even for a moment. For falling like a helpless cripple, when a sound woman would have swirled away from him in proudful disdain.

But mostly—seeing the false, simpering smile on his face—she felt shame for having allowed herself to be deceived all these weeks. She saw the truth in a sudden blinding revelation. He'd played her for a fool, with his namby-pamby ways and his feigned gentility. And he was *still* hoping to play the game. She could read it in his eyes. See it in the strong body that deliberately curled into a cringe. Blast his hide, even his voice had just gone up an octave!

She snatched the cane from his hand and struggled to her feet with as much dignity as she could muster. "Don't you 'Oh, fudge' me, Horace Perkins!" she said, her lip curling in disgust. "You mealy-mouthed scoundrel with your mock-modest face! You may have been meek and genteel when Mr. Collins knew you in Baltimore. But somewhere along the way you learned to know exactly what you want, and go after it. And devil take the consequences!"

He hesitated, rubbing the red spot on his cheek. "Now, Miss Callie . . ." he said in an ingratiating whine.

"Stop it!" She stamped her foot on the ground. "Who the hell *are* you, Jace Perkins?" She couldn't believe she was swearing like a street tough.

He smiled sheepishly and shrugged in surrender. Then he began to chuckle—a sly laugh completely out of character with the Horace Perkins she'd come to know in the past month. He let his eyes travel up and down her body in a brazen appraisal that was all too easy to interpret.

"You're right, darlin'," he drawled at last. "I *do* know what I want. So if I were you, I'd get me on that horse right quick, and skedaddle out of here."

She shivered and turned toward the creek and Milkweed. She didn't need to be told twice.

Chapter Thirteen

"Well, now, Mousekin, what's this all about?" Big Jim settled himself beside Callie in the wagon and picked up the reins. "I've never known you to come fetching me for dinner before."

Callie put up her parasol against the harsh midday sun. She could feel the heat of her body, encased by her tight corsets. "I've been wanting to talk to you alone for days," she began hesitantly.

He gave a hearty laugh. "Well, girl, it's not as though I've been away!"

"No. No, of course not." But when he came in for dinner, he was eager to spend time with all his children. And when he came home in the evenings, Jace was always by his side.

Jace. Callie frowned and chewed at her lower lip. In the few days since their dreadful meeting in the mountains, he had been reserved and distant, eyeing her warily as though he was waiting for her to make the first move. She'd been aware of a noticeable lessening of his prissy manner—perhaps he no longer thought it necessary to keep up the pretense.

Poppy guided the horse out of town and glanced at her. "Well?"

She found herself losing courage. *Poppy will think I'm daft, no doubt.* She gave a forced laugh and looked up at the clear sky. "My, it's going to be a scorcher today, isn't it? I'm glad I brought my parasol."

"Well, maybe when it gets cold, I'll buy us a nice closed-in chaise, like we had in Boston. Good for next summer, too."

"I'd like that," she said. "Something with enough seats for the whole family."

"Beth *likes* the back of the wagon."

"But it isn't ladylike, and . . ."

"Dagnabit!" he bellowed suddenly. "You didn't come all this way to talk about Beth and chaises and the weather. Out with it, girl!"

She rubbed her hand across her mouth. "It's just that . . ." She gulped. "Oh, Poppy, I'm scared!"

"Scared?" He leaned over and patted her hand. "What's troubling my little girl?"

"It's . . . it's Jace. He's not the man we thought he was."

Poppy began to chuckle. "Is that all? Well of course he's not, thank God!"

"But the man in his letters, the man Mr. Collins knew . . . All his genteel ways, his . . . his softness. Not the man I've begun to see."

"Sweetie, I think that *other* man died in the war. The man who works beside me every day has a backbone. And a shrewd head on his shoulders. Just the man I hoped he'd be."

She gaped at Big Jim. "You *knew?*"

"The first day he came to town with me."

"But then, why all the pretense?"

"I reckon it was for you, Mousekin," he said, patting her hand again. "Because you're shy. You said you wanted a genteel man. Maybe he thought you'd be skittish if he showed there was more to him than just polite ways. At least until you got to know him better."

"I know him about as well as I want to," she said with a sniff of disgust.

"That doesn't sound very friendly-like, girl. Let me tell you about the man *I've* seen. He's strong and tough. Bright as a whip. Runs that store as though he were born to it. Splendid. Splendid! He's a hard-headed businessman, but he's got more charm than any ten men I've met. You should see him with the customers. Gets them to buy things they never even knew they wanted!"

"I've seen his charm," she said bitterly. "He only uses it to get what he wants."

"Well, he's a clever devil. Nothing wrong with that, by jingo! Stands up to me, too. But not like some hell-for-leather rowdy. Just quiet and solid and stubborn." Big Jim chuckled again. "He knows I like him, the rapscallion. Talked me into a raise in salary after the second week, by God!"

"If he's so clever, why couldn't he keep a job?"

"Lots of men have been rootless since the war, girl! But I think he's settling in nicely here."

"But he *gambles*, Poppy!"

Big Jim roared with laughter. "And wins, by thunder! He's skunked many a sharper, from what I've heard in town."

"And he sneaks out to prospect for gold."

"What in the Sam Hill do you mean by *sneak?* Last Sunday? He told me where he was going. I think it tickles his fancy— the thought of making a strike. It's just a harmless diversion to him."

She felt like she was in a shooting gallery, watching all her arguments being demolished like clay ducks. She tried again. "I . . . was in his room this morning. Looking for Mummy's old lace antimacassars on top of the linen cupboard. I knocked down his hatbox by mistake."

She shivered, remembering her horrible discovery. "Poppy, there were *guns* in it! One of those little ones the gamblers hide in their sleeves. And a big pistol, with a fancy holster that looks like it's been used a lot. What if he's a . . . a criminal?"

Poppy snorted. "That's all my eye and Betty Martin! He's knocked around a lot. Probably found himself in more than one scrape. A fellow needs to defend himself."

"But he told me he didn't own a gun."

"Told me the same. But Mousekin! Why do you fret? Every man has a few secrets."

"And I'm not supposed to be frightened of him?"

"All I know is the man I see. A damn fine fellow." He raised a quizzical eyebrow. "Has he ever been anything but polite and honorable to you? You tell me, and I'll fix his wagon!"

How could she tell him about the shameless kiss near the creek? She'd have to confess that a part of her had enjoyed it. "N-no," she stammered.

He beamed and threw his hand in the air in an expansive gesture. "Well then, there you are! You'd be a dad-blamed fool not to take him for a husband."

Husband. She felt her fear like a hard lump in her throat. Strong and tough, Poppy had called him. And overpowering. She'd found that out in the mountains. Husband. And then shy, crippled Callie would become a cipher, bending to his every wish. *Just like Mummy.*

They rode in silence for a while. She knew that Big Jim watched her, poised to speak, but perhaps reluctant.

At last he cleared his throat. "Look, sweetie," he said gruffly. "Is it because of . . . the traffic between men and women? Is that what has you so all-fired jumpy?"

She felt the heat of embarrassment on her cheeks. "Poppy, please," she whispered.

"No point in beating around the bush, girl! That's a part of marriage you'll have to get used to. Now Jace strikes me as the kind of man who hasn't had much experience in that direction. He's always a perfect gentleman around the ladies. Nothing to be frightened of there, by thunder!"

She wasn't so sure. She'd seen Jace with the sporting girl.

"If I marry, I'm prepared to take on the obligations of a wife," she said stiffly. *If* she married.

"And well you ought, girl!" He gave a sly laugh. "Not like your mother and me, of course. A smack on the rump now and again. A good tickle or a pinch. I knew how to please her." He sighed. "My God, there was a lusty woman! How I miss her."

She stared at him in shock. All those terrifying sounds coming from their room ... *And Mummy had* enjoyed *it?* It was a new and frightening thought. *Perhaps* that *was why Mummy willingly traded her free will in their marriage—for the pleasures of the bedroom.*

She herself had succumbed to Jace's passionate kiss, trembling like a spineless fool. If she married him, would his more intimate caresses reduce her to utter helplessness? "Poppy, I don't think I want ..." she began.

He interrupted her with a firm arm around her shoulder. He pulled her close and gave her a loving hug. "I'm glad we had this talk, Mousekin. You see how foolish your fears were? Jace will make you a damn fine husband. And the sooner the better!"

Her heart sank. Poppy had already made up his mind. And she didn't have the courage to cross him.

"I'll be jiggered, Jace." Beth swallowed her mouthful of food and pointed across the table at him. "I can't hardly see where that desperado plugged you. It ain't nothing but a little line on your head anymore."

Callie frowned and opened her mouth to correct Beth's grammar. Then she sighed. What was the use? The few hours a day that she taught Beth her lessons couldn't offset the time her sister spent at the store, in the company of rough-talking Westerners. If only Dark Creek had enough children to warrant a school!

Jace laughed and rubbed at his scar. "I reckon I just heal fast, Princess." He reached for a platter and helped himself to more potatoes. "I surely do like Mrs. Ackland's cooking." He pulled his plate closer and dug into the potatoes with single-minded gusto.

Weedy looked over at Big Jim. "You think they'll ever catch those road agents?"

His father shrugged. "Mr. Hepworth doesn't see how. They could be anywhere from here to California by now." He chuckled. "Not that Ralph Driscoll minds."

Jace interrupted his eating to scowl at Poppy. "What's Driscoll have to do with it?"

"That was a payroll from the Eureka Mine they stole. The manager told me they had to borrow from the bank to pay their men. And Driscoll, being the only banker in town, slapped on a fat interest rate."

Jace snorted. "He would, that son of a . . ." His eyes shot to Callie's face. "Son of a gun," he finished lamely.

She pursed her lips in annoyance. "Don't hold back on my account, Jace," she said sarcastically. He'd dropped every other pretense. He might as well swear in her presence as well!

Weedy thrust out a belligerent chin. "All I know is, if those varmints ever showed their faces in Dark Creek, I'd shoot them down. By jingo, I'd wring their necks with my bare hands!"

Big Jim smacked his hand on the table. "Weedy, that's no way to carry on! You're going to be a Harvard man. Why don't you show a little restraint and civility, like Jace here?"

Two bright spots of angry color appeared on Weedy's cheeks. Callie bit her lip. It was bad enough that Big Jim ignored Weedy most of the time. But to compare him with Jace, as though the outsider had become the favored son . . .

"Now, Big Jim," said Jace with a gentle laugh, "you ought to be right proud of Weedy. He shows a lot of spunk. Darned if *I* was that bold at his age."

Callie stared in surprise. She wouldn't have expected Jace to defend Weedy like that—certainly not at his own expense.

Big Jim hesitated, then gave his son a nod of approval. "You're right. Damned if he's not tougher than I thought."

Weedy basked in the unexpected compliment, seeming to grow an inch in his chair. *Thank you, Poppy,* thought Callie. Then, with more reluctance, *Thank you, Jace.* He might be a two-faced scoundrel, but sometimes he showed a flash of kindliness that surprised her.

Big Jim pushed away his plate. "I couldn't eat another mouthful. That's fine cooking, Mrs. Ackland," he said, as the housekeeper began to clear away the dishes.

Mrs. Ackland glanced at Jace, then back to Big Jim. "Will you take your whiskey now?"

"I think we'll take it in the parlor tonight," he replied.

Beth slid from her chair, skipped around the table, and tugged at Jace's sleeve. "Come play the piano for me. I want to hear that song again—the one you sang the other day."

Callie pricked up her ears. Lord knew what corrupting influence the man was having on Beth! "What song is that, Jace?" she asked sharply.

His blue eyes were as innocent as a newborn babe's. " 'My Wife Is a Most Knowing Woman,' " he said.

"Hmph! It sounds like something they'd sing in a variety hall."

The innocence had a mocking gleam behind it. "Now, Miss Callie, you know I'd never frequent those wicked places." He contrived to look mournful. Hoping for her pity, no doubt! "We sang Mr. Foster's gayest songs around the campfires to lift our spirits. A soldier's comfort, alas, far from hearth and home."

Big Jim shook his head. "No. No songs tonight." He dismissed Weedy and Beth with a wave of his hand. "Go along with you. I want to talk to Jace and Callie alone in the parlor."

Callie felt the blood drain from her face. Was it to be *tonight?* So soon? It seemed as though her talk with Big Jim last week had meant nothing to him.

Beth thrust out her lower lip in a pout. "Oh, botheration!"

"Skedaddle, I said!"

Jace tweaked Beth's nose. "We'll sing tomorrow night, Princess."

"Promise?"

He grinned and held out his little finger. Beth hooked her finger through his. "'Pinky, pinky, bow-bell, Whoever tells a lie,'" he began.

Beth's eyes were bright with adoration. "Oh, Jace!" she burst out. "I want you to stay forever and ever! Can we make that part of the promise?"

"I don't see why not." They finished the doggerel in a solemn singsong, then Jace smiled again and tugged at her pigtail. "Now scoot, like your father says."

Callie trailed the two men into the parlor, her heart weighted with dread. She watched them down their whiskey, wishing for the first time that she could indulge in the false courage of liquor.

Poppy leaned back in his chair and tapped his fingers together. "Well, have you made up your minds yet?"

Jace looked startled. "Sir?"

"Dagnabit, we've had enough shilly-shallying! You've been here a month and a half, son. Time enough to decide. I want to get those papers drawn up. You and Callie will own half the store, as I promised in my letter."

Callie stole a glance at Jace's face. He looked as stunned by her father's precipitous haste as she was.

"P-Poppy," she stammered, "this is so sudden."

"By jingo, how long do you need? It's time for you to get married! I can't wait forever."

"But if I'm not ready to decide . . ." she said in a timid voice.

"Jumping Jehoshaphat! That's why we got him out here, isn't it? If you say no, I can't let him stay the winter. It wouldn't be right. I'd have to find someone else—and right quick, before the snows come. Now make up your mind, girl!"

She felt as though the walls were closing in on her. She couldn't look at Jace. He was so quiet. *Oh, God,* she thought, overwhelmed by a new and frightening notion. What if he didn't want *her?* She'd die of shame. "Must it be tonight?" Her voice trembled.

"What better time?" Big Jim stirred impatiently in his chair and poured himself another drink.

Jace put down his glass and cleared his throat. "If I may be so bold, sir." He stood up, crossed the room to where Callie sat in abject misery, and took her hand. "Miss Callie, I'd be proud and honored to be chosen by you."

Her heart skipped a beat. He looked so solemn and intense, his eyes filled with warmth, that she wondered why she hesitated. He *must* care for her. Hadn't he played his milksop's role only to please her?

And then a darker thought—all unbidden—crept into her brain. Was *she* what he wanted? Or merely the partnership in the store? The chance to have the money he craved.

As usual, Poppy decided for her. "Well, there you are!" he boomed. "That's the finest proposal I've heard in a long time. We'll make the wedding in the middle of August. Before Weedy goes off to school."

Jace knelt before her and looked deep into her eyes. "It's what you want, isn't it, Callie?"

She looked at her father, then at Jace. Caught between two strong men, she felt as though she were fading into invisibility.

"Yes, of course," she whispered. And suppressed the small voice inside her that screamed, *"No!"*

The moon was nearly full, outshining the bright stars that crowded the night sky. The distant howl of a coyote reverberated in the stillness, and crickets chirped in the nearby mountain stream. The wind, deserted by the warm sun, blew fresh and cold, but the spicy scent of spruce bark it carried gave promise of the summer day to follow.

Jace exhaled a mouthful of cigar smoke; it caught the moonlight for a moment, hanging suspended like a silvery cloud, before the breeze swirled it away. He scowled up at the sky. It was too dark to read his watch, but it must be well after midnight, to judge from the position of the constellations. He wondered if he'd ever be able to sleep tonight.

What had he gotten himself into? *Marriage,* for Christ's sake! A wife and a settled life. No better than a starch-collared drudge who lived out his life in quiet desperation—as that writer, Thoreau, had said. If he had any sense, he'd steal one of Big Jim's horses and head for Nevada.

He laughed ruefully. That son of a bitch Perkins had been a sly one—gabbing about everything in his life except the fact that he'd been bought, like a slab of meat at the butcher's. Bought to be Callie's husband. He'd damn near dropped his whiskey glass when Big Jim had come out with it tonight! He hoped they hadn't noticed his surprise.

Not that he hadn't surprised himself by making the first move. Like a goody-goody suitor, on his knees. He'd done everything but sigh and hand her flowers! But Callie had looked so forlorn, so humiliated by Big Jim's unthinking brashness. And so uncertain and scared, he'd suddenly felt the need to resolve the matter.

He shook his head. *Poor Mousekin. No wonder she's been so angry and hostile all this time, knowing that this night was coming.* She might want him—and he was sure she did—but she couldn't have welcomed it. Not on Big Jim's terms. He'd never known a woman, no matter how plain or self-conscious, who didn't want to feel she could snag a man without help.

"Jesus," he muttered aloud, as a sudden thought struck him. All these weeks he'd worked the confidence game on her, simpering like a damned fool, scheming to steal kisses, just to get her to the point where she'd fall into bed with him. But all he'd really needed to do was keep her from hating him outright. The bedding—legal at that!—had been practically guaranteed from the first day.

Not that the game hadn't been fun. At least until last week, when he'd kissed her like that at the creek. He felt his body growing warm with the memory. The sweetest mouth he'd tasted in years. And that flash of fire when she'd slapped his face. If she brought that much passion to the marriage bed, he'd be a lucky man. Damned if he wouldn't!

Still, she'd changed since then. She was peeved at him; that was natural enough. He'd let Horace's mask slip once too often. He was almost sure she knew he'd been shamming all this time. He'd gotten used to her contempt for "Horace's" manner; it amused him in a queer way. And he'd expected the anger he'd seen in her eyes this week.

Yet there was something new in her behavior as well, something that unsettled him. *Fear,* or he missed his guess—though he couldn't figure why. She hadn't feared "Horace." But that whisper of fear had kept him distant and wary all week, wondering how to deal with such an unfamiliar response from a woman.

"Hell," he said, flinging the stub of his cigar to the ground. Why should he care? He'd have what he wanted, at least for now. That ripe body beneath him in a bed, the unexpected contentment of his life here, and—to sweeten the pot—a half interest in the store. He could put aside a heap of money, fatten his grubstake at the faro table, then light out for greener pastures if the marriage became too restricting.

He took a satisfying breath of the clean air, feeling at peace with himself. He could sleep now.

He was suddenly aware of a strange noise. He strained his ears, listening. He could hear the sound of the aspen leaves rattling in the breeze. And, from farther up the canyon, the mournful sough of the wind through the evergreens.

But this was a different sound—faint and disturbing. Like hiccuping sobs, low and irregular. He moved cautiously around the side of the house, putting himself into the building's shadow.

Behind the house was the table and chairs that Callie used for Beth's lessons. Huddled on one of the chairs, her face buried in her hands, was Callie. She was weeping bitterly, her shoulders shaking with grief. The breeze riffled her hair, and her nightdress gleamed like snow beneath the bright moon.

"Son of a gun," he muttered, hurrying toward her. "What ails you, Miss Callie?"

She gave a jump of alarm and looked up at him, hastily wiping her sleeve across her eyes. "Wh-what are you doing here?" she said, and sniffled.

"I heard you crying." When she looked in dismay toward the darkened house, he reassured her. "I was outside, taking the night air. I'm sure they didn't hear you."

She seemed to be recovering her composure bit by bit. She took a deep breath and squared her shoulders. "They weren't meant to. Nor were you. Go away."

"Cheese in crackers, ma'am. A lady in distress shouldn't ought to weep alone."

She reached for the shawl on the chair behind her. "Oh, do stop playing your games!" she snapped. "You might have deceived me at first, but no longer."

He was curious to see how much she suspected. "What games?" he asked innocently.

"Oh!" She swirled the shawl around her shoulders with an impatient gesture, took hold of her cane, and stood up. "Do you deny you're not what I thought you were? A . . . a . . ." She sputtered to a stop.

He found it hard to suppress his smile. "A twiddlepoop? No, I suppose I'm not." But *Horace* had been, and Cooper had told them that, no doubt. "At least not since the war," he amended. "It tends to toughen up a man."

"Yet you found it necessary to deceive me."

"It was my error. For which I beg forgiveness." He meant it truly, much to his own surprise. "I should have trusted your generosity of spirit to accept me for what I am."

"And what *are* you, Horace Perkins?"

Horace Perkins. Even his name was false. "Just what you see, Miss Southgate," he lied. "An ordinary man who's led an ordinary life. A man who hopes to start anew in this brave new territory. With you."

He could see the bitter curl of her lip in the glow of the moonlight. "In this absurd forced marriage?"

He stared at her, bewildered. *"Forced?* Would you prefer to change your mind and refuse me?"

She shook her head. Her curls shone like silvered gold. "No," she said softly.

"But you don't much cotton to this marriage."

Her voice was softer still. "No."

That hurt his pride. *He* should be the one with doubts, not she. "Is it me? Or the idea of a husband?"

She shrugged tiredly. "Both, I reckon."

"Then why did you agree to it?"

She started to turn away. "Oh, what does it matter?"

He took her by the shoulders and forced her to face him again. "Damn it, tell me!" He could feel her shoulders shaking under his hands, see the remnants of tears still on her cheeks. He fought the urge to hold her close and comfort her against her unknown grief.

"It's what Poppy wants," she said at last. "Someone to take over the store. And a strong hand for Weedy."

He scowled. He'd thought she had more backbone than that. "Your father may be a tyrant. But he's a loving tyrant. And he means well. If you're unhappy, tell him you don't want to marry me. He'll understand."

She began to weep again. "I . . . I can't!" she cried.

"Why the devil not?"

She choked on a sob. "Because Poppy's dying. And this may be the last thing I can do for him."

He dropped his arms and fell back a step, stunned. Dying? That vigorous man, so filled with joyous life, was *dying?* "That's absurd," he said gruffly. "What is he? Fifty-five? Six? In his prime!"

She rubbed her hand across her eyes. "He has a bad heart. The doctor thinks he could have a couple of years, if God wills it. The children don't know. But it's the least I owe him—to obey his wishes in this. If I hadn't been born, he would have taken my mother and come West years ago. And now it's almost too late for him."

"You can't atone for his life."

She sighed heavily. "But I can give him what he wants before he dies. A son-in-law to run his store." Her voice thickened. "And a grandson, if he lives that long."

Before he dies. He found himself shaking at the thought of it, his blood running cold. He'd never given a damn before. People had come and gone, lived and died around him. And as long as Jace Greer survived, what else mattered? But the thought of losing that good man, a man who called him "son," tore through his guts.

He reached out to stroke her curls—as much to comfort himself as her. Their velvety softness soothed the ache in his heart. "Then I reckon we'll have to give him what he wants, won't we, honey?"

She shook free of his touch. "Don't go getting any high-and-mighty ideas, Mr. Perkins! I'd as lief marry a snake as marry you! But I'll do it for Poppy. And you'll have what you want. The store. And all the money you can charm out of the customers."

He heard the bitter note in her voice. She must feel like a helpless pawn to her father's dreams. Maybe a bit of his special charm right about now would perk her up. "I'll have *you*," he said gently. "The prettiest little wife a man could have. And that's what I want."

He slipped his hand around her neck to pull her head near, and bent his own head to her lips. "Shall we seal our bargain with a kiss?" His mouth was beginning to water at the thought of the sweet taste of her. And she was wearing nothing but a thin nightdress. He might risk a bold caress or two, if it didn't frighten her. He hoped his hungry body would be satisfied with that. She was so damned seductive in the moonlight.

She pushed roughly at him to free herself. "I don't want your kisses. Quite frankly, I don't want you!" she cried in a high, angry voice.

His own anger was rising along with his desire. Never had a woman treated him with such contempt. Refused his kisses. Not ever! He didn't like it one bit. He felt like a cross-eyed Saturday-night whore, chosen only because there was no one else available. He pulled her savagely into his arms. "Don't press your luck, darlin'," he growled, and crushed her mouth with his own.

She struggled for a moment in his embrace, and then was still, stiff and passive under his burning kiss. He pressed more insistently, moving his lips against her mouth with rough, passionate strokes. It was like kissing a stone wall. *The ornery bitch!* he thought. He choked on his fury and released her.

At once, she swirled away from him and took a hobbling step toward the house. She turned and looked back at him over her shoulder. In the bright moonlight, he could see her sneer of disgust.

"Don't think for a minute that I consider this marriage anything more than my duty to Poppy," she said scornfully.

His anger bubbled close to the surface, hot and searing, but he forced himself to smile. "Cal, honey, I think we're going to make a right fine couple," he drawled.

And then—because he was so furious and humiliated and frustrated, and because his hands were aching to touch her—he reached out and gave her a sharp smack across her rump. The soft, yielding mounds beneath his fingers nearly drove him wild. *Slap my face now, darlin',* he thought grimly. Waiting, hoping, for her explosion. By God, she'd find herself on the grass within a minute. And he'd be inside her within two, easing the throbbing pain in his loins.

Instead, she stared, her eyes wide with fright. Then her face crumpled into a mask of grief, the fresh tears sparkling like jewels in the moonlight. "Oh, go away, Jace," she sobbed. "Before I do something foolish and break Poppy's heart."

He spun around, his thoughts whirling in confusion, and sprinted for the house.

What the hell had he gotten himself into?

Chapter Fourteen

Callie set down her coffee cup on the parlor table and fingered the cane lying on her lap. She glanced nervously across the room toward Big Jim. "Please, Poppy. I *can't* walk down the aisle today with . . . with this. Why can't I just sit in the front, and get up when Jace comes in?"

"Dagnabit girl, what kind of a bride will you look like? I want the whole world to see how proud I am of you, in your mother's wedding gown."

"But everyone will stare at me."

Big Jim gave a hearty laugh. "Well, of course they will! You're the bride." He smiled in that way that melted her heart. "Come on, sweetie. You don't want to disappoint your old Poppy. I expect you to come down the aisle with me. And no arguments. Understand?"

Needing support, she looked desperately to Jace; he was just finishing his second lunchtime whiskey. Did he need the courage to face the afternoon? she thought in bitterness. "*You* don't want me to walk down the aisle, do you, Jace?" Her eyes held a silent plea.

"Cal, darlin', I'd be right honored to look up and see you coming toward me on your father's arm." He gave an easy smile, but stubborn determination glittered in his eyes.

She sighed. There was no support from *him,* the scoundrel! She felt trapped. Jace had called her father a loving tyrant. Now here she was—caught between *two* tyrants, each eager to bend her to his will.

Jace put down his glass. "What say Weedy takes your other arm to steady you? I can hold your cane until you reach me."

She cringed. She could picture the scene. "Oh, don't be absurd! I'd look ridiculous, propped up like a rag doll. I'm not that helpless. I only need *one* cane, not two!"

He grinned. "Precisely. Then you only need one arm. Big Jim's. Matter of fact, If I keep my arm around you all during the ceremony, you don't have to bring the cane to the church at all."

"Go without my cane?" The thought was terrifying. She'd feel as exposed as if she were standing there in her shift!

"Then Beth can hold it until you need it again. She'll like that." He chuckled. "She's been complaining that a maid of honor 'don't hardly get to do nothin,' by cracky!'"

Callie rolled her eyes. "Except learn to speak like a ruffian."

Big Jim banged his fist on the arm of the chair and beamed. "Well, I think it's a splendid idea, Jace. Splendid! That's what we'll do."

Callie felt her protests die in her throat. What was the use? She swallowed her frustration and started to rise from her chair. "Maybe I should start to dress now."

Jace shook his head. "Not yet. I've only been home from Chicago for two days. I've scarcely had the chance to be with you." Was that a possessive gleam in his eye already?

"You'll have lots of chances when we're married," she said sourly.

"By thunder, I think the Chicago trip was the best thing you've done," said Big Jim. "Why should the folks in these

arts have to go to Cheyenne or Kansas City to get good beef,
when we can get it sent direct?''

Jace shrugged modestly, but couldn't resist a smug smile.
'Well, with the Kansas Pacific Railroad opening up that line
o Denver this month, it made no sense to deal with a middle-
aan. Now, if they'd build a spur from Denver to Dark Creek,
he trip would be even faster. Save that last ride up the canyon
y stage. We could even open up another store just for fancy
astern foods. The town is growing, and I met a lot of business-
en in Chicago who'd be happy to deal with us.''

''Any trouble on the stage?''

Jace rubbed his scar and laughed ruefully. ''No. It took a
ew more holdups after mine, but they finally got wise. There
vas someone riding shotgun this time.''

''Sheriff Hepworth's really riled up about that last one. *Two*
ayrolls, by jingo, and another good man shot.'' Big Jim shook
is head. ''Well, it's a wild land.''

Jace nodded. ''But ripe for the taming.'' He grinned at Callie.
'Just like a wife.''

His oozing self-confidence pricked her like a burr. So over-
earing, so autocratic, now that he didn't have to pretend any-
nore. Clearly, he already considered himself her master, even
efore the wedding. And she hadn't forgotten that slap to her
ear, the brute! She'd given him frosty silence in the week
efore he left for Chicago, and had avoided him since his return.

''And you think this wild land is ready for your fancy foods?''
he asked sarcastically.

He seemed to be deliberately ignoring her rising anger. He
ave her a warm smile. ''Why not? Every man, no matter how
owly, aspires to a better life. Why shouldn't he want a few
elicacies on his table? A finer house? Just like a beautiful
voman should know she's beautiful, and show herself off once
n a while.''

Her head snapped up at his words. ''Is that a criticism?''

''No, darlin', a suggestion,'' he drawled. ''And more than
hat.'' He crossed the room to a table near the door and picked

up a large, bulky package. "You've been ducking me since I came back from Chicago. I haven't had the chance to give this to you."

She gaped in surprise. "For me?"

"It's not much. I wish I could give you more." His eyes were dark with sincerity. "To show you how proud I am, how honored to become your husband."

His self-effacing kindness, so unexpected, caught her off guard. She opened the package with nervous fingers. Within was a magnificent gown of copper silk twill trimmed with velvet bands of the same color. She held it up before her. The neckline was far lower than anything she usually wore; she made a mental note to fill it in with a muslin chemisette. "It's . . . it's beautiful," she stammered.

Jace beamed. "There's a hooped petticoat, puffed out in back, to go with it."

"Thank you so much," she said, regretting her hostility. Perhaps she had misjudged him again, her own fears seeing a tyrant where there was none.

And then he nodded briskly, in command once more. "You'll wear it the first time we give a dinner party. Hear?"

Just like that—with no ifs or buts. Her heart sank. She was right to fear his domination.

Big Jim exploded in a good-natured laugh and lumbered to his feet. "Well, now that we're giving gifts . . ." He fished in his vest pocket, crossing the room to Jace and Callie. "I'd thought to wait until just before the ceremony. But, what the devil." Awkwardly, he thrust a small box into Callie's hand. "Your mother's amber eardrops. They'll look mighty fine with your new gown."

She smiled up at him with tears in her eyes. "Oh, Poppy, that they will. Thank you. Thank you!"

He actually began to blush. "Don't start getting all sentimental!" he said gruffly "Here, Jace." He tossed another small box at the younger man. "A junior partner of a fine emporium needs a *proper* watch."

Jace pulled out a large, finely chased gold watch. "You didn't have to, Big Jim," he said, turning over the watch in his hand. "I . . ." He gulped and blinked, as though he had something in his eye. "Shit," he muttered, and turned away.

Callie stared in wonderment. She'd never seen him so unnerved—to forget himself, use such vulgarity in her presence! What could have upset him so? "What is it?" she asked.

He held out the watch in a trembling hand, his back still to her. On the reverse, carved in bold letters, was the inscription: "To my new son Jace. August 14, 1870. Welcome to the family."

Big Jim looked even more embarrassed than before. "Hell, man! It's just a fancy timepiece. It's not as though . . ."

"Thunderation!" Beth bounded into the room, clutching a large straw hat trimmed with flowers and tiny silk birds. "I *hate* this hat. It looks like I cotch'd a whole nest of critters! Danged if it don't!"

The dark, troubled look on Jace's face vanished. He grinned and knelt to Beth. He took the hat and perched it on top of her head. "I think it's mighty pretty. Just what a maid of honor should wear. Of course, if it was up to me, Princess, I'd tell you to wear the bowler. But we don't want to scandalize Dark Creek, do we?"

She snorted. "Don't be daft, Jace. I'd look like a dad-blamed fool. So don't go funning me!"

He opened his eyes wide with innocence. "I? Funning you? I wouldn't think of it, Princess."

She giggled, then threw her arms exuberantly around his neck. "I'm so glad you're going to be my brother!"

"Well, somebody has to," grumbled Weedy from the doorway. "Now that I won't be around."

Big Jim exhaled an angry puff of air. "Are you going to kick up a fuss again? And on your sister's wedding day? You're leaving for Harvard in a week, and I don't want to hear another word about it!"

Seeing the look of dismay on her brother's face, Callie tried to be cheerful. "The Thompsons will help you get settled. They were always nice to us in Boston. Remember how Mrs. Thompson baked your favorite pie after Mummy died?"

Weedy scowled at her. "That old biddy is worse than a nursemaid. I don't need school. It'll be worse than a prison. Meantime, Jace'll be running the store. And the sign will read 'Southgate and Perkins.' Who needs that?"

Jace put his arm around Weedy's shoulder. "There won't be a sign that says 'Perkins.' Not ever. I promise you that. I want you to get a real fine education back East. Times are changing. A man can't make it with just brains anymore. And one of these days, I'll need a real smart partner. When . . ."

Callie raised a warning hand. He mustn't tell them about Big Jim!

Jace smiled easily. "When Big Jim decides he's had enough of pots and pans," he finished.

Weedy was beginning to brighten. "You'd make me your partner?"

"Hell, I'd let you run the whole store. In the meantime, we'll see you at Christmas. They say the deer make fine hunting in the snow. Look around in Boston. See if you can find us some first-rate rifles."

Weedy beamed. "I'll surely do that."

Callie felt the familiar pang of envy. Then unease. Jace was so smooth, so comfortable with people. Conquering them with a word, a smile. All the while getting them to do exactly what he wanted. Big Jim had merely cowed them all, ruled with the force of his personality. She wondered whether Jace would undo her with his charm, rather than with his strength.

No, by heaven! she thought. Not if she kept her wits about her. If she remembered her mother. She'd fight his domination. Resist his charm. And keep her independence—even if their marriage became a battleground.

And she'd have an ally, she thought suddenly. Sissy had come toddling into the parlor, followed by Mrs. Ackland. Now she stood, pudgy legs firmly planted on the carpet, and pouted at Jace.

He smiled and turned to the little girl. "Here's my new little sister," he said in a jovial voice. It was the same voice he used on the others, but it never seemed to work with Sissy. "Well, little one. Did you like the toy I brought you from Chicago?"

"No!" She scowled and kicked his shin, then held up a grimy fist wrapped in a length of bandage. "It cutted me."

Jace looked dismayed, rubbed his shin, and appealed to the housekeeper. "Can't you do anything with her temper, Mrs. A.?"

"Now, now, boy," said Big Jim. "She's just a baby. Callie had a temper like hers at that age. She'll grow out of it."

Mrs. Ackland smiled serenely. "She knows who she likes, and who she don't like. Charm ain't everythin'." She chuckled. "You may be able to soft-sawder the rest of us—and I'm not sayin' I ain't susceptible—but you'll have to do better with Sissy here."

Callie wanted to whoop for joy at the look of chagrin on Jace's face. She herself might not resort to kicking his shin, but she'd make him stand up and take notice of her, not squash her into the dust. Devil take her if she wouldn't!

"If you'll both just sign here." The Reverend Maples rested the paper on the small table outside the church tent and handed a pen to Callie.

She dipped it in the ink, took a deep breath, and signed her name. It was too late to back out now.

"Mr. Perkins?"

Jace took the pen from Callie. "Horace Perkins," he wrote, then frowned. Dipping the pen again, he drew a long, black line through his name. "I forgot," he said sheepishly. "Horace *Jason* Perkins," he corrected himself, and wrote it under the first name.

Callie wrinkled her brow in thought. "I never noticed before.

Your handwriting is so different from your letters. They were all tight and spidery.''

He gave an easy laugh. ''I reckon I was always writing them on trains or stagecoaches. It's a marvel you could read them at all.''

The Reverend Maples pulled aside the tent flap. Soft music came from within, mingled with the murmurs of the assembled guests—the doctor, Sheriff Hepworth, and most of the important people of Dark Creek. Not Ralph Driscoll, though Callie had wanted him; Jace had been very insistent on his exclusion. Callie was surprised to see fashionable hats on several wives of the mill managers; except for the crude tent, they could almost have been in Boston.

The reverend gave a signal to the organist. At once, the muted strains of the melodeon became more lively, playing a stirring hymn. The reverend smiled at the Southgate family, gathered around the table. ''Shall we begin?''

Clutching her cane like a beleaguered soldier with his only weapon, Callie gulped and slipped her other hand through Big Jim's arm. Her small bouquet was pinned firmly to her bodice, and her loose hair was covered with a lace veil that stirred in the afternoon breeze.

How had this day arrived? she wondered, anguished. She'd meant to be stronger than this. She felt as though she were betraying her ladies' circle, her women's rights friends.

The Reverend Maples nodded at Weedy. ''You'll follow me down, young man. And then the groom.''

Beth jumped up and down and held out her own bouquet of meadow flowers. ''And then I'm next!''

Jace straightened her hat and tapped her on the tip of her nose. ''In the prettiest goldurned bonnet I've ever seen. Even if you do hate it.''

Beth wriggled in delight. ''I don't hate it anymore.''

The reverend turned to Poppy. ''Wait for the bride's march, Big Jim.'' He gestured toward the tent flap. ''Weedy?''

''Just a minute.'' Jace moved to Callie and gave her a long, searching appraisal, his eyes crinkling in pleasure. "Your mama couldn't have looked any more beautiful in that dress." His glance took in her cane. "But I thought we had an agreement."

"I can't . . ." she began.

He shook his head. "You can, and you will." While she bleated in protest, he pulled the cane from her hand and tucked it under his arm. Then he unpinned her bouquet and put it in her free hand. "Now you look just right."

He turned to Beth. "Princess, I'll carry the cane down the aisle, then give it to you when you get to the altar. You can hold it for Callie until she needs it."

Callie clung more tightly to Big Jim's arm, feeling as though she would teeter and fall at any minute. She made one last attempt to have her way. "You can't do this, Jace. I won't be ordered around!"

He grinned, tipped up her chin, and planted a soft kiss on her lips. "I'll be waiting for you, darlin'."

She hated him. She watched him follow the reverend and Weedy into the tent, swaggering like a cock of the walk. "Poppy, I can't," she whispered.

Big Jim squeezed her arm in reassurance. "I've got you, sweetie. You won't fall."

The melodeon began to pipe out the bride's march. Callie took a hesitant step forward, then squared her shoulders and forced her mouth into a smile. She might fall flat on her face halfway down the aisle, but she wasn't going to make a fool of herself by looking like a coward.

It was Jace who sustained her. Standing tall and handsome at the altar, splendid in his best suit, he smiled with such confidence and radiant pride that she found herself almost floating down the aisle on Big Jim's arm. She forgot her shyness, ignoring the whispers of the townsfolk as she passed. All she saw was his smile.

When her father handed her over to Jace at the end of their walk, he slipped his arm around her waist and held her close.

"I'm so proud of you I could kiss you right now," he whispered. His eyes were a dazzling blue that took her breath away.

She didn't notice the service after that. She was only aware of his strong arm, the masculine scent of his cologne, the deep timbre of his voice as he made his responses. His solid support—her rock and salvation.

Is this what marriage is? she thought in wonder. Someone you could cling to, so you didn't have to stand alone? Perhaps it mightn't be so bad after all. He was strong and kind and . . . She trembled at the sudden memory of his impassioned kiss. Marriage to him might be *very* pleasant.

Her glow of contentment held until the service was concluded and Jace had kissed her gently. She turned to Beth. "Give me my cane now."

Jace tightened his arm around her. "No. You'll walk back with me."

The romantic bubble burst. She glared at him. "I will not!"

His eyes hardened. "You made it down the aisle. You'll make it back. Without a fuss."

"Is this to be our first married quarrel?" she sputtered.

"If you want it that way, darlin'."

"I refuse to move," she said, digging her heels into the soft ground. "You can't very well walk with a deadweight."

He chuckled. "Like hell I can't." He slipped his arm under her knees and scooped her up, cradling her against his hard chest.

"Mercy sakes!" she gasped, burning with embarrassment. "Put me down! You can't do this."

He laughed again. "Honey, it's my wedding day, and I don't plan to have another. I can do anything I damn well please."

"In the name of pity, Jace," she said, cringing at the smirks on the faces of the spectators. "Let me go. What will people say?"

"What do you care? But if they say anything, they'll probably say that I can't wait to get my wife home." He stared at her mouth with eyes suddenly grown hot and intense. "Sweet as sugar,'' he said hoarsely. "Maybe I can persuade Mrs. Ackland to serve the food in a hurry, so's they'll all go home pronto.''

She shivered at the possessive look in his eyes, feeling the panic rise in her throat. He'd already taken over the wedding, willy-nilly. Run roughshod over her feelings. God knew what awaited her in the bedroom, when he'd be free to put his seal on her once and for all.

He started up the aisle with her, nodding cheerfully to the guests along the way. It was small comfort to Callie that they were greeted with happy nods and smiles of approval.

She was trapped like her mother—in a marriage she'd never wanted.

Chapter Fifteen

"Don't you worry, Mousekin," said Big Jim, giving Callie a smothering hug that nearly swept her off her feet. "There'll be no shivaree tonight. Hepworth and I will break a few heads if anyone is planning to disturb my little girl."

Big Jim released her with a kiss, waved to the last departing guests, and hoisted himself up on his horse beside the deputy sheriff. "Come on, Hepworth. Let's head for town. I've had enough fancy French champagne. I'm ready for some whiskey."

Callie bit her lip. Big Jim was so careless of his health, despite the doctor's warnings. "Don't stay up all night," she pleaded. "Get a room in the hotel."

He laughed and winked at Jace, standing on the veranda beside Callie. "I reckon I'll get more sleep than some folks, tonight!"

Callie was glad the torches in the yard had burnt low; she knew her face must be bright red. "Poppy, please," she whispered.

Jace draped a proprietary arm over her shoulder and gave a

smug chuckle. "I may be a little late to the store tomorrow, Big Jim."

She ground her teeth together in sudden fury. That was really the last straw! He was already beginning to act as though she were his possession, with his sly words and his open embraces.

He'd had a perfectly lovely time at the wedding party, the scoundrel, ignoring her own less than joyous mood. He'd gobbled down Mrs. Ackland's cooking as though he thought it would vanish, danced with every twittering matron who batted her eyes at him. Why shouldn't he be self-satisfied? Well fed, doted on by every blamed fool he could charm. And he was a *partner* now, a bigwig coming up in the business world—after a shamefully brief period of time.

And tonight she was to be his final triumph, the feather in his cap. Her stomach gave a sickening lurch—part anger, part resentment. If she had the courage, she'd lock him out of her bedroom. But Big Jim expected a grandchild. And Jace expected a wife. She sighed. And Callie had no backbone.

Big Jim and Hepworth wheeled their horses around and headed for Dark Creek. Callie waved a final good-bye, wishing she could call her father back, delay the inevitable.

Jace indicated the rows of trestle tables set up in the front yard. "Weedy and I can put those away in the morning."

She surveyed the stained tablecloths. "Mrs. Ackland and I will be doing wash for a week," she said sourly.

"But it was a damn fine party. Big Jim knows how to treat his guests."

"Hmph! The 'cream' of Dark Creek." She'd never seen such coarse manners, such abandoned dancing, in all her life.

"I keep telling you, Cal, there are some fine people here, if you'd let yourself look for them."

"Why should I bother?"

He took her roughly by the shoulders and frowned down at her. "I don't think you're a snob, but you sure as hell sound like one sometimes."

"Of course I'm not!" she sputtered. "I'm simply accustomed to a finer class of people."

"Or maybe you just keep them at arm's length because you're scared."

She shook off his hands. "Don't be absurd. Did you see them? Do you think people dance like . . . like *elephants* in Boston?"

"Son of a gun. I think the dancing riles you up only because you're jealous."

She flinched. That came too close to the truth. "I'm sure I don't know what you're talking about," she said in a haughty voice.

He laughed and patted her familiarly on the rump. "Never mind, honey. I got you to walk down the aisle. I'll get you to dance, one of these days."

"You'll do no such thing! I . . ."

"Mrs. Perkins?" The housekeeper stood in the doorway with a sleeping Sissy in her arms. Beth drooped beside her, her eyes half-closed.

Callie turned. *Mrs. Perkins.* It grated on her ears. "Are you going now?"

Mrs. Ackland nodded. "I put the food away in the pantry. I'll get to the rest of the dishes in the mornin'. And I folded your lace veil in tissue paper and put it in the linen chest."

"Thank you. You're sure it's no bother to take the girls?"

"My land! It wouldn't be fittin' for them to stay here tonight. And my man's off prospectin', so the cabin's empty. We'll be as snug as fleas on a sheepdog."

Jace knelt before Beth. "See you in the morning, Princess." As she smiled sleepily, he kissed her on the forehead and stood up. "Mrs. A., did Weedy hitch up the wagon for you before he lit out for town?"

"Sure enough." She clicked her tongue. "Him and those bummer friends of his. I wish you was with him tonight. You're the only one I know keeps him from raisin' Cain."

He gave a sly laugh. "Well, *I* sure am glad I'm not with him. Not tonight!"

She looked scandalized. "Get along with you, Mr. Perkins. You're a devil! I knew it the minute I laid eyes on you."

He grinned. "Devil or not, you feed me well, Mrs. A. Now get along with *you*, before Beth falls asleep on her feet."

He watched them go off into the dark toward the stable, then turned to Callie. "Well, darlin', it's just you and me now."

She couldn't look him in the eye. "I . . . I don't really know what we should do next," she said, nervously touching the shiny new ring on her finger.

He chuckled. "I have a pretty fair idea. Grab tight to your cane, Mrs. Perkins." He reached out and lifted her in his arms.

She held her body rigid in his embrace, conscious of their isolation, the overwhelming masculinity of the man. "Sh-shouldn't we douse the torches?"

"They'll burn out." He moved through the doorway and into the vestibule. "It would be right friendly of you if you put your arm around my neck," he said.

She slid her hand up his shoulder to curl around his neck. The hairs on his nape were silky-soft, but the muscles were as hard as steel. "Are you sure I'm not straining your ribs?" she ventured, as he started up the stairs.

"I heal fast. The doctor took the bandages off weeks ago." He ducked through the doorway of her room and set her on her feet.

Mrs. Ackland had left a single kerosene lamp burning by the bed and had turned down the sheets. Callie felt her mouth go dry. "We'll move your clothes down here tomorrow," she said quickly, to cover her chaotic emotions. "I'll have to make a space in my bureau, but I'm sure that . . ."

His eyes were on her lips. "Yes, of course," he said absently. He reached out and stroked her shoulders above the edge of the wide lace bertha that trimmed the bodice of her gown.

She shivered at his sensual touch, the intimate warmth of his fingers on her flesh. She found herself babbling. "We might have to put another bureau in the room, of course, if this one . . .''

''I'm sure you'll know what to do,'' he said, and kissed her on the neck, his hot mouth gliding to the hollow of her throat.

She trembled and rocked on her feet, leaning heavily on her cane to steady herself. ''P-Poppy has a handsome chest that will fit nicely . . .''

This time, his kiss found her lips, silencing her mouth in mid-sentence. He wrapped his arms around her waist and pulled her close; his body was hard and solid against hers.

Oh, mercy, she thought, losing herself in the wonders of his kiss. His mouth was firm yet gentle as it moved over hers, urging her to respond; when she pursed her lips to enjoy his more fully, he deepened his kiss, sucking at her mouth with ever-increasing fervor.

She gasped and jerked her head away from his. Something alarming was happening to her body—a tension, a wild throbbing that seemed to be centered in her most private regions.

He smiled in understanding, deepening the seductive dimple in his cheek. The sharp angles of his face were softened by the dim light, and his eyes glowed like blue fire. ''Don't be frightened, darlin','' he murmured. ''Pretty little Callie.''

He kissed her again, his hands caressing the back of her gown and the trembling, eager flesh of her shoulders. She sighed and melted against him, wrapping one arm around his neck to draw herself closer to his sustaining warmth. She felt as though she were drowning, lost and enveloped in his sweet embrace, his passionate kiss.

Then she felt his fingers at her shoulder blades, working on the brass-wire hooks of her gown. ''No!'' she cried, pushing frantically at his chest. ''I can do it myself. I *want* to do it myself.''

He chuckled and released her, shaking his head in wonder. ''You sly Mousekin. Who would have thought there was a Siren lurking beneath your prim laces?'' He stepped back, grinning, and crossed his arms against his chest. "Well, then, show me what I've married."

She felt the blood drain from her face. "Surely you don't expect me to . . . ." She could scarcely say the words. "To . . . to disrobe in front of you."

He looked bewildered. "I thought that's what you meant."

She opened her eyes wide in shock. Were there actually women who did such shameless things? "I never could," she whispered. "Can't you grant me a bit of privacy?"

He studied her for a moment, then gave a heavy sigh. "Would you prefer me to change in my own room, as well?"

"Yes, please," she choked.

It usually took her a long time to undress, leaning up against the bed or a chair to keep her balance. But tonight she had fear to spur her on. God forbid he should come back while she was naked. She didn't even bother to fold her clothing, but left it piled in a heap on a settee. She buttoned her prim nightdress to her throat, limped to the bed and crawled in, pulling the sheet and quilt up to her neck.

He took a long time returning. She burrowed in the bed, wishing she could sink through the mattress. What if she hated it—the thing he intended to do? Her mother had spoken frankly of a man's needs and practices without making it seem like a woman's burden; but Callie's women friends had told whispered tales of wives who submitted unhappily, and only out of duty.

Oh, God, she thought suddenly, as another more terrifying thought struck her. What if she *liked* it? He would put himself inside her with his rigid manhood—she knew that much. The very thought of it made her shiver. But was it a shiver of fear? Or anticipation? His kisses had made her weak. If she discovered that she liked being made love to, she'd spend her days following him around like a docile puppy dog, surrendering her independence without a struggle.

"That was mighty fine champagne tonight. I thought we could have a bit more." Jace stood in the doorway, holding out two filled glasses. His nightshirt, reaching only to his knees, revealed firm-muscled calves, as thickly covered with dark hairs as the patch of chest exposed by his open neckline. The linen was so thin that Callie could almost see the outline of his strong body. The fabric clung to him; she knew what lay beneath the large bulge at his groin.

She squeezed shut her eyes in horror. "I don't want any champagne," she said. "It makes me dizzy. And could you please put out the lamp?"

She heard the sound of the glasses being set on the night table beside her—a sharp click, as though he'd banged them down in a fit of annoyance. She heard the impatient puff of his breath as he leaned over the glass chimney and blew out the flame.

She opened her eyes to the safety of darkness. The watery half-moon shone through the windows, giving the room a faint, silvery glow. She saw the shape of Jace's white nightshirt as he moved around to the other side of the bed. She was even more grateful for the darkness when she saw him lift his arms and pull the nightshirt over his head. His body was just a dark, hazy form, with blacker patches at his chest and loins.

He climbed in beside her and gently tugged the bedding from her fists. "Cal, honey, don't be afraid," he murmured. He bent and kissed her, his tongue stroking her lips until she reluctantly opened her mouth to his.

This time, there was no pleasure in his kiss. The thrusting movement of his tongue was too vivid a reminder of what was to follow. She pushed at him, breaking the contact of his mouth. "Don't kiss me like that," she said, gasping. "It takes my breath away."

He laughed. "It's supposed to."

"No. I mean, I don't like it. Could we just . . . get on with it?" The sooner this night was over, the more relieved she'd be.

"Son of a gun," he muttered. His voice held an edge. He

reached out to the buttons of her nightdress, working at them with impatient fingers.

She clutched the garment to her breast. "Please. I'd rather you didn't. Do you mind?"

"As a matter of fact, I do," he growled. He sighed heavily. "You're not making this very easy, Cal." His voice softened. "But I reckon a virgin is a different creature. I'll try to be as gentle as I can." He pulled at her nightdress, sliding it up to her waist.

She stiffened and gritted her teeth. It was all so unpleasant and awkward. And when he spread her legs and knelt between them, she held her breath. His hands went around her buttocks to cradle and lift her hips. She felt his male member prodding, probing, searching for entrance. She flinched at the hot, insistent feel of him.

"God, how I've wanted you," he said, and plunged into her with a sudden, violent push.

She gasped in surprise and arched her back. There had been none of the pain that her mother had warned her of, but the fullness of his manhood within her was so alien, so intrusive, that she wondered how women had always tolerated it. And when he began to move—hard, jerking thrusts that jolted her against the bed—she fought the urge to ask him to stop.

He began to pant, soft grunts coming from his throat. The thrusts became more and more rapid, ending abruptly in his muffled cry and a flooding warmth. He gave a groan that sounded like disappointment, then rolled away. "Damn," he muttered, sitting up to put his head in his hand.

She lay quietly for a moment, feeling the tension leave her body. It was over, thank God. She was aware of the hot moisture between her legs, the foreign seed that seemed to defile her flesh. She smoothed down her nightdress and sat up in her turn. "I want to wash," she said in a choked voice. "I'll go to Beth's room."

She reached for her cane that leaned against the night table, stood up, and limped from the room. She lit a lamp in Beth's

room and poured out a bit of water into the washbasin. The
water was cold and uncomfortable, but at least she felt clean
again.

She gazed at herself in Beth's mirror, half-expecting her face
to reflect the monumental change in her life. To her surprise,
she looked the same. Maybe it was because she had felt almost
nothing. A slight discomfort, a sense of embarrassment, to be
sure—but nothing more.

Still, the experience wasn't so unpleasant that she couldn't
endure it whenever he made demands on her body. And perhaps
it was for the best. She might have to call him "husband," but
at least she wouldn't lose her independence to the nonexistent
joys of the bedroom.

Jace stared at a patch of moonlight on the floor and scowled.
What did the woman want? He'd tried to be gentle and quiet
her fears, tried to court her, flatter her, use all the charm at his
command to let her know she was desirable.

He reached out to the night table and grabbed a glass of
champagne, tossing it down in one gulp. Hell, he'd even tried
to relax her with liquor, break down her shy reserve as he'd
done that night behind the store. And all he'd gotten for his
pains was chilly indifference. And a nagging feeling of dissatis-
faction.

Damn it, he hadn't treated her like a bit of fluff in a
whorehouse, had he? It was his usual way: a few kisses to get
the juices flowing, a boisterous romp with a tickle or a playful
whack or two—and then he was free to seek his own sexual
release. It had always been enough to leave him feeling drained
and comfortably sated.

No. He hadn't behaved that way. He'd treated her like a
lady. And she'd responded like a martyr on the Cross, suffering
him with fortitude. He swore softly and downed the other glass
of champagne. He'd come too fast, that was for damn sure.
Shot the bishop before he'd hardly begun. But he'd hungered

for her for weeks, while his loins ached and his guts twisted with frustrated desire. He hadn't had a woman for months, except for that whore on the Fourth of July, and she'd been a coarse slut.

He thought of Callie lying passive beneath him, and felt his anger growing. Damn her! He'd felt so good all day, so filled with joy and optimism—the sight of her walking toward him without her cane, the beaming approval of Big Jim, the gaiety and the laughter. He'd wanted to share it all with her—his warm contentment, his unforeseen pleasure at their marriage.

Instead, ''Miss Don't'' had come into the bedroom with him. *Don't* kiss her with passion, *don't* touch her body, *don't* look at her in the light. It was a wonder he could get his cock up at all, with that lack of encouragement!

He'd gone wandering all over Chicago—taking the risk of being recognized—just to find the right gift for her. Had she even noticed that he'd chosen a gown to match her hair? And she'd treated him like dirt tonight, as though he were some kind of disgusting lothario, out to steal her precious virginity. He gnashed his teeth. He had half a mind to take her over his knee and give her a good spanking, just to show her who was boss!

Son of a bitch, he thought, shaking his head. He sighed. He'd never felt so helpless with a woman in all his life.

He frowned. The patch of moonlight had moved halfway across the floor. Where the hell was she? Weeping in Beth's room? Or writing another letter to one of her silly, emancipated friends in Boston, complaining of how she'd been violated by a man?

He rolled off the bed and got to his feet, grabbing for his discarded nightshirt. Slipping it over his head, he stomped down the hall to Beth's room. To his surprise, it was dark. He glanced at the bed, half-expecting to see Callie asleep there, making her discontent crystal clear. The bed was empty.

Concerned now, he started back to her bedroom, meaning

to light the lamp and search for her. As he passed the head of the staircase, he saw a faint glow of light from the floor below.

The glow came from a small fire burning in the parlor grate. In one corner of the large sofa, Callie lay curled up asleep. Her knees were drawn up to her chest, her graceful arms wrapped around them. Her head tilted to one shoulder, a posture that was both provocative and demure. Her hair was tousled, tumbling onto the bosom of her nightdress—a mass of riotous curls that shimmered copper in the firelight. She was exquisite.

His anger evaporated. He felt the same jolt of desire he'd felt the first time Perkins had shown him her picture. He sat down carefully at the edge of the sofa and stroked her cheek. "Cal, honey?"

She stirred and opened her eyes. "Oh. Jace. I must have fallen asleep. I just came down to sit for a little while. I shouldn't have lit the fire. Staring at it made me so sleepy."

"Well, it's been a long day."

She shivered and rubbed her shoulders. "It's cold. I should have covered myself with the throw."

He settled back on the sofa and pulled her into his arms, holding her close to warm her. "Let me be your blanket."

She sighed and snuggled against him, tucking her legs up under her. "That feels nice and warm. They say the winters here are a caution."

He glanced down at her. She looked like a sweet kitten, nestled in his arms. He frowned at the look on her face. No. A *lost* kitten, far from the security of her old home and friends. Poor lonely Mousekin. Tonight couldn't have been easy for her. He felt a surge of protectiveness. "You have a husband, now, darlin'," he said, wondering why his voice had suddenly gone hoarse. "And I'll take care of you, and keep you warm."

She stared up at him, then looked away. "I just hope I wasn't . . . a disappointment to you tonight."

He felt a pang of guilt. While he'd been busy blaming her, she'd been blaming herself, as if the burden were all hers. Maybe he hadn't been as accommodating as he should have been. "It sometimes takes getting used to. Did I hurt you?" He hadn't thought of *that* before, either.

She shook her head. "I thought it would, but it didn't." She gave him a shy smile. "Thank you."

Jesus, he thought. He'd been so horny, he hadn't stopped to wonder about her. Now here she was, gazing at him with trusting eyes, and *thanking* him, for God's sake! "You're the sweetest woman I've ever known," he said humbly. "I'm right proud to be your husband."

She chewed at her lip. "Don't," she said. "You'll make me blush."

He stared at her mouth. Her teeth were white and even, pressing a ridge into her full lower lip. He felt his heartbeat quicken. He wanted her lips—right this minute. But he'd been clumsy before, demanding too much, perhaps. And now he was afraid even to kiss her, hesitating as though he were as green and helpless as that fool Horace would have been.

Horace. Why not? He smiled timidly, fluttered his eyes, and pitched his voice higher. "Oh, my stars, Miss Callie. Do you suppose you'd allow me a kiss?"

She giggled, relaxing in his arms. "Mrs. Ackland was right. You really are a devil."

"I thought it would please you. I wanted you to like me." He was suddenly hot with desire, his blood coursing through him with enough force to cause a stirring in his groin. "And let me kiss you," he added, fighting to keep his voice calm.

"I . . . I suppose so." She drew her brows together in an adorable frown. "Oh, dear. That sounds so cold. Of course you may."

He grinned and lifted her onto his lap, bending her across his arm. He kissed her as gently as his raging hunger would allow. He took her lips, then let his mouth explore her face, tasting the fragrant softness of her cheeks, kissing the feathery lashes of her closed eyes. He buried his head in her neck and inhaled the intoxicating scent of her perfume, then found her earlobe and teased it with the tip of his tongue.

She sighed in pleasure and slid her hand up his arm, kneading his shoulder through his nightshirt. Then he felt the glide of her cool fingers on the nape of his neck—delicate strokes that gave him chills. His cock went rigid.

He felt a thrill of confidence. Perhaps it had just been the newness, that first time, that had made her so skittish. He put a tentative hand on her breast. He was pleased to see that—though she opened her eyes in alarm for a moment—she allowed his hand to stay. Her breast was full and round and eager; even through her nightdress he could feel the nipple hardening at his caresses. It drove him wild.

He kissed her again, with more passion. And when he pushed gently at her closed lips, she opened for his searching tongue. He reveled in the exquisite taste of her mouth.

Son of a gun. She'd never be more ready. More ripe for the taking. He hesitated, then glided his hand down her belly to clutch at her furry softness.

She stiffened at his intimate touch and pushed his hand away, then twisted off his lap and sat up. "Mercy sakes. Again?"

The resentful edge to her voice revived his anger. The little tease didn't mind taking *her* pleasure with him, welcoming his kisses with contented sighs. But she balked when it came to *his* needs! "Yes, again," he growled. A man had a right to his wedding night, damn it!

He stood up and pulled off his nightshirt. He was hard and erect—and as well favored by nature as any man. Maybe more so. Perhaps the sight of him would excite her; he'd been complimented often enough by the whores he'd bedded.

She gasped and turned her head aside. "Wh-what if I don't want to?" she stammered.

Hell's bells! He'd have to try another tack. He knelt in front of the sofa, putting his hands on either side of her knees. "Cal, honey, I'm just aching for you. My sweet wife."

"But twice in one night?"

He gave her his most charming smile. "Blame it on yourself, darlin'. You're a man's dream come true."

She jutted her chin at him. "A pretty little speech. But I don't see why I should give in."

Damn it, he *would* spank her in another moment! He tried once more to be reasonable. "It's my right, as your husband." He managed a stiff smile. "It was part of your vow today. Remember? To honor and obey."

He could see the spark of rebellion die in her eyes. She sighed. "Very well," she said in a resigned voice. She stretched out on the sofa, arranging herself in a comfortable position, and raised her nightdress to her waist. Like a sacrificial lamb.

Damn her! If it weren't for his throbbing prick, he'd go back upstairs and just sleep. Well, if he couldn't please her, he'd damn well find his own satisfaction tonight—at least one time. What had happened in the bedroom hadn't exactly felt like pleasure.

And maybe, just maybe, he could arouse her in spite of her stubborn resistance. Even in this dim light, he would see it on her face—the moment when her inflamed senses overwhelmed her indifference. But as he took his position between her legs, she threw up her arm and covered her face.

That final act of defiance was more than he could tolerate. He slammed into her with all the power of his frustrated passion. She was dry and tight; it excited him even more to be enclosed so firmly.

But he hadn't counted on his endurance. He'd already spilled his seed once tonight; it was more difficult the second time. He found himself pumping in and out of her like a madman, while the sweat poured down his back and his cock grew sore. *Come on, Jace,* he thought, screwing up his face into a grimace, *you can do it.*

Just as he was ready to quit in frustration, he exploded in a drenching rush. A release that felt more like defeat than satisfaction. He leaned back on his heels and stared at her. She had never made a sound. Never moved a muscle. Just lain there stiff and passive, an unwilling vessel for his lust.

He remembered all the whores who had moaned and cried

out in delight, praising his skill. His masculine prowess. He passed a hand across his mouth. He was almost afraid to speak to her. "You didn't enjoy that, did you?" he asked at last.

She lowered her arm. Her eyes were dark and unreadable by the firelight. "Was I supposed to?"

Son of a bitch! He didn't even know if she was being sarcastic, or just innocent. "Some women do," he muttered, standing up to put on his nightshirt.

She pushed down her nightdress. "It took a long time," she said hesitantly. "Longer than before. And it made me sore." She reached for her cane and stood up, putting one hand on her lame hip. "And I can't hold the same position forever, without my hip hurting."

He felt like the lowest dog that had ever walked the earth. A randy bastard who had used her for his own selfish needs. She had tried to refuse, to rebel for a brief moment, and he'd run roughshod over her wishes. "Perhaps the next time . . ." he began, knowing how inept his words sounded.

She hobbled to the door, then stopped and gave him a bright, hopeful smile. "Well, if we made a baby tonight, Poppy will be happy."

He flinched and turned away from her. She couldn't have destroyed him more if she'd taken a knife and lopped off his balls.

Chapter Sixteen

"I'll be hornswoggled! Ain't Jace the most amazin' handsome man you've ever seen?" Seated beside Callie in the wagon, Beth pointed to the front yard where Jace stood, ax in hand, splitting logs into firewood.

Callie stared at him and gulped, her rebuke of Beth's language dying on her lips. He was stripped to the waist, his galluses hanging loose, his hairy chest covered with sweat. His flesh was firm and golden in the afternoon sun.

She hadn't seen his naked torso since their wedding night, and the sight of his powerful body, muscles bulging, gave her a jolt. It was the same sensation she always felt when he kissed her—a trembling thrill that surged through her and flooded her with warmth.

She sighed. Now, of course, he seldom kissed her, except as a prelude to the sex act. And then his kisses were always cursory, impatient, as though he were simply trying to work himself into the proper mood. He always readied for bed in the spare room, and waited until she had settled under the quilt before he returned. He would extinguish the lamp and get in beside her. And then, in the dark, she would feel a hand on her shoulder, his fingers on her chin, turning her head for a kiss. His silent signal that he wanted her.

It was always over quickly. Neither pleasant nor unpleasant, except for her awareness of the weight of his body on hers. She didn't mind. It was her duty as a wife to give him her willing body; if it brought him satisfaction, she felt a certain pleasure, knowing she'd fulfilled her obligation.

She chewed at her lip with uncertainty. But *did* it bring him satisfaction? More and more it seemed that he performed the act with an angry haste. And afterward he would roll off of her, pull down his nightshirt with an edgy impatience, and drift off to sleep without a word. If she worked up the courage to ask him if he was contented, she imagined she heard a note of disappointment in his voice. Moreover, in the three weeks since they'd been married, his silent requests had become less frequent, as though she was no longer worth the effort he had to expend for his release.

She sighed again. It was all so bewildering. She gave him what he wanted, didn't she? Then why did she feel like a failure?

She brought the wagon to a halt beside the front door and handed Beth her Bible. "Go and change out of your good clothes, and put away my Bible. If I know you, you'll want to help Jace with the chopping. And I don't want you to soil your Sunday best."

Beth pouted. "Oh, botheration. When I'm just bustin' to tell Jace about that all-fired cracked galoot in the front row? The one who nearly gave Reverend Maples a conniption fit?"

Callie gave her a warning scowl. "Get along with you. If I had any sense, I'd make you spend the afternoon with your grammar books. Heaven knows you've forgotten what a proper young lady should sound like!"

Beth grumbled, but she hopped down from the wagon and scurried toward the door. "Be sure to tell Jace not to finish until I get there!" she called.

At the sound of his name, Jace looked up from his work and hurried toward the wagon, smiling warmly. Callie returned his smile. It was strange, but somehow what happened in their bedroom scarcely seemed a part of their lives. There was an unspoken undercurrent between them, of course. Something she couldn't quite understand. But she found it easy to be civil to him, enjoying his company.

For his part, Jace had been nothing but helpful and kind these past few weeks, settling comfortably into the bosom of the family. He'd taken over Weedy's chores when her brother had left for school—tending the horses, seeing that the house had enough firewood, helping Mrs. Ackland haul water from the well.

And of course he was busy in the store with her father. They were making money hand over fist, Big Jim had boasted to her. Callie sometimes wondered if it was Jace's enthusiasm— or his self-confessed desire for riches—that urged him on. She would often retire late to bed, leaving him and Big Jim sitting up long into the night and excitedly talking of expanding the store, or opening another.

Jace reached up and helped her down from the wagon. Her senses were overwhelmed by his masculine presence—his musky scent, the strength of the arms that held her, the firm-jawed smile that played around his lips and gave her shivers. She suddenly ached to feel those lips on hers. She lingered in his embrace for as long as she could, deliberately fumbling for her cane to prolong the moment. Why didn't he want to kiss her? She felt so green and inexperienced. Was the sex act meant to take the place of kisses in marriage? An unequal exchange, to her way of thinking.

Jace released her and stretched his arms over his head. "Son of a gun, it feels good to exercise again. I thought my damn ribs would never heal."

She frowned. Swearing seemed to be second nature to him. She wondered how he had managed to suppress his foul language when he'd first come to them. Merely to impress her, she thought sourly. Then she chided herself for her uncharitable thoughts—and on the Lord's day! Her father had always sworn, and it had never disturbed her. Perhaps her discontent with Jace had more to do with what she dimly perceived as the uneasy state of their marriage.

She glanced over at the neatly stacked pile of logs. "You've chopped a great deal of wood this morning. Do we need so much?"

He waved his hand toward the hills. The quivering aspens were beginning to turn—lemon yellow and pinkish orange. "It's September already," he said. "It won't be long before the winter sets in. We'll need all the wood we can gather now, for when the snows come."

She took off her gloves and tucked them in her pocket. "You should have come to church. The sermon was very enlightening."

He smirked. "Temperance?"

She snorted in disgust. "In Dark Creek? I swan, there were more men falling in and out of the saloons and gambling halls than bothered to come to church. We'll never find enough pious souls to pay for a proper building. But that's no excuse for you not to come."

"God has never been a big part of my life," he growled. "I can't see the need to worship in His house."

She stared in dismay. He'd never spoken so frankly of religion before. And in his early weeks at Dark Creek, he'd dutifully attended church with them, even singing along with the hymns. "But if you don't embrace God, how can you see the good in His creatures? Your fellow man?"

He gave a dark, cynical laugh. "I seldom have."

The sudden anguish in his eyes touched her heart. "Jace," she said softly, putting a hand on his arm. "What can have made you so bitter?"

He frowned, searching her face as though he debated with himself. Then he waved away her question with an impatient

4 BESTSELLING HISTORICAL ROMANCES BY YOUR FAVORITE AUTHORS CAN BE YOURS, FREE!

Kensington Choice brings you historical romances by your favorite bestselling authors including Janelle Taylor, Shannon Drake, Rosanne Bittner, Jo Beverley, and Georgina Gentry, just to name a few! Each book is filled with passion, adventure and the excitement of bygone times!

To introduce you to this great club which is part of Zebra Home Subscription Service, we'd like to send you your first 4 bestselling historical romances, absolutely free! And once you get these 4 free books to savor at home, we'll rush you the next 4 brand-new books at the lowest prices available, as soon as they are published.

The way the club works is that after your initial FREE shipment, you will get our 4 newest bestselling historical romances delivered to you

doorstep each month at the preferred subscriber's rate of only $4.20 per book, a savings of up to $8.16 per month (since these titles sell in bookstores for $4.99-$6.99)! All books are sent on a 10-day free examination basis and there is no minimum number of books to buy. (And no charge for shipping.) Plus as a regular

subscriber, you'll receive our FREE monthly newsletter, *Zebra/Pinnacle Romance News*, which features author profiles, subscriber benefits, book previews and more!

So start today by returning the FREE BOOK CERTIFICATE provided. We'll send you 4 FREE BOOKS with no further obligation: A FREE gift offering you hours of reading pleasure with no obligation...how can you lose?

*We have 4 FREE BOOKS for you
as your introduction to
KENSINGTON CHOICE!
To get your FREE BOOKS, worth
up to $24.96, mail the card below.*

FREE BOOK CERTIFICATE

Yes! Please send me 4 Kensington Choice (the best of Zebra and Pinnacle Books) Historical Romances without cost or obligation (worth up to $24.96). As a Kensington Choice subscriber, I will then receive 4 brand-new romances to preview each month for 10 days FREE. I can return any books I decide not to keep and owe nothing. The publisher's prices for Kensington Choice romances range from $4.99-$6.99, but as a preferred subscriber I will get these books for only $4.20 per book or $16.80 for all four titles. There is no minimum number of books to buy and I may cancel my subscription at any time, plus there is no additional charge for postage and handling. No matter what I decide to do, my first 4 books are mine to keep, absolutely FREE!

Name _____

Address _____ Apt. _____

City _____ State _____ Zip _____

Telephone (_____) _____

Signature _____

(If under 18, parent or guardian must sign)

Subscription subject to acceptance. Terms and prices subject to change.

KF1097

AFFIX
STAMP
HERE

KENSINGTON CHOICE
Zebra Home Subscription Service, Inc.
120 Brighton Road
P.O.Box 5214
Clifton, NJ 07015-5214

flick of his hand. "It scarcely matters anymore." He bent and retrieved his ax.

"But . . ."

He set a log on the block and split it with such savagery that the splinters went flying. She felt as though he'd closed a door on his soul. She watched him in silence, grieving and wondering if she should leave him to his own black thoughts.

Then he looked up and smiled blandly at her. The dark mood had been banished. "I invited Mrs. Watts to supper tonight," he said. "I've already told Mrs. Ackland."

She gaped in surprise. "Mrs. Watts?"

"She's the woman who owns the boardinghouse. The one you waited on in the store that day."

Callie remembered only that Mrs. Watts had been a timid, plain woman in a shabby dress. "Why on earth would you do that?"

"She doesn't have many friends. She's a widow. I thought it would be right neighborly. And Big Jim agreed."

She puffed in annoyance. "What could we possibly have in common with her? Good grief, I've never even seen her in church!"

He threw down the axe and scowled at her. "Dammit, Cal, sometimes you can be the worst snob! She doesn't come to church because seven days a week she's bent over a hot stove in her boardinghouse. Cooking for a bunch of louts so she can keep body and soul together. Do you have any idea what it's like to be without money?"

That touched a chord of guilt. Big Jim had always been successful; the Southgates had never known want. "I'll welcome her, of course," she said stiffly, uncomfortable with his criticism, justified though she knew it was.

A hard muscle worked on the side of his cheek. "You'll do more than that! You'll be downright gracious, just as though she were one of your high-toned Boston friends."

His autocratic tone set off warning bells in her head. "Don't tell me how to behave," she snapped.

"Then don't behave like a prig!"

"Oh!" Did he think she'd tolerate such insults? She clenched her fist tightly, half-tempted to strike him.

His eyes flicked to her quivering hand, then back to her face. "Go ahead, darlin'," he said softly. "I've been wondering for a while now if a few swats on your bustle wouldn't make you a more agreeable wife."

She blanched at the look in his eyes and uncurled her fist. She swallowed her fear, then managed to glare at him, finding an unexpected spark of independence deep within her. "Do you plan to rule me by brute force?"

He looked disgusted. "I don't plan to rule you at all. You're a grown woman, when you act like it." He sighed and turned away, shoulders sagging. "But this sure as hell isn't what I thought marriage would be."

The implied accusation in his words cut deep. And it was so unjust! "What have I done wrong?" she said, her voice beginning to tremble. "I've tried to be cheerful and . . . and agreeable. I'm sorry for sounding like a snob about Mrs. Watts. You were right to chide me. But what more do you expect from me?"

He whirled about and grabbed her by the shoulders. "Dammit, I *expect* . . ." He stopped, the anger draining from his face, then shook his head in resignation. "What the hell does it matter? You wouldn't understand. And maybe I'm just a fool for expecting more."

She stared in bewilderment. "Jace, please . . ." she began, barely above a whisper. Surely there was something she was doing wrong, to make him so angry. Perhaps if he could explain it to her, the uneasy undercurrent would vanish.

"No," he said, and dropped his hands. "Beth's coming."

Beth skipped up to him and grinned. "Did you leave me anything to do?"

He patted her on the top of her ever-present bowler. "Just one more log to split, Princess. And I saved it for you."

Beth giggled and launched into a colorful description of the church worshipers, punctuated by exclamations of delight from Jace. As always, Callie felt excluded from their cheery banter. She turned to go into the house. Perhaps she and Jace could have their talk another time.

"No, don't leave," said Beth. "I want you to see how all-fired strong I am." She lifted the ax with difficulty, waited while Jace upended a log on the chopping block, then swung with all her might.

Callie held her breath, seeing Jace's long-fingered hand on the log; she exhaled with relief as he pulled his hand away at the last moment and the ax cut cleanly through the wood.

Jace laughed, picked up the pieces, and tossed them onto the woodpile. "You're your father's child, Princess. Didn't he used to be a woodcutter?"

Beth beamed. "What shall we do now?"

He rubbed at his damp chest. "Well, I ought to get washed up for Sunday dinner. And I thought I'd go hunting for a few hours this afternoon."

Beth thrust out her lower lip in a pout. "Just one game."

Callie pulled off her straw hat, fighting the hollowness in the pit of her stomach. She wasn't wanted here. "I think I'll just put away my bonnet. And see if Mrs. Ackland needs help with dinner."

"No. Don't go in yet, Cal," he said, his eyes warm on her face. "Have a little fun with us. I reckon you missed it as a kid."

She remembered the years of lonely watching, too shy to intrude herself, while the neighborhood children laughed and played. "Of course not," she said defensively. "I had heaps of fun."

His eyes were dark with understanding. "To be sure. But Beth and I want you to be our playmate now."

She smiled timidly, her heart swelling with gratitude. How was it he could see into her soul, when no one else ever had?

He grinned at Beth. "Let's make stars."

"Oh, I love that game!" Beth pointed toward the back of

the house. "I'll get a big shovel from the toolshed. Will that do?"

Jace tweaked her nose. "Splendidly! But it's too heavy for you. I'll get it. In the meantime . . ." He turned to Callie and pointed at the scraps around the chopping block. "We'll need splinters. As thin as you can find them. About this long." He held up two fingers and measured out five or six inches.

Callie nodded and dropped to her knees, searching on the ground with Beth, who could scarcely conceal her glee. By the time Jace had returned, toting a large shovel over one shoulder, she had collected more than a dozen thin strips of wood, and Beth had a fistful.

Jace set the shovel on the chopping block, back-side up, and squinted along its smooth surface to make sure its flat bottom was level. Then he showed Callie how to carefully crack the splinters in the middle so they bent without separating and formed a deep V. He and Beth arranged six or seven of them in a circular pattern on the shovel back, cracked edges inward, sides touching. The design resembled a spiked blossom. They made several more, then Jace looked at Callie.

"Now what?" she asked.

"Oh, let her do the first one!" cried Beth, her eyes shining.

"Right you are," said Jace with a chuckle. "Now then, Cal, I want you to spit."

"Spit?"

He pointed to the center of one of the arrangements. "Right there. Work up a good, juicy mouthful, and let fly."

"Oh!" she huffed. "That's disgusting! And this is what you've been teaching Beth?"

"Beth will know how to be a lady, when the time comes. In the meantime, I think you're just scared to look undignified." His blue eyes gleamed with amusement.

"Is that a challenge, Mr. Perkins?"

"Yes, Mrs. Perkins," he drawled. "It sure is. You're always going on about female emancipation. Let's see if you can emancipate yourself enough to do something unladylike."

She could scarcely back down *now*. She hesitated, then swirled the saliva around in her mouth and allowed it to drop onto the center of the splinters.

There was an instant transformation. The splinters began to straighten under the effects of the moisture, pressing against one another and expanding the arrangement into an uneven star.

Callie gaped. "I'll be jiggered! That's astonishing!"

"Ain't it just some pumpkins?" Beth burbled. "Can I do the rest myself? *Please,* Jace?"

"Why not?" He smiled at Callie, his eyes crinkling. "That wasn't so hard, was it? No one's watching you every minute, to see that you do things right. Maybe if you learned to unbend a little, Cal, *lots* of things would be better." He reached out and stroked the side of her cheek.

She shivered at his tantalizing touch. If Beth wasn't there, she'd beg him for a kiss right this minute! And devil take propriety.

"Hurry up, Callie! I see the lantern on the wagon already. It's Jace, with our company." Beth stood in the doorway of Callie's bedroom, shaking her hands with excitement.

"In a minute." Callie licked closed the envelope of her letter and picked up her pen again. She didn't know why she'd even bothered to answer Anabelle's last, acid-dipped letter. It was clear her ladies' group in Boston had merely been fair-weather friends.

She wondered why she hadn't realized it before. All that brave talk about emancipation! Bosh! All they'd been was just a bunch of frightened women, railing against the opposite sex because they were ignorant of men. Afraid to venture into the world. And now that she was married, they viewed her as a traitor.

Since she'd begun to write about Jace—even before the wedding—there had been fewer and fewer letters coming from back East. And the ones that arrived were filled with reproaches and thinly disguised scorn.

What do I care? she thought. Let *them* try maintaining their independence within a marriage. That was the real challenge. And she'd acquitted herself rather well on that score, she thought.

Still, she felt an emptiness, a loneliness she hadn't felt in years. Deluded or not, she had enjoyed the first circle of friends she'd ever known.

Beth stamped her foot. "Come *on,* Callie!"

She put the letter aside. She'd address it later. She followed Beth down the stairs, arriving in the vestibule just in time to meet Jace coming in with Mrs. Watts.

The sight of the woman, so nervous and uncomfortable in her surroundings, touched a chord in Callie's heart. She limped forward and held out her hand. "Mrs. Watts. So glad you could come."

"Please. Call me Dora," she said shyly.

Dora had clearly taken great care with her toilette. Her black serge gown, though shiny with long usage, had been neatly pressed, and she had fashioned her dark brown hair into a smooth, if severe, coil at her nape. Her eardrops were of inexpensive cut steel, but she had fastened a sprig of reddish gold cone flowers to her bodice, which lent a bit of color to her sallow complexion.

"It was so kind of you to invite me through Mr. Perkins," she added.

That took Callie by surprise. She looked questioningly at Jace.

He smiled, his eyes wide and innocent. "Just as you said, honey, I told Dora you were pining for companionship, and would be honored to receive her. As a worthy substitute for your absent Boston friends."

The black-hearted devil. He *would* twist the knife! "Thank you," she said sweetly.

He glanced around the vestibule. "Where's Big Jim?"

"Right here, son." Big Jim came in from the kitchen, waving a large bottle. "I thought it would be fitting to open a bottle of good French wine, in honor of the first company we've had in this house."

"No she's not," Beth piped up. "What about the wedding guests?"

While Mrs. Watts turned red with embarrassment, Callie glared at her sister. Then she smiled apologetically to the other woman. "I . . . don't know how we could have neglected to invite you," she said.

Mrs. Watts looked down at her boots. They were scuffed and worn. "That's all right, Mrs. Perkins. I couldn't have come anyway. My boarders need their meals on time." She gave a soft laugh. "As it is, I've left my hired girl to see to their supper tonight. I expect to come home to *le diable à quatre.*"

Callie stared in surprise. "You speak French, Mrs. Watts? Dora," she corrected herself.

"I had hoped to go abroad, as a governess. But the very week I completed my studies, I met Mr. Watts."

Jace looked pointedly at Callie. "You were formally educated, then, Dora?"

She rubbed at her work-roughened hands. "I was a member of the first graduating class of Vassar College in '65."

He grinned. "Do tell! What do you think of that, Cal, honey?"

"Well I, for one, think it's time to eat!" boomed Big Jim. He held out his arm to Dora. "Ma'am? Callie, sweetie, if you'll lead the way . . ."

Supper was more enjoyable than Callie would have imagined. Though self-effacing, Mrs. Watts was gracious and knowledge-able, conversing on any number of erudite topics. Between Jace's gentle prodding and Beth's artless questions, she gradually told her history.

Her husband had been a dreamer, a luckless adventurer who had always imagined that his El Dorado lay beyond the next mountain, and the next. They had haunted the diggings for years—California, Nevada, and finally Colorado—living off her modest family inheritance. And when at last the money had run out, Dora had turned to baking pies—setting up crude tents in the mine fields, living in rickety shacks in wild new towns, while she supplied the miners with cakes and pies to supplement their monotonous diets. The money she'd earned had kept them going.

Dora sighed. "He made one good strike in Russell Gulch, and then was cheated out of his claim. He went to work for a big mine owner, but then he was killed in an explosion last year. They paid me a small sum in compensation." She smiled apologetically at Callie. "I suppose I could have taken the money and gone back East, but I discovered I wasn't fit for anything but baking pies and feeding men. So I used the money to buy the boardinghouse."

Callie gazed at her with pity. "But such a difficult life."

Dora raised her chin to a proud angle. "I manage very well. The house is warm in winter, and there's always ample food on my table. And enough boarders to keep me in staples, if not indulge in luxury."

Jace eyed her thoughtfully. "If it's a matter of a new hat or a fancy dress now and again, I'm sure we could make some accommodation for you at the store."

"Goodness, no! I'm far too plain for vanity." She gave a wistful sigh. "I miss my books. We had to sell them when Charles needed a grubstake."

Callie laughed in delight. "But that's the simplest request of all! I have more books than I know what to do with. I'd be honored to share them with you." She hesitated, wondering if she could be so forward as to make a proposal. She took a deep breath. "If . . . if it pleases you, and you have the time, perhaps we could meet once a week and discuss our reading."

Dora gave her a radiant smile that lit up her face. "It would please me greatly, Mrs. Perkins. I'm usually at liberty on Thursday afternoons."

"I'll plan to come into town, then, since I have the wagon. And do call me Callie."

Her heart was filled with warmth and gratitude, a glow that lasted even after Dora had gone. She had a new friend, thanks to Jace. She wondered how much he had known of the woman's history before he'd invited her to supper. Callie rocked impatiently on the veranda, in the chill autumn night, waiting for him to return from taking Dora home.

Big Jim had already gone inside to have his "nightcap." And a second one, "the string to tie it with," as he called it. She wished he wasn't so insistent on his whiskey and his cigars. Surely they weren't good for his heart. She wondered if she could ask Jace to persuade her father to practice a little moderation.

She heard the creak of wheels, saw the glimmer of the lantern. At last! She stood up and waited, tapping her cane on the veranda in impatience, until he had stopped the wagon and jumped down.

He climbed the stairs to the veranda and grinned at her. "Dora surely had a good time tonight."

"I'm glad. She was delightful company." Inadequate words to express her joy at her newfound friend.

"Indeed. She has a fine mind."

"But how did you know that . . . ?"

"She comes into the store all the time. She didn't sound like a yokel."

"I'm so pleased. I . . .." She threw her free hand around his neck in an excess of emotion. "Oh, thank you. Thank you." She hesitated, then kissed him shyly on the mouth.

He looked surprised, then pleased. He wrapped his arms around her waist and drew her close. He bent his head and kissed her the way he hadn't kissed her in weeks—a hot, passionate kiss that took her breath away. His mouth inhaled hers like a man slaking his thirst after a long dry spell.

She dropped her cane and leaned into him, clutching him with eager hands. She opened her mouth to his kiss, and when he slipped his tongue between her lips, she met it with her own. She was in ecstasy.

He broke the kiss at last and stared at her, his eyes dark in the dim light from the house, the crescent moon. She could feel the rise and fall of his heavy breathing against her breasts. "Callie," he said in a husky voice. "Why can't we . . . ?"

"Oh, just keep kissing me, Jace," she said, pulling his head down to hers once more. She couldn't get enough of his burning mouth.

And then she felt his hand on her buttocks, kneading furiously at the soft mounds beneath her bustle. She gave a start of alarm and drew away from him. She had felt equal to him tonight, partners in the joy of a new friendship. But that one lustful gesture had shown her that she was to be his inferior once more, helpless beneath him while he took his pleasure. All her warm feelings fled, to be replaced by growing rebellion. Resentment at his domination in the bedroom.

"I suppose you won't want to sleep tonight," she said irritably.

He swore softly and pushed her away from him. She wobbled for a minute before finding the safety of the rocking chair and sitting down. "No, darlin'," he said in a low, even voice. "I'm not tired. I think I'll go back into town."

Oh, God. *Those women* were in town. She chewed at her thumbnail, torn with indecision and a gnawing sense of inadequacy. "Do you . . . find more pleasure there than in my bed?" she asked at last.

He gave a dark laugh. "Honey, you don't want to know the answer to that." He turned on his heel and stomped back to the wagon.

She buried her face in her hands. What kind of a woman was she, when her own husband no longer even wanted her?

Chapter Seventeen

Dawn was a silver-gray light that filled the room with melancholy sadness. It had drifted in through the windows on the last of the chill night air, settling into every corner as though it would never leave.

Jace tossed impatiently in the bed, then sighed and sat up. It was useless. His churning thoughts refused to allow him to return to sleep.

He looked to where Callie slept beside him, her glorious hair spilling over the pillow, her hands cradled under one cheek. Her full lips were gently parted—lush and inviting. He fought the urge to capture them in a kiss, taste their sweetness.

Christ, he thought. How had it come to this? Had he so misread her desires? There had been a time when she'd trembled at his kisses, pressing her body to his as though she yearned for more than just his mouth. But the woman who lay beneath him each time he put himself into her had no life, no passion. She submitted in rigid silence, so that he prayed for release quickly, taking no pleasure in an act that once had been his joy, his affirmation of survival.

And then, as if she hadn't unmanned him enough with her passivity, she always made him feel as though he were a vile despoiler, soiling the purity of her flesh. She would rise in the dark—he'd hear the click of her cane as she made her way to the washbasin—and sponge away his seed.

And there was no satisfaction to be found elsewhere. He'd intended to bed that prostitute last week, when he'd ridden back to town in a rage. To show the cold bitch he'd married that he didn't give a damn. But he'd choked on the whore's cheap perfume, turned aside from her tobacco-stinking kisses. And when she'd groped at his trousers and grabbed his balls, he'd damn near tossed her clear across the room.

Maybe he was getting soft, with his comfortable middle-class life, his respectable wife. But the world of the barroom and the saloon had taken on a tawdry edge that sickened him. He smiled ruefully in the gloom. Old Sam Trimble had always said he'd turn himself into a proper gentleman someday.

But hell! Even a proper gentleman needed a little horizontal refreshment once in a while. And it was Callie he wanted. Callie he ached for—wild and hot in his embrace. The more frustrated he became, the more his desire grew. But he seemed incapable of rousing her to passion. Perhaps he'd only imagined it—that woman of fire lurking beneath her prim ways.

It was worse when Big Jim questioned him at the store, poking him slyly in the ribs and asking if married life agreed with him. He would always put on a face of bravado and strut around like a rooster in a henhouse, suggesting by his silence that he was more than satisfied. It made him feel cheap. He'd never before minded using lies, charm, whatever it took to deceive the people he dealt with. But Big Jim had trusted him, called him "son." The man deserved better than a fraudulent bastard for a partner and a son-in-law.

Callie sighed and turned in her sleep. Her wedding ring had left a small dent on her cheek, marring the perfection of her porcelain skin. He bent over to kiss it, brushing his lips back and forth on her velvety flesh.

He felt the familiar tightness at his groin and stifled a groan. Son of a gun. Did she even know what she was doing to him? Did she *care*? He moved to the safety of his own side of the bed. He'd be a damn fool to wake her now, to demand his marital rights, to risk his pride one more time tonight.

He hadn't come near her for over a week. Not since the night with the whore. But he'd been so hungry for her he was cross-eyed with desire, and tonight had been special. Their anniversary. One month to the day since they'd been married.

He'd come home early, bringing gifts. A bouquet of flowers he'd picked from a meadow, and a fancy, lace-trimmed chemise that had come in the new shipment from Denver. He'd thought she'd be pleased that he wanted her to have pretty things. But when he'd suggested that he'd be right proud to see her in the shift, she had looked horrified, as though the sight of her in her undergarments was more than he had a right to expect. He'd even chilled a bottle of champagne and brought it into their bedroom—"to celebrate," he'd said. She'd obliged him by drinking half a glass, then complained that it gave her dyspepsia.

He'd still tried to play the romantic fool, kissing her more than he usually did and praising her sweetness and beauty. It had made no difference—not even his kisses, which she'd received coldly. He had succeeded only in working himself into a fervor, without arousing her in the slightest degree. And when he'd put his hand on her breast, she had pushed his fingers away.

After that final rebuff, he had taken her as he was accustomed to taking a whore—with no more overtures, no finesse, seeking his own release as quickly as possible. And feeling like hell afterward.

No, he thought bitterly, he wasn't about to try again tonight.

He heard a noise from beyond their closed bedroom door. An unhappy wail. Callie gave a start and sat up. "Oh, my! That's Sissy. She's having another one of her dreams." She shook her head to clear away the sleepiness.

He pushed her gently back to her pillow. "No. I'll see to her. I'm already wide-awake."

She yawned and rubbed her eyes. "Are you sure?"

"Go back to sleep," he said, climbing out of bed to search for his dressing gown. He shrugged into it, found his slippers, and hurried next door to Sissy's room.

The little girl was on her knees, sobbing in terror. He scooped her into his arms and held her tightly until the sobs had subsided to soft hiccups. "Nothing to fear, Sissy," he said, wiping her cheeks and putting her back on her bed.

Only then did she seem to remember that she didn't much like him. She scowled, her rosebud lips twisting into a pout. "Want Callie. Don't want you."

He gave her a friendly smile, though his guts churned at her unending animosity. "Callie's sleeping. We don't want to disturb her, do we?"

"Want Callie!"

He tried to sound even more friendly. "Now, sweetie, we don't want to wake her up." He had a sudden thought. "Do you want some milk?" Maybe that would put her back to sleep.

She nodded. "A big cup."

He beamed. "Good! You wait right here and I'll fetch it."

She started to climb off the bed. "No! Want to come with you."

Jesus! Was every little kid so perverse? He stroked her honey blond hair and tried again. "Why don't you stay here while big brother Jace gets the milk?" he said with false cheer. "Maybe you'll even fall asleep again while I'm gone."

She shook her head free of his touch. "Don't *wanta* sleep!" She looked like she was about to scream. She pointed toward the window, where the sky was beginning to brighten. "It's morning."

The smile was now frozen on his face. "No it's not, honey. It just *looks* that way. But Poppy is still asleep, and Callie is still asleep. And the sun is still asleep. Mr. Sun won't be up for hours! Now listen to big brother Jace and lie down."

Her chubby face was beginning to turn red. "You're not my brother! *Weedy's* my brother. Stupid!"

He'd seen her tantrums more than once. He sighed in defeat. "Do you want to come downstairs with me?"

She nodded and held out her arms. "Pink me up." She looked like an angel in her full-sleeved nightdress, but he wasn't deceived.

He held her—at arm's length—like a stick of dynamite that he feared would explode in another minute. He carried her through the kitchen to the pantry and sat her on the sideboard. He found a tumbler and a covered pitcher of milk, and poured out a small quantity. She put her pudgy fists on her hips and glared at him. He poured some more.

He watched her drink, depositing a mustache of milk on her upper lip. When she had finished, he found a towel, dabbed at her mouth, then held out his arms. "Now, sweetie, are we ready to go back to bed?"

She scrambled to her hands and knees and wriggled off the sideboard, using the drawer pulls as toeholds. She gave him a wicked grin and skipped into the parlor.

Son of a gun! "Now what?" he said tiredly, following her.

She pointed to the large upholstered armchair in front of the fireplace. "Want to sit in Poppy's chair." She hopped up onto the chair, squashing herself against the cushions. "I'm Poppy," she announced proudly. She pointed to the mantel. "Need my Habana cigar."

He snorted. "Like hell you do."

She held out her hands, squeezing them into impatient fists. *"Gimmie!"*

He shook his head in exasperation, then pulled a smoke from the cigar box and handed it to her. She pretended to puff at it, making exaggerated blowing sounds with her mouth.

Christ! he thought. If she wanted to play Big Jim, maybe he should have put some whiskey into her milk. At least it might have made her sleepy. As it was, she seemed wide-awake, and ready to assault a new day.

He shivered. It was cold in here. He hated to be cold. And who knew how long Sissy would want to sit there, staring contemptuously at him as though he were a bug crawling along the floor? Might as well light a fire. He reckoned it was nearly six o'clock by now. And Mrs. Ackland would be along soon and want to light one anyway, to take the chill out of the room.

He built the fire and squatted before the hearth, conscious that Sissy watched him. He felt utterly defeated. By Callie, by this sour girl-child. He glanced back over his shoulder to see the hostility in her eyes. He sighed. "Why don't you like me, Sissy?" he said, then gave a bitter laugh. "Why doesn't Callie like me?"

She stared at him, uncomprehending.

"You don't know what I'm talking about, do you? You don't know what it's like—to be without people who care for you. You have your safe little world. But I have a wife. And that *should* be enough, shouldn't it?" He felt as lonesome as a stray dog in the mountains.

Sissy frowned in bewilderment. "Callie sleeping?"

"Yes, honey. Callie's sleeping. Like the beautiful princess in the fairy tale. Only I don't seem to be her prince. I sure as hell can't wake her with my kisses. And I don't even know what I'm doing wrong."

Sissy made a face at the cigar and put it down. "I like Callie," she said.

"So do I," he said hoarsely. "I've never known any women like her. Not up close. Jace Greer wasn't exactly their type." He turned, swore softly in frustration, and threw another log on the fire. "Now here I am with a stolen life, everything I thought I ever wanted. And my guts are twisted in knots."

She blinked. "I had a stomachache once. It hurted."

"It sure as hell does, honey." *Son of a gun, I must be cracked,* he thought. Talking to a kid who didn't understand a word, saying things he'd even been afraid to admit to himself, let alone say to someone else.

"Maybe I should just leave," he muttered. He heard the

anguish in his own voice and bent his head. "But I don't want to." He covered his eyes with his hand, fighting the tears that threatened to rob him of the last vestiges of his pride. "Oh, God, I don't want to," he groaned.

He felt her soft little hand on his shoulder, looked up to see her large, baby eyes brimming with tears. "Don't cry," she said. "Don't cry."

He gathered her to his breast and held her tightly, filled with awe and gratitude. A beggar who'd just been thrown a bone. "Funny little Sissy," he said, his voice cracking.

She stroked his cheek with her plump fingers. "Don't cry," she whispered. "Sissy loves Jace."

"What do you think, Big Jim?" Jace plunked down a fist-sized piece of rock beside Big Jim's dessert plate and eyed the older man, his eyes glowing with expectation.

The older man held up the jagged chunk, turning it this way and that in the light. He frowned. "I don't know. You can take it into Dark Creek to be assayed. But I don't think there's enough gold there to fill a thimble. And if it's the most you found after a foot of digging . . ." He scratched his thumbnail along the glittering seam running through the rock. "And it looks like the kind of ore that'll need smelting. A big operation. I wouldn't bother filing a claim. Where'd you find it?"

"Five, six miles west of Central City."

"Hell, man! That area pinched out years ago. Most of those claims were abandoned."

Jace's face fell. "I'm sorry I took the whole day off from the store. I could have made more money selling boots." He pulled his plate toward himself and began to work on his pie, shoveling a thick slab into his mouth with single-minded concentration.

Callie turned her head aside in disgust. He was nothing but a greedy, selfish little boy. All that mattered to him was making money, and eating, and finding gold! His hawknose was red from sunburn; he'd clearly been too intent on the search for riches today to have the sense to wear his hat. He might have Big Jim fooled, with his talk of "harmless diversions." But she'd long since seen his ferocious self-interest in everything he did.

As for his other hunger—his need of her body—she still couldn't forgive him for that night he'd gone into town. His shirt had reeked of some saloon girl's perfume, sweet and sickening. She wondered how he had the temerity to smile innocently at her, let alone expect her to welcome him in bed.

Not that he hadn't tried, last week, on their anniversary. With his gifts and his champagne and his honey-voiced flattery. Did he think she was a fool, to be cajoled so easily?

She felt a sudden flush of warmth, remembering that night. She'd nearly succumbed to his kisses, thrilling to the touch of his mouth on hers, his darting tongue that sent her into a frenzy. But then she'd imagined the other woman with her spangled dress, her painted face. And her mouth had turned to stone, feeling nothing, desiring nothing.

She felt a twinge of resentment as Sissy came toddling into the dining room with Mrs. Ackland to say good night. She'd even lost her last ally. Her baby sister no longer glared at Jace, ran from his presence, greeted him with sour frowns. Now she was all shy smiles and coy looks. And Jace had abandoned his previous hearty manner toward her; his false laughter and oily charm had been exchanged for a quiet intimacy that seemed to draw a private circle around him and Sissy. More than once, this past week, Callie had come upon them in a room—Sissy on his lap, stroking his cheek, while he spoke low to her, his eyes dark with sincerity.

Big Jim lifted Sissy into his lap and wrapped his large arms around her, nearly swallowing her in his embrace. "Now say good night to your sisters and brother," he said, setting her back on her feet.

Sissy waved good night to Beth, came around the table to receive Callie's gentle kiss, then skipped to Jace. He kissed her on the cheek, then whispered something in her ear. The little girl ducked her head and smiled in pleasure.

Mrs. Ackland shook her head. "Land sakes! Who would of thunk it? Mr. Perkins, you sure you weren't ever a drummer with a carnival? Or some sort of fancy magician?"

He smirked at the housekeeper. "You're just jealous, Mrs. A."

"Get on with you. You're too slick by half. You'd best temper your ways, or you'll be catawamptiously chawed up by your own charm one of these days."

He looked smugly pleased with himself, kissed Sissy once more, then turned back to his pie.

Beth finished the last of her milk and stood up. "Can we sing tonight, Jace?"

"Sure enough, Princess. If you're not getting tired of Mr. Foster's songs." He smiled warmly at Callie—a look that was supposed to melt her, no doubt. "Will you join us, darlin'?"

She gave him a withering stare. She'd had more than enough of his charm for one night. "I want to read," she said stiffly. "Dora and I plan to discuss La Fontaine on Thursday."

He shrugged. "Suit yourself."

She sat in the parlor, trying not to hear his laughter as he and Beth sang at the piano together. Why should she care if Beth adored him, if Sissy had been won over? They could scarcely know that he was a two-faced deceiver, a man who had no respect for his marriage vows. But her anger grew as the evening wore on, and she knew that her discontent had very little to do with her sisters, or even the painted hussy he'd spent the night with.

She hadn't expected to be so *lonely*. She hadn't wanted a tyrant, to be sure. But somehow she'd thought that a husband would be a companion. Oh, he laughed and joked with her. But something was missing. *What does he think? What does he feel, behind that mask of charm?* She didn't know. She only knew there was an emptiness at the core of their marriage that dismayed and bewildered her.

When Beth had gone to bed and Poppy cheerfully pulled out the checkerboard and suggested a game with Jace, she admitted defeat. There must be something wrong with *her,* she thought, if she was the only one in the family who wasn't taken by him. Good grief, even Mrs. Ackland had slyly confessed that, if she were a few years younger, she wouldn't mind putting her slippers under his bed!

She closed her book and got to her feet. "I'm going off now," she said. "Good night, Poppy. Jace."

Engrossed in their game, they barely nodded as she limped from the room.

She took a long time readying for bed. Her nerves felt jangled, her body filled with an edgy impatience. Was this to be how they'd spend their lives—in a bland, distant state of civility? She was ready to explode, scream at him, do *something* to crack that mask.

Perched on the edge of her bed, she pulled off her shift and reached for her nightdress. She looked up in alarm as the door opened and Jace came into the room, wearing his dressing gown. She gasped and clutched her nightdress to her naked body.

He closed the door behind him, but made no attempt to avert his gaze. "I'm sorry," he said. "I thought you'd be in bed by now."

She threw her nightdress over her head and pulled it down as far as she could. She felt stupid and uncomfortable. There was no way to cover her bare legs without standing up—a normally awkward maneuver unless her cane was at hand. And she'd left it leaning against the night table.

"Why are you here?" she said. "I thought you were playing checkers with Poppy."

"Big Jim was tired. We decided to quit."

She pursed her lips in annoyance. "Will you please turn your back?"

He grinned, his glance traveling the length of her. "Why? You have beautiful legs."

"Are you deliberately trying to provoke me?"

The smile vanished. "I don't think I could," he said tiredly.

She waited for a moment. Then, seeing that he had no intention of turning away, she reached for the bedpost and hauled herself to her feet, impatiently smoothing down her nightdress to its modest length.

He stared at her neckline. "Don't forget the buttons," he said with sarcasm. "I might catch a glimpse of your collarbone."

"I have a right to my modesty!" she said in a huff.

"Or prudery." He untied the sash of his dressing gown. "Cheese in crackers, will it insult your sensibilities to see me in my nightshirt?" he simpered.

"Oh, don't play the buffoon with me. I'm not my silly sisters." She slid along the edge of the bed to keep her balance, and crawled under the covers. "How *did* you manage to win over Sissy?"

He gave a small laugh, filled with wonderment. "I asked her to be my friend," he said softly.

"Hmph! Will you get the light, or should I?"

He tossed his dressing gown on the end of the bed, kicked off his slippers, and came around to her side. He blew out the lamp, then padded around to his side of the bed. She heard the frame squeak as he climbed in, felt the mattress sag from his weight.

The room was bright with the glow of the moon. Callie could see its silvery face through the window. "I don't think I'll ever sleep tonight with that moon in my eyes," she said peevishly.

She felt his hand on her shoulder. "Let's not sleep, then, darlin'," he said. "Those legs of yours were mighty tempting. Not to mention the glimpse I had of the rest of you."

The last thing she wanted tonight was to submit to him! "I

suppose the next thing you'll want is for me to prance around naked in front of you. Like some disgusting variety-hall girl!''

"Jesus," he muttered. "What put a burr under your saddle tonight? Your eyes threw darts every time you looked up from your book, in the parlor.''

"I get tired of hearing the same songs you play. Over and over.''

"I apologize for my limited repertoire," he growled. "But you could have joined us.''

"And come between you and Beth?" She snorted and turned away from him, curling up on her side.

"Damn! She's only a kid. Are you jealous?''

"Must you swear? I don't like it." She was beginning to hate him.

"Son of a bitch!" he exploded, clutching her by the shoulder and rolling her onto her back. "I'll swear as much as I damn well please! There's a heap of things I don't like about *you*. But I don't go around with a sour face all day!''

She wondered if he'd hear the anger in her voice. "Whatever I may, or may not, have done to displease you, I'm sure it doesn't include infidelity!''

"What is that supposed to mean?" He sounded as angry as she was.

"Did you enjoy your soiled dove that night?" she said scornfully. She was almost sorry the lamp was out; she would have enjoyed seeing if he turned red with shame.

He swore again—low and savage. "Don't be absurd.''

Her lip curled in contempt. "Do me the honor, at least, to be honest. I smelled her perfume on your shirt the next morning.''

"Is that what this is all about? Why you've been sulking for days?" She could see the disgusted shake of his head by the light of the moon. "Nothing happened, except that she put her arms around me. I didn't betray my vows.''

She cringed at the mental picture. Jace in the arms of some

. . . some creature! "But you *wanted* to." She was choking on her bitterness and rage.

He bent over her and gripped her fiercely by the shoulders. "Yes, I wanted to. Because I was so damn sick of living with a woman who doesn't know she's a woman!"

She felt his condemnation like a knife to her heart. It hadn't taken him long to regret his marriage to shy, crippled Callie. "Take your hands off me," she said, her voice shaking. "You're nothing but a selfish, lustful libertine, hiding behind a mask of charm!"

His fingers tightened on her shoulders. "Now, by God . . . !"

She hated feeling helpless, a prisoner of his brute strength. She turned her hands into claws and raked her fingernails across the hands that gripped her so possessively. "Let me go, I said!"

He winced in pain, jerking his hands away, and growled— a sound of fury that rumbled in his chest and sent chills of fear running down her spine. He pulled her roughly toward him and rolled her onto her face, then threw back the quilt and placed his hand firmly on the small of her back. She gasped as she felt his other hand push her nightdress up to her waist, felt the sudden rush of cold air on her bare buttocks.

"No!" she squeaked, wriggling furiously against the hand that pinned her to the bed. He couldn't! He wouldn't dare. She tensed in terror, powerless to escape him.

He hesitated, while her panic grew. She'd pushed him to the edge tonight, half-hoping for a confrontation to clear the air between them. But, dear heaven, she'd scarcely expected to feel his anger in such a humiliating way!

"Jace, for pity's sake," she whispered in a trembling voice.

To her shocked surprise, there was no painful slap. Instead, she felt his hand part her thighs, felt his fingers probe her intimate core. She stiffened, suddenly breathless, as his fingers penetrated her with savage intensity. Deep and hard, with pulsing strokes that set her on fire. He seemed to touch a part of her that she had never known existed. A sensitive bud of pleasure that tingled and sent waves of feeling coursing through her body with each violent thrust of his hand.

She clutched her pillow in tight fists, burying her face in its downy softness to stifle the cries that threatened to burst from her throat. She found herself raising her hips to meet the exquisite, tantalizing surge of his fingers, conscious of a rising tide within her that lifted her to a peak of unbearable tension. Again and again his fingers assaulted her, working her into a frenzy.

She moaned softly. She wondered how much more she could endure without crying out in frustration and delight. And then his fingers were gone, and she was on her back, opening to receive the hard thickness of his manhood. She gasped at the feel of him, full and vigorous and potent within her, pulsing with a pounding rhythm that sent her senses reeling out of control. Her heart throbbed wildly, her brain whirled in confusion, her body grew hot with a fire that seemed to consume her. She tossed her head from side to side, uttering little squeaking noises.

He grabbed her breasts and kneaded them with strong, demanding hands, and groaned with each impassioned thrust of his hips. He quickened his thrusts, then suddenly stiffened, threw back his head, and inhaled sharply through his teeth. She felt the flood of his hot seed.

At the same moment, something exploded within her; she felt a violent, shuddering release, as though a string drawn taut had abruptly snapped. She cried out—a sound that was both a sob and a scream—and sagged against the mattress.

She was dimly aware that he had withdrawn from her and moved to his side of the bed. She was trembling too much even to think clearly. She managed to push down her nightdress, curl away from him. She rubbed a shaking hand against her face and across the back of her neck; she was bathed in sweat.

It seemed forever until her racing heart slowed, her thoughts returned to a semblance of reason. She covered herself with the quilt, grateful that he felt no need to break the silence.

What in the name of heaven had happened to her? She had

so completely lost control of herself that she'd screamed like a primitive beast. She burned with shame. Surely his silence was disgust—that the proper lady he thought he'd married was no better than an animal!

Chapter Eighteen

The frost still clung to the grass of the meadow like a white haze, giving off diamond-sparks where the sun caught a crystal of ice. Callie shivered in the crisp morning air and folded her wrapper more tightly against her nightdress. The first day of autumn, she thought, and already the air was tangy with the promise of winter. It would warm up later, of course. Even now, the sun shone with the warmth of summer; it would chase away the night chill long before noon.

She adjusted the bucket on her arm and hobbled toward the pump in the backyard. Jace had filled the water barrel in the kitchen, as usual, before he'd gone off to town. But Mrs. Ackland planned to bake this morning, and Big Jim had promised to bring home live lobsters for dinner from the shipment he was expecting today. It didn't seem right to use up the kitchen water for her own indulgence. But she felt the need for a thorough sponge bath this morning, not just a quick wash. Jace's scent still clung to her every pore.

He had left the house even before she'd awakened. She was glad. Even now, the memory of her shameless behavior last night made her cheeks burn. It would have been more than she could bear to face him today. Perhaps she'd even plead a sick headache and take to her room to avoid sitting at the supper table with him.

She set the bucket under the pump spout, worked the handle until the water gushed out, and filled it nearly to the top. It would be awkward, carrying the heavy pail back to the house while she balanced herself with her cane, but it was easier than making two trips.

She steadied herself, picked up the bucket, and struggled toward the back door. She heard the sound of a horse's hooves and looked up.

Jace came riding into the meadow, his coattails flapping, and halted beside her. He dismounted and reached for her pail. "I'll take that."

She jerked it out of his reach. "I thought you had gone off to work."

"I went for a ride instead. I had a heap of thinking to do. I reckon Big Jim can do without me for an hour or two."

She turned her head away, avoiding his piercing glance. "And did your thinking prove to be enlightening?"

"Not by a long shot. There were too many questions that needed answers. About what happened last night."

She pressed her lips into a prim line. "I'm not about to engage in a conversation on a topic I consider unseemly to discuss."

"Jesus, Callie, we're husband and wife! There's nothing unseemly about it. You cried out last night. You never have before."

"I did no such thing!" she said indignantly.

He scowled. "Dammit, don't play games with me. Did you find pleasure in the act? Is that why?"

She was dying of embarrassment. She closed her eyes as though she could shut out his words. "I won't listen," she said. "It's perverted to talk about it."

"No!" His hands gripped her shoulders. "Open your eyes and look at me. I want to know if you enjoyed it."

She opened her eyes with reluctance. "I did my duty as your wife. What more do you expect of me?"

"I expect honesty, damn it! *Did you enjoy it?*"

She wavered before the burning intensity of his gaze. How could she lie? "I didn't ... that is, it wasn't entirely ... unpleasant."

"And when you cried out ... Did I hurt you?"

She shook her head, too mortified to answer.

"Then why?" he demanded.

She stared at the dew-kissed grass at her feet. "I felt ... just for a moment ..." She gulped. "The most extraordinary sensation." Her voice was barely above a whisper.

"Has it not happened before?"

"N-no."

"And when I kiss you?"

She couldn't endure another humiliating question. She shook off his hands and gave a shiver. "Please, may I go inside? It's cold, and I'm practically naked. And this bucket is heavy."

"Damn!" he roared. He snatched the pail from her hand and flung it across the meadow. The water made a sparkling arc in the air. "What happens when I kiss you?"

She found her courage and thrust out a defiant chin. "It isn't right, all your prying questions. You shame us both. I won't listen to another word."

For the first time, he looked uncertain. "Callie," he said softly, reaching out to touch her sleeve.

"No!" She slapped at his fingers and whirled away toward the house.

His voice, low and ragged with emotion, stopped her. "I wanted to see your face."

She chewed at her lip. He suddenly sounded so lost, so unsure of himself. She waited.

She could hear his heavy sigh behind her. "I ... I never thought of it before," he said, stumbling over his words. "A woman's pleasure. A . . . a whore teaches a man to be selfish, I suppose. *Did* I pleasure you?''

She caught her breath in wonder. A woman's pleasure. That's what he'd said. Was she *meant* to enjoy it?

"In the name of God, Callie, say something." He stepped nearer and wrapped his arms around her. She could feel the heat of his body on her back. He bent and put his head close to her ear. "I hate it in the dark with you," he said in a choked voice. "So sad. So damned alone."

Her thoughts were churning. She needed time to think. "Please, Jace, let me go."

He gave an angry growl and spun her around. "Damn it, I wanted to see your face! I wanted to know you took pleasure in what we do. Is that so perverted of me?" He pulled her close and ground his mouth down on hers—a long, searching kiss that left her breathless and trembling.

She had to be alone. She clenched her jaw to still the quivering of her chin. "I need water for my bath," she said. "Will you fill the bucket for me again?"

He stiffened, his blue eyes turning as frosty as the meadow. "Of course." He filled the pail without a word, set it inside the back door, then turned to his horse. She watched him ride out to the road, his back rigid with injured pride.

It was only after he'd gone that she remembered the look in his eyes. Humble, almost pleading for a moment. He'd wanted to please her. And yet—and this was what was so strange— he seemed to want her reassurance as well. The affirmation of her pleasure.

The thought stunned her. He *needed* her reassurance. All this time, she'd felt that he was the strong one, ready to overwhelm her with the force of his will. Someone to be resisted lest she lose her own selfhood.

She felt a sudden wild surge of power, a dawning awareness of her strength as a woman. She laughed softly. *Perhaps Mummy hadn't been the weak-willed creature she'd always appeared to be.*

And Mousekin herself could become a queen, ruling her subject. At least in the bedroom.

"Dang my britches, Jace! Where'd you get those scratches?" Beth pointed to Jace's hands on the piano keys as he finished his song.

Callie felt herself blushing, remembering how she'd attacked him with her nails last night. She held her breath, waiting for his answer.

"Well, Princess," he drawled, "it's like this. A fearsome critter came snarling out of the forest as I was riding home tonight. Leaped up on me and fought me tooth and nail. But I pulled out my trusty revolver and plugged the varmint."

"Bosh! You don't have a gun."

He pulled back his coat to reveal a small holster. "As a matter of fact, I do." He shrugged apologetically to Big Jim. "It seemed the wise thing to do, since I'm so often carrying around large sums of cash."

His father-in-law nodded. "A capital idea. Capital! But then I've always said you've got a head on your shoulders."

"That still don't explain the scratches," said Beth.

"*Doesn't,*" corrected Callie. "And I'm sure that Jace must have hurt his hands in the store, carrying sharp wire or some such." She felt the need to end Beth's questioning before Jace said something that embarrassed them both.

He smirked at her, his dimple showing. "If you say so, darlin'."

Big Jim harrumphed loudly, barely hiding his knowing smile. "I think it's time for bed, Beth. And you, too, Callie. You're looking peaked this evening." He lumbered to his feet. "Matter of fact, I think I'll turn in myself. How about you, Jace? We have a long day tomorrow, with that load of tools coming in."

Callie tensed, watching Jace's face. Normally, her father's obvious hint would have riled her; she would have seen it as just one step short of an imperious command. At the very least, it would have embarrassed her that he took such an unseemly interest in her and Jace's marital relations. But not tonight.

She'd been in a ferment all day, impatient for Jace to come home, eager to confess that she *wanted* him in bed. He had been frank and open with her this morning, painfully revealing the secrets of his heart. She wanted him to know that she was no longer afraid to seek pleasure with him, if he could make her feel as wonderful as he had last night.

But he'd been so distant since he'd come home—filled with a jollity that seemed forced—that she hadn't known how to approach him. She wanted to hug Big Jim for playing matchmaker. For giving her an opening.

She contrived to stifle a yawn with her fingers. "Oh, my. I *am* tired. Are you coming, Jace?"

He smiled, but his eyes were guarded. "No. I'm not tired. And I haven't read the *Rocky Mountain News* today. Go on up. I'll not disturb you."

Her heart sank. Had his pride been so badly hurt this morning? Or was it more than just his pride that was wounded?

She climbed slowly to their room, filled with regret for the way she'd treated him. What an innocent fool she'd been! Why shouldn't he want to please her—in every way? Didn't she sit with Mrs. Ackland every day to plan the supper menu to please *him?* And perhaps he was trying to please her most of all through the intimacy they shared in the bedroom.

Well, tonight she would try to be the wife he wanted. She undressed quickly and slipped between the sheets. She lay down and stared at the ceiling, watching the flicker of the lamp on the beams. She mustn't fall asleep. Not tonight.

But she was already drifting on a tide of somnolence, her eyes heavy, when she finally heard him come in. She stirred, watching through half-closed eyes as he draped his dressing gown at the foot of the bed and came around to put out the light.

"No," she said. "Don't."

He turned sharply and frowned, seeming dismayed to find her still awake.

She gave him a shy smile. "Don't put out the light."

He eyed her warily. "Why not?"

"How will you see my face?"

He stared, his eyes lighting up with wonder. "Callie," he whispered, and bent low to kiss her.

She held him off. "Wait. Tell me first . . ." She couldn't go on.

He smiled tenderly. "That you're the sweetest darlin' in the world?"

"No. That . . . that it's quite proper for a lady to . . . enjoy this sort of thing."

He perched on the edge of the bed and stroked her hair. "It's the greatest gift you can give a man," he said hoarsely.

Tears welled in her eyes. For the sincerity of his words. For her own lack of understanding. "I've been a dreadful wife to you."

He managed a mock frown. "Oh, dreadful."

"No, truly, Jace. How you must have hated me."

"I wasn't exactly blameless, honey. I forgot how green you were. And behaved like a cad."

"And . . . and it wasn't shameful of me to . . . cry out last night? Like some savage creature?"

He threw back his head and roared with laughter. "*Shameful?* Hell, Callie, it was the most welcome sound I ever heard."

Her heart flooded with relief. "And you won't mind if I . . ."

"Son of a gun, woman! Are you going to talk about it all night? Or do it?"

She still felt awkward. She lifted her arms and twined them around his neck. "Kiss me first," she said shyly.

He put his lips on hers, stroking with a tantalizing softness that sent shivers up her spine. His mouth was gentle and unde-manding, as though he were doing homage, not taking what was his due. He brushed her lips, then trailed feathery kisses across her cheek and against her closed eyes. She sighed and relaxed beneath his tender care.

He was content to kiss her for a long time, each kiss deeper and more impassioned. His hands went around her waist to hold her close to the hardness of his chest. She wriggled her breasts against him, stirred by his nearness, even through the layers of their clothing.

He straightened, and pulled her to a sitting position. His hands moved to the buttons at her throat.

She curled her hand over his to stop him. "Please, I'm not sure . . ."

The warmth in his eyes touched her to her very soul. "Cal, honey. You've no cause to be shy with me. I think you're beautiful. Grant me the right to enjoy that beauty."

She dropped her hand and allowed him to open the first few buttons of her nightdress. He slipped it low on her shoulders, so it rested on the first swell of her bosom. "I want to see you in a ball gown someday. Cut just like this. With your shoulders bare and glowing in the lamplight. Every man will envy me my exquisite wife."

She had never felt so admired, so warmly praised. Never felt more like a woman than she did at this moment. It made her feel flirtatious, and slightly wicked. "Wouldn't you be jealous of the other men?" she asked coyly.

He chuckled. "Why should I? While they could only look, I can do this." He pressed his burning mouth to the curve of her bosom. "Sweet," he murmured. "You smell of lavender."

She leaned her head back and gasped in pleasure as he covered her with kisses—her neck, her shoulders, the sensitive area above her bosom. She was in heaven. And when he carefully undid the rest of her buttons and parted her nightdress to expose her breasts, she felt a shiver of anticipation.

He gazed at her body, taking in a sharp breath. "Jesus, but you're one hell of a woman. Do you know how often I wanted to see you like this?"

She felt the hot blush on her cheeks. "I was always afraid you'd be disappointed."

He curled his hands around her breasts and caressed them softly. His thumbs found her nipples, circling the rosy points with ever-increasing intensity until she gasped in wonder and delight.

"Oh, merciful heaven," she said breathlessly. "I must have been mad. Was this what you wanted to do—and I wouldn't let you?"

He laughed, his eyes filled with pleasure at her words. "And this," he said, and planted a kiss on her breast. His tongue repeated the tantalizing movements of his thumb, teasing her nipple with hot, wet strokes until she felt weak.

She sank back against the pillows, trembling. She could already feel a tingling in her intimate core, a yearning for the feel of his hard length within her. She resisted the urge to tell him so. Her ignorance and unthinking prohibitions had spoiled too many nights between them.

He seemed to have the same thought in mind. "Well, Miss Don't," he said, "can we agree that nightclothes are no longer necessary?"

She nodded. She should never have felt embarrassed to let him see her body. Not when he treated it with such honor. While she wriggled out of her nightdress, he whipped back the quilts and sheet. She giggled. "It feels like we're warriors, preparing to go to battle."

He grinned and gestured to the broad expanse of the bed. "A large battlefield, for a fateful encounter."

She eyed his nightshirt with distaste. Now that she was naked, she had a sudden desire to see his powerful body. "And will you remove your battle raimant and arm yourself, milord?"

He gave a sly laugh. "I think I'm already armed." He pulled his nightshirt over his head and stood before her. He was hard and erect. She examined him shamelessly, astonished at her own boldness. Astonished even more at how the sight of his strong body, his potent manhood, quickened her pulse and increased the throbbing deep within her.

She was filled with wonderment. Tonight was a revelation. If the sight of him could stir her so, surely her body had the same effect on him! Small wonder he had seemed so disappointed, all those nights when she had smugly told herself she was doing her wifely duty merely by allowing him access to her lower regions. As he lay down beside her, she parted her legs, eager to show her willingness.

"Not yet," he said. "I haven't tasted enough of you." He kissed her, sought her mouth with his tongue, ran his firm hands along the length of her flanks and across her heaving breasts. His kisses made her weak; his caresses sent her into ecstasy. And when his fingers dropped lower to gently push their way inside her, she gasped and arched her hips in an excess of emotion.

His fingers moved gently, gliding and teasing with a rhythm that increased the delicious tension of her body with each tantalizing stroke. She began to moan and whimper softly, giving sound to her pleasure. It was as much for herself as for him. Somehow, when she'd suppressed her voice in the past, she'd also suppressed her body's natural responses.

But, after a while, she felt an odd disappointment. She was beginning to lose the glow. His fingers, though thrilling to her senses, were so hesitant. "Mercy sakes," she panted. "I'm not fragile!" She groped for his hand and pushed wildly against it, forcing his fingers more deeply into her moist core.

He grinned in surprise and delight. "A tiger cat?"

She suddenly felt ashamed of her boldness. "Well, you weren't so . . . so genteel, last night," she said hesitantly.

He chuckled. "I take it you don't want a twiddlepoop. Is this more to your liking?" He removed his fingers, then thrust them back with such force that she uttered a sharp cry and clutched at his bare shoulder.

"Oh, God, yes," she breathed. She closed her eyes and tossed her head back and forth on the pillow while his hand worked her into a frenzy. And when he rolled on top of her and replaced his fingers with his manhood, she wanted to die for sheer pleasure.

He rode her wildly, while her senses reeled out of control and her body shook with spasms. She felt the same explosion within her as before, the same delicious release. She thrust her hips against his, gave a final, satisfied cry, and collapsed into a quivering heap, feeling the warm flood of Jace's release at the same time.

They lay exhausted, side by side, too spent even to cover themselves. At last, Callie stirred. "It was like last night," she said in wonder. "Oh, Jace. Will it always be like that?"

He leaned up on one elbow and kissed her. "I hope so, darlin'."

"And is it always like that for you?"

He stared at her, frowning, then sat up and turned away.

"Jace?" she said, alarmed.

She saw the heave of his shoulders as he sighed. "It was *never* like that before. In all the years ..." He cleared his throat, as though he were having trouble controlling his voice. "It always left me feeling sad and alone. No matter how satisfied my body."

"And tonight?" she asked softly.

He turned. His eyes glistened with tears. "Cal, honey, I don't know how I lived until I met you." He swept her into his arms and pressed her close to his heart. She could feel the trembling of his strong body.

He held her for a long time. She said nothing. She was suddenly aware that he had opened a door for a brief moment, exposed his vulnerable core. And he was a proud man. It seemed only decent to allow him his privacy.

At last he stirred and released her. The smile on his face was easy, but oddly distant, as though he'd shut the door again. "Damn," he said. "If I'd known you were going to wait for me tonight, I'd have brought up a bottle of your father's wine."

She rose to her knees and put her hands on her hips. "Good

grief,'' she said with a snort. ''Are you so unsure of your charm
that you need to get me drunk, as you did that night near the
storeroom?''

He got to his knees in his turn and smirked. ''I could have
had you without the whiskey, if I'd pressed a little harder.''

She gave him a withering stare. ''Not as Mr. Twiddlepoop,
you couldn't!''

''Why you little saucebox!'' he said. He reached out and
smacked her playfully on her backside.

''Oh!'' She rubbed at the spot, surprised at the delicious
tingle. She leaped for him and pushed him onto his back, then
perched over him, her hands curled into claws. She managed
to hold back her giggle and put a ferocious scowl on her face.
''I scratched you last night,'' she said. ''Wasn't it enough?''
She raked her fingers across his hairy chest in long, teasing
strokes—just deep enough to leave white marks on his flesh.

He grunted in pleasure and wriggled beneath her hands. ''My
lord, you *are* a tiger cat. I knew it all along.''

''And what do you intend to do about it?'' she taunted.

He laughed and glanced down at himself. ''I'll give you one
guess.''

She saw the trembling of his member as it grew with his
rising desire. ''Again?'' she said mockingly, remembering their
wedding night. She had been dismayed then by his endurance;
tonight she was ecstatic.

He was clearly recalling that night as well. ''Yes, again. I
promise that your hip won't get stiff this time.'' He grabbed
her around the waist and flipped her onto her hands and knees,
then knelt behind her.

''What are you doing?'' she said.

He laughed softly. ''Honey, you'd be surprised how many
positions I know. And we'll keep trying 'em until we find the
one that makes you comfortable.''

She glanced back at him and gave him a nervous smile.
She'd just begun to enjoy *one* position; she wasn't sure she
was ready for more. ''I don't know . . .'' she began.

She gasped as he thrust into her, a hot, savage entrance that ignited her like a match to tinder. "Oh, criminy," she whispered. She had thought she'd experienced everything tonight. But this was new, and even more wonderful.

He thrust again, as hard and pounding as before. She let out a squeal of delight. "In case I forgot to mention it, darlin'," he drawled, "I also promise that I won't be so gentle this time, since my tiger cat doesn't want a namby-pamby." He emphasized his words with another thrust of his potent hips.

She groaned and buried her face in the pillow. "You're a devil," she gasped. "But don't stop."

He laughed in pleasure. "Glad to oblige. But I sure hope these walls are thick. I'm going to make you shriek like a wildcat tonight!"

Chapter Nineteen

"Come on, Cal, let go of the goddamned cane." Jace tightened his fingers around her waist and gave her an encouraging smile.

"I *can't!*" she wailed.

"You walked down the aisle on Big Jim's arm. Why can't you try to dance with me?"

"Dancing isn't the same as walking. How can I balance myself and concentrate on the rhythm at the same time? I need my cane."

"Just because you're accustomed to it, doesn't mean your legs aren't strong enough to support you, if you try."

Callie looked wistfully toward the parlor door, wishing she could escape. "Please, Jace. Don't make me do this."

"It's only a cane, darlin'. Not a shield. You can't hide behind it forever."

She bristled at that. She'd been through this argument with doctors a hundred times. As if they knew what her lame leg was capable of! "Don't bully me," she said in a huffish tone.

He grinned slyly. "I wouldn't dream of bullying an emancipated woman. However, I'm not above a little blackmail. I reckon the bed in the spare room will suit me just fine tonight.''

She narrowed her eyes. ''You wouldn't dare.''

''I might,'' he said with a smirk.

''Hmph! Don't you look so cocky with me, Jace Perkins. Wild horses wouldn't keep you away from our bedroom. And you know it.''

He grinned. ''Lordy, woman, but you're getting full of yourself! Scarcely a week, and you've become a shameless hussy.''

She ducked her head and blushed. It had been a week of glorious pleasures and hot, wild nights. Each evening, they had raced through supper, exchanging veiled glances, and yawned and feigned sleepiness when Big Jim suggested another game of three-handed cribbage, or Beth begged for more songs around the piano. And when at last they reached the welcome of their cozy room, they tore off their clothes and fell into each other's arms.

Encouraged by Callie's willingness, Jace had become an exciting lover—boisterous and exuberant sometimes, unexpectedly tender at others, so that Callie wanted to weep for joy. She didn't imagine that any man could be more wonderful than he was.

At least in the bedroom. For now, he was being far too difficult on the matter of her dancing, the scoundrel! She fixed him with a superior smile. ''Blackmail is useless. I refuse to dance. I may be a hussy, but you're a man who doesn't want to be deprived. You can't win *this* argument.''

''I reckon so. However . . .'' his eyes twinkled, ''I know a wonderful game with molasses . . . But, no. I'm sure you're not interested.''

That piqued her curiosity. She giggled and tugged at a black curl on his forehead. *''Molasses?* Oh, tell me!''

''Dance with me first.''

Her light mood vanished. ''No, truly, Jace. I can't.''

He scowled. ''You can try.''

"You don't know what it's like," she said bitterly. "Or you wouldn't badger me this way."

"Don't I? When I was in the Reb camp, both my legs were broken. The only one who could set them was another prisoner, an old rummy taken at Sharpsburg. He was a doctor till his love of drink made his hands shake too much. He warned me I'd probably never walk straight again. Even rigged up a jerry-built cart on wheels so I could get around."

"Oh, Jace," she murmured.

"I don't need your pity," he growled. "It was a long time ago. But, by God, I threw that cart away and learned to stand on my own again. And walk."

She felt humbled and ashamed. "I suppose I could try," she said, reluctantly setting her cane on a table.

He grinned. "That's my girl. We'll try a slow waltz. Put your hands on my shoulders. I'll not let go of your waist."

While he counted out the beat, she followed his steps, tentatively placing her feet as he directed, and holding her breath each time she had to shift her weight to her lame hip. They took several turns around the room before she collapsed against him.

"No more," she said. "My limbs are beginning to shake."

He beamed his approval. "You were wonderful. We'll try again tomorrow. Maybe next month, when they have the church sociable, you'll be ready to step out onto the floor with me."

She had been feeling inordinately proud of herself, but his words struck terror in her heart. "In front of all those people? I never could. I never will!"

His eyes grew cold. "When will you ever learn that folks aren't staring at you all the time? Only a fool lives his life fretting over what others think of him. You'll dance with me at the sociable. You surely will."

His autocratic tone raised her hackles. She felt the sudden need to assert her independence. She might not have the courage to refuse his demand, but she could at least make one of her own.

"Only if you allow me to teach you to read music," she said boldly. "I don't know where you learned to play, but you ought to know more songs than you do." She held her breath, waiting for his explosion.

Instead, he smiled and nodded. "Fair enough." He looked around the empty parlor. "Now, I think while Big Jim is still taking the night air on the veranda, we'll sneak upstairs." He pulled her close and gave her a searching kiss, demanding more and more of her mouth until she shivered with the anticipation of their lovemaking.

Still supporting her, he picked up her cane. "Here you are, honey. You go on upstairs. I'll be there in a minute."

"What do you . . . ?"

"I'll just tell Big Jim we're retiring for the night." He grinned wickedly. "And then I reckon I'll stop by the kitchen, darlin'. And see what Mrs. A. keeps in the pantry."

Jace looked up Front Street, then turned to Callie. "That's Mrs. Llewellyn coming toward us. Her husband manages the Eureka Mine."

Callie linked her arm more tightly in his and leaned against him for support. She sighed and eyed her cane, tucked firmly under his other arm. They had made an unequal agreement, as far as she was concerned: He wouldn't leave the cane in the wagon, if she agreed to a stroll along the entire length of the main street. "How do you know her?" she asked.

"She comes into the store. Matter of fact, I sold her that hat."

She dimpled up at him. "With your usual charm, no doubt."

He ran his tongue along the edge of his lip. "Don't dare look at me like that again, darlin', or I'll kiss you right here on the street."

She'd learned enough about him to know it wasn't wise to dare him! The rascal would probably *enjoy* making her self-conscious. "It's a charming hat," she said primly, to change the subject.

He chuckled. "Fraid-cat." He nodded toward Mrs. Llewellyn. "I'll introduce you."

"Oh, Jace, you wouldn't! What will I say to her?"

"Good day, or some such. Nice weather for the end of September. We can't very well cross the street, Cal. That would be rude."

She gasped as a sudden thought struck her. "Is that why you wanted to take this stroll?"

"Well, I wanted to show you off in that dress I bought in Chicago. My beautiful wife. And then, I thought it was about time you got to meet your neighbors."

"Oh, Jace, how could you? Knowing I'm so shy?"

He shrugged. "I was shy, too, as a kid. But you don't get over it unless you make the effort."

He'd never spoken about his childhood. "You? Shy? I don't believe it. Tell me."

He hesitated for a moment. "Well," he said at last, "there I was every Sunday, in my churchgoing best, shined and polished. The proper little gentleman. My papa would take me for a ride in his open chaise."

"In Baltimore?"

"Yes. We'd go up Lexington Street to Fayette, and past city hall. The old one," he added hastily. "They didn't build the new one till after the war. Papa would stop every few yards, and make me say howdy-do to everyone. And what do you know? It wasn't so long before I stopped being shy." He glanced back at her bustle and smirked. "Of course, if I balked, I knew I was in for a walloping."

She was *almost* sure he didn't mean it as a threat, but—to be safe—she contrived to be gracious to Mrs. Llewellyn, even managing to compliment the woman on her hat. And with each succeeding cluster of people they met and greeted, she found it easier to think of something to say. It gave her an air of confidence she'd never known before. But, of course, it was probably Jace's presence that emboldened her.

They had nearly reached the end of the street. Jace stopped and gathered her into his arms. "Son of a gun. I'm proud of you. You sailed through that like a frigate in a fine wind. I want everyone to know what a pippin I married." Despite her protests, he kissed her. Long and hard. Her protests died away at the feel of his burning mouth on hers.

"Mercy!" she said, catching her breath at last and glancing nervously around. "What will people think?"

"Hang them," he said. "They know we're just married. Now, if I can just get you into the store . . ."

The store. She remembered feeling humiliated and lost that day. Out of her depth in the unfamiliar surroundings. She shook her head. "I draw the line at that. There's no way you can persuade me. Or bully me."

"As you wish." He shrugged and kissed her again, more passionately than before. Her knees went weak. "Oh, sweet woman! What I'm going to do to you tonight." His voice was low and thrilling.

She shivered, then felt her face grow hot with remembrance. She would never have believed there were so many ways to make love. "I can scarcely wait," she whispered.

He anchored her arm in the crook of his elbow, and steered her down the rest of the street. "But only if you come to the store," he said in an offhand voice.

She stopped in her tracks. "I won't yield on that," she said peevishly. She glanced at his darkening expression. She didn't want to quarrel. Not on such a bright autumn day. Perhaps a little blackmail of her own . . . . "If you promise to stop pestering me about the store, I might undress *very* slowly for you tonight." She gave him a coy smile.

He sighed and shook his head in defeat. "You've conquered me, woman. I'd have to be a fool to . . ."

She interrupted him as she saw a familiar face across the street. "There's Dora!"

Dora Watts waved and crossed to them, exchanging warm kisses with Callie and nodding to Jace. The two women chatted for a few minutes, then Dora fidgeted with her shawl fringe and smiled uneasily. "I don't know if I should ask this of you, Callie. I suppose I should have asked yesterday. But it's such a dreadful imposition . . ."

Callie put a reassuring hand on her friend's sleeve. "I'll help you if I can."

"You know I've been tutoring the little Raglan boys. For a bit of extra money. But now Mrs. Raglan's sister, Mary O'Neill, has asked if I'd be willing to teach her children as well. I don't see where I can find the time. The O'Neill children are much older. They couldn't possibly study together. But I know how wonderful you are with Beth, and . . ."

Callie thought of the cozy Thursday afternoons she'd spent sitting at the worn table in Dora's boardinghouse, sipping tea and discussing great works of literature. How could she refuse the best friend she'd found in years? And she wasn't shy around children, so there was nothing to make her uneasy with the arrangement.

"Of course I'll do it," she said. "Ask Mrs. O'Neill to stop into the store and tell Jace what day would be agreeable for me to call upon her and meet her children."

The door to the saloon down the street opened and Ralph Driscoll came swaggering out, followed by several rough-looking ranch hands.

Jace muttered under his breath. He turned to Dora. "Take my other arm, Mrs. Watts. I think we should cross the street."

Callie frowned. "I don't know why you're so disagreeable when it comes to Mr. Driscoll. He's a fine man."

Jace snorted in disgust. "Is that why he surrounds himself with the worst pack of mongrels I've seen this side of the Mississippi?" He tugged at her arm. "Come along."

Callie glared at him. "I won't. You've been carrying on about my being friendly. Well, I don't see why we can't be friendly to him." In truth, she was eager to meet Driscoll again. She hadn't seen him since before her wedding. But she remembered his patronizing manner. Would he think so little of her now—now that she was a married woman?

She knew that Jace had given her an air of confidence that had been absent before. And the new copper gown—thanks to Jace's unerring taste—accented her coloring and figure as none of her gowns had ever done before. She wondered if Driscoll would notice and admire her.

She smiled as the banker approached them on the boardwalk. "Mrs. Perkins," he said smoothly, tipping his silk hat. "Mrs. Watts." He paused, favoring Jace with a cold-eyed look. "Perkins."

Jace returned his icy formality. "Driscoll."

The older man managed a sour smile. "You're making quite a name for yourself in Dark Creek, sir. The best salesman since the last raree-show came to town."

Jace clenched his jaw in a tight grimace and surveyed the cluster of men behind Driscoll. "I reckon I'll need an entourage like yours, one of these days. Where did you find them? Behind a saloon, in some refuse barrel?"

One of the men growled and leaped forward, his hand going to the pistol at his hip. "Why you ornery . . ."

Jace skewered him with a look. "Carl, isn't it? Driscoll's foreman? I remember the last time we met you were free and easy with that pistol." He indicated the two women on his arms. "You see I'm occupied with the ladies at the moment. But my challenge still stands."

"I can plug you anytime I want," sneered Carl, pulling his gun half-out of his holster.

Jace eyed him up and down with a look of supreme contempt. "Yes. That would be your way. A craven, slippery backshooter." He scanned the rest of the men. "And only if your pards are there to lend support. I told you once before, you mangy dog. Either have the guts to meet me in a fair fight, or don't show your face or your pistol around me."

Carl wavered, his bulldog jaw thrust forward, then moved his hand away from his gun.

Callie stared in surprise and alarm. This was an aspect of Jace she'd never seen before. Cold-blooded and ruthless. And reckless, dear heaven! She didn't fancy having him ambushed some night in town.

She turned to Driscoll with a nervous smile. "I find the presence of your men offensive, sir. I'm sure Mrs. Watts agrees with me." Her courage was growing. She tilted her chin at a proud angle. "Will you please ask them to leave?"

Driscoll looked at her as though he were seeing her for the first time. "I admire your spunk in speaking up, ma'am. You're quite right. There was no call for Carl to be so huffish." He jerked his head in the direction of his men. "Get back to the ranch."

Jace watched Driscoll's men shuffle down the street to their tethered horses, then turned back to the banker with a scowl. "Tell Carl that if he threatens me one more time, I'll rip his head off." He nodded apologetically to Callie and Dora. "Your pardon, ladies, for this unfortunate scene. You might ask Mr. Driscoll why he chooses to associate with such men."

Driscoll looked decidedly unhappy with the criticism. "You can scarcely blame me," he said in an aggrieved tone. "It's not easy to get men of quality out here. What with the wild territory, and this, that, and the other thing." He smiled briefly at Dora, then allowed his eyes to linger on Callie's face. "I trust you haven't been upset needlessly, Mrs. Perkins. Perhaps you'd care to take tea at my ranch some afternoon. I'd like to show you I haven't completely forgotten the civility of Eastern ways."

The glint in his eye surprised Callie. There had been a time when she yearned for him to look at her with interest. Now, clinging firmly to Jace's arm, she no longer needed his approbation. Still, his offer was generous. "Perhaps Dora and I can . . ." she began.

''No!'' Jace's voice was like a hard rock scraping against a wall.

Driscoll stiffened. ''As you wish.'' He tipped his hat again and made his way down the street.

Dora looked at the tight expression on Jace's face and let go of his arm. ''I really must be going,'' she said. With a blown kiss to Callie, she hurried away.

Callie glared at Jace. ''How could you presume to answer for me? I have a mind of my own. That was a very gracious offer on Mr. Driscoll's part. I'm sure he wanted to make amends.''

Jace snorted. ''He has a slick and genteel way about him, that's for damn sure. But I didn't think you'd be so easily taken in.''

''Or maybe you're just allowing your dislike of him to warp your judgment.''

He puffed in exasperation. ''Jesus, Callie! Use the mind you're boasting of! Who do you think you'd find at his ranch? A dozen or so Ralph Driscolls, with his proper manners? Or a heap of men like Carl? A man is known by the company he keeps. Isn't that the maxim?''

''Don't be absurd! He *told* us he had difficulty finding good men.''

''An easy excuse, but not very credible.''

She stared at him. Why was he being so impossible? Ralph Driscoll was a perfectly fine man. ''I swan!'' she exclaimed, as the sudden thought struck her. ''I think you're *jealous,* Jace Perkins!''

He frowned, studying her face. Then he relaxed into a tight smile, grabbed her, and kissed her possessively on the mouth. ''Damn right I am,'' he growled.

Chapter Twenty

Perched over Jace in the large bed, Callie tried to look stern. "Don't laugh so loudly," she scolded. "The little ones might hear you."

Jace made a face and wriggled under the assault of her fingers. "If you'd stop tickling me, darlin' . . ."

She suppressed a giggle. "It's your own fault. Waking me up at dawn because you were so lustful." She tickled him again, burrowing her fingers under his armpits. His body was golden in the fresh morning sunlight that streamed through the windows. Golden—and strong and beautiful, from the broad shoulders to the segmented ridges of muscle on his belly, to the quivering thickness that awaited her pleasure.

She felt wicked and kittenish this morning. And more than a little smug. They'd made love for hours last night. And still he wanted her again. Wanted her enough to kiss her awake, then tease her into a frenzy with his hot mouth, his rapacious hands.

But she was in no hurry to end the delicious game he'd begun. She traced a finger across his chest, scratching at his deep pink nipples, then circled his navel while he twitched in delight. She'd never touched him so boldly before. She hesitated, then allowed her finger to continue its descent. The curls at his groin were dense and coarse; she tugged playfully at them and was entranced when he uttered a groan of blissful agony.

Encouraged by his response, she ran her finger along the rigid length of his manhood, marveling at the softness of the skin beneath her touch.

"Jesus," he said in a strangled voice.

This time she giggled aloud. "I never realized what fun it is to tease *you.*" She curled her hand around his throbbing member and squeezed.

He jerked beneath her as though he'd been struck by a thunderbolt. "You're playing with fire, woman."

She smirked. "Is that its name?" And squeezed again.

"Its name is retribution, you saucy miss," he muttered, reaching up to grab her by the waist. He threw her onto her back, scrambled to his knees, and separated her legs with impatient hands. "I have my own way of tickling," he said, and plunged into her.

She raised her hips, eager to receive his usual pounding thrusts. Instead, he withdrew, and slowly slid back into her with a tantalizing softness that made her gasp. He lingered for a moment, then withdrew again, gliding in and out with a deliberate, teasing motion that drove her wild with anticipation.

"You villain," she choked.

He chuckled wickedly. "Not at all. I . . ."

They were startled by a sudden pounding on the bedroom door. "By jingo, Jace! Aren't you up yet? Mrs. Ackland has chicken-fixings, ham-doings, and corn slapjacks this morning! And if you and Callie are going for your ride, you ought to be up!"

Jace collapsed against her, smothering his laughter. "We'll be down soon, Big Jim," he managed to get out.

Callie clapped a hand to her mouth to smother her own

laughter. "That sounds like a mighty fine breakfast," she whispered. "Now, which hunger do you want to satisfy first?"

He pinched her bottom so she squeaked, and then called out. "Don't wait for us, Big Jim!"

Callie's body was still tingling in pleasure when they finally trooped down to breakfast. She took her seat, trying not to see her father's knowing smirk as he finished the last of his coffee.

"About time you got here," he grumbled.

Jace smiled blandly and reached for the stack of pancakes. "Well, Sunday morning. A body likes to catch up on sleep. Hell's bells, I thought I'd never wake Cal. Do you know the only thing that will rouse her?"

Callie's eyes opened wide with alarm. It would be just like Jace to try to embarrass her with some wicked remark! "Where do you want to ride today?" she said quickly.

He grinned. "I was only going to tell your father that I have to shake you out of a sound sleep." He piled his plate with chicken fricassee. "I thought we'd go up north, toward Caribou."

Big Jim frowned. "Take a rifle, then. Maybe even a pistol. Hepworth reckons that after that cold spell last week, the bears may be on the prowl. They know winter's coming."

Jace grunted in assent and attacked his breakfast.

"I have your picnic, Jace." Beth came from the kitchen, staggering with a large oilcloth-wrapped package tied with string. She gave a happy laugh. "And ain't it amazin' fine? Mrs. Ackland promised to bake this afternoon. Gingerbread!"

Jace put down his fork and tugged at her pigtail. "Just be sure you leave some for us, Princess. I'll be mighty wolfish by suppertime."

They rode off into the sunny morning, taking a trail that led up toward the snowy peaks. The day was warm, with a gentle breeze—October making a last defiant stand against the coming rigors of winter. Most of the aspens had already dropped their golden raiment; the deep green of the pines stood out vividly against the bare branches and the carpet of amber-and-brown leaves at their feet. Here and there, huddled against sheltering rocks, were clumps of blue gentian and a few reddish brown cone flowers that had miraculously escaped the early frosts.

Callie slowed Milkweed for a minute to adjust her split riding skirt over her saddle. She was almost sorry she'd worn her heavy trousers on such a fine day; she could feel the perspiration under her seat.

She glanced over at Jace. He looked so handsome that her heart caught in her throat. He had taken off his coat and rolled up his shirtsleeves, exposing his sinewy arms. His tight leather vest served to accentuate the broadness of his back and shoulders. And his trousers fit snugly against legs that were thick with muscles. She felt an absurd rush of pride. *She* had seen the masculine body beneath those clothes, had tasted of its glories. *He's all mine,* she thought in wonder. That perfect specimen of a man belonged to her as surely as she belonged to him.

She frowned, seeing the holster he had strapped to his hip. It looked so natural, resting comfortably against his thigh, with the large, pearl-handled pistol jutting aggressively from it.

"How long have you worn a gun?" she asked.

He looked at her, startled by the question and a bit defensive. "Since the war," he said. "Off and on."

"And are you a good shot?"

"Pretty fair."

She dropped her gaze, suddenly embarrassed by her thoughts. "Have you ever . . . killed a man?"

"In the war, yes. And I probably killed that road agent, the day of the holdup." He scowled. "But I'm not a gunman, if that's what you're thinking. Or a killer."

She felt a twinge of guilt. "I didn't mean that at all. I was merely curious." She gave him a sidelong glance. "I knew about the guns, you know. I found them in the spare room by accident one day."

He tugged uncomfortably at his collar and loosened his necktie. "While I was still being a twiddlepoop?" He gave an uneasy laugh when she nodded. "That must have put a crimp in your bustle."

She chewed at her lip. "You must have had a jolly time funning me, all those weeks."

His eyes went dark and serious. "I didn't. Lots of times it was hell, knowing I was deceiving you. But I wanted you, Callie. Jesus, I wanted you. The first time I looked at your picture." He reached across the space that separated their horses and gripped her hand. "I wanted to say 'This is what I am. Take me.'" He looked away. "But I was plumb scared."

She lifted his hand to her lips and kissed it. "You didn't have to be," she whispered.

"You can say that now. But your father's letters were very clear. A genteel man. The man Mr. Collins remembered from before the war. And the California Southgate who met me in town that first day was prim and straitlaced."

She smiled sheepishly. "And full of 'don'ts.'"

"And shy and adorable and everything I'd ever wanted in a woman," he said with fervor. "Not the sort who'd appreciate a rough, knock-round fellow like me."

"I *was* suspicious," she said. "You slipped a few times."

He chuckled. "I know."

"When you kissed me in my bedroom. And the 'friend' who kept me warm and fed me liquor and tried to kiss me outside the storeroom. And all those times you 'accidentally' got me in your arms. Very suspicious. You'll never have a career on the stage."

He puffed out his chest like a little boy who'd brought back first prize at a county fair. "I think I was a right good playactor. Considering what I *really* wanted to do every time I had you in my arms!"

She had a sudden recollection. "And you don't snore!" she said in amazement.

"I never have, far as I know."

"Except that first night in my bed. Bless my soul, what a racket! I thought I'd have to listen to it the rest of my life."

He grinned. "It wasn't easy. Damn near tore my throat to shreds."

"Was it a relief to stop pretending?"

"It was a surprise. Is that what won you over, when I stopped being so priggish?"

She found herself blushing. "No. It was that morning at the pump. When you seemed so lost. So *real.*"

He tried to sound lighthearted, but his voice shook. "Is that what conquers a woman? A man's weaknesses?"

"No. A man's honesty," she said simply.

He sighed. "I never would have believed it. But Sissy knew I was shamming right away."

Her heart overflowed with joy and happiness. "Oh, Jace! I'm glad you're not what I thought you were in the beginning."

"I'm glad you *are,*" he said hoarsely. "Don't ever change, Cal."

It was a moment of such painful intimacy she almost couldn't bear it. "Mercy sakes," she said in a bright voice. "Are you going to get all sentimental, or are we going to ride?"

They moved on up the trail, stopping to admire a circling hawk, then found a shortcut through a stand of junipers that led them to a clear stream. They followed its path as it meandered up the mountainside, tumbling and sparkling under the bright sun.

They rode in silence. There was nothing more to say that they hadn't said with their eyes, with their fervent bodies, dozens of times in the past two weeks. Callie stared in wonder at the crystal water, the deep blue sky, the small puffs of clouds that sailed serenely across the heavens. Had there ever been a day more glorious than this? Or was it only his presence that made it so beautiful?

She could see that the trees up ahead thinned out and gave way to a high mountain meadow. She pointed with her whip. "Can we gallop when we get there?"

He was staring intently at the stream. "Sure, honey," he said in a distracted voice. He frowned and leaned over in the saddle. "Son of a gun!"

"What is it?"

He halted his horse and leaped from the saddle. "I think I see 'color'! Right there, on the edge of that large rock."

She tightened her mouth. "Jace, must you . . . ?" she began.

But he had already waded into the stream and was tugging at the rock with impatient hands. He scooped up a fistful of silt and sifted it through his fingers. "Damn! I wish I had my pan."

She felt the edge of annoyance. This was to be their special day. No interruptions, no work to distract them. Only a ride, a picnic, the chance to be alone together for a whole day. And he was willing to forego it for a gambler's chance at *gold?*

"Is that all that matters to you?" she asked in a petulant voice.

He looked up at her. His eyes were shining with a light she'd only seen when he was in the throes of passion. "Cal, honey. It could be a strike! Think of it—if we had all the gold we wanted!"

"*You* think of it," she said in disgust. "I'm going to ride." She gave Milkweed a savage kick and made for the open meadow. *Devil take him,* she thought. Why did he want to spoil their day?

She looked behind her. He was racing to catch up. Though she spurred on Milkweed, Jace reached her, then passed her. She glared at him, prodded Milkweed once more, and overtook him.

The meadow stretched out for a good half mile. By the time she reached the edge of it—neck and neck with Jace—she was breathless and Milkweed was foaming.

Jace pulled his horse to a stop, slid from the saddle, and grabbed Milkweed's bridle. "Whoa, there, Callie." He held out his arms to help her down. "You're as het up as Milkweed."

"Shouldn't I be?" Reluctantly, she swung her leg over the saddle and allowed him to lift her down. She reached for her cane in its sling, eager to be free of his hands.

He held her fast. "Sorry, darlin'. I reckon I wasn't thinking."

He gave her a sheepish smile, the naughty child hoping to be forgiven.

How could she be angry when his eyes were so soft and pleading? He might not be a *perfect* specimen, after all, but he was still the finest man she'd ever met. She kissed him softly to show him he was forgiven, then grinned wickedly. "I beat you in the race."

"You had a head start."

She tossed her curls. "It doesn't matter."

"Like hell it doesn't," he said with a snort. "You may be the finest damn horsewoman I've ever seen, but I'll beat you on the ride back."

She glowed at his compliment, but managed a mock frown. "Hmph! You'll need all your strength even to keep up with me. I suppose we ought to see what Mrs. Ackland packed for our picnic. Just to fortify you."

While Jace spread a saddle blanket on the ground, Callie unwrapped the oilcloth package. She found cold roast duck and dried mountain plums, corn bread, and a large jar of lemonade.

Jace shook his head in disappointment. "I didn't think Mrs. Ackland was 'temperance.'"

"Mrs. Ackland is sensible," she said primly.

"Well, I'm not." He crossed to where his horse stood contentedly nibbling on the grass, and pulled a small flask from his saddlebag. Before Callie could stop him, he had poured a generous amount of liquor into the lemonade. "Do you good, honey," he said to her bleated protests. "And it'll wear off long before we ride back."

She put her hand on her hip. "Were you born wicked?"

He chuckled. "I suspect I was. Either that, or I was some drunkard's kid, exchanged at birth so no one would know."

That set her to wondering. He was always so close-mouthed about himself. "Were you born in Baltimore?"

The smile vanished from his face. "Do we have to talk about this? I'm starved."

"You're always ducking when I ask you about your childhood."

He stroked the side of her face, his eyes filled with an unfathomable sadness. "Maybe I'll tell you the whole story someday, Cal." He smiled away the darkness and tapped the tip of her nose with his finger. "In the meantime, let's eat."

Callie didn't know if it was his company, the satisfying food, the warm, bright day—or the whiskey-laced lemonade—that made the simple meal taste like a banquet. She only knew she was filled with a heartwarming glow, a sense of completeness in her life.

Jace stretched out on the blanket, hands behind his head, and sighed. "Son of a gun. Now all I need is a good cigar."

"Didn't you bring one?"

He sat up reluctantly. "I left it in my saddlebag."

She leaned on her cane and struggled to her feet. "No. I'll get it. I need to walk off the effects of that lemonade. My head is still spinning." She smiled down at him, taking in his laughing eyes, his full, sensuous mouth. "Besides, I can barter it for a kiss."

He grinned back. "They're free, darlin'. As many as you want."

She was ready to pounce on him, right this minute, and demand payment. Then she remembered his cigar. It always made him even more mellow after a meal. And the thought of waiting for his kisses gave her a shiver of anticipation that was almost as delicious as the kisses themselves.

Bursting with a happiness she could scarcely contain, she made her way across the meadow toward the horses. To her shocked surprise, her cane caught in a gopher hole, giving a jerking twist to her body. She cried out and crashed to the ground.

All her joy vanished. Crippled Callie. She buried her face in her hands and began to sob.

He was beside her in a moment. "Callie, honey. Are you hurt?"

She shook her head, too miserable to speak.

He gathered her into his arms and held her close. "Don't cry, darlin'. Hush, little Callie." He rocked her gently and kissed her forehead and rubbed her back, all the while murmuring tender endearments.

She stilled at last, sniffled, and wiped at her tears. "That was foolish. I'm sorry."

He took her face in his hands and stared deep into her eyes. She had never seen such warmth and understanding before. "Callie, honey, you're perfection in my eyes. I thought so the first time I saw you."

"A lame wife?" she said bitterly.

"You're as perfect as I need you to be. Do you think I give a damn that it takes you longer to get around?" He grinned and kissed the tears from her eyes. "The slower you walk, darlin', the longer I can look at you." The grin deepened. "And then, you can't get away from me so easily."

She managed a small laugh. "Don't be a buffoon."

"You think I don't mean it? Any other woman might run away before I could do . . . this." He slipped his hand under her skirt and grabbed at the juncture between her legs, jiggling the fabric of her trousers against her so she twitched in delight.

"Don't you dare!" she said.

His eyes shone with benign innocence. "Dare what, Miss Don't?" His hand moved upward to the waistband of her trousers and worked on the buttons. "I'm so glad you don't bother with a corset when you ride."

"Good grief, Jace. We couldn't. You wouldn't! Not *here.*"

He laughed. "I reckon we have as much privacy here as in the house. Maybe more. You can shriek as loud as you want."

She felt the grass around her. With the coming of autumn, it had begun to turn dry and brown. "The grass will scratch me," she protested, clinging desperately to her last vestiges of propriety. In daylight! And out of doors, mercy sakes!

He clicked his tongue. "We wouldn't want that, of course. Not on your pretty little bottom." He finished unbuttoning her

rousers and pulled them down to her knees. Then he tugged
at her boots and slipped them off her feet.

"Jace?" she said in a tentative voice.

"Never fear, darlin'," he said, and stripped the trousers from
her legs. He searched her drawers, finding the split between
the two legs. His fingers teased her delicate flesh, awakening
her desire.

She moaned softly. She was beginning to weaken. She supposed she could protect herself with the back of her riding
skirt, and the broad meadow was deserted, with no one to see,
but still . . .

He withdrew his hand abruptly, unbuckled his gun belt, and
lay down on the grass. He fumbled with the buttons of his
trousers, plunged his hand inside and worked on his shirt and
drawers until he could draw out his erect member. He grinned
up at her and spread his arms. "I'm all yours, honey."

She stared in surprise. "You want me to . . . ?"

"As far as I know, the parts work just as well this way."

She hesitated, then straddled his body, pulling aside her skirt
and drawers to expose her tender core. She lowered herself on
him and gasped as her softness enclosed him. "Oh, my," she
breathed, closing her eyes in pleasure.

He put his hands around her waist, guiding her body up and
down on his. It was a new and wondrous sensation—to control
the rhythm of their lovemaking, to take her pleasure at her own
tempo. She found her senses quickening, rising to a fever pitch
as she rode him with ever more passionate intensity, until cries
of ecstasy were torn from her throat. She could hear his own
rapturous gasps, feel the frenzied thrusts of his hips as he rose
to meet hers.

"Open your eyes, Cal," he said hoarsely. "See how I take
pleasure in you."

She wanted to weep for joy at the look on his face. Impassioned, ecstatic, adoring. It was as though the traffic of their
bodies had opened the window onto his soul. She gave a cry
of release—her own soul soaring in transport—and collapsed

against him as he jerked upward in the final spasms of h
climax.

His eyes sparkled with unshed tears. He had felt it too. Th
magical moment that had passed between them. "God, Cal
he said in a choked voice. "It just keeps getting better a
better."

They lay together for a long time, too moved by what h
happened to want to be parted. At last he stirred reluctant
and lifted her from him. "Let's go back to the blanket. I cou
sleep, right about now."

She nodded, filled with a delicious lethargy, a sleepy conter
ment that flooded her body with warmth.

They slept for half the afternoon, clinging to each other, a
woke to a strange shyness. They packed up the remains of th
picnic, mounted their horses, started for home. The silen
between them quivered with words yet unspoken.

Callie stole a glance at his angular profile and felt her hea
pounding in her breast. *I love him*, she thought in wonder. *A*
he loves me. And no day would ever be as special as this da
They'd talk about it to their children someday—the day th
knew they loved each other.

She thought of what she'd been, just a short time ago.
woman who feared to be dominated. And yet today, face-t
face with him, she had been his equal. His partner in glorio
love. And more than that. In some strange way, their positio
had made *her* the dominant one, looming above him, controllir
their lovemaking. Foolish Callie. How baseless her fears h
been.

I'll tell him tonight, she thought. When they were in b
together, sharing kisses and caresses, she'd confess her lov
And he would tell her the same.

Jace reined in his horse in front of the house and frowne
"I thought Beth would have spotted us halfway down the ro

and come running out." He shrugged. "Well, maybe she's busy with the gingerbread."

Callie shook her head. "No," she said, feeling a tickle of unease. "I just realized there's no smoke coming from the kitchen chimney."

Jace helped her down and left their horses at the door. "I'm sure nothing's happened," he said, stepping across the threshold into the vestibule.

She heard the uneasy note in his voice. "Still, it's strange," she said, limping in behind him. "And so quiet."

"Is there anybody home?" he called.

Callie sniffed the air. It should have been heavy with the aroma of gingerbread. Instead, all she smelled was cigar smoke and the scent of the pine planking.

The parlor door was closed. Jace strode to it and threw it open. "Damn," he muttered.

Callie gasped. Big Jim was sitting in his armchair, bound and gagged. Beth clung to his knees, her face as white as paste. Mrs. Ackland sat stiffly on the sofa, clutching a red-faced Sissy to her ample bosom.

And leaning against the unlit fireplace, one elbow draped over the mantel, was the ugliest man Callie had ever seen. His chin was sooty with the growth of a several days' beard, and his dark eyes were small and glittering with malevolence. His hair was long and scraggly, and his filthy clothes covered a body that was as thin and wiry as a ferret.

The hand on the mantel held a lit cigar. The other held a large pistol, pointed straight at Big Jim.

The man looked up as they entered and gave an evil laugh. "Jace, you old son of a whore," he drawled. " 'Bout time you showed up. I was gettin' mighty tired of hearin' the brat scream." He scowled at Mrs. Ackland. "And you better keep her quiet, grandmaw. Or I'll plug the little bitch."

Poppy grunted in anger and strained against the ropes that held him.

The man laughed again. "Well, Jace, old man. Not a word for your pard? After you left me'n Ethan in the lurch?"

"What the hell are you doing here, Ben?" growled Jace. His hand hovered over the pistol at his hip.

Ben smiled. His front teeth were rotted and black. "Ain't no call for you to be ornery, pard. You go for your gun, and I'll draw the pops on the old man afore you can slap leather." He jerked his chin at Beth, trembling beside Poppy. "Might get off *two* shots."

Jace moved his hand away from his pistol. "This has nothing to do with them. Let's you and me go outside and settle it."

"You're a sly man, chummie. I'm not gonna risk a shoot-out with you. Unhook that fancy holster of yourn and drop it to the floor. And no tricks."

Jace scowled and did as he was ordered. "I only want to talk."

Ben snickered. "You reckon you can soft-soap me? *Me,* what knows all your dodges?" He eyed Jace up and down. "You look different-like. Heard tell you'd shaved off your whiskers. And well fed, you polecat. While me'n Ethan was starvin'." He snickered again, a sound filled with hatred and malice. *"Mr. Perkins."*

Callie found her voice at last. "Who is this man, Jace?" she asked unsteadily.

Jace looked at her and rubbed a hand across his mouth. "His name's Ben Wagstaff," he said in a tired voice. "The worst plug-ugly who ever came out of Baltimore. Except maybe for his brother."

Wagstaff took a long puff of his cigar and waved it in Poppy's direction. "Mighty fine smoke you carry, mister." He glared at Jace. "Me'n my brother ain't had the money to afford a fine Havana in months. Some son of a bitch robbed us blind."

Jace looked warily around the room. "And where's Ethan?"

"Hell, man. Don't get your britches in knots. Me'n Ethan's been on the shadow ever since you lit out of Chicago. Ethan's up to Omaha. Ain't heard from him in a while. I was nosin' around Kansas City, ready to quit, figgerin' you'd give us the slip good.''

Callie limped across the room toward her father. Heaven knew how many hours he'd been tied up like that.

''Hold it right there, doll,'' snarled Wagstaff, turning his gun on her. ''I ain't never minded shootin' a cripple.''

Instead of intimidating her, his words fired her temper. ''My father isn't well!'' she snapped. ''I intend to remove his gag.''

He brandished his gun. ''You'll damn well stay where you're at.'' His eyes raked her body with a look that made her flesh crawl. ''You're a mighty fine-lookin' filly, doll. But just who the hell *are* you?''

She drew herself up in outrage. *How dare he prevent me from helping Poppy?* ''I'm Mrs. Horace Perkins. And you have no right to be in our house. My husband . . .''

Wagstaff roared with laughter and jerked his thumb in Jace's direction. ''If you mean *this* galoot, you better think again.''

''Ben,'' said Jace with a warning scowl, taking a step toward the man.

Wagstaff trained his gun on Big Jim once more. ''Don't move, chummie, I said, or the old man gets it.'' He turned to Callie with a self-satisfied grin. ''Hate to break your heart, doll. But the only name they ever pinned on that bastard was Jace Greer.''

Chapter Twenty-One

Callie sank into a chair, almost too stunned to breathe. "That's . . . that's absurd," she said. "He's Horace Jason Perkins. From Baltimore."

Wagstaff flicked his cigar end into the cold fireplace. "I don't give a damn what he told you, doll. When me'n Ethan met him in a Baltimore whorehouse last year, he was just plain Jace Greer, out of Philadelphia. And crooked as a Virginia fence."

She was desperate for reassurance. She looked hopefully toward Jace. "There *was* a good reason you changed your name after the war, wasn't there? Some little scrape or other?" Surely this was all a terrible mistake.

"Callie . . . it's so difficult to explain. I didn't want . . ." He shook his head. "Oh, hell."

Wagstaff chuckled. "Still can't believe it, can you, doll? I told you. He's always been Jace Greer, far's I know. We was down in New Orleans in April. Tryin' to fleece a greenhorn out of a pile of tin for somethin' we called the Union Veterans Fund. And when the man balked, old Jace there—slick as grease—whips out his enlistment papers with a tear in his eye. Saw them myself. 'Jace Greer,' they says. And within five minutes, he's got that pigeon blubberin' and scrapin' the bottom of his pocket for his last nickel. I gotta hand it to you, Jace. You may be a back-stabbin' skunk, but you're *flash*, man.''

Jace curled his hands into fists. His face had gone ashen. ''Shut up, damn it.''

Wagstaff grinned, clearly enjoying Jace's discomfort. ''Why Jace, old pard. You mean you ain't never told them what a slick confidence man you are? Best man to pull a dead suck I ever met. Whether it was swindles or whores or cards, you did all right for yourself.''

''For Christ's sake, man,'' said Jace in a choked voice. ''Let's go outside and get this over with.''

''All in good time.'' Wagstaff glanced around the well-furnished parlor. ''Looks to me like you just worked the best game of your life. A pig in slop. Damn sight easier than a crooked hand of faro, eh? Though you were a mighty fine dealer, I'll give you that. Me'n Ethan ate good on your winnin's, that we did, pard.''

He grinned at Callie and hooked a thumb in his vest. ''Course he had the best damned bodyguards in case of trouble. We cut a swath through every gamblin' hall east of the Mississippi. Didn't we, pard?''

Callie's head was spinning in confusion. It *couldn't* be true, all the things he was saying about Jace. ''Why are you here?'' she asked Wagstaff, almost afraid to hear the answer.

''Well, doll, it's a matter of five thousand dollars. From a bank outside St. Louis.''

Oh, God. She looked at Jace in horror. ''You robbed a bank?'' she whispered.

''Cal . . .'' His eyes beseeched her understanding.

Wagstaff grunted. ''Not that he'd do the dirty work. Not our refined gentleman, Jace. That was for me'n Ethan. But he has a head on his shoulders. Ethan found this little bank, see? But we couldn't never figger how to crack it. All them gates and bars." He laughed. "But here comes Jace with a plan."

"Enough," growled Jace. "Let's talk about the money."

Callie banged her cane on the floor. "No! I want to hear this plan."

"Well, see, doll, Jace here done some acting on a stage in Philadelphia once. So he plays like he's a bigwig, lookin' to borrow a pile of greenbacks from the bank. Flashes a box of jewels he's puttin' up for collateral." He snickered. "That theatrical company never knew he nabbed 'em. Slick, Jace. Slick. So he pulls the banker and his clerk out from behind the cage for a closer look, and they leaves the door open."

Jace groaned and covered his eyes with his hand.

Wagstaff laughed. "No call to hang your head, Jace. You honey-fogled 'em good." He grinned at Callie. "I reckon you didn't know what you married. By the time me'n Ethan gets to the bank, the banker and his clerk is droolin' over the box, just waitin' for Jace to open it again. We draws our Colts and . . ." He shrugged. "Like takin' candy from a baby. We're out of there like greased lightnin'. Five thousand richer."

Jace raised his head, his lip curling in disgust. "But it wasn't enough for you."

"Jace, old buddy. That damn banker mouthed off to me afore we left."

"So you had to go back and kill him."

"I made the bastard crawl on his belly first, beggin' for his life. And then . . ." Wagstaff pointed with his finger held like a gun and squinted down the "barrel," ". . . *Bang!* Straight through the eye."

Sissy jumped at the sound and was immediately soothed by Mrs. Ackland.

Callie felt sick. She turned to Jace with accusing eyes. "And you allowed it? A murder?"

"I didn't know about it until we got to Chicago," he muttered, unable to look at her. "Drinking in a barroom with this rummy and his brother. And they got to bragging like kids pulling the wings off flies.''

Wagstaff poked his thumb against his chest. "*I* was the one done the shootin'. Ethan just watched my back.'' His thick brows darkened into a scowl. "And for what, Jace? So's you could light out with our dough, knife me'n Ethan in the back after all we done for you?''

Jace sighed wearily. "How did you find me?''

Wagstaff laughed. "Your own fault, pard. You couldn't stay away from the cards in Chicago this summer. One of the Kansas City fellers thought he spotted you one night. A Mr. Perkins, they told him. From somewhere west of Denver. Took me a while to find you. But here I am on your doorstep, just itchin' for our five thousand.''

Jace spread his hands. "I don't have the money. There was a holdup outside of town. They cleaned me out.''

"But now you got yourself a business, I hear. And a fine house. I reckon you can rustle up the money in jig time. Whyn't I just keep myself a guarantee until you make good?'' He crooked a finger at Beth, who had been listening and watching everything with saucer eyes. "Come here, kid.''

Callie jumped to her feet. "No!''

Big Jim writhed against his bonds in frustration, groaning. Suddenly he gasped, his face turning gray.

"Poppy!'' she shrieked in alarm, and limped toward him. As she passed Jace, he abruptly threw his body against hers, pushing her to the floor. She cried out, and her cane clattered noisily across the room.

Wagstaff looked startled by the sudden confusion. In that moment, Jace reached under his vest, pulled out his derringer, and fired. Wagstaff dropped like a lead weight, a bright red spot over his heart. Beth screamed, while Sissy began to wail.

"I'll be jiggered,'' said Mrs. Ackland in awe, staring at Jace. She crossed herself quickly, then turned her attention to Sissy, rocking her until she calmed. At the same time, she held out her free arm to Beth. "Come to me, dearie. Nothin' to fear now."

Beth ran to her comforting embrace and buried her face in the woman's neck.

Jace retrieved Callie's cane, then bent to help her up. She glared at him and snatched away her cane. "I don't need your help."

He looked at her for a moment, naked anguish in his eyes, then turned to untie Poppy. "Are you ailing, Big Jim?"

Big Jim rubbed the stiffness from his arms and ran his tongue around his dry lips. "I'll be fine," he growled. "It was just a twinge."

Mrs. Ackland patted the two little girls, stood up from the sofa, and reached for the throw. She tossed it over Wagstaff's body. "No call to be lookin' at this heap of garbage."

Poppy glowered up at Jace. "All this time you've been pretending to be someone you're not?"

Jace shrugged in resignation. "Yes."

"And Horace Perkins?"

"You buried him the day you buried 'Mr. Johnson.' That was the name I was using."

"And everything Wagstaff said was true?"

"Yes."

"You cheated at cards?"

"Never in Dark Creek, sir. I swear it."

"And you robbed a bank?"

Jace ran a hand through his hair. He looked utterly defeated. Callie had never seen such a wretched expression on his face. "Only that one time in St. Louis," he answered. "But I've stolen. Yes, I didn't have a damn thing after the war. I make no apologies for what I was. But I never stooped to murder. I quit the Wagstaffs as soon as I found out, because it sickened me."

Callie fought against her tears. It was as though her life had crumbled in the brief space of a half hour. "And all your lies?" she said bitterly.

He was trembling as he looked at her. "I didn't want to tell them," he said hoarsely. "This was a new life for me here. The chance to start again. Clean, and free of the past."

Beth scrambled down from the sofa, staring at him in bewilderment. "I don't understand. You're *Jace*. You've always been Jace. And I love you," she added in a whisper, holding out her arms and reaching for him.

Callie stopped her. He didn't deserve *anyone's* love. Not after all he'd done.

Jace turned away, his shoulders sagging. "I thought I'd found a home here," he said in a choked voice. "I never wanted to lie. You were all too damned decent for that." He turned to Big Jim, his face twisted in anguish. "I tried to do the best I could to make you proud of me, sir."

Big Jim harrumphed and moved to the sideboard. "I think we could both use some whiskey, right about now." He poured two glasses and held one out to Jace without looking at him.

Callie leaned into her cane, feeling as though the floor was falling away from her. "I want him out of our house."

Big Jim swallowed his whiskey and poured another glass. "No," he said at last. "I don't give a damn who he was. We all know the man we've lived with all these months. A good man. An *honest* man. I'd stake my life on that."

Mrs. Ackland nodded. "Horace or Jace. It don't make no nevermind. A man's intentions are what count, not his name."

Callie shook her head in protest. Were they actually going to *forgive* him? "But all those lies, and the things he's done . . ."

"Dammit, the past is past, girl!" bellowed Poppy. "Have the sense to know what you've got. A fine man! Worthy of our forgiveness. I, for one, won't stand in judgment. I've seen too many good men broken by the war. And Jace, at least, had the gumption to turn his life around!"

Would she ever learn to stand up to her father? "But Poppy . . ." she whispered.

"Not another word! It's settled. I don't see why anyone ever

. to know what happened here. As far as I'm concerned,
s Jace Perkins. That's good enough for me.''

ace blinked his eyes and swallowed hard. ''I . . . I don't
ow what to say, sir,'' he muttered gruffly.

'Bosh! Just keep being the Jace we've come to know.'' He
ned to the housekeeper. ''Can you keep the secret, Mrs.
kland?''

She gave a soft, indulgent laugh. ''I always knew he was a
undrel. Just never knew how much. But there's many a man
o's done worse.'' She gave Beth a little shove in Jace's
ection. ''He's still your Jace, dearie.''

Eyes lighting up, Beth ran to him and threw her arms around
waist. ''I *knew* it. I don't know what that ornery, all-fired
cal was jawing about. Like you were another man, or some-
ng. When any blamed fool can see you're the only Jace we
er knew!''

ace returned Beth's hug, his eyes strangely bright, then
ssed the distance to Callie and put a tentative hand on her
n. ''Cal?''

She couldn't look at him. She was too upset. ''If Poppy
nks it's best . . .'' she murmured.

Big Jim gave a hearty laugh. ''Good! It's settled. I'll ride
o town and get Hepworth. Wind this up tonight.''

ace shook his head. ''No. I'll go. You've had too much of
train for one day. You look like you could use a rest.'' He
wned in thought. ''Did Wagstaff have a horse?''

'I think he left it out back.''

ace grunted. ''Then Hepworth can have something to carry
body back on.''

''Tell Hepworth the man was a *stranger,* you understand.
armed desperado who came to rob us. He tied me up. You
ot him. There might be an inquest. Just a formality. And then
whole thing can be forgotten.''

ace went to the door, then turned back. ''Thank you, Big
,'' he said humbly. ''I won't let you down.''

''By jingo, you can thank me by doing your job as my

partner. As far as I'm concerned, you were born the day y⟨
rode into Dark Creek.'' He waved his arm toward the bo⟨
near the fireplace. ''Tell Hepworth to get the undertaker
ready a coffin. We'll pay for the burial.''

Mrs. Ackland snorted in disgust. ''The goldurned bumm⟨
will probably leave a bloodstain on the carpet. And did y⟨
see him with his cigar ash? Higgledy-piggledy, all over t⟨
floor! I wanted to box his ears.''

Jace managed a thin smile and left the house.

Callie dragged herself through the next few hours as thou⟨
she were in a dream, a nightmare that would surely end wi⟨
Jace kissing her awake.

While Mrs. Ackland fed Sissy and got her to bed, Callie a⟨
her father picked at supper. He looked exhausted, and she w⟨
too sick at heart to eat. She had trusted Jace, had been rea⟨
to give him her love. But how could she love a man she did⟨
even know?

Only Beth was filled with happy exuberance, chattering aw⟨
with shining eyes. With the danger past, she seemed to ha⟨
forgotten her fear, dwelling only on Jace's heroic rescue.

''Ain't he some pumpkins with a gun!'' she exclaimed.
reckon he could even be the hero in one of those dime nove⟨
Poppy has in the store.''

''Mercy sakes, Beth,'' said Callie, rolling her eyes. ''You'⟨
not reading *those,* are you?''

''Well, most of the words are too big,'' she said, clear⟨
disappointed. ''But the pictures are nice.'' She grinned. ''I b⟨
you none of those heroes could hold a candle to Jace. The w⟨
he whipped out his gun and everything. Kerpop! Kerchun⟨
And the bristle-headed varmint bit the dust!''

Big Jim looked thoughtful as he pushed away his pla⟨
''About what happened today, Beth . . . I think it would be b⟨
if you didn't talk about it too much. That 'varmint' said a ⟨
of queer things. And if you start blabbing to the customers ⟨
the store, it could make Jace mighty uncomfortable.''

Beth screwed up her face in bewilderment. ''I wouldn't kn⟨

at to tell, mostly. I was so scared, I didn't hardly hear what
yone was saying.''

''Well . . . names, cities, things like that. It was all blarney,
t I'd just as soon you said nothing.''

She nodded solemnly, her fingers going to her lips. ''Tick
ck, double-lock.'' She looked at her father with sudden rebel-
n in her eyes. ''But I can tell about the *shooting,* can't I?''

''If you make Jace sound too good, every gunman in the
ritory will want to call him out.''

Her eyes opened wide in alarm. ''I never thought of that!''

''Best you say nothing, pet. Now scoot on up to bed.''

It seemed forever until Jace returned with the deputy sheriff.
pworth examined Wagstaff's body, listened to Big Jim's
ory, asked to see Jace's derringer. ''You didn't happen to get
ame off this rascal, did you?''

Jace opened his mouth to speak, but Big Jim cut in quickly.
Not a hint.''

Hepworth scratched his ear. ''I didn't find no papers on him,
ither. And his clothes was all rags. No tellin' what city they
me from. Wal, we got us a few John Does in the cemetery.
eckon we can have one more.''

Big Jim nodded. ''Likely he was just some passing rowdy,
uring we were an easy mark to rob.''

''I reckon so. You bein' isolated out here, and all. And he
ly had six bits in his pocket.''

''Give it to the church for a donation,'' said Big Jim. ''Since
n paying for his burial.''

''No,'' said Jace firmly. ''I'll pay. I shot him. It's the least
an do.''

''How noble of you.'' Callie could scarcely keep the sarcasm
om her voice. Jace wasn't much better than Wagstaff had
en. And probably a lot worse, with his dishonest ways and
s slick charm—all in the service of lining his pockets. No
nder he'd gone after gold with such single-minded purpose!

Satisfied at length, Hepworth tied Wagstaff's body to his
rse and climbed into his own saddle. ''I don't think we'll

bother you fellers with an inquest. Looks open and shut
me.'' He waved good night and headed off into the darknes

Big Jim closed the front door and turned to Jace. "You mu
be hungry. There's fixings in the pantry."

Jace shook his head. "No. I want to talk to Callie."

She rubbed her forehead tiredly. "I can't think anymo
tonight. Do you mind?"

His eyes narrowed. "I think we ought to talk. And now.'

"Splendid idea," said Big Jim, giving them a push towa
the parlor. "Clear the air. I'll go on up to bed." He put b
arm around Callie and kissed her on the forehead. "You g
this settled, now, Mousekin. Hear? And that's an order!
Despite his tone, his gray eyes were filled with concern. "Dor
cut off your nose to spite your face, sweetie," he added softl

He released her and turned to Jace. "I'm mighty tired. I ma
sleep in for an hour or two in the morning."

Jace nodded. "I'll open the store as usual. Good night, B
Jim." He hesitated, his eyes troubled, then held out his han

Big Jim clasped it warmly. "Good night, son."

Callie hobbled into the parlor and waited while Jace close
the door. The throw had been left over the bloodstains on t
carpet, but it served as a bitter reminder of Wagstaff and a
he'd told them. "I don't know what we have to talk about,
she said.

He sighed heavily. "Sit down, Cal."

She glared at him. "I'll stand."

He crossed to the window and stared out into the night. "I'
hoping you can forgive me. But you don't make this easy.'

"Why should I? Was *anything* you ever said the truth?"

He turned. His eyes were filled with desolation. "Try
understand. I haven't had a soft life like you. Not even lil
Horace." He gave a wry laugh. "You would have hated him.

"And yet you found it very convenient to fill his shoes.''

"I didn't have much choice. Those road agents took the fi
thousand as well as the payroll. I could either be Jace Gre
without a nickel, or Horace Perkins with a job waiting."

"I'm glad they took the money," she said. "You're nothing
ut a lowlife thief. You deserved to have it stolen from you."

He shrugged. "God's punishment, I suppose. If God bothers
ith someone like me."

Her anger boiled inside her. "A gambler and a cheat and
. . ." she sputtered over her words.

He flinched at every epithet. "Say it all," he said raggedly.
If it will make you feel better."

She wasn't about to spare him. "A liar and a swindler and
mealy-mouthed, sweet-talking sham! Did you have any con-
cience at all?"

"Damn it, I couldn't undo my past when I came to you. But
tried to live with more honor than I ever had before. Doesn't
at count for something?"

"Honor?" Her lip curled in disgust. "Is that why you lied
me, every chance you had?" It made her sick to think how
e'd deceived her. "Your broken legs. That fairy tale about
altimore, and riding in the carriage with your father. Was any
f that true?"

"I did live in Baltimore for a spell," he said. "I played the
iano in a whorehouse. That's how I learned Mr. Foster's songs.
lived in *lots* of whorehouses."

She gasped and put her free hand over her ear. "I won't
sten to this!"

He strode to her and grasped her by the shoulders. "You
on't want lies?" he growled. "Then you'll damn well listen
the truth."

"And what is the truth? That you'd do anything for money?"

He swore softly. "Do you know what it's like to starve? Do
ou know what it's like to be cold and lonely? You get to
inking that if you don't look out for yourself, no one else
ill."

"Is that how you justify what you did? You worked your
onfidence game on the whole Southgate family. Honey-fogled
e into a sham marriage, so you could get your hands on
oppy's store!"

His grip tightened. "I never thought of this as a sham marriage." His eyes bored into her, blue and intense. "You're the best thing that ever happened to me, Cal. And that's the truth. I want your forgiveness. I *need* your forgiveness."

"You'll never have anything but my contempt and scorn until the day I die!" she said shrilly.

"Damn your stubborn pride!" he burst out. "What is it about me you can never forgive? What makes you so hard?"

"I *trusted* you!" she cried. It made her sick with self-loathing and humiliation. She'd stood naked before him, shared the deepest secrets of her heart, given him her willing body in ways that now shamed her to recall. And tonight she would have given him her avowal of love.

She shook off his hands, choking on her bitterness and regret. "Did *you* ever trust anyone in your whole misspent life?"

He gave a cynical laugh. "Only once. In Belle Isle, that hell on earth prison near Richmond. Where the Reb soldiers hated us Yanks so much you could smell it in the air along with the other stinks. I found a man I thought was a friend. We'd planned an escape—a bunch of us. Through the swamp outside the camp. So I told my new friend. *Trusted* him. And he betrayed us."

"Then you're no stranger to betrayal," she said with acrimony. "Perhaps you can begin to understand my hurt."

His eyes burned with rage. "You self-pitying little prig!" he roared. "The only thing that's hurt here is your pride. My misguided trust cost the lives of six good men! The Rebs were waiting with dogs to drive us back into the swamp. To flounder and drown in panic. And when they saw that I wouldn't die, they stretched me across a plank and smashed both my legs with an iron bar. As a warning to others. And you expect me to trust again?"

She gasped in horror, her eyes flying to his legs.

He laughed darkly. "You see, I did manage to tell you a few truths."

She was filled with anguish and doubts. "How do I know

's true?'' she cried, near tears. ''How do I know anything ou ever told me is true?''

''Because I *tell* you it's so!''

''You told me you were Horace, too. You played a part ithin a part, conspiring with Poppy to keep me from seeing hat you were. And even *that* was false. The 'Horace' who as changed by the war.''

''Damn,'' he muttered, exasperated.

''How does it feel to drown in the swamp of your own lies?''

He took a steadying breath. ''Cal,'' he said, putting a gentle and on her arm, ''we can start again.''

''I don't want to start again!'' She swirled away from him d hobbled toward the door. ''I don't want you!''

His jaw tightened. ''You have no choice, honey,'' he said. As long as Big Jim is agreed, I stay.''

She wanted to scream aloud in frustration. She felt trapped— y her father's hold on her life, by Jace's arrogant certainty. he was where she had always feared to be, helpless and subser- ient to a man. ''I'm not your honey!'' she shrieked. *And I'm ot Poppy's Mousekin, either, by God!*

She saw a book on a table near the door. She picked it up d hurled it at him with all her might; it missed him and ppled a jug filled with dried grasses, sending shards of pottery ashing to the floor.

''You damned hellion,'' he growled, striding across the room take her roughly by the shoulders. ''Is this how you want play the game?''

She trembled at the fury in his eyes. She tore at his fingers. Let me go! You can't . . .''

The door banged open. Big Jim stood on the threshold in is dressing gown, his fists jammed on his hips. ''What in e Sam Hill is going on here? I expected you to settle your fferences, not wake the dead!''

Jace dropped his hands and turned away, his jaw working anger. ''I'm not sure, but I think you just saved your daughter om a good licking.''

"That's no way to make peace!" Big Jim glared at one stony face, then the other. "Get off to bed! Both of you. We'll talk in the morning."

Callie was still quivering, but she managed to draw herself up, thrusting a belligerent chin in Jace's direction. "I'll leave your nightclothes outside the door. The spare room bed is made up."

"Can't say as how I approve," said Big Jim with a scowl.

Jace's eyes were like ice. "It suits me fine."

Big Jim made a face and drew a sharp breath through his teeth. "There's no reason why you can't . . ." He grimaced again and put one hand to his chest.

Jace leaped forward to clutch him by the elbow. "Jesus, what is it?"

"Nothing. Just a twinge. I . . . Oh, God!" Big Jim groaned in pain and sank to his knees.

"Poppy!" Callie knelt beside him and stroked his forehead. His skin was cold and clammy.

"Oh, Christ." Jace's face had gone white. He put his arm around Big Jim's waist and draped the elder man's arm across his shoulders. "Can you walk?" he said in a tight voice.

Big Jim nodded. He seemed to be having trouble breathing, but he managed to get to his feet with Jace's help.

Jace pulled Big Jim against him to support the greater part of his weight. "Cal, go on ahead to be sure his bed is ready. We'll get him settled in, and then I'll ride for the doctor."

She hurried up the stairs, her heart filled with dread. She could still see the stricken look on her father's face.

"Oh, Poppy," she whispered. "Don't die."

Chapter Twenty-Two

Mrs. Ackland closed Big Jim's bedroom door with a soft click and shook her head. "I don't know, missus. I think you ought to telegraph Weedy and get him home right quick. Your papa scarcely had the strength to hold Sissy before she went to bed tonight."

Callie limped up the last few steps and indicated the door. "Is Beth in there now?"

"Yes. Poor little tyke. She's the one will suffer most. Sissy's too young to understand."

"Don't talk that way. He's going to be fine."

"You sound like Mr. Perkins, all hopeful-like. Mr. Jace," she corrected herself. "But we all heard what the doctor said."

Callie fought against her tears. It had been over two weeks since Poppy's attack, and he only seemed to grow weaker by the day—breathing laboriously and struggling even to sit up and take a bit of food.

"Where is Mr. Jace?" she asked.

"Sleepin'. The poor soul. Up all night again with your father. And then spendin' the whole day in town, to keep the store runnin'. Land sakes! He didn't even want supper this evenin'. Just fell into bed with his clothes on, and asked me to wake him before I go home tonight. In case Mr. Southgate is restless.''

"I don't know why you don't wake *me*."

The housekeeper shook her head. "Mr. Jace wouldn't hear of it. You have enough to do all day, he says what, with mindin' the girls and seein' to your father."

"I have you to help," she said sharply. "And Mr. Jace isn't my keeper!" It rankled her that he had so easily slipped into the role of head of the household since Big Jim had fallen ill. It was Jace who decided when they should eat. Jace who determined when to send for the doctor. Jace who arranged the schedule of the girls' visits so their father wouldn't get too exhausted.

And she allowed it, deferring to him like a meek wife, though she seethed with resentment. To think she'd almost persuaded herself that she was in *love* with that overbearing man! A devious trickster who had wormed his way into their lives and seemed determined to stay.

Mrs. Ackland crossed her arms against her bosom. "If I can speak plain, missus . . . You hadn't ought to treat Mr. Jace the way you do. Broke my heart to see his face when I helped him move his clothes to the spare room. He looked as forlorn as an unmated coon.''

"It's only what he deserves," she said defensively. "If he's suffering, I'm sure that's not my concern."

"It's givin' him a heap of grief. I can see it in his eyes. He wants to make it up to you. No call to be so crotchical around him.''

"It really isn't your concern, Mrs. Ackland," she said stiffly.

"Hmph!" Mrs. Ackland snorted. "Pride don't keep you warm on a winter night."

The door to Big Jim's room opened and Beth came out. Bright tears brimmed in her eyes. "Oh, Callie," she said, her chin quivering.

Callie knelt on the floor and gathered her sister into her arms.

"There, there. We don't want Poppy to hear you crying, do we?"

"But is he going to die?"

What could she say? She needed as much comfort as Beth did. "When it's his time, and God decides He wants him," she said gently. "It's the natural order of things."

Beth stamped her foot. "Then I don't ever want to grow up!"

Mrs. Ackland held out her hand to Beth. "Come along, dearie. Let me fix you a nice cup of hot cider before bed, while Callie makes your papa comfortable."

Her heart heavy with grief, Callie watched them go downstairs to the kitchen. Then she stood up, squared her shoulders, and hobbled into Big Jim's room.

Big Jim lay among the pillows of his bed, taking in short gasps of air. He looked almost ethereal—his snowy hair against the white pillowcase, his skin pale and glowing with an odd translucence. His gray eyes were open and calm.

"Mousekin," he whispered.

She hurried to his side. "Did you enjoy your supper?" she asked brightly, trying not to look at the nearly full tray beside his bed.

He nodded. "Splendid! As usual, that woman is a wonder in the kitchen." His once-robust voice trembled and cracked. He frowned and turned away from the bright lamp on his night table.

At once, Callie lowered the wick so the light in the room was muted. "Can I bring you anything else?"

He lifted shaking fingers. "Just sit and hold my hand."

She straightened the pillows beneath his head, smoothed back his hair, then pulled up a chair to the bed. The flesh of his hand felt waxen and dry. She stroked it gently and smiled at him.

"You look like your mother," he said. He glanced toward the window, where the bright moon shone clear in the sky. "She's waiting for me. Up there."

"She'll have to wait a little longer."

He gave a soft cough and smiled wistfully. "How she would have loved this land. I should have listened to her."

"What do you mean?"

"She was always begging me to take her West. We dreamed about it together when we were younger. But the years just seemed to pass. And then she got so frail, and I wouldn't risk her health."

Callie stared in astonishment. "She *wanted* to come West?"

He sighed. "I should have listened to her," he said once more. He squeezed Callie's hand. "Don't let the years pass, sweetie. Grab hold of life while you have it. And Jace ..." He coughed again, his body shaking with heartrending spasms.

She bit her lip, hesitant to sound so final. "Poppy, let's send for Weedy."

He took a steadying breath. "Nonsense, girl. Let him finish the term. He'll be home for Christmas."

Two months. She wondered if Big Jim would last that long. "Maybe just a short visit?"

He laughed, a hollow rattle that came from deep in his chest. "You always knew the way to get around me. Tell you what. Don't you have a birthday soon?"

"Next week." She'd almost forgotten.

"Then send for him. We'll have a grand party. Like we did when your mother was alive."

"That doesn't mean we won't have a ripsnorting Christmas!" Jace stood in the doorway, grinning. "We got in some good French cognac today that will just plain amaze you."

Callie pursed her lips. Was Jace a foolish dreamer, talking about Christmas that way? Anyone could tell that Big Jim might never even see the first snowfall. She studied his face. Perhaps he was only pretending for Big Jim's sake. But no. Though he looked haggard from lack of sleep, his eyes were clear and untroubled, as though he'd convinced himself that Big Jim would be hale and hearty again by holiday time.

Jace crossed the room and put his hand on Callie's shoulder. "Did Big Jim have a good day?"

She moved her shoulder away from his touch. "Tolerable," she said coldly.

Big Jim frowned, a bit of the old fire returning to his eyes. "Dammit, are you two still at loggerheads?"

She didn't want to upset him. Not at a time like this. "We'll work it out, Poppy," she said. "I promise."

He looked intently at Jace. "We ought to get one thing straightened out." He took a shallow breath and grimaced. "Your name. It says Horace Jason Perkins on the store papers. And your marriage license. What do you want to do about it? Change it to Greer?"

"Isn't Jace Greer wanted for a bank robbery?" asked Callie with an edge to her voice.

Jace gritted his teeth at her tone. "I doubt it. If Ben Wagstaff was throwing his name around so freely, I don't reckon the Pinkertons ever picked up on our trail. I suppose I could use my own name now."

"Still," said Big Jim, "it would raise a few eyebrows in town."

Jace shrugged. "Then I'll stay Perkins. It's all the same to me."

Big Jim managed a feeble nod. "Let sleeping dogs lie, I always say. You won't be the first man who ever took a new name out here." He sighed. "Jumping Jehoshaphat, but I'm tired tonight. You two skedaddle, and let me get some rest."

They lingered over their good-nights; Callie was reluctant to leave. He looked so small and helpless in his bed, all his strength and vigor gone. She kissed him, pulled his quilt up to his chin, dimmed the lamp to a tiny flame. Then she followed Jace into the hallway.

"Why don't you go downstairs and get yourself some supper?" she said stiffly, hoping to be rid of him as quickly as possible. "Mrs. Ackland said you never ate."

He put his hand on her arm. "Cal," he said, "I can't stand

much more of this coldness between us. You promised Big Jim we'd work it out. Can't we begin to try right now?''

"I never promised we'd be friends again," she said. She wasn't ready to forgive him—if she ever would. "We have time to think about it after . . ." She couldn't finish. The "after" was too dreadful to contemplate.

He took her by the shoulders. His touch was warm and gentle. She wondered if he was going to try to kiss her. She wondered if she would still melt at his kisses, now that everything had changed. He bent his head to hers, his eyes glowing.

Just then, Mrs. Ackland came out of Beth's room and moved toward them. "Is Mr. Southgate asleep?" At Callie's nod, she opened his door. "I'll just tiptoe in and fetch out his supper tray."

The intimate moment had passed. Jace sighed tiredly and dropped his hands from Callie's shoulders.

There was a loud crash from Big Jim's room, the sound of breaking crockery and glass. Mrs. Ackland came out slowly, wringing her hands. "Saints preserve us. He's gone. Quiet as a whisper."

Callie clapped a hand over her mouth, stifling her wail of pain.

"God damn it, *no!*" cried Jace. He turned to the wall and drove his fist into the planking.

Callie punched at her pillows and tried to settle herself once more in the large bed. If she didn't sleep tonight, she wouldn't have the strength to face another day. Not after last night.

Last night had been the time for weeping. For hours, alone, in her room. Soul-wrenching tears, her face buried in her pillow. And then, still wide-awake at dawn, she'd gone downstairs for tea, and found a mournful Mrs. Ackland there, and wept again, leaning her head against that comforting bosom.

Jace had spent the night in cold isolation, sitting in Big Jim's chair in the darkened parlor, smoking one cigar after another.

She could scarcely look for solace there, even if she'd wanted to breach the wall around him. She wondered what he was thinking.

Today had been so busy and chaotic she hadn't had time to think of her grief, nor to give way to exhaustion. She had done what she had to do, with a strange numbness that had been a comfort in its way. And Jace's unemotional distance had made it even easier.

They had dispassionately picked out her father's burial suit, as though they were outfitting him for a Sunday visit, sat with Mrs. Ackland to discuss the food they'd need for the visitors who would surely wish to call and pay their respects. They had gone out behind the house and chosen a grassy knoll—rimed with frost and sheltered by a large cottonwood—for Poppy's final resting place.

After that, Jace had hitched up the wagon and they'd gone to town. To telegraph Weedy, to talk about the eulogy with the Reverend Maples, to make arrangements with the undertaker, who had sent his assistants out to the house to pick up Big Jim's body. They had agreed to delay the funeral until Weedy should arrive—in three or four days, if there were no problems with the railroad.

Dora Watts had imperceptibly extended the boundaries of their friendship, listening in sympathy and promising to bake pies. And more than one citizen of Dark Creek had stopped them on the street to express condolences. Big Jim had been loved; he would be missed.

The most difficult part had been to tell Beth. She had screamed and struck out at them, her grief turning to a disbelieving anger that had persisted all day. Neither Callie nor Jace had been able to calm her, let alone give her comfort. Only Mrs. Ackland, in her homey way, had managed to soothe Beth, however briefly.

Callie sighed and rolled onto her back. She didn't know what she would have done without Mrs. Ackland. They had found a hot supper waiting for them when they'd returned from town,

a sullen-eyed but compliant Beth, a cheerful Sissy. And then
Mrs. Ackland had left, taking the girls back to her cabin for
the night, so Jace and Callie could have a restful sleep.

Callie sighed again. And still sleep wouldn't come. Her
thoughts were in turmoil. Not even her mother's death had
been so devastating. She'd been frail for such a long time they'd
come to expect it. But Big Jim, so vigorous, so full of life . . .
It had been easy to forget that within that powerful body had
reposed an imperfect heart.

Callie sat up in alarm at the sound of a loud crash above
her. Jace's room. Surely he was asleep by now. He had stretched
and yawned and gone up hours ago, leaving her to douse the
lights in the parlor.

She fumbled for her slippers and reached for her cane. The
room was bright with moonlight. She wouldn't need a candle
or a lamp to see her up the stairs to the spare room.

Jace's door was ajar, lamplight spilling onto the narrow
landing. She pushed open the door and stared, aghast.

The room was in shambles. The bedding had been tossed
into a heap in the center of the floor—pillows and quilts in
wild confusion—and a chair was overturned. In one corner of
the room was a smashed whiskey bottle; the amber liquid
running down the wall above it made it plain Jace had hurled
it across the room.

He sat on the bare mattress of his bed, naked except for his
drawers. His bare arms were wrapped around his head and he
sobbed bitterly, rocking back and forth in an agony of grief.
Beside him on the mattress was the watch Big Jim had given
him on their wedding day.

The sight of him left her untouched, indifferent to his distress.
To the contrary, it ignited a spark of anger within her, a pent-
up rage that had been smoldering since Big Jim's attack. A
bonfire of fury she'd managed to contain until now. "How
dare you presume to grieve, after what you've done?" she
fumed.

He looked up at her, clearly startled by her intrusion. He

shook his head, blinked his eyes, reached for his discarded shirt to wipe his face. He stood up and staggered to the window, leaning his forehead against the pane. "For God's sake, go away," he said at last. His voice was thick and unsteady.

The room reeked of alcohol, and she noted that he swayed on his feet. "How drunk *are* you?" she asked in disgust.

His back heaved with a heavy sigh. "Not drunk enough."

"If Poppy could see you now," she said, her lip curling. "But he was too good, too kind, to see what you really were. Selfish and dishonest, shamelessly taking advantage of his goodwill for your own purposes."

He whirled around; his eyes glowed with blue fire and his hands curled into fists. "Dammit, I *loved* that man!" he roared.

It was too much. That he could even use the word! The suppressed fury flared up within her and exploded in a shriek of outrage. "Loved him? He *died* because of you!"

He flinched, his face draining of color. "No." He shook his head vehemently *"No!"*

She choked back a sob. "Yes! You and your evil ways, and your evil friends. He could have lived for years, the doctor said."

"Or he could have gone at any time," he said defensively. "He knew it was chancy. He'd had more than one twinge in the store."

"How contemptible you are! You hid behind Horace's identity, and now you flee from your own guilt. It was you who brought Ben Wagstaff to our house—to torment Poppy until his poor heart gave out."

He seemed to shrink with every word she spoke. He clenched his teeth and rubbed at his eyes. "Don't do this to me, Cal," he said hoarsely. "I'll mourn that man till the day I die."

She had no pity for his anguish. She was too filled with bitterness and despair. "And I'll hate you till the day *I* die." She started to turn to the door.

He moved toward her, stumbling over the bedding in the

center of the room. He stretched out his arms like a starving beggar. "Don't go, Cal. I need you tonight."

"Sleep with your conscience," she spit.

"No." He covered the distance between them and pulled her into his arms, hungrily pressing his mouth on hers. His touch brought remembrance, awakened her numbed body. She felt the familiar thrill at the warmth of his lips, the throbbing of her loins. There was comfort in his mouth, in the powerful arms that held her close. She sighed and leaned into him, drawing strength from his impassioned kiss. How she needed his lips, his body.

He buried his head in the curls at her neck. "We're both hurting, darlin'," he murmured. "I don't want to be alone tonight."

His words brought her to her senses. She wasn't about to ease his pain by succumbing to him. Not after what he'd done! She pushed at his chest, tore herself from his arms. She was aware suddenly that his eyes—already red from weeping—were unfocused, glazed by drink. And he reeked of alcohol. Her belly curdled with loathing. Had she been prepared to give herself to *this?*

She backed up toward the door, banging her cane angrily with every step. "Don't touch me, you drunken thief," she said. She remembered the shameful stories of his past. The sight of a lewd embrace lit by fireworks. "You disgusting whoremonger. If you want a woman tonight, go to town. Find your own kind. Those hussies are more than you deserve."

He growled menacingly and took a step toward her. "You damned cold bitch. You may not have a heart, but, by God, you have a body! And I want it tonight."

He reached for her with both hands, grabbed her nightdress, and clawed at it with frenzied fingers until she stood naked and trembling before him.

She shrieked in outrage. Heedless of her balance, she raised her cane and swung it at his head with all her might. It opened a bloody gash above his eyebrow. He clutched at the wound, swearing loudly, and staggered back a step.

She struggled to steady herself with her cane. In that moment, he lifted her in his arms, turned about, and pitched her onto the bedding. She scrambled to her hands and knees, desperate to crawl away, to escape him. But he jammed his hand onto her back, pushing her flat. She gurgled, her face half-smothered by a pillow.

She felt his hands on her naked body, roughly turning her over. The plank floor was cold on her back and buttocks. He threw himself on top of her and ground his mouth down on hers. She pummeled him with her fists, tore at his hair, writhed and twisted beneath him, fighting her own desire. His mouth was hot and demanding, stirring her in spite of herself.

Abruptly, he released her mouth to assault her breasts with his teeth and tongue, sucking at the tender nipples until she surrendered and screamed in pleasure. His fingers found her moist core and plunged deep—hard, savage thrusts that roused her senses to a fever pitch. And when he returned to her mouth, pushing his tongue between her teeth with fierce intensity, she knew she was totally conquered.

She returned his burning kisses, inhaling his lips and nipping sharply at the tip of his tongue with her teeth. She raised her breasts to meet the hardness of his chest and wrapped her arms around his torso, feeling a jolt of pleasure at the intimate contact of flesh to flesh.

He stood up and tore off his drawers, then lifted her and positioned her over the mound of bedding so her back arched and her quivering core lay open to his assault. He knelt between her thighs, grasped her legs, and pulled her roughly to his rigid manhood. He entered her with a wild, frenzied thrust that made her gasp.

She had never been more aware of the power of their lovemaking, more alert to every sense: the scratch of his hairy skin against hers, the fullness of his thick member within her, his scent, the feel of his hard muscles beneath silken flesh.

She felt a surge of inexplicable joy. He was warm and alive, and so was she. And they were affirming life in the face of death. She suddenly wanted to draw him into her so their bodies were one, strong and secure against the darkness. She clasped his buttocks to hold him closer, raked her nails across his skin. She wanted to feel, to taste, to *live*.

He was as insatiable as she. Again and again he plunged into her, until her head was swimming and her body dripped with sweat. She lost all sense of time, conscious only of his pounding thrusts, the almost unbearable tension that built within her to a wrenching climax. Her scream of release was matched by his animal roar.

They lay quietly, like seafarers cast up on shore after a violent storm. He was still within her, and his arms held her close—a calming and comforting presence that was like a sweet narcotic. She felt the pain drain from her heart for the first time in two days, felt a merciful heaviness creep into her limbs and dim her eyes. Her body was content, her soul was at peace.

She awoke in her own bed, still naked. The sun was bright in the room, and the curtains blew softly in the morning breeze. From somewhere beyond her door, she could hear Beth's voice, Sissy's happy shrieks as she played her games. Mrs. Ackland would already be cooking, no doubt, or straightening the parlor in anticipation of their visitors.

It took her a moment to remember what had happened last night. And another moment to wonder if their lovemaking had been the beginning of a better understanding between them, or the closing of a door. They had needed each other, but she wasn't sure if she could forgive him. Wasn't sure if she wouldn't always blame him for Big Jim's death, picking remorselessly at a wound that could only grow and fester over time.

She felt a desperate need to speak to Jace this morning, suddenly remembering the blood on his face as he'd made love to her. It shamed her to think of how she'd attacked him. She could apologize for that, at least. They had both been slightly mad from grief last night, but that was no excuse for her savage behavior.

She sat up to reach for her dressing gown, and saw the letter on her night table. Hands shaking with sudden dread, she tore it open.

It was from Jace. "Dear Callie," he wrote. "I didn't want to humiliate you further by forcing you to throw me out. I've done a lot of bad things in my life, but I've never taken a woman by force before. That's only one more reason for you to hate me.

"I've taken my horse, in lieu of the salary I was owed this month. Otherwise, my account with the Southgates is free and clear. All I've taken, I've paid for, with the exception of the watch from your father. Forgive me for that, but it's too precious for me to part with.

"Since Horace Perkins doesn't exist, I give you leave to seek an annulment of our marriage. I've signed over my share of the store to you. You'll find the papers in Big Jim's desk in the parlor.

"Try to forgive me for the pain I've caused you, if you can. Jace Greer."

She read it over half a dozen times, growing angrier with each reading. She had been prepared to apologize to *him*? He had practically raped her, she thought self-righteously. That was clear enough, once she thought about it. And in a state of drunkenness that was nothing short of disgusting!

She was well rid of him, she thought, and tried to ignore the serpent voice that hissed in her ear: He had abandoned her. She had meant no more to him than one of his painted women.

She closed her eyes to stem the tears. When she put her father in his grave, she would be burying two men.

Chapter Twenty-Three

"Oh, Callie, that's wonderful! Try again." Dora smiled at Callie, her eyes shining.

Leaning against the shop counter, Callie handed her cane to the other woman. She chewed at her lip, inhaled deeply, and moved away from the counter. She stood still for a moment, establishing her balance, then took half a dozen hesitant steps before clutching at Dora's arm for support. She gave a shaky laugh and retrieved her cane. "I don't know what's happened to me, but my hip doesn't seem to lock the way it did. I've been practicing every morning, and it's getting easier and easier."

Dora beamed. "Well, I've heard tell that a woman's bones loosen up, or some such, when she's in the family way."

"That sounds like an old wives' tale. Still, I must say, I've never felt more healthy."

Dora looked around the well-stocked shop. "How long do you intend to work?"

Callie patted the slight protuberance of her belly beneath her loosely laced corset. She'd only had to let out her black crape mourning dress a little bit. The one she'd first worn for her mother. "Thank heavens I haven't really begun to show yet. And I'm more than five months along. But the miners' wives don't hide in their houses just because they're pregnant. I don't see why I can't work in the shop right up till my confinement, if I have the strength. This isn't like Boston."

"July is a good month to have a baby out here. Time for the little tyke to grow and bloom before the hard winter sets in."

Callie glanced at the window and the day beyond. Large flakes of snow had begun to fall again, drifting softly down and settling in little pockets beneath the panes. "Nature is set on playing an April Fools' Day joke. I swan, I thought spring had finally come last week. And now this!"

Dora laughed. "I've been here when it snowed in May. But it won't last long. Not these spring snows."

"I hope you're right. I found wake-robins sprouting around Poppy's grave yesterday. They looked so pretty."

"Do you miss him?" asked Dora softly.

Callie limped to a shelf and began to straighten a stack of cartridge boxes. She still felt shy, speaking of pesonal matters wth Dora. But sh'd felt so alone after Jace had gone that she'd found herself confiding more and more in her new friend. "Yes," she said. "Very much." She swallowed and blinked away her tears. "But, God forgive me," she blurted out, "I miss Jace more!"

"Oh, my dear." Dora hurried across the room and embraced her. "Have you never heard a word?"

She shook her head. "Why should he want to return, after the cruel things I said to him?"

"You had cause." Except for Mrs. Ackland and Weedy, Dora was the only soul who knew the truth about Jace's deception. "You're probably well rid of him. Will you get an annulment one of these days?"

Callie stared in horror. "Mercy sakes, no! Not when I'm carrying his baby. It's bad enough that folks pity me for being deserted by my husband. Poor Mrs. Perkins. Can you imagine what they'd call me and my child if they knew the marriage was less than proper? Mrs. O'Neill would snatch her children from my tutelage in about a minute.''

Dora smiled in reassurance. ''Nonsense. I've heard too many good things about your teaching through Mrs. Raglan. And there are several new families who came to town last week. With a passel of children.'' She giggled. ''I think we'll have to start a school one of these days, if Dark Creek keeps growing.''

Callie rolled her eyes. ''I have enough to do in the store.''

Dora's eyes went dark with sympathy. ''Are you managing?''

She sighed. ''Not as well as I'd like.'' It had been painful for her at first, to overcome her shyness, to take charge of the store the way Big Jim would have wanted. But at least her difficulties had kept her from dwelling on her misery those first few months.

The winter had been more severe than she could have imagined. There had been mornings when the snow had been so deep that she could scarcely struggle to the stable with Weedy to reach the horse and wagon, let alone make the treacherous journey into town—even with runners instead of wheels. She had spent long hours combing the shelves and rooting around the storeroom to familiarize herself with the stock. She had pored over account books, working at Big Jim's desk far into the night, and written letters to suppliers and sent out bills. She hadn't imagined there was so much to know about running a store.

She sighed again. ''We're still losing business to Mr. Hauptmann down the street. I don't have Jace's charm. And the last tin supplier sent me an order that was short. I reckon he thought a woman could be more easily gulled.''

''Isn't Billy Dee of any use?''

''Oh, he can run the store. When he's sober. But I can't depend on him. Jace was the only one who could keep him in line.''

''And Weedy?''

She shook her head, filled with despair. "I don't know what to do with him. He doesn't want to return to Harvard. I thought he'd be pleased to work in the store. He always wanted to. But he's gone back to his wild ways. Some days I have to send Billy Dee up and down the street, hunting in every barroom and sporting palace to find him. And he can't talk to me without a quarrel. I think he blames me for driving Jace away."

"And you blame yourself."

"Maybe I do." She shook off her melancholy. No sense dwelling on the past. She picked up a package from the counter and held it out to Dora. "But I don't want to keep you from your boarders. Don't forget your linen towels."

Dora laughed. "I'll be cooking all afternoon. They always expect a big feed on Saturday night."

She thought of Jace. "So they'll have the strength to roister with their saloon girls till dawn," she said bitterly. Was that where he was now?

"Perk up, lovey." Dora kissed her on both cheeks, pulled her shawl around her shoulders, and went out into the snowy day.

Callie spent the next hour waiting on the customers who had braved the weather to come shopping. She felt witless and lost in a sea of unfamiliarity when a ranch hand demanded a Starr carbine: she finally admitted defeat and waved her hand in the direction of the rifles, asking him to pick out what he wanted. She managed better with a sporting girl who wanted some laces, though it still outraged her sensibilities that such creatures paraded themselves freely around town as though they were respectable.

Mrs. Llewellyn, the mine manager's wife, swept into the store, stamping the snow from her boots. Callie greeted her warmly, inquiring after her needs. They spent the next quarter of an hour discussing the merits of the various corsets in stock, finally deciding on a serviceable white cotton twill. To Callie's astonishment, she even managed to persuade the woman to choose a blue satin corset as well. "So pretty and fresh for spring," she said.

She felt an unexpected glow of satisfaction as the woman left the shop. To think she'd once been afraid to set foot in the store! Perhaps there was more of Big Jim in her than she supposed. Or perhaps Jace had given her the courage, all those months ago, to seek within herself for strength.

The door opened and Beth and Sissy came in, followed by Mrs. Ackland, brushing the snow from her gray woolen cloak.

"Land sakes!" said the housekeeper. "I ain't seen such big flakes in April since the day I buried my second husband."

Callie covered a smile. Mrs. Ackland never ceased to amaze her. The woman had had four husbands, and spoke as cheerfully of the dead ones as the ones who had just "wandered off," as she put it. She had shown up at the house two weeks after Big Jim's funeral, valise in hand, and announced that she was moving in to stay. Her last man, bitten with gold fever, had simply neglected to come home one night.

She was a godsend. Callie could never have run the store and tended her sisters at the same time. There were too many late nights, too many exhausting days. And only Mrs. Ackland seemed able to reach Beth since Jace had gone.

Callie frowned in concern at Mrs. Ackland. "Does the dentist think your tooth can be saved?"

Mrs. Ackland rubbed her jaw. "It hurts like blazes, but 'taint nothin' but an abscess. He lanced it and give me some salve to rub on it."

Callie knelt before Beth and wiped the damp snow from her cheeks. "And what did you do while Mrs. Ackland was in the dentist's chair? Explore the town?"

Beth gave her a morose look. "I minded Sissy."

Callie sighed. It had been easier to patch together her own broken heart than to mend Beth's. Jace's bowler hat had been relegated to the darkest corner of the little girl's wardrobe, and she ran from the room whenever she heard Callie and Mrs. Ackland mention his name. She seldom came to the store now, and her riotous conversation—once so exuberant and filled with high spirits and colorful slang—had withered to sullen monosyllables.

"You'll never believe what I heard, pet," Callie said brightly. "The funniest slang from a mule skinner who came in yesterday. Do you know what he called a bump in the road?"

Beth shrugged.

Callie forced herself to keep smiling. "Why, he called it a thank-you-ma'am! Isn't that the queerest thing? Because when you hit it, your head bobs forward as though you were bowing!"

Beth pointed to the jars on the counter. "Can Sissy and I have some rock candy?"

Callie stood up and threw Mrs. Ackland a look of dismay. "Of course," she said tiredly.

"Just one piece," said Mrs. Ackland. "I don't want you spoilin' your supper." She glanced out of the window. "And then I reckon we ought to get on home, before the snow starts comin' down lickety-split. If I was you, missus, I'd close up early."

"A splendid idea." Callie tried again with Beth. "Tell you what, pet. We'll sit at the piano and play songs for hours tonight." She held out her pinky for Beth's game. "Promise."

Beth glared at her and took a ferocious bite of her candy. "That's a stupid baby game!"

Callie's heart sank. How could she have forgotten? Jace had played the game, and promised to stay forever and ever. "Get on home with you," she said in a choked voice. She fastened Sissy's bonnet more firmly under her chin, then accompanied them to the door and watched unhappily from the sidewalk as Beth trailed Mrs. Ackland and Sissy down the street, kicking at the mounds of snow.

"Go back inside, little lady, or you'll catch a chill." The voice was warm but commanding.

Callie looked up in surprise. She had been so intent on her family that she hadn't seen Ralph Driscoll coming down the other side of the boardwalk. She smiled uneasily. Of all the friends she'd made in town these past few months, only he had the power to make her feel shy and insecure. Perhaps it was the air of fatherly authority about him, the craggy good looks that she always found unsettlingly attractive.

"M-Mr. Driscoll," she stammered.

He held the door wide and made a sweeping gesture with his hand. "Inside, now. That's a good girl."

She hobbled back into the shop, searching for something to say that wouldn't make her sound foolish. "My mother always called this the dangerous weather. When you think it's spring, but it isn't."

He banged his silk hat against the counter to dislodge the snow, then smoothed the damp nap with his sleeve. "And particularly dangerous for someone in your delicate condition."

Her eyes shot to his face while a hot flush rose to her cheeks. "How did you . . . ?"

He laughed gently. "I've heard whispers. The ladies can't keep a secret. I reckon the story was making the rounds the first day you visited the doctor."

The blush deepened. "Oh, my."

"No call for you to feel shame, little lady. There's not a man in Dark Creek wouldn't like to take a horsewhip to Perkins for leaving you in the lurch."

His words took her aback. "That's . . . that's very gallant of them."

His eyes were dark with feeling as they searched her face. "More than gallant. I wonder if you know how many hearts you've broken in this town?"

She looked down at the tips of her shoes. "I didn't think anyone noticed me," she murmured.

He gave an easy laugh. "Not notice you? By gum, you came into this store like a house afire after Big Jim died and your husband left. Took the reins where even a man might have thrown up his hands in despair and walked away."

She felt a surge of pride; her efforts hadn't been wasted. It gave her the courage to face him eye to eye. "I only did what I had to."

"You have old Hauptmann on the run. He came into the bank yesterday complaining that you were stealing all of his business."

"There's room for both of us in Dark Creek. The town just keeps growing." She felt suddenly shy again. But, after all, he was being so complimentary . . . "I haven't seen you in the store much these past few months," she ventured. "Or your men." Perhaps they'd begun to go to Hauptmann's, despite his flattery.

"I minded how Carl and the others disturbed you with their rough ways. I've given strict orders that they're not to come in here for this, that, and the other supplies. Not unless Billy Dee is here."

That made her blush again. "That's very considerate of you."

He put his hand on her sleeve. "I want you to think well of me. And consider me your friend."

"Oh, but I do!" she burst out, then sucked on her lip in consternation. What on earth had prompted her to be so frank? Perhaps it was the way he looked at her, the comfort of his hand, the moving sincerity in his voice.

"Dash it all," he exclaimed suddenly, "I think you get prettier by the day!"

She felt completely flustered by his unexpected words. "Please, Mr. Driscoll . . ."

He smiled warmly and slipped his arm through hers. "My friends call me Ralph. And you're downright beautiful."

She managed to disengage his arm and scurry behind the safety of the counter. If he meant to court her, it was too soon. She was too defenseless. "Was there . . . something you wanted in the store today?" she asked, desperate to turn him away from further intimacies.

He smoothed the graying hairs at his temple. "In point of

fact, I came to tell you that I'm taking up a subscription for a new church. It's time we had a proper edifice in this town.''

She relaxed into a smile of pleasure. ''Oh, that would be splendid! I've so longed to see a real church on Front Street. I don't know how much I can give, but you can rely on my support.''

''I knew it would please you. Reverend Maples told me it was a topic much in your conversation these past few months.''

She laughed nervously. ''But surely you're not doing this merely to please *me!*''

His dark eyes bored into her. ''Yes.''

She groped for the chair behind her and sat down. ''I . . . I find your haste disconcerting, Mr. Driscoll. Ralph.''

''I expected you would. A woman of your sensibilities needs time to adjust, given your recent tragedies. And I scarcely mean to press you. But I want to be your friend, for now. And I entertain hopes that I may be more than that someday.''

Dear heaven, how could she respond to that? She cast around in her mind for something to say, and was spared by the sudden slam of the door.

Weedy stood in the doorway, swaying slightly and clutching a newspaper in his fist. ''Callie!'' he said in an excited voice. His clothing was in disarray, as though he'd just dressed, and he smelled of alcohol.

Callie didn't know which was worse—her distress at seeing Weedy in this condition, or her embarrassment that Ralph should see it as well. ''Where have you been?'' she scolded, rising to her feet and moving to the front of the counter. ''You promised you'd come back right after lunch. And only look at you! How can you serve customers in that state?''

Weedy scowled and threw the paper on the counter. ''They're not *my* customers. They're yours. Big Jim didn't even trust me enough to leave me anything in his will.''

She glanced nervously at Ralph. She wished he'd leave. ''Poppy meant it for the best,'' she said in a conciliatory tone. ''When you're old enough . . .''

"I'm not a kid!" he burst out. "I'm already sixteen. Lots of fellows have good jobs, even wives at sixteen! But I'm just a clerk, with a sister for a boss." His lip curled in bitterness. "Jace would have understood."

She felt as though she were losing control of him. "The minute you show yourself capable of the responsibilities," she said firmly, "we can talk about a partnership. And not a minute before."

"Jace would have put me in as a partner right away. If you hadn't made him leave."

Her distress was now acute. Weedy had always viewed the episode with Ben Wagstaff as an example of Jace's heroic courage, glossing over the account of his deception and his unsavory past as mere details. "I-I never did," she stammered. "He chose . . ." She took a steadying breath. "This is a family matter. Scarcely a topic to be discussed in front of Mr. Driscoll. And Jace is gone. There's no point in wondering how he would have dealt with it."

He gave a scornful laugh. "*He* would have know what to do. He always did." He picked up the newspaper and brandished it angrily. "And he still does. Look at this! The *Rocky Mountain News,* out of Denver just this morning."

She felt her mouth go dry. News of Jace? "What is it?" she croaked.

Weedy squinted at the paper through drink-bleared eyes and read aloud. " 'Mr. Jace Greer, owner of the Trimble Silver Mine near Loveland Pass, has just opened a fancy new saloon and restaurant in Silver Plume. Mr. Greer promises that his establishment, the Philadelphia Saloon, will offer hearty fare and the finest French champagnes and Irish whiskeys, as well as every sporting game of chance a gentleman might desire'." He glared at Callie, dark accusation written on his face. "He found silver! Enough to make himself rich. And you always mocked his prospecting."

Ralph took the paper from his hand and frowned at it. "Greer? Jace *Greer?*"

Callie stiffened in alarm. It wouldn't do for the truth to come ut now! "His . . . his mother's name," she said quickly. "He metimes used it in the past."

Ralph perused the article. "Silver Plume. That's east of erman Mountain. He's been so close. All this time, while u struggled to keep shop. Never a minute's concern for your rries." He gave Callie a pitying look. "I always knew he s a scoundrel. But to take another name, to make a clean eak with the past, as though he had no responsibilities to u . . ." He shook his head. "Shameful!"

Weedy snatched away the paper. "He's a damn sight better an any man who ever came into this town, by jingo!" He ode to a shelf behind the counter and pulled down a bottle whiskey.

Callie stared in dismay. "Weedy, you can't!"

"Take it out of my clerk's pay, *boss*," he growled, and mped to the door.

"Will you be home for supper?"

"I might." He gave a harsh laugh. "Then again, I might t be home at all tonight." With a final contemptuous glance their direction, he stormed out the door, slamming it behind m.

She could scarcely look at Ralph. She gave him a weak ile. "He's still upset about Poppy's death. I'm sure he'll ow out of it."

"I hope he doesn't ruin his life first."

"What do you mean?"

"It pains me to be the bearer of bad news. But I think you ght to be warned. I've heard your brother spends much of his ne at the Red Bull. In the company of a half-breed woman."

She gasped. "Oh, my Lord!"

"They say she's a fine-looking woman, as sporting gals go, t her mother was an Arapaho squaw."

She fought back her tears. She was the head of the household, d she couldn't rein in Weedy, couldn't console Beth, couldn't en run the shop as Big Jim had done.

Ralph put his arm around her. His embrace was strong and firm, and deeply comforting. "Oh, my dear child. Weedy needs a father. And you need a man. You shouldn't have to work like this, in your condition."

She looked up into his eyes—so filled with earnest concern. It would be very easy to give in, to let herself be cared for. She was so tired of her burdens.

He bent his head to hers and kissed her softly on the mouth. "Poor Callie," he murmured. "Poor little girl."

It was too soon. Her lips still recalled the glory of Jace's kisses. "Please, not yet," she said, pushing him gently away.

He reached for his hat. "I quite understand. Will you allow me at least to call on you?"

"Let me think about it."

He sighed, took her hand and kissed it, then left the store.

She allowed herself to weep then, overwhelmed by despair. Her hopes were shattered. In some secret corner of her mind she had always thought that Jace might return, to seek and receive her forgiveness. To exult in the news of their unborn child. She'd even imagined he might come before July, when the baby was due.

But he had a silver mine now. Probably all the money he had ever wished for. And a saloon, with dozens of painted women, no doubt. He had everything he'd ever wanted. Why should he need *her?*

She stared mournfully at the closed door. Perhaps she'd encourage Ralph after all.

"Oh, God," she whispered. "I'm so lonely."

Chapter Twenty-Four

"Jace, sugar, are you just going to chatter away all night, like a li'l old chickaree?"

Jace took a deep drag on his Havana and looked up at the woman with narrowed eyes. She might be a lively bit of jam bed, but she had damn little else to recommend her. Too oad across the rump, too picayunish up top, with a waistline at would soon vanish if she didn't stop swilling beer. Her air was an unnatural shade of black—probably washed-out own underneath, he thought, recalling the thick tuft at her oin. And her face, though strikingly beautiful, masked a blank ind; it was covered with so much rouge and powder that she oked like a wax figure in a raree-show.

"Netta, honey," he said, trying to contain his annoyance, I told you never to disturb me when I'm talking business. Go up to the room."

"It's too hot," she said with a whining sigh. "I thought July as bad, but this month's a scorcher."

He clenched his jaw. "Get Sweeney to fix you a cool bath, en."

"I don't want one." She leaned over the table so her modes breasts sagged above the line of her low-cut gown. She gav him a coy smile. "Aren't you going to introduce me to you li'l old company, sugar?"

Son of a bitch! Even her Southern drawl was beginning t grate on him tonight. "No," he growled. "Go find somethin else to do." He jerked his head in the direction of the long ba its polished-mahogany length lit by cut-glass lanterns. "Talk t the bartender. He looks bored, listening to drunks all night.'

Netta tossed her shoulder at him. The little silver bells tha trimmed the neckline of her garish red dress gave off a tinn sound. She made a face, her rouged lips forming into an exag gerated pout. "Saints alive, I don't know *why* I let you trea me so poorly."

Because if he didn't keep her here, he thought, she'd be a the nickel saloon across the street. Getting drunk every night, th way she had when he'd found her, the poor bitch. "Skedaddl honey," he said, trying to keep the edge from his voice.

She wasn't about to be placated. "Hmph! I just might n wait for you tonight."

He was beginning to lose patience. "You'll wait," he mu tered. "And scrub off that damned paint." He silenced h protest with a scowl. She whirled around and flounced away

Jace turned his attention back to the man who sat opposi him. "You were saying, Mr. Saint-James . . . ?"

The man, nattily dressed in a gray English suit, took a swa low of his whiskey. "The company I represent, the East Londo Smelting and Refining Works, is prepared to pay you eigh thousand dollars for your claim to the Trimble Mine," he sai in his cultured British accent.

"I wouldn't settle for less than one hundred twenty."

"Come, come, Mr. Greer. I have it on good authority th you've already pulled out nearly a quarter of a million dolla from those diggings."

Jace waved his hand around the saloon, crowded with nois customers. "And most of it is here."

It had cost him a pretty penny, but it was the finest damned
tablishment in Silver Plume. The barroom was richly paneled,
ith gilt-edged mirrors and paintings around the walls, and the
aming tables were covered in green baize and surrounded by
oled-leather chairs. The pianist, brought direct from New
ork, plunked out his tunes on a Steinway, and the front win-
ws boasted more glass than any other saloon in town.

The dining room next door was even more elegant—pat-
rned inlaid floors and wainscoting, bronze nymphs on carved
edestals, lush floral paintings in soft colors. And, in the center
the room, surrounded by tables set with fine linen and china,
as a bubbling fountain. Jace's own suite of rooms upstairs
as as beautifully and expensively furnished—a restrained
astern style more at home in Boston than Colorado.

"You didn't stint, by jove," said Saint-James, casting an
miring glance around the room.

Jace shrugged. "I like my comforts." One of his dealers came
er to the table and stood politely, waiting to be acknowledged.
What is it, Bartlett?" he asked.

Bartlett crooked his thumb in the direction of the faro table,
hich was crowded with men. "Richards, there, is asking for
edit."

"How much has he dropped tonight?"

"Ten thousand."

Jace rubbed the scar over his brow. It always itched when
e weather turned hot. "Give him another five. But tell him
xpect him to pay off before he runs up debts anywhere else.
r he won't be allowed back at my tables." Bartlett nodded
d withdrew.

"You're a shrewd man, Greer," said Saint-James with a
oughtful gleam in his eye. "I wonder why you're ready to
ll. Is the vein about to pinch out?"

"Hell, man, I'm not cheating you. It's worth every penny
u'll pay for it. You saw it yourself. A vein of carbonate of
ad that carries forty ounces of silver to the ton. It doesn't get
uch richer than that."

"Then why would you sell it?"

"It costs me too much to send off the ore to be refined. You have your own works in Denver. You'll see a better profit than I do."

Saint-James leaned back in his chair and tapped his finger together. "A hundred and twenty, you say?"

"That's my hardpan price."

Saint-James studied his face for a moment, then laughed wryly. "By jove, there's no moving you, I see. I'll have to wire my board of directors, of course. But I think they'll agree It might take a few weeks for all the papers . . ."

"I can wait."

"It's a deal, then." Saint-James saluted him with his glass then downed the rest of his whiskey. "That's a capital drink sir. I couldn't get a finer one in Dublin."

"I have a taste for the good life," said Jace sardonically, "Must have been my upbringing."

They shook hands and Saint-James rose to go. "I still think you're a fool for selling."

Jace watched him amble out of the saloon, then stared gloom ily into his whiskey glass. *Was* he a fool? The mine had pro duced from the first day he'd dug his pick into the loose shale— high-grade silver that sold at a premium. And even after he' begun hard-rock mining, hiring workers at four dollars a da to blast tunnels into the mountain, there'd been no letup. Ther could still be a fortune in silver to be found.

Still, to be practical . . . His manager had begun to worr about the shafts and tunnels. They couldn't dynamite muc more without stopping to shore up what was already there. An a big company could do it better.

He lit another cigar and blew a smoke ring into the ai staring up at the crystal chandelier. He'd come a far piece i ten months. He could almost forget the long, cold, hardness o the winter, huddled in the shack he'd built on the sheer sid of Sherman Mountain. Every time the snow let up, he'd trudg through drifts, lugging his tools, and stop and clear a patc

herever he saw a bulge under the snow that seemed to be an
utcropping of stratified rock. Half the time it was just a stunted
ush or a granite boulder. It was backbreaking work, and he'd
nd himself sweating and gasping, feeling his lungs about to
urst from the lack of oxygen at that height.

And when he'd finally struck silver, he'd gone down to Silver
lume and registered his claim and bought himself an ore
agon and a pack mule, hauling the day's find to town every
vening and dragging himself back at dawn to dig once more.
le didn't ever want to go through that hell again.

But at least it had given him something to fill his days. Once
e'd hired a manager and a bunch of workers, he'd found the
xcitement of his find fading.

He laughed softly. Maybe that's why he wanted to sell. He
as just plain bored with the damned mine. The exhiliaration
f the search had fired his blood; the reality of owning a mine
eft him strangely disappointed, troubled by a hollowness in
ae pit of his stomach, the aching hunger that he'd never shaken.

He looked around the busy barroom. It was a novelty for
im, at least. He'd play with his new toy for a while. And, in
ae meantime, he'd have $120,000 in his safe, and time enough
o consider what he wanted to do next.

He pulled out his watch and flicked it open. Ten o'clock.
e felt too restless to sit in on a game of poker. Maybe he'd
o to his rooms, have some oysters and champagne sent up.
artlett could close up when the gamblers and drinkers finally
ot tired and decided to leave. Not for him a stable of whores
a the premises. Let the townsfolk carouse elsewhere through
ae night; he liked a few hours of quiet and peace.

Yes. Oysters and champagne. And a long, leisurely romp in
ed with Netta. He could feel his cock beginning to grow hard
the thought of it. He'd take his pleasure of her till the moon
t.

He looked at his watch again and felt a sharp and familiar
ang of remorse. If only he hadn't gambled that one night in
hicago. Wagstaff would never have been able to find him,

and maybe Big Jim would still be alive. He sighed. He reckoned he'd carry that guilt to the grave.

He turned over the watch and read the inscription for the hundredth time. "To my new son Jace. August 14, 1870. Welcome to the family." He swallowed hard. Son of a bitch, he was getting softer and more sentimental by the day! He'd never owned anything in his whole life that he couldn't part with. He'd lost more than one keepsake at a gambling table and never turned a hair. But he'd kill anyone who tried to take this watch.

He read the inscription again. August fourteenth. "Damn!" he muttered in surprise. That was only a few days away! Their first anniversary—his and Callie's.

Callie. Would she have the same regrets as he, when that day arrived? Would she think of the joy they'd shared, the laughing days, the magic nights? He hadn't heard much about her. Weedy was home, and working in the store. And Callie helped out. That much he'd learned from an old prospector who'd come over from Dark Creek. And there had been no annulment, as far as his lawyer could ascertain.

Callie. He leaned back and closed his eyes, seeing her once more in his visions. Those silver-green eyes, so filled with trust. The glory of her golden copper hair. The passion in her sweet kisses, her pliant body. He found himself torn between hope and despair, suddenly yearning to see her again. To start over fresh and new, and court her as he had in the past.

He groaned. But he'd killed her father and just about raped her that last night. She might not have forgotten him yet, but she sure as hell must hate him thoroughly. And all his fabled charm wouldn't win her back.

"You look tired, sugar. Come on up to bed, and Netta will take care of you."

He opened his eyes to the whore and felt his desire ebb. All her practiced arts couldn't make him forget her shallow greediness tonight. She might be just a convenient bit of calico to him, but he was simply a jack-at-a-pinch for her. A bankroll, and not much else.

He fished in his vest pocket, pulled out a hundred-dollar bill, and slapped it on the table.

Her eyes lit up. "Does my li'l old Jace want something special in bed tonight?" she drawled. She sat down on his lap and rubbed her hands suggestively against his chest.

He pushed her roughly away. "No," he growled. "I want you to go shopping in the morning. Buy yourself a few new dresses."

She took the bill and slipped it into her bosom. "You want to see me in anything in particular, sugar?"

His stomach churned at the coarseness of the woman. When had women like this stopped appealing to him? "Something *ladylike,* for Christ's sake," he muttered.

He must be out of his mind. Jace shivered and pulled up the collar of his oilskin coat, urging his horse forward along the muddy trail. The rain pelted his broad Stetson hat and dripped like a curtain six inches in front of his face. His trousers were soaked at the knees, and he could already feel the dampness through the toes of his boots.

He glanced up at the leaden sky. It would soon be dark. And if he was on a fool's errand, he'd have to make the three-hour trip home over treacherous trails in the pitch-black. Son of a gun, he hadn't even thought to bring a lantern!

He hadn't thought of *anything* that made sense these past few days. Only of Callie—and their anniversary. And every fresh thought had buoyed his hopes, finally sending him barreling out of the Philadelphia this gray afternoon and onto the trail for Dark Creek.

She hadn't annulled their marriage. Could she still care for him? Would he find her reading, sad and distracted, in the parlor tonight? Or weeping in her room—mourning this unhappy anniversary day as he did?

He could almost picture the scene. He'd take her in his arms, beg her forgiveness for all he'd done, comfort her grief. And then . . . hell! He knew how to make love to her, if nothing else. And when they were both feeling mellow and contented, he'd tell her that he wanted to try again. That his life just wasn't the same without her, no matter what he did.

He'd visit Big Jim's grave in the morning. He had always regretted not being there for the old man's funeral. And then he'd sit with Beth and Sissy and the others, before a warm fire. Back in the bosom of his family.

He prodded his horse and began to whistle, heedless of the rain on his face, the cold drizzle that worked its way under his collar. Hell's bells, he wouldn't need a lantern tonight after all!

It was dark when he finally saw the Southgate house, down the gulch. The windows were bright with lamplight, and a plume of smoke came from the chimney. They would have eaten supper by now, but maybe good old Mrs. Ackland had something for him in the pantry. Perhaps even one of her special berry pies.

He shivered. It was raining harder now, with a cold wind that came down from the peaks and cut through his clothing. It felt more like October than August. But unless Callie had gone "temperance" with a vengeance, there would be blood-warming whiskey from Big Jim's supply.

He guided his horse carefully in the dark, trying to still the rising excitement in his breast. How he'd missed them! All of them. Missed the warm routine his life had become, in the brief months he'd spent in this house. He found himself grinning, rehearsing the words he'd say, imagining his welcome from the children, Callie's impassioned kisses.

But the closer he drew to the house, the more his uneasiness grew. Perhaps Callie's sadness had turned to anger by now, and she viewed this anniversary as the occasion for venting her rage. He *had* walked out on her, after all, though he'd known in his heart it was what she wanted.

Maybe he'd look in at a window first. If he knew her mood, he could more easily shape his own behavior. He approached the house from the back, climbed down from the saddle, and walked his horse around to the parlor windows on the side.

He saw Sissy first, seated on the carpet, happily playing with her blocks. My God, how much she'd grown! She must be four by now. His funny little Sissy, who'd bedeviled him for such a long time.

He edged closer to the window. There was Beth, standing by the piano. She'd sprouted two inches, at least, and her rounded child's face had begun to take on the subtle contours of budding womanhood. She'd be a beauty, one of these days. Just like her sister. She seemed to be singing, though the tattoo of the rain around him drowned out the sound.

And then he saw Callie at the piano, and his heart thumped wildly in his chest. His memories hadn't done her justice. She was blooming, with a lush roundness to her figure that only heightened her loveliness. The somber black of her dress only served to accentuate her striking coloring; her hair seemed to shimmer in the lamplight. The golden glow bathed him with warmth, driving away the chill of the rain.

Callie finished the song, closed her book, and rose from the piano bench. It took him a moment—watching her cross to a table to pour out a cup of coffee—before he realized that she didn't have her cane. Her steps were slow, punctuated with pauses, but she was walking unaided.

Oh, Cal! he thought, bursting with pride. *Good for you!*

He couldn't get enough of looking at her. So serene, so self-assured, as though she'd finally put Mousekin to rest. He'd expected to find her sad. But the sight of her, content with her family, was even more heartening. Forgiveness might come easier for her if she wasn't still harboring resentment against him.

And then a sturdy figure came into Jace's line of view and he muttered a curse. Ralph Driscoll! What the hell was he doing here? And on *this* day, of all days?

Driscoll moved to Beth, smiled at her, patted her on the head. Beth ducked her head, and turned away shyly, twisting her fingers in her pinafore. Jace fought the urge to break through the window and smash the man's face. Beth was *his* little princess! Did that bastard Driscoll know how to play silly games with her?

Driscoll bent to Sissy, picked her up, and gave her a big kiss. The little girl threw her pudgy arms around his neck and kissed him back. Jace wanted to die. *But Sissy loves Jace,* he thought, anguished, remembering that morning in the parlor. Clearly the memory had faded for Sissy, as transient as the flowers that had bloomed in the meadow last summer.

Callie put down her coffee and picked up Driscoll's hat and coat from a chair near the door. She handed them to him with a smile, watched him dress for the weather, straightened the edge of his coat collar for him.

When they vanished from Jace's sight into the vestibule, he crept around the side of the house to watch the veranda. Driscoll's horse was tethered there, tossing its head to shake off the rain. Jace felt like a Peeping Tom, watching in dread for something he didn't want to see.

The door opened. Callie and Driscoll were silhouetted in the doorway; Jace could hear the murmur of their voices. Then Driscoll leaned over and kissed her firmly on the mouth. Jace covered his eyes with his hand and groaned.

He heard the sound of Driscoll's horse fading into the night. He turned away from the house and groped for his own horse's reins. He had seen enough. He scrambled into the saddle, turned his animal toward the trail. His heart was as cold and bleak as the night.

Why should she mourn? Why should *any* of them need or miss a knockabout like Jace Greer? He'd been an outsider from the first, fooling himself into thinking he'd found a family at last. Well, what the hell. He'd been alone all his life. It was nothing he wasn't used to.

But . . . *Sissy loves Jace.* He groaned again, filled with a new and sharp awareness. And Jace loved Sissy—and Beth and Weedy. And *Callie. Oh God, yes, Callie!* He'd never loved before. But they'd crept softly into his heart, like a morning mist invading the gulch. Silently occupied the empty place that he'd lived with forever.

He should have known he loved her. He should have realized—every time the sight of her made his heart sing. How often had he kissed her, when he could have said the words? How many opportunities had he let pass him by? And now it was too late.

He made his way up the trail in the pouring rain. And soon the cold drops on his face were joined by scalding tears.

Chapter Twenty-Five

"Why do I have to let him pat me on the head? I *hate* it!" Beth tore a bright orange leaf from the cottonwood tree and savagely ripped it to shreds.

The soft September breeze caught at Callie's hair and blew a curl across her cheek. She brushed it away and sighed. "I expect you to be civil to Mr. Driscoll when he arrives."

Beth pouted. "Even when he calls me missy? Dang my britches, it's just plain stupid!"

Callie rolled her eyes. She was glad Beth was finally getting some of her old spunk back, but the child who was emerging from her gloom had a sharp edge that the old Beth had lacked. Perhaps it was her way of dealing with Big Jim's death and the loss of Jace, but she tried Callie's patience as she never had before.

And Ralph seemed to view her the same way. More than once, in the past few weeks when he'd visited, he'd gently chided Callie for allowing the child to run wild. She knew he didn't mean it as a criticism, of course, but it made her feel helpless nonetheless.

She managed a bright smile and tweaked Beth's nose. "Now, pet, let me see a cheery face. It's a beautiful day for a picnic. Don't spoil it by pouting." She chewed at her lip, hearing her own words. She'd promised herself not to be "Miss Don't" with Beth.

"It would be more fun if he weren't coming. Just you and me and Sissy. He's *always* here."

"Mr. Driscoll has been a good friend to us." And a welcome companion, she thought, now that she wasn't going in to the store. He'd helped her while away many a lonely afternoon, reading aloud to her or lending a hand with little chores around the house. "And it was gracious of him to invite us on a picnic today," she added. "And on such a glorious Sunday morning."

The day was indeed beautiful. August had been a dreadful month: days of suffocating heat, then drenching rains that weighed on her spirit. And the last heavy rain, in the middle of the month, had brought with it a cold spell that had persisted for weeks. The trees had turned color overnight, and the delicate meadow blossoms had withered.

But September had come in on a zephyr, sweet and mild, smelling of pine smoke and crackling autumn leaves. The sun beamed down from a crystal blue sky. It reminded Callie of Jace's eyes.

No! she thought suddenly. She'd promised herself she wouldn't think of him again. Ever since the night of their anniversary, when she'd blithely kissed Ralph good night, then wept in her bed for hours, recalling Jace. *I've shed enough tears over him,* she thought.

Mrs. Ackland came out of the house, carrying Little Jim in his basket. She put it on the table under the tree. "I thought the wee one could take his morning nap out here," she said, "while I peel apples for the pies. We can both enjoy the fresh air."

Callie pulled back the edge of the blanket and gently stroked the side of her baby's face. He slept in blissful innocence, his shock of black hair curling sweetly over his forehead. Nearly

wo months, and her heart still swelled with the wonder of this
iny, precious creature. *If only Poppy had lived to see him.*

"Did he take his nursing bottle?" she asked. It had taken
her little more than a week to realize that her breasts could
never supply him with enough nourishment. A small goat had
been installed in a penned-up corner of the stable; Mrs. Ackland
milked it every morning.

"Land sakes, yes!" exclaimed the housekeeper. "Gobbled
it down. Every blessed drop. He has the appetite of his . . ."
She stopped and looked uncertainly toward Beth. "Dearie,"
she said with a smile, "fetch that bowl of apples from the
kitchen for me. And see that Sissy is still sleepin'. That's a
good girl."

Callie watched Beth skip into the house. "I wonder if she'll
ever forgive him," she said with a sigh.

Mrs. Ackland snorted. "No more'n you. 'Tain't right that
he doesn't know he has a son."

"I'm sure he doesn't care," she said stiffly. "Besides, the
father's name is Jace *Perkins*. It says so on his birth registra-
ion."

"Don't you split hairs with me, missus. You're still sittin'
on the fence, and you know it!"

She could scarcely deny that. Not when she still dreamed of
Jace, despite her resolve to forget him. She gave a wry laugh.
"Well, Ralph is certainly pushing hard enough to get me off
that fence."

The housekeeper nodded. "He's taken a shine to you. Any
blamed fool can see that. Do you fancy him?"

"I don't know. He's kind. And good company. And he keeps
saying he can arrange a quiet divorce for me, now that we
know where Jace is. His lawyer could fix it without my ever
having to see Jace." She laughed uneasily. "He keeps talking
about making an honest woman of me. As though Jace's deser-
ion had somehow soiled my reputation. But it would be nice
o rely on a man again."

Mrs. Ackland brushed a fallen leaf from Little Jim's basket

and settled herself in a nearby chair. "Then do it, if you're set on it. He's rich enough to keep you well."

Callie found her own chair and sat. Despite her growing mobility, her hip sometimes troubled her if she stood for too long. "I don't know," she said. She still had a thirst for independence, a lingering wariness of a man's domination. "He'd want me to give up the shop, stay at home to care for the little ones. Just as I've begun to enjoy it." She was already looking forward to going back to the store next week.

"Weedy can still run it."

She shook her head. "How can I depend on him? He's getting wilder and wilder. These last few months, since my confinement . . . Most of the time, it's Billy Dee who keeps things going. I can see by the account books that we're losing money. Weedy seems to be spending most of his time with that . . . woman of his."

Mrs. Ackland shrugged. "Well, there's worse things than a half-breed."

"That's not the part that disturbs me." She stared morosely at the sky, beset anew by her worries.

"My land! Don't go mopin' on such a fine day." Mrs. Ackland smiled as Beth came out of the house, carrying a large bowl of apples. "Thank you, dearie." She chose a round, shiny one and held it out to the little girl. "I reckon I can spare one."

Beth grinned and crunched into the apple.

"Is Weedy comin' on the picnic with you?" asked Mrs. Ackland.

Callie hesitated. She didn't really want to answer in front of Beth. "No," she said at last. "He came in late and we quarreled last night. As usual. He doesn't much like Ralph. All he talks about is Jace. How rich he must be, what a good friend he was. Do you know he even threatened to go and live with him? And then I'd be sorry, he said."

"Bosh! That's just big talk. He's feelin' his oats, is all. He wouldn't leave."

Beth frowned and stopped her munching. "But I reckon he *did.*"

"Did what?" asked Callie in alarm.

"Go to Jace. I heard a noise this morning, before the sun was up, and peeked out the window. It was Weedy, making a straight shirttail for the stable. With his valise and everything."

"Mercy sakes! Why didn't you tell us?"

Beth looked bewildered. "Well, I was so sleepy. I thought it was a dream. But I reckon it really happened. His hat wasn't on the peg near the door just now."

Callie jumped up from her chair. "Dear heaven, I must go after him, before he does something foolish! I'll go upstairs to change. Can you saddle Milkweed, Mrs. Ackland?"

"Land sakes! What'll I tell Mr. Driscoll when he gets here?"

Her head was spinning. Too many thoughts. Too many confused emotions crowding in. "Tell him I've gone to find Weedy," she said impatiently.

"At Mr. Jace's?"

She groaned. She had enough complications in her life without worrying about Ralph's jealousy if he knew she was going to Jace. "No. Just tell him Weedy's run away, and I've gone to fetch him back."

Mrs. Ackland shook her head. "You must be tetched. I think the whole notion is ruinacious. I surely do!"

"Philadelphia Saloon. Jace Greer, prop.," read the sign.

Callie rode past closed shops and busy barrooms, and reined in Milkweed before the false front of a large, sturdy, clapboard building. It had wide plate-glass windows and a double door with a fanlight, and the elaborately lettered sign above was striking without being gaudy.

Jace certainly had a finely developed sense of taste, thought Callie, remembering his impeccable style of dress, his refined manners, his familiarity with good food, wine, furniture.

Despite his checkered background, he surely had had high-toned beginnings. She need have no fear for Little Jim's lineage.

Still, she was almost sorry that his establishment was so elegant. She felt intimidated and self-conscious stepping up to the door. Her riding habit, which she hadn't worn for months, fit her newly rounded figure rather too snugly to be ladylike, and it was covered with dust and still smelled of camphor from its months of storage. Moreover, she'd lost her hat to an overhanging branch on her ride, and her hair was windblown and tangled. Her stomach churned uneasily: Mrs. Ackland had given her a lunch of bread and cheese, which she'd gulped hastily in the high mountain canyon just outside of Silver Plume.

She took a deep breath to give herself courage and went through the door. After all, why should she care how she looked? She was here to find Weedy, not to charm Jace.

The interior of Jace's saloon was even more grand than the outside. Except for the knots of spurred and booted men around the gaming tables, and the pall of cigar smoke that hung in the air, it could be a respectable drinking establishment in Boston. Though of course men wouldn't gamble or drink on a Sunday in *Boston*. But the few women in the place, chatting at the bar with patrons, or leaning over the gamblers' shoulders to watch them play, seemed a shade less garish than the creatures she encountered in Dark Creek. Thank heaven Jace didn't run a brothel as well!

She made her way toward the bar, conscious that her nervousness exaggerated her slight limp. But the barkeep looked friendly—a heavyset man with a weather-beaten, honest face. "I'm looking for Mr. Greer," she said.

He raised his voice and called to one of the women at the end of the long bar. "Netta. Someone here looking for Jace."

The woman strutted toward Callie, eyeing her up and down with distaste. She had a seductive figure, raven hair elaborately dressed, and the most beautiful features Callie had ever seen.

ler gown was clearly expensive, and the drops at her ears were
f finely chased gold. "Who wants to know?" she drawled.

Callie was painfully aware of how she herself must look.
Cinderella among the ashes, next to a beautiful stepsister. She
ound herself blushing. "I'm . . . I'm a friend," she stammered.
'But I must see Jace."

The woman snorted. "You don't look like the sort of friend
e'd choose." She jerked her thumb toward the staircase at the
ack of the room. "He's still asleep."

The large enameled clock behind the bar showed nearly two.
"At this hour?" said Callie in surprise. "He never slept so
ate when . . ." She stopped, feeling her blush deepen.

Netta's eyes flickered with sudden jealousy. "I reckon I
now how he sleeps, sugar."

Callie's heart sank. There could be no misunderstanding the
voman's words. "Would it be possible to wake him?" she
aid, barely above a whisper.

The woman smiled smugly and patted her curls. "I don't
now, sugar. Jace has been a li'l old devil these past few weeks,
porting all night long until I don't know *what's* gotten into
im!"

Callie winced and forced herself to think of Weedy. That
vas why she was here. "Please," she begged, burning with
umiliation.

"Callie?"

She turned at the familiar voice, feeling a thrill of remem-
rance. He was even more handsome than she recalled, with
n air of polish and a proud arrogance in his bearing that hadn't
een there before. The successful man, with all the money he
eeded.

"What are you doing here?" he said coldly.

She noticed the scar above his brow, where she'd struck him
hat night. Her lingering guilt only added to her distress. "It's
Veedy," she said, her voice quivering. "He's gone."

He raised a mocking eyebrow. "Can't Driscoll find him?"

That bewildered her. "Why should I ask him to? Weedy's

always talking about you. He saw the article in the paper months ago. And he threatened to run away to you. I felt sure that . . .'' She was too devastated to go on. Weedy was gone, and Jace hated her. She could see it in his eyes.

He motioned to the barkeep. ''Give the lady a drink. A big one.''

''Oh, but I . . .''

''Drink it!'' he ordered, handing her the glass. ''When did he leave?''

''Probably before six this morning.'' The whiskey soothed her and calmed her nerves.

''Sweeney,'' he said to the barkeep, ''did a young man come in here this morning asking for me? Reddish brown hair. Tall. Fifteen, and looks it.''

''Sixteen,'' Callie corrected.

Jace looked disconcerted at that. ''Of course,'' he muttered.

Sweeney frowned. ''Jeez, Jace. I didn't know you were upstairs. I kinder thought you were at the mine, cleaning out your gear. That's what I told him.''

Jace smacked his hand on the bar. ''You sent him to the mine? I closed it a week ago. Before I even sold it. Those beams are ready to give way.''

Callie stared in horror. ''And Weedy went there?''

''We'll find him,'' he growled. ''Sweeney, you were a pretty fair miner in your time. Can Charlie take over for you here?''

''Sure, Jace.''

''Good. Get my horse. And one for yourself. I want you with me in case there's trouble.''

Netta pouted and put her hand on Jace's arm. ''But you promised to take me for a stroll down Main Street this afternoon, sugar.''

He glanced at Callie, hesitated, then deliberately kissed Netta full on the mouth. ''I'll be back in a while, honey.'' He smiled at her. ''You're looking mighty pert in that dress.'' He glanced at Callie once more, his eyes turning to ice. ''I assume you want to come with us.''

Her heart was in splinters. "Yes," she whispered. "Milkweed is outside."

They made their way up the mountainside in strained silence,
Jace leading the way, Sweeney bringing up the rear. They
passed half a dozen shafts and tunnels, where giant mounds of
mine tailings corrupted the beauty of the slope and bore witness
to the systematic rape of the countryside.

At last they came to a crude shack, nestled against a hill.
Beside it was the opening to a tunnel, with the words "Trimble
Silver Mine" scrawled on a plank above the entrance.

Callie gasped, pointing to a gelding near the mine. "That's
Weedy's horse!"

Jace gestured toward the shack. "Sweeney, see if the kid is
in there. If not, find a lantern." While Sweeney went to the
cabin, Jace dismounted and held out his arms to help Callie
down.

She had forgotten the feel of him, the warm strength that
made her feel protected. His hard length pressing so close to
hers. Her body trembled as she looked into his eyes. But there
was nothing there except icy hostility. "I don't need your
support," she said stiffly.

He dropped his arms. "I see you don't use your cane anymore."

She thought of his intimacy with Netta. "A year can bring
many changes," she said bitterly. "You've finally found your
dream."

He nodded. "It was time." He looked toward Sweeney, who
had emerged from the cabin carrying a lantern. "Let's go in."

The tunnel was dry, with a dustiness in the air that made
Callie cough. She saw the anxious looks that passed between
Jace and Sweeney, and frowned. "What is it?"

Sweeney clicked his tongue. "The shaft don't usually kick
up dust like this less'n there's been a cave-in."

"Don't go spooking the lady," growled Jace, as Callie stared
in alarm.

They made their cautious way along the tunnel, guided by

the golden glow of the lantern. The walls were rough-hewn, and supported here and there by sturdy beams. Between the thin mountain air and the dust, which seemed to grow thicker as they progressed, Callie found breathing difficult. More than once, Jace stopped to let her rest, though she protested she wasn't helpless.

They came at last to a divide in the tunnel. Sweeney pointed to one fork, dense with choking dust. "The cave-in's that way. If we take a look, the lady shouldn't come. Too dangerous."

"Damn right," agreed Jace. "Wait here," he said, pointing to a spot on the tunnel floor.

"No!" she said, raising her voice in anger. A domineering husband was bad enough. But to take orders from a man who consorted with a woman like *that* one was more than she could endure. "I'll go with you!" she cried. Her shrill words bounced off the stone of the tunnel walls and echoed in the gloom.

From somewhere beyond the cloud of dust came a quavering voice. "C-Callie?"

"Oh, my God, that's Weedy," she whispered.

"Come on, then," grumbled Jace, holding tight to her hand. "There'll be no keeping you away."

The dust was like a thick fog as they made their way through the tunnel, guiding themselves as much by the feel of the walls as by the light of the lantern, which penetrated only a few feet. Jace called out to Weedy, and grunted in satisfaction when they heard a faint response.

They turned a sudden corner and saw a flickering light. Callie could just make out Weedy's form, buried among a jumble of rocks. Near him was a sputtering lantern. She dropped to her knees beside him. "Are you hurt?"

He lay on his face, his back and legs covered with debris and splintered beams. The tunnel beyond him was half filled with boulders. He lifted his head and gave her a thin smile. "I sprained my ankle when the walls started to give way. I couldn' un fast enough. And now I can't move. But I don't think nything's broken." He looked up at Jace. "By jingo, I'm glad o see you!"

"Lie still. Sweeney and I will try to dig you out. But the haft could go at any time."

Sweeney set the lantern on the floor and rolled up his sleeves. ace reached for a rock and lifted it from Weedy's legs, then notioned to Sweeney. "Let's see if we can lift this beam."

Callie watched them as they worked, clasping her hands ogether in concern. The task seemed to take forever. They runted and strained—pushing aside debris, moving rocks, pry-ng beams out of the way—and gasped in the choking dust. As they removed the last rock from Weedy's legs, Callie heard n ominous creaking from the tunnel beyond.

"There goes the rest of it," muttered Jace. He dragged Weedy to his feet and threw him against Sweeney. "Help him out of here. Cal, pick up that lantern."

She barely had time to snatch it up before Jace scooped her nto his arms. He raced for safety, calling back to Sweeney to be sure he was following with Weedy. They could hear the rash and rumble of the tunnel walls behind them as they umbled out of the mine entrance into the bright sunshine. There was a final earth-shuddering roar, and a large cloud of dust uffed out of the opening.

Jace set Callie on her feet and wiped the grime and sweat rom his face. "Saint-James isn't going to like the mess we eft him!" he said with a wry laugh. He turned to Weedy, who at on the ground, still stunned and shaking. "We'll get you ack to town pronto. Can you sit your horse?"

Weedy wiggled his foot and grimaced. "It's only my ankle. don't reckon it's broken. But I sure could use something to at and drink. And a rest, first. I'm plumb worn-out from trying o get loose." He looked at Jace, his eyes bright with gratitude. 'I was scared! It felt like hours, and the lantern was ready to lie."

"You were a damn fool," said Jace gruffly. "Scaring you sister like that. You might have been killed." He looked toward the cabin. "There's a cot inside. As long as you don't need doctor in a hurry, we could wait until you sleep a spell." H lifted Weedy easily in his arms and started for the cabin. " don't know if there's water inside. Sweeney, get the cantee from my saddlebag."

Callie felt helpless, shaking with relief, but useless to he brother with Jace here. "I still have some bread and cheese," she said, turning toward Milkweed. At least there was *something* she could do.

While Sweeney found the canteen, she pulled out the remain of her lunch. She glanced at the man beside her. Except fo the dust on his face, and a few scratches on his hands and arms he looked as serene as though he'd just come from a picnic "Didn't that frighten you?"

Sweeney gave a hearty laugh. "Jeez, ma'am, me and Jac have been through worse than that. We was oncet nearly blow to kingdom come by a dynamite blast. Hell, I could hav spent the rest of my life working at the digging, if Jace hadn convinced me I was safer as a barkeep."

They made their way to the cabin. Jace had left the doo ajar. Callie stepped over the threshold and choked on a scream dropping her package from limp hands. Behind her she coul hear Sweeney grunt in anger.

Jace lay on the floor unconscious, blood streaming from cut on his head. Weedy sat huddled in the center of the room his dusty face white with fear, his body shaking all over.

Behind them stood a smiling man, holding a large pistol i each hand. He was of medium height, slender and wiry, wit beady black eyes that moved restlessly around the room an came to light on Callie and Sweeney.

"Come in, folks," he said. "No call to hang back." H looked down at Jace's inert form and laughed. "Sashayed righ in, he did, like a bug into a spider's web." He kicked Jace' egs savagely. ''Like a big, money-grubbin', back-stabbin' bug. Me and Ben is been lookin' fer this son of a bitch fer more'n a year.''

Callie's heart sank. This had to be Ethan Wagstaff, and none other.

Chapter Twenty-Six

Callie glared at Ethan Wagstaff. "In the name of pity, why can't I see to Jace's injury?" She looked toward Jace, sitting groggily in a chair, his hands and feet firmly tied with rope, his face covered with blood. She bit her lip, surveying Sweeney and Weedy similarly tied to chairs. If Wagstaff hadn't been holding a pistol to her temple at every moment, she couldn't have forced herself to help him tie up the men.

Ethan laughed. "Sweet on him, ain't you? But I reckon Jace has suffered worse. And done to others." He brandished his pistol at Callie. "Don't go near him."

"At least let me tend my brother," she pleaded. "He was caught in a cave-in. He hasn't had anything to eat or drink all day."

Wagstaff nodded reluctantly. "I ain't got no quarrel with the kid. But no tricks. Hear?"

Callie retrieved the canteen and the food packet, and contrived to feed Weedy as best she could, breaking off small bites of the bread and cheese and drizzling the water into his dry mouth. She smoothed back his dust-covered hair. "Don't lose heart," she whispered.

Jace shook his head and swore softly, fighting to focus his eyes. "Jesus, Ethan, you damn near broke my skull."

"It was a pleasure, old buddy." Ethan chuckled. "Damn, but it does a man good to set his peepers on you once again."

"Can't say I share your sentiment," said Jace dryly.

"And you're gettin' soft, buddy. What's happened to that Colt of yourn, and that fancy holster?"

"I didn't think we'd find rattlesnakes in these mountains."

"Now, Jace, that ain't sociable of you. After all the trouble I went to, to find you."

"I never set much store by your brainpower, Ethan. How did you manage it?"

Ethan scowled. "Don't give me your sass. Not when I got a bead on you. But it was that thing in the paper that done did it. Jace Greer and his Philadelphia Saloon. Hell, you left a callin' card a blind man could find."

"I thought you'd quit mousing around by now."

"Not me. Ben, mebbe. I lost track of him nigh on to a year ago. Probably whorin' it up in some cow town, forgettin' his brother, like he always done. Mebbe he even cashed in by now."

Jace shrugged. "No great loss. The son of a bitch deserved it for killing that banker."

"I don't give a tinker's damn. When I'm rich, he can go to hell. He'd do the same fer me."

"Brotherly loyalty," said Jace with a sneer. "I always knew there was something about you two I liked."

Wagstaff growled. "Don't go high-handin' me, buddy. come fer my money. I hear tell you're mighty rich now."

Jace looked bored. "Rich enough. You want your five thousand? You can have it."

"Hold on just a dog-boned minute. Mebbe I want a bonus after all this time." He crossed to where Callie still stood near Weedy, and grabbed her around the waist. "I always did fancy

our women, Jace. None of 'em never give me a tumble when
ou was around.''

Callie struggled in his hold, cringing at the feel of his rough
and, the smell of his breath.

Jace wrenched his body against his ropes, his eyes glittering
vith rage. ''Get your hands off her!''

Wagstaff laughed and pulled Callie back against his chest,
unning his hand up her bodice to clutch her breast. She squealed
n dismay and felt the cold barrel of his pistol against her
emple. ''I can take you dead or alive, girlie,'' he growled in
er ear. ''It's up to you.''

Jace's face had turned white. ''What do you want?'' he said
n a rasping voice. ''Name it. But let go of the girl!''

Ethan released Callie and laughed again. ''What do I want?
everythin' you got.''

Jace sighed and leaned his head back against his chair, closing
is eyes for a moment. ''Will I have your word not to touch
er?'' He glared at Wagstaff with burning eyes.

Wagstaff scratched the stubble on his chin. ''I reckon so.
Vhat's the deal?''

Jace searched his face for a minute, then nodded. ''You were
lways good for your word, Ethan,'' he said. ''Can't say the
ame for Ben.''

Wagstaff grinned. ''Ben were always a snake in the grass.
3ut what's the deal?''

''If I give you what you want, I want your word you'll light
ut for Wyoming or California. And never show your ugly
nug in Colorado again.''

''Fer enough money, I reckon I could melt away like the
now.''

Jace looked at Weedy and Sweeney, then allowed his gaze
o linger on Callie's face. ''And you won't harm any of us.
especially not the girl.''

''You got my word. But I don't want no tricks.''

''My word is good, too. You know that.''

''I reckon I do. I won't touch no woman of yourn.''

Jace gave a nonchalant laugh. "Hell, she's not my woman. I was just helping her find her brother in the mine. But there's no call for her to be mixed up in this. Let her go to town to get the money."

Wagstaff snickered. "What a damn liar you are, Jace. I seen the way you look at her. You think I'm as dumb as Ben? The minute she's safe away, you'll do somethin' crazy. I reckon she's my best insurance. She stays till the deal is done. *You* can go, old buddy."

"I'm not as dumb as Ben either. You may be a man of your word, but not when your cock is involved." He jerked his chin in Sweeney's direction. "Untie my man. He can go."

"Well . . ." Wagstaff looked doubtfully at Sweeney. "I don't want no half-cracked heroics."

Sweeney scowled. "I'll do whatever Mr. Greer tells me to do."

"Right," said Jace. "Don't get the sheriff. And don't tell anyone. Just go to my rooms. There's a safe behind the picture over the bed. They key is here, in my vest pocket."

Ethan grinned. "You're a good man, old pal. I knew I could depend on you."

Jace cast him a contemptuous look, then addressed Sweeney once more. "There's one hundred fifty thousand in the safe. Get it, and come right back here with it."

Sweeney's jaw dropped. "Jeez, Jace, ain't that all you got?"

"What of it? I want this bastard far away. For good and all I don't want to look over my shoulder the rest of my life. Or worry that Callie might be harmed."

Ethan had been licking his lips in anticipation of his windfall. Now he narrowed his eyes at Jace. "Hold on. He won't bring me no package of queer, will he?"

"No. They're the real shiners."

Still holding his pistol on the alert, Wagstaff pulled a bowie knife from his belt at the small of his back and cut Sweeney's ropes. He watched, with suspicious eyes, as Sweeney found the safe key in Jace's pocket and went to the door. "I don't want

o slip-ups,'' he warned. "I'll be watchin' from the window. If
even smell trouble, I'll cut her throat faster'n you can say
ack Robinson. And take her tits fer a souvenir.''

Sweeney turned back to Jace, a worried frown on his face.
"Are you serious about the amount, Mr. Greer?''

Jace gaved a tired sigh. "It's only money, man. Now get
he hell out of here.''

When Sweeney had gone, Wagstaff forced Callie into his
hair, facing Jace, and tied her with fresh rope. He gave a sly
augh. "Now you two lovebirds can watch each other.''

Callie blushed and looked around the cabin—anything to
void Jace's intense gaze. Besides the chairs and a cot, the
hack contained a rickety table and a small fireplace. The room
vas crowded with supplies a miner might need to see him
hrough a long winter—foods in tins, prospecting tools, gun-
owder, and a box of dynamite with blasting caps. She frowned,
vatching Wagstaff light up a cigarillo. If she could somehow
vork her chair over to the gunpowder . . . She threw Jace a
onspiratorial glance.

He scowled back. "Don't do anything foolish. It's not worth
our life.'' There was a gentleness in his voice, despite his
ark look.

She felt her heart quicken, felt the anguish of the last few
nonths fading away. Nothing had changed. She still loved him,
nd everything he'd done today had shown her he felt the same.
Even the defiant kiss to Netta had been the action of a man
vho feared to have his tender emotions trampled. And to give
way all he owned to save her . . . ! "Jace,'' she said softly.
"About the money.''

"That's my worry, not yours,'' he muttered.

"Shut up!'' barked Ethan. "Or I'll put a button or two on
our lips.''

Callie sagged in her chair. She was exhausted, drained of
motion. When this dreadful ordeal was over, perhaps she and
ace could talk.

The time seemed to drag. The sun hung low, filling the cabin

with an amber light. Callie's head drooped and her eyelid:
fluttered with the need for sleep. She sighed. Perhaps a few
minutes . . .

"Not a peep, girlie." Callie was awakened by the feel o
cold steel at her throat, and the grating voice of Wagstaff behind
her. Jace sat stiffly in his chair, his shoulders taut, his jaw
working furiously. Even Weedy had roused himself from hi:
torpor to prick up his ears.

Callie tried to draw back from the knife at her neck. "Wha
are you doing?" she said with a gasp of alarm.

"Shut yer trap," growled Wagstaff. "I seen Jace's mar
comin' up the trail. You better pray he ain't got the law wit
him."

"Jace!" Sweeney's voice called from outside the door
"Everything okay in there? I ain't coming in less'n you're
safe."

"Come ahead," said Jace. "We're all in one piece."

Sweeney came in. Alone. In his hand he gripped a larg
sack. "Stop right there," barked Ethan.

"Was there trouble?" asked Jace.

Sweeney shook his head. "They was all too busy with th
faro. Richards was working on a bundle. And Netta was havin;
a conniption fit 'cause you're gone, is all."

Jace stiffened. "Damn! She wasn't suspicious, was she?
don't fancy a posse right about now. Not with my friend ove
there so ready to kill."

Sweeney snorted. "Suspicious? No. But she sure as hell wa
jealous."

Ethan moved away from Callie and pointed his pistol a
Sweeney. "Drop the sack right there. You wasn't so stupid a
to bring a gun, was you?"

Sweeney spread his arms and sneered at Wagstaff. "Yo
can search me if you want."

"You ain't worth the trouble. Turn around." As Sweene:
obeyed, a perplexed frown on his face, Wagstaff raised the bu

of his pistol and gave the man a savage blow across the back of his head. Sweeney crumpled.

"You bastard," muttered Jace.

Ethan scurried to the sack and scooped it up. He plunged in a hand and came up with a fistful of bills. "Son of a bitch!" he gloated, "if you're not a man of your word, old buddy!"

"Then keep *your* word, and make tracks out of here," snarled Jace. "I swear, on your mother's miserable grave, if I ever see your face again in this life, I'll blow your head off your shoulders."

Wagstaff grinned. "No call to be ornery. I reckon we're quits." He tied up the sack and slung it over one shoulder. "Fer this kinda tin, you won't never hear another peep from Ethan Wagstaff." He swaggered to the door, turned, and gave a mocking bow. "So long, old buddy. I'm sure gonna miss your style." Then he was gone.

Jace muttered a string of curses and fought at his ropes. He puffed in exasperation and stared at Sweeney, still lying motionless on the floor. "Come on, man," he said. Raising the chair behind him, he managed at length to scrape and bounce across the floor to Sweeney. He stretched out a booted foot and prodded the other man gently. "Get up, Sweeney, for Christ's sake."

The room was nearly in darkness before Sweeney groaned and stirred, pulling himself painfully to his feet. He rubbed the back of his head and grimaced. "Jeez, what hit me?" He looked around the room. "Is he gone?" At Jace's nod, Sweeney wobbled toward the door. "I'll ride for the sheriff."

"No! I gave my word. And the bastard's probably long gone by now. Just free us. And light the lanterns."

Sweeney untied Jace, then moved unsteadily to Weedy. Jace was at Callie's side in a minute, working furiously at her bonds. He lifted her to her feet and held her for a moment, his eyes dark with concern. "Are you all right?"

"Just a bit stiff and shaken," she said. She glanced toward her brother, who was attempting with little success to stand on his sprained ankle. He gave up at last and sank onto the cot. His face was pale and drawn. "But Weedy looks dreadful."

Jace grunted. "And Sweeney looks worse. Staggering like a drunkard. He could have a concussion."

She reached up and stroked his blood-covered face. "You don't look much better yourself," she said with a gentle smile. It felt so comfortable to be in his arms. So natural.

He shuddered at her touch and released her. "My head is used to it," he said gruffly. The scar above his brow gleamed pale in the light.

She swallowed hard. "Jace, about that night," she began.

The eyes that focused on hers had turned cool and distant. "It was long ago. And we have more serious concerns." He turned toward the others. "It's already dark out. And the two of you aren't fit to ride. I propose we stay here for the night. There are tins of food on that shelf, and plenty of blankets. Callie will take the cot. I reckon we can pad the floor enough to make it comfortable for the rest of us."

While Jace built a fire, Callie found a roll of bandages and bound Weedy's ankle. They heated cans of beans, found a pot, and brewed up coffee. They ate in silence. Weedy was already nodding from exhaustion, and Sweeney was too lethargic to do more than just pick at his supper.

Jace pushed away his plate and stood up, reaching for a lantern. "There's a creek out back," he said. "I'll water the horses and bed them down, then bring back a bucket of water for the morning." He pulled a pail from a shelf.

Callie stood up in her turn, smoothing her riding habit. "I think I need a few minutes of privacy outside," she said delicately. "I'll go when you come back."

"We'll go together," he said. "I don't want you wandering this mountain alone at night." He took her by the elbow and steered her out the door.

"Mercy sakes!" she said, shaking off his hand. "This is quite improper!"

His mouth quirked in a smile. "Cal, honey, after all we've

been through, don't you think I know you're a living, breathing human being? With human needs, like the rest of us?''

She covered her answering smile. Her prudery was absurd, after the intimacies they had shared.

They walked in the direction of the mine. Then Jace set the lantern in a clearing. ''You can go behind those bushes,'' he said, ''while I tend the horses. Then we'll fetch the water.''

In a few minutes, they were picking their way along a narrow path toward the creek. The night was cool and clear, and the half-moon hung like a bright letter D in the sky. The wind sighed through the evergreens with a gentle murmur, and the scents of the pine and the smoke from the cabin hearth blended into a heady perfume that intoxicated Callie's senses. She felt a surge of tenderness toward Jace. Whatever he had done, no matter her past grievances, there was nothing that could separate them again. He had willingly given up his fortune to save her. Could he have shown his love more clearly than that? Even Wagstaff had seen it in his eyes.

Jace knelt by the creek and filled the bucket, then stood and handed the lantern to Callie. He took her other hand in his and led her back toward the cabin.

His fingers were warm and comfortable in hers, and his strong face, lit by the golden light of the lantern, wore an expression of serenity. *We belong together*, she thought in wonder. *We always did.*

As they neared the cabin door, she put down the lantern. ''Wait,'' she said, unwrapping the neckerchief from her riding shirt. ''You look like a hobgoblin.'' She dipped the neckerchief in the bucket of water and gently washed away the blood from his face. ''I did this once before. Do you remember, 'Horace'? That first night?''

''I remember I thought that you were . . .'' His voice was shaking. He took a steadying breath. ''That was a long time ago,'' he muttered.

''Why did you let Wagstaff have all your money?'' she asked softly. ''Without a fight?''

He avoided her glance. "There wasn't much I could do."

"Nonsense. You outsmarted Ben. You could have made sure Sweeney came back with men to surround the cabin."

"And risk your life? Besides, I didn't want Ethan telling about that bank in St. Louis."

"Bosh. No one would have believed him, and you know it. Was it worth every single penny you own?"

"I still have the saloon," he blustered.

She blotted his face with a dry corner of her neckerchief, turning the humble gesture into a kind of caress. Why was he being so stubborn? "Did you do it for me?" she whispered.

He clenched his teeth, clearly fighting his desire. "Let it be," he said in a ragged voice.

She rested her hand on his shoulder. "Jace, we have to talk. There's so much unsaid between us."

"No," he said suddenly, bending toward her. "Not talk, damn it."

She trembled with longing. His deep voice beguiled her senses, and his soft breath, so close to her mouth, was a sigh of promise. *Please kiss me,* she thought.

He shivered and jerked upright. "This is madness. We're all dog-tired. We'll talk in the morning."

"Jace?" All her yearning was in the word.

He stroked the side of her face, his eyes warm and tender. "You're looking well. I meant to tell you." He turned and strode into the cabin. "We'll talk in the morning," he said again.

She went to sleep on a bed of hope.

It had to be the most idiotic thing he'd ever done. Every penny he'd worked for—gone! All those months of labor, all those years of dreaming. Gone in a moment of madness.

The saloon would never make much of a profit; he'd sunk too much money into it. And the silver boom would die out as the mountains were stripped of their treasure. It had happened before, at other diggings. He should probably sell off the Philadelphia soon, before Silver Plume became just another dead town. But he'd have to take a loss. And start over, one more time.

Yet, oddly, it didn't disturb him in the least. He looked toward the cot, where Callie slept sweetly, her copper-gold hair bright in the dawn light that filled the cabin. Perhaps it was the way she had looked at him last night, her eyes soft and trusting. And she had come to him, not Driscoll, to find Weedy. She could have sent someone else. But she'd come riding over the mountains herself to find *him,* to beg his help.

He felt a pang of guilt. He shouldn't have kissed Netta in front of her. That was cruel. To show her he didn't care, he supposed. Though any blamed fool—even that polecat Wagstaff—could see the truth.

He was glad he'd put off their talk last night. They'd all been worn out. And he wanted his wits about him, needed every bit of his charm this morning to persuade her that they should try again. He grinned suddenly, remembering. If he'd kissed her last night, taken those sweet lips, he never would have been able to stop. And she would have welcomed it—he was sure of that. His dear Callie.

He heard the soft nickering of a horse outside and frowned. It sounded as though it was right near the cabin door. But he'd tethered the animals next to a patch of grass. Maybe one of them had gotten loose.

He sat up quietly from the floor and slipped his stockinged feet into his boots, tiptoeing across the room to keep from disturbing the others. He opened the door and swore softly.

Ralph Driscoll rode into the clearing and climbed down from his horse. He signaled to his foreman Carl and handed over his reins before the other man had even dismounted. "You stay here," he said.

Jace stepped out into the early-morning sunshine. "What are you doing here?" he said with a scowl.

Driscoll turned and gave him an oily smile. "Mr. . . . ah,

Greer, isn't it? I came looking for Callie. Mrs. Ackland said she'd gone after Weedy. It took me a spell to realize that Weedy would come running to you. You seem to have become something of a god in his eyes,'' he added with a sneer.

Jace clenched his fists, controlling his anger. ''Weedy is here with me. And safe.''

''You caused quite a stir, and this, that, and the other, when you didn't come back to town last night. I understand the sheriff is getting up a posse this morning to look for you.''

''There was an accident in the mine. No one was hurt, but it seemed wise to spend the night and rest up here.''

''And Callie's with you?'' Driscoll's eyes glittered with jealousy.

''I'm sure you knew that,'' he said sardonically. ''You wouldn't have come for Weedy's sake.''

Driscoll brushed the dust from his coat in a gesture of studied nonchalance. ''I must confess to a certain unease, thinking her alone with you. A woman can't be too careful of her reputation. Particularly if she's alone with a man like you.''

''She's still my wife,'' he growled. He hadn't thought of that until now. *Damn fool Jace,* he thought. He *should* have kissed her last night. And made love to her.

Driscoll eyed him with contempt. ''I think you forfeited the right to call her your wife the day you deserted her.'' He shrugged. ''In any event, the point will soon be moot. You can expect a visit from my lawyer one of these days. To arrange a divorce.''

He felt a stirring of dread. ''What are you talking about?''

''Didn't Callie tell you? We're engaged to be married.''

''The devil you say.'' It *couldn't* be true. Not when she'd looked at him the way she had last night.

''Well, perhaps Callie has been reluctant to tell you until the formalities of the divorce were concluded. She's a woman of refined sensibilities and propriety.''

He felt as though he'd been disemboweled with a rusty knife. Then shock gave way to anger. A woman of sensibilities? Hell, she was a two-faced witch! Leading him on the way she had. And all the while knowing she'd already pledged herself to this snake! Had she done it to amuse herself? Or merely to guarantee his help with Weedy?

He fought to appear calm. He wasn't about to show a flicker of emotion to this son of a whore. He turned toward the tethered horses. "I reckon I should head off that posse. No point in their making the trip up here for nothing."

"And Callie?"

He jerked his thumb toward the cabin. "They're all asleep. When my man wakes up, you can tell him I've gone back to town. Weedy sprained his ankle. He might need a doctor when you get back. To Dark Creek," he added pointedly.

Driscoll nodded. "That sounds wise. No point in distressing Callie further by stopping at Silver Plume." He gave Jace a smile of smug triumph. "You didn't invite me to your wedding. I don't reckon you ought to expect an invitation to ours."

His anger was boiling near the surface. What a fool he'd been, to think she still cared. How she must be laughing at him! "There's a big mountain between Dark Creek and Silver Plume," he growled. "I'd just as soon keep it that way. I have no desire to tangle with you *or* Callie. Ever again!"

She awoke to the sense that someone was watching her. She opened her eyes and started in alarm. "Ralph?"

Driscoll knelt before the cot, a look of deep concern in his eyes. "I'm so grateful you're safe. Don't ever frighten me like that again, dearest."

She sat up and scrubbed the sleep from her eyes. "How did you find me?"

"Mrs. Ackland told me you'd gone to find Weedy. I knew that misguided boy has never had the sense to see Greer for what he is." He groped for her hand and brought it to his lips. "So I came after you. What else could I do?"

She pursed her lips, wishing she were more wide-awake to

think clearly. She couldn't allow Ralph to court her like this. Not after what had happened last night. She looked anxiously around the room. "Where's Jace?"

"Don't trouble yourself, my dear. He's gone back to his own **kind**. Water finds its own level. Even foul water."

She felt the blood drain from her face. "He's . . . he's gone back to Silver Plume?" To his vile woman?

"I saw him leaving as I rode up."

"Without a word to me?" She was devastated.

He looked away, seeming to be embarrassed. "It's of no importance."

"Yes! What did he say?"

"He said . . . forgive me, my dear. He said he never wanted to see you again."

She put her hand over her eyes, trembling in every nerve. She had misunderstood. Misread his easy charm for true affection. Allowed him to beguile her into thinking he still cared for her, when clearly he was happy in his new life. With his new woman.

Curse him! "I never want to see him again, either!" she said defiantly.

Chapter Twenty-Seven

The large red elk lifted its head from its supper of bare willow branches beside the creek and uttered a shrill scream. The sound—like whinnying horses—reverberated across the gulch and left a mournful echo lingering in the air.

Looking for a mate, the poor thing, thought Callie. She slowed the wagon to a halt and gazed out over the gulch, deep in afternoon shadow.

She hadn't made this trip in daylight for weeks—not since she'd begun going back to the store. The morning ride was always shrouded in fog, and it was dark before she locked the shop and started for home. Now she looked out at the countryside and marveled at the changes a few weeks had brought.

The trees were almost bare, and the long stretches of meadow grass had turned dry and yellow. The birds had flown, except for a few hardy chickadees, flitting among the stark branches and calling out their harsh cries. Gone were the green patches of thimbleberries beneath the aspens, and the clumps of rabbitbrush, so lush in summer, had become lacy pin cushions, stripped of their leaves.

Callie sighed. Another winter coming. And although October might bring a brief respite of Indian summer, the snows would follow soon enough. As bleak and lonely as her heart.

She sighed again. Not that it didn't feel good to be back at work. The town had grown over the summer, and the newcomers—unlike the miners and prospectors who came and went—clearly intended to put down roots. They wanted fine furniture, "citified" fabrics, fancy tools for elegant woodworking. And although she'd still have to learn the difference between a gunpaper cartridge and a minié ball, she felt more familiar with the new stock.

And of course she had Dave Culkin to help now. Billy Dee had slipped back into his old drunken ways. Completely useless. She was grateful to Ralph for suggesting Culkin. He had just come to town and needed a job. He'd been sick for more than a year—lung problems, Ralph had said. And although he seemed to have been a rancher before his troubles, he had taken to shop work with enough competence so she could feel comfortable in trusting him.

Comfortable enough to leave him in charge and come home early today. She was restless and unhappy, unable to concentrate. Three weeks since she'd seen Jace again, and she couldn't forget him. The sight of him had revived all her old feelings, reminded her of the few glorious weeks last year when she'd loved and felt loved in return.

Foolish Callie! Why was she still hoping for something that could never be? Jace was gone. She might as well get on with her life. And Ralph was so doggedly persistent, pushing her to announce their engagement, to allow him to arrange her divorce. Well, perhaps she'd give in. The thought of facing another cold winter alone was too disheartening.

She clicked to the horse and started down the road again. Maybe an hour or two at the piano would cheer her. Ralph was coming to supper—an almost nightly event these past few weeks—and his presence had begun to make her feel crowded in. A couple of hours of solitude was just what she needed.

She put away the horse and wagon herself; she couldn't depend on Weedy, whose appearances at home and the store had become sporadic. She was surprised to meet him in the vestibule, pacing nervously, when she came in the door.

"I missed you at the store again today," she said, trying to keep the disapproval from her voice. "Don't you intend to make a future there?"

He ran his hand through his hair, avoiding her eyes. "I want to get married," he muttered.

She gasped. "What do you mean?"

"I love Alice, and she loves me. And she doesn't belong in that place."

"But you're only sixteen!"

He clenched his jaw. "I'm a *man!* Or hadn't you noticed?"

"And how old is your . . . Alice?"

"She's fifteen. She needs someone to look after her."

Her head was reeling. "I won't allow it!"

"Is it because she's a half-breed?" he said bitterly. "Is my big sister as intolerant as that?"

"Don't be absurd. My ladies' circle and I always championed the cause of downtrodden peoples. We rejoiced in the emancipation of the slaves. I'd willingly embrace her as a sister if you were older, and if . . ."

"It's because she's a whore, isn't it!" he burst out.

"That . . . sort of woman is entirely unsuitable," she said primly. "Poppy would be horrified."

His eyes blazed with resentment. "First it's Big Jim, and now it's you, trying to run my life! Jace would have understood."

"Oh, I'm sure he would have!" she snapped, remembering Netta with disgust. "But I won't have you marrying a creature who thinks so little of herself that she can sell her body. It's disgusting! To think of all the men she has . . . accommodated. She's not fit to be around decent folk."

He looked at her with pure hatred. "Go to hell," he said, and stormed upstairs to his room.

She watched him go with a sinking heart. How could she

persuade him that what he proposed was intolerable? To marry a *whore?* A woman who spent her life thinking only of how to please a man in bed! Heaven alone knew what arts they employed, what vile practices they allowed themselves.

She tried to ignore the unwelcome thought that nagged at her. Before they were married, she had thought Jace was relatively inexperienced in bed. It had been a comfort to her virginal mind. But "Horace" the twiddlepoop had turned out to be Jace the confidence man, a man at home in brothels and gambling halls. And—if she admitted the truth to herself—she had looked back in retrospect and wondered if he had found her inadequate. Perhaps her own sexual insecurity made her resent women like that.

She sighed and went into the kitchen. Sissy sat on the floor, looking at a picture book. She picked her up and kissed her, then smiled at Little Jim in his cradle. "Has he been good today?" she asked, bending to caress his downy cheek.

Mrs. Ackland turned from the hot stove and rubbed her damp forehead against her sleeve. "A love, as always," she said. "Don't wake him. He'll want his supper soon, and I need to finish peelin' the potatoes."

"Perhaps I'll give him his bottle and his bath. I don't spend near enough time with him."

"He's the spit and image of his father," said Mrs. Ackland with a pointed look.

"Don't start badgering me again."

"Why not? When you've been mopin' about this house ever since you come back from Silver Plume? But maybe you still don't know what you had. A good man. And after he saved Weedy's bacon, and all . . ."

She chewed at her lip to keep it from trembling. "He doesn't want me. He made that clear enough."

"Land sakes! Then *make* him want you. You've got Driscoll buzzin' around you like a bee to honey. And you're a looker. What ails you, that you can't go after the man you really want? Are you content to settle for Driscoll?"

This conversation was pointless, and too painful. "Where's Beth?" she asked.

"Dunno. Probably prancin' around in Jace's hat. *She's* got sense, at least."

Callie sighed, feeling assaulted from all sides. Ever since they had come back from Silver Plume, filled with stories of Jace's rescue of Weedy and his noble surrender of his fortune to save them, Beth had become a changed child. Where before she had refused to talk about Jace, now she spoke of nothing else, extolling his virtues and pleading with Callie to bring him back. And the hat had emerged from its hiding place.

"I'm going to play the piano," she said tiredly. "Call me when Little Jim wakes up."

She played in a listless fashion; her heart wasn't in it. Her thoughts were far away, drifting on a tide of remembrance. She was startled by a tap on the parlor door.

"May I come in?" Ralph came striding into the room and tossed his hat and overcoat on a chair. "Dearest," he said, pulling her from the piano bench to hold her in his arms.

He bent and kissed her, his mouth hungry and demanding. She tried to respond with warmth. After all, when they married, he'd expect much more of her—though the thought of making love with him gave her an uneasy thrill.

"What are you doing here so early?" she asked, when he finally released her.

"Culkin said you'd gone home. There's a traveling theater troupe in town this week. I thought we might have a hasty supper, then go back to see them."

She hesitated. "I don't know. I have to be in Dark Creek early tomorrow morning. Dora is bringing over several new students to be tutored."

His brow darkened. "I thought I asked you not to take on more pupils. You have enough to do as it is."

"But Dora can't manage alone. And if we should decide to open a school . . ."

"There'll be no school. You don't have the time."

His sharp tone raised her hackles. She hadn't even agreed to their formal engagement yet. "I don't have to take orders from you," she said with some heat. "Not until we're married."

His expression softened. "Callie, dearest," he said, stroking her hair, "I only want what's best for you. Aren't you busy enough with the church? Tell me I haven't made a mistake by giving all my time and money to a project I thought would please you."

She felt a pang of guilt. Thanks to Ralph's money, the new church was already half-built. She and some of the women had even formed a committee, and spent hours poring over plans and consulting with the Reverend Maples. "Of course I'm pleased," she said. "But I'm sure I have time for more pupils as well."

His mouth drooped with unhappiness. "You have time for everything but me."

Her guilt was now acute. "Oh, Ralph, that's not so!"

He brightened. "That cheers me. And perhaps, when we're married, we can sell the store."

Sell Poppy's store? "I never could!"

"Why not? I expect a wife of mine to stay home where she belongs. And that man Culkin can't run it alone, as far as I can see."

"Well, there's Weedy," she said hesitantly.

"Come now, Callie, we both know he's not mature enough yet."

She sagged in despair. "I know. I don't know what to do with him. And now he's talking about marrying that woman of his."

He scowled. "Dash it all, I won't have it! That young man needs a good talking to!"

"I wish it did any good."

He gave her a comforting pat on the shoulder. "There, there, little girl. I'll take care of it."

"Howdy!" Beth came bounding into the room, clutching

her hat to her head. Her bright smile faded at the sight of Ralph. She gave a sullen curtsy. "Hello, Mr. Driscoll."

"Well, now, missy," he said in a hearty voice. "Didn't I ask you to call me Uncle Ralph?"

"You're not my uncle," she said in disgust. "And even if you marry Callie, you won't be my uncle."

"Beth!" said Callie in horror. "Don't talk to Mr. Driscoll that way."

Beth pouted. "You stopped being Miss Don't when *Jace* was here."

"I won't have that man's name mentioned in this house," said Ralph sternly. "He's caused your sister enough grief."

"I *liked* Jace. Dang my britches, but he knew how to laugh. *He* wasn't an old killjoy!"

Ralph's eyes had gone cold. "Your sister doesn't like you to use slang. And I don't want you wearing that hat in my presence anymore."

Beth stamped her foot. "I'll do what I want. I *hate* you!" She gave him a last defiant glower and raced from the room.

Callie twisted her hands in dismay and embarrassment. "I'm so sorry," she said. "I don't know what's gotten into that child."

"She has become painfully precocious and obnoxious," he said stiffly. "I don't know why you can't control her."

She felt his words as a condemnation. Why did he always make her feel so uncomfortable and edgy? He always seemed to be pushing her to do things she didn't want to do. Or couldn't do, without his support. She'd never felt so helpless with Jace, or even Big Jim. They might have tried to dominate her, but it wasn't the same. They pushed her to make her stronger and more independent, not to make her feel inadequate, useless without their strength.

"I do the best I can," she said defensively. "It can't be easy for any of the children. To have lost both Mummy and Poppy in less than two years."

He put his arm around her. "I quite understand. And I'm

Sylvia Halliday

proud of you for managing as well as you have. And now that you have me to help you, things will be better. Tell you what. Why don't you go and change for the theater, and I'll have a talk with Weedy.''

She dressed slowly, filled with misgivings. On the one hand, it was nice to share her burdens. But was it worth giving up her independence? She'd managed to be strong since Jace had left, to learn to stand on her own two feet—in every way. Now here she was meekly dressing to go to an evening affair she had earlier refused.

Her mother had allowed Big Jim to rule her because there had been love between them. She knew that now. But did Ralph love her enough to be a gentle tyrant, as her father had been? Or would he simply squash her—and Beth as well?

Beth came racing into the room, her face twisted in dismay. "Callie, come quick to the shed!" she cried. "Mr. Driscoll is beating Weedy! I can hear it through the door."

"Oh, my Lord!" Callie dashed down the stairs and ran outside. She could hear the terrible noise from the toolshed even before she reached it: a loud whack followed by a yelp of pain from Weedy. She tried the latch on the door, groaning in frustration as it refused to give. There was the sound of another blow. This time Weedy howled.

Callie pounded on the door. "Ralph! Stop that! Open this door!" She was sobbing with rage. Beth jumped up and down beside her, squealing in anguish.

The punishment continued, Weedy's cries following each sharp crack. She pounded again, screaming Ralph's name until her throat was sore. She was ready to send Beth for Mrs. Ackland. Perhaps, between the two of them, they could force the inside lock.

The noises stopped abruptly. Callie heard the sound of the bolt being pushed back, then Ralph emerged from the shed, buckling on his wide leather belt. In another moment, Weedy came limping out, pulling up his galluses. His face was a bright red of shame, his cheeks wet with tears.

He wiped angrily at his face and glared at Callie. "Damn you!" he spit, and turned and raced for the stable. Beth whimpered his name and followed him.

Callie whirled to Ralph in outrage, her hands clenched into shaking fists. "How could you?"

He seemed insulted by her anger. "What do you mean? You wanted me to take care of Weedy for you. Well, by gum, he'll think twice now before he marries that girl of his. Isn't that what you wanted?"

"I didn't want you to *beat* him."

He shrugged. "Sometimes it's the only way to keep people in line." He gave her a wry smile. "When we're married, little girl, you'll feel my hand from time to time, if it's necessary."

She stared at him, dumbfounded. "Marry *you?* My God, I'd have to be mad!"

He frowned in bewilderment. "But Callie, I only gave him what he deserved."

"Don't say another word," she said, holding up her hands as if to shield herself from his vile presence. "Or I'll lose what little respect I still have for you."

She heard Beth's voice, crying Weedy's name, and turned. Weedy was on his horse, galloping around the house toward the front gate. Beth ran after him sobbing, her pigtails flying, her bowler hat long since gone. As Callie watched in horror, Beth tripped over a large boulder and went sprawling. She screamed, then lay still.

Callie was at her side as fast as she could reach her. She knelt before her sister. "Beth, sweetie, what is it?"

Beth pointed a shaking finger to her arm. It was bent at an unnatural angle, as though she'd suddenly developed another elbow on her forearm. She looked up at Callie with terror-filled eyes. "It hurts bad," she whispered.

Ralph came running up. "I'll go into town and fetch the doctor. We'll have the little missy fixed in no time."

Callie rose and faced him, her lip curling in disgust. "Don't you dare to come back with him," she said, "or I'll run you off with a shotgun!"

Callie gestured to the man on the ladder. "Culkin, if you're finished with those tubs, go out back to the storeroom and unpack that case of calico."

"Sure enough, Miz Perkins," wheezed Culkin, climbing slowly down from his perch. He nodded politely at Dora, then shuffled into the other room.

Dora watched him go. "He seems to be working out just fine," she said.

Callie straightened a stack of boxes on the counter. "He's slow, of course. I don't know what happened to his lungs, except that he nearly died. But he gets to the work in his own time, and he's clever enough. And sober, thank heaven." She smiled knowingly at Dora. "But you didn't interrupt your busy morning to come and talk about Culkin."

Dora stirred uncomfortably. "No. First of all, when the Ladies' Church Committee met yesterday, we agreed that we could hold the opening social in a month. Mrs. O'Neill thought the pews would be finished by then, and Mrs. Llewellyn feels sure the cushions and draperies will arrive in time. And Mr. Driscoll . . ." She paused and looked at Callie. "I'm sorry. I don't know if you want to talk about it."

Callie had stayed home since Beth's accident; her curiosity was aroused. "What did Ralph say?"

"Only that he no longer entertains hopes of your marriage. What happened the other day, Callie?"

She snorted. "I came to my senses. I've spent these last two days feeling more free than I have in months, as though that man had been a stone around my neck, and I didn't even know it." She shook her head. "I don't know how I'm going to be able to work alongside him on the committee after this."

"Well, we can't very well ask him to leave! Not after all the money he's raised. And given from his own pocket, as well.

Mercy me! I never saw a man grow so rich in such a short time. When he came to Dark Creek two years ago, his bank was struggling.''

''Maybe he struck silver, like Jace,'' she said with sarcasm.

''But would he give it all up for you?'' asked Dora softly. Callie had told her the whole story of Ethan Wagstaff.

She felt her pain anew. ''Don't, Dora. He didn't give it up for me. He gave it up so he wouldn't have to be tormented by Wagstaff the rest of his life. And maybe it still troubles his conscience that he killed Ethan's brother and stole their money in the first place.'' She sighed, remembering the hard and cynical Jace she'd seen in his saloon. ''If he still has a conscience,'' she added.

There was an uncomfortable silence. ''How's Beth?'' Dora asked at last. ''The doctor says it's not a bad break.''

Callie swallowed hard. ''She's in pain. And crying for Jace. It breaks my heart. I almost didn't want to come in today.''

''Oh, my dear. I'm sorry.''

She could no longer stem the tears. ''Oh, Dora,'' she cried, ''it just gets worse. I don't know where Weedy is!'' She didn't have the courage to tell Dora of Weedy's beating at Ralph's hands. His pain and terrible humiliation. Not when she felt so responsible for it. Somehow, she should have seen Ralph's dark streak a long time ago.

Dora stared in surprise. ''He's been in town since Monday. I thought you knew. He married that girl Alice. He's living with her in . . . her establishment.''

That was the final blow. ''What am I to do?'' she sobbed. ''I feel so helpless. Jace was the only one who could reason with Weedy. I feel as though it's all my fault. The children had Poppy and Jace. And now, because of me, they have no one.''

Dora shrugged. ''Then get him back. For the children's sake.''

She chewed at her lip, sniffling back her tears. For the children's sake. Yes, of course. Jace had a responsibility to the family, didn't he? They depended upon him. How dare he cut them out of his life! Because he found his new life more pleasant?

"Yes, indeed," she said firmly. "He had his nerve, running off that way and leaving the children to mourn. I intend to make him aware of his obligations. Including his son!"

She had a sudden disquieting memory of Netta, dazzling in her fancy gown. It would take more than words to persuade Jace. She crossed to a shelf and took down a large box, rummaging among its contents until she found what she wanted. She pulled out a bright violet dress, low-cut and figure-revealing, and lavishly trimmed with bows and ruffles. The sort of dress the sporting girls came to buy every day in the shop. "For ammunition," she said, in answer to Dora's startled look.

Dora laughed. "Good for you, lovey."

She must be mad—to dress like a tart! "It's only for the children," she said.

Then why did Big Jim's dying words come back to her at this very moment? *Grab hold of life while you have it.*

Chapter Twenty-Eight

Callie pulled off her hat and long coat and draped them over her saddle. *Drat!* she thought, putting a hand to her hair. She must look a sight. She'd dressed her curls in the latest fashion before she'd left Dark Creek—front piled high on top of her head, back twisted into a thick chignon—but several strands had come loose. She tucked them into place, then smoothed down her skirts and petticoat, praying that her bustle didn't look too crushed, nor her skirts too rumpled. It had been an uncomfortable trip, what with her tight corset, and her skirts hiked up to her knees so she could ride astride. And she wasn't used to thin drawers against the saddle.

She hesitated, staring down at the bodice of her dress, then adjusted it so her breasts rose more provocatively above the low neckline. If she was going to play this part, she might as well play it to a fare-thee-well! She ignored the stares of the passersby. "Sporting gals" weren't afraid to exhibit their charms.

She laughed softly, ironically. *What would Poppy think of his Mousekin now?* She'd come a long way from the shy Callie of a year ago. Still, her nervousness increased her slight limp as she made her way to the door of Jace's saloon.

Though it was still only midafternoon, the barroom was crowded with drinkers and gamblers, filling the air with their noise and tobacco smoke. She cast her eyes quickly around the room. No Jace. She was working up the courage to speak to one of the dealers, when she saw Sweeney behind the bar.

He gaped as she came up to him, staring at her flamboyant gown. "M-Mrs. Perkins?"

She nodded in recognition. "Mr. Sweeney. I'm looking for Mr. Greer."

He shook his head. "Hell, ma'am, you oughtn't to come in here dressed like that, or folks'll get the wrong idea." He shrugged. "Well, it's your call. Jace is in the dining room next door. He don't usually get up for dinner until now."

Head held high, she sailed across the room, conscious of the murmurs of approval. It might be an inappropriate emotion for Boston, but she felt an unfamiliar thrill of pride to be noticed and admired. Even as a tart!

The dining room—a finely appointed space, she noted with surprise—was nearly empty at this hour. Several men sat at a corner table, eating and chatting, and a solitary diner perused the menu.

In the center of the room was a magnificent fountain. Jace sat at a table next to it, the remains of his dinner on a plate before him. In one hand, he held a delicate crystal glass of wine; the other hand held a large cigar, which he puffed in contentment. Netta sat on his lap, her arm draped possessively around his shoulder.

All of Callie's nervousness vanished, to be replaced by rage and burning jealousy. *Look at him,* she thought in disgust. Like some great potentate. The king of his castle. No, by heaven— of his *harem!*

She stormed across the room, her teeth clenched, her blood coursing with angry courage. She ignored the startled jerk of ce's head as he caught sight of her. "If you want this trollop," he shrilled, "you had better divorce me first!"

Netta jumped to her feet. Her eyes scanned Callie, filled with bvious jealousy. "Who do you think you are, sugar, calling e names?"

It pleased her to know she looked so much better than this eature. "I'm his *wife,* you painted slut. And I don't intend see him go to the likes of you!"

Jace gave a low growl. "Callie . . ."

Netta waved a hand at him. "Never you mind, sugar. I reckon etta can take care of this li'l old bitch."

Callie cast her a withering look. "This 'li'l old bitch' has ad just about enough of you." She reached out and gave Netta savage push, tumbling her into the fountain.

Netta screamed and sputtered, thrashing about as the water scaded over her. She struggled to her feet and surveyed her ined gown. "Jace!" she wailed, plucking at her wet hair.

His eyes glittered coldly. He put down his wine and his cigar ith deliberate slowness, then uncurled himself from his chair d rose to his feet, towering over Callie. Without taking his aleful gaze from her, he fished in his vest pocket and threw handful of coins on the table. "Go get yourself a drink from e bar, Netta. *Now!*" he barked, as she bleated a protest.

Netta whimpered, snatched up the coins, and scurried from e room, dripping as she went.

Jace's eyes traveled from the top of Callie's head to the tips f her shoes, lingering on her shameless bosom. "Would you are to explain this?" he drawled.

His cold indifference only fired her anger the more. "You npossible man! How *dare* you abandon us and take up with at whore? Weedy needs you. Beth needs you. The store needs ou. And, damn it, your son needs you!"

He looked stunned, then outraged. "Son of a bitch!" he ared. His eyes shot burning sparks. He grabbed her savagely ound the hips and tossed her over one shoulder.

She shrieked and bucked, pounding on his back, but he

smacked her once on her bustle and she yelped and kept still
suddenly filled with dread. What in God's name had she been
thinking of, to challenge him like this? She didn't feel quite
so brave anymore.

With Callie bobbing helplessly over his shoulder, he stormed
out of the dining room, marched resolutely through the crowded
bar—ignoring the snickers of the patrons—and bounded up
the staircase at the end of the barroom. He kicked open a door
at the top of the stairs, slammed it shut behind them, and set
her roughly on her feet. "Now, what the hell is this about?"
he bellowed.

She stood rocking for a moment, dizzy from hanging upside
down, and wondered why she'd ever come.

"I have a *son?*" he said through gritted teeth.

She gulped. "Since . . . since July."

"Damn! Did you ever intend to tell me?"

She recovered her courage. "I'm telling you now!" she shot
back.

"And why now? Who the hell do you think you are, coming
here to disturb my life, dressed like that?" He scanned her
once more, his eyes narrowing. "And, by God, if you ever
dress like that again . . . !"

She found herself sputtering. "You . . . you tyrant! You have
no right to sound like a husband if you can't act like one! I
came because you have a responsibility. To me. To the family.
Weedy's gone off and married a *whore!* Isn't that shameful
enough to bring you back to your obligations?"

She had never seen such towering rage on his face. He
grabbed her by the shoulders and shook her violently. "I was
raised by whores, damn it! And those women were kinder and
more decent than half the upstanding females I've met since!"
He growled in disgust and pushed her away. "Hell! How would
you begin to understand, with your easy life?"

For all his anger, he suddenly looked lost and abandoned.
Callie felt her own burning anger die, like a flame being doused

he was filled with an aching sympathy. "You never told us," he murmured.

He crossed the room—a small parlor, Callie noticed now—nd stood at the window, gazing out at the street. His stiff oulders were a hostile wall against her. "Of course," he said ockingly. "How careless of me. I should have told you at nce that I'm a bastard. That I don't even know who my parents ere." He gave a sardonic laugh. "I'm sure Big Jim would ave welcomed me with open arms."

She heard the shame and anguish behind his bravado, and ished she could touch him at this moment. "Poppy knew hat you were from the beginning," she said softly. "A good an. That's all that mattered to him. Whether you were Jace r Horace . . . he didn't care. He looked at a person's soul, not is family tree." She burned with remorse. "I was the snob. was the fool. In some secret part of my heart, I could never uite forgive you for pretending to be Horace. It was the lie at colored everything else. I should have trusted you. Under-ood—without having to *know*—what drove you to it."

"When you've led the kind of chancy life I did, you catch t any straw." He shrugged, feigning indifference, though she uld hear the pain in his voice. "The only good things I ever d—enlisting in the army and pretending to be Horace—ended disaster." He spun around, defiance on his face. "Jace Greer oks after himself! That's the only way to live."

"That's not the Jace I knew. Nor Beth, or Weedy. Or Big m. We saw a kindly man, who was always there to help."

He snorted. "That was just the Jace Greer charm. Taking ou in. Playing you all for fools." He swaggered toward her, otioning to the door. "Why don't you get home to Dark reek, where you belong?"

Dear God, he's so fragile! she thought in astonishment. errified of being hurt again. She felt suddenly strong and rotective, guided by her heart, not by his defensive words. You can't chase me away so easily," she whispered.

He turned pale. "What must I do to get you to leave?" he asked in a ragged voice.

She stared at him for a long time, wondering how she could reach him. "Tell me about your mother," she said at last. "Was she a . . . a fallen woman?"

He gave a heavy sigh. "I wish I knew." He sank into a chair, dropping his head in his hand. "I was raised in a brothel in Philadelphia. The only place I ever called home. But I spent the first six years of my life in the hell of an orphanage. We never had enough to eat, but lots of beatings if we complained." He laughed bitterly. "Even in that miserable place, there was seniority. And I was at the bottom of the heap. A foundling. A bastard. Most of the kids had names. Birthdays. Some even had the memory of parents. I had nothing. Only a name they'd given me, that came on the apple crate they found me in. Greer's Orchards."

"Oh, Jace," she choked. She moved to him and knelt before his chair.

He rubbed the sharp angle of his nose. "I got beaten up every other day by the kids for as far back as I can remember. The worthless bastard. The butt of all their jokes. And when one snot-faced tough finally broke my nose, I ran away. I lived on the streets for a while, like a savage, until the whores took me in. I was their good-luck charm. Played the piano, flattered them, listened to all their secrets."

She ached for the little boy suddenly forced to grow up, to see and know far more than he should have. She smiled tenderly and put her hand on his knee. "And learned to charm people. And learned to laugh. How on earth did you do it?"

"An instinct for survival, I suppose. But I damn near didn't make it, except for Sam Trimble."

She stared in surprise. "You named your mine for him!"

"I was turning into a drunken bummer. Like Weedy. Then Trimble came to play piano at the brothel. He'd been a school teacher, fallen on hard times. But he came from a fine upbringing. With a good mind. And God knows I had a lot to learn.

e looked at her, his face haggard. "He was the closest thing
a father I ever had. Except for Big Jim." He swallowed hard
d blinked his eyes.

She found her own eyes filling with tears. The Southgate
ildren had mourned Big Jim. But she saw now that Jace's
in had been infinitely deeper and more poignant. "Jace, my
earest . . ." she began.

He clenched his jaw, shutting the door to his pain, and
enced her with a glare. "Why did you come back into my
fe? To remind me of what I lost? Why haven't you married
riscoll by now?"

"Why should I ever marry him? He was nothing but a bully."

"Then why did you get engaged to him?"

She gasped. "I never did!"

"That's what he told me at the mine, three weeks ago."

"That scoundrel! Is that why you went away and said you
ever wanted to see me again?"

"It seemed like a good idea at the time," he said gruffly.
e studied her face, his eyes dark and unreadable, then reached
t a hand and stroked the side of her cheek. "Why did you
me here?"

She felt suddenly shy and flustered. "I told you. Beth, the
ildren . . . they need you."

He ran a sensual finger across the swell of her breasts.
Dressed like that, as if you thought the old Callie wouldn't
ease me? You could have sent a letter. I would have come."

"I . . . I never thought . . ."

"*Why* did you come?" he said hoarsely.

She looked away, frightened at the intimacy of the moment.
Why did you choose me over your money?"

"I couldn't bear Wagstaff pawing at you," he growled.

She stared at his beautiful face, as filled with uncertainty as
er own. They were two children, standing on the threshold of
wondrous land, fearful to cross over. "Would it make it easier
I said it first?" she whispered. "I love you, Jace Greer."

He reached down and pulled her into his lap, wrapping his

arms tightly around her as though he'd never let her go. "C
Cal, it was so lonely without you. I never thought I knew ho
to be lonely. But it was like someone turned off the sun." I
lifted her chin and kissed her hungrily on the mouth. "I thir
I always loved you. I just didn't know what love felt like."

She returned his kiss, glorying in the sweetness of his mout
"And do you know now?"

"This . . ." he caressed her face, his eyes soft and tend
"and this . . ." he kissed her again ". . . and the warmth I fe
whenever I look at you."

"And you're not sorry about losing all that money?"

"Once upon a time, I thought it was all I needed in life. B
I've got silver shining from your eyes, and the gold of yo
hair. And it's the only treasure that matters to me."

He suddenly grinned and stood up, still holding her in h
arms. "God forgive me," he said with a joyful laugh, "I'
about to take another man's wife to bed!"

She wrapped her arms around his neck and managed a moc
frown. "I don't think that's proper."

He returned her expression with a solemn look of his ow
"Well, then, allow me to be more formal. Mrs. Perkins, w
you marry Jace Greer?"

She glanced toward a partially opened door. "Is that a be
room?"

"It sure is, darlin'."

"Then I think you're going to have to prove to me first th
you're worth marrying."

He kissed her and started for the bedroom. "Is that a cha
lenge?"

She giggled. "It sure is, darlin'."

They smiled and laughed as they tore off their clothes, pull
back the quilts, closed the shutters against the late-afternoo
sun. But when they lay side by side in bed, embracing, Ja
suddenly buried his face in her neck.

"Oh, Callie," he groaned, "I never thought this mome

ould come again.'' He kissed her softly, reverently, his lips
iding over her throat and shoulders and coming to rest on
e round fullness of her breast. He circled her nipple with his
ngue, tasting her like a starving man. All the while his hand
amed her body with thrilling caresses, as though he could
ver get enough of the feel of her.

His lovemaking had never been more tender and gentle. Her
art was moved to tears even as her body responded to him
ith ever-growing ecstasy. He unpinned her hair, ran his fingers
rough the long tresses, inhaled their sweetness. And when he
ally parted her legs and entered her, it was with the same
hurried joy, prolonging their rapture until the final frenzied
oments.

She gasped at his last hard thrusts, raising her hips to enclose
m more fully, more deeply. They were one body, one heart,
e soul. And as the sweet fires of release raced through her
d she cried out, she clasped him to her breast and held him
st. He thrust once more, moaned, then lay still.

Her swelling heart burst with happiness; she dissolved in a
od of tears. ''Oh, Jace, I love you so much,'' she sobbed.

''Tears?'' he said with a quirk to his mouth. ''I've never
d that effect on women before.''

''Tears of happiness.'' She sniffled and smiled up at him,
en chewed at her lip, thinking about what he'd said. ''Am I
disappointment, after all the women you've known?''

His eyes were strangely bright. ''A disappointment?'' he
id, his voice thick with emotion. ''I never made *love* in my
hole life, Cal. Not until you.''

She still felt a pang of doubt. ''And all those other women?''

''What other women? There's only my sweet Callie. And
ways will be.'' He grinned suddenly and propped himself on
e elbow, beaming down at her. ''Now, darlin', are we going
waste time on foolishness, or are you going to tell me about
y son?''

* * *

Mrs. Ackland stood at the door, her hands on her hips, he stout body silhouetted by the lamp in the vestibule. ''Lan sakes! About time you dragged your carcass back here, M Jace!''

Jace jumped from his horse, grabbed Mrs. Ackland aroun the waist, and gave her an exuberant kiss. ''I knew you couldn live without me, Mrs. A.''

''Hmph! You just come back for my cookin'!''

''You've found me out,'' he said with a laugh, reaching help Callie from her horse. His eyes twinkled. ''Besides, m gentle wife, my little Mousekin, engaged in hand-to-hand con bat for my affections. What else could I do?''

''Jace, don't,'' Callie said, feeling herself blush. It still asto ished her, the way the proper and shy Callie had become tigress defending her own.

He winked at Mrs. Ackland. ''I'll tell you the whole sto later, when she's not around.''

The housekeeper looked askance at Jace, then at Callie, the back to Jace. ''You ought to know I'm livin' here now. I' in the spare room.'' It sounded more like a question than statement.

He grinned. ''Don't you fret. I have a bed.''

Mrs. Ackland nodded in satisfaction. ''And about time, to I was afeared Little Jim would never have a brother or sister. She looked out at the night sky. ''It's mighty late. Have y et?''

''We had supper before we left Silver Plume. In my resta rant.'' He shook his head, his eyes mischievous. ''Mighty fi cook I've got there.''

''Get on with you. Can't hold a candle to me, I reckon.''

He fought to hide his smile. ''Oh, I don't know.''

''I'll just go put on a fresh pot of coffee,'' she said nonch lantly. ''And cut a slab or two of my apple pie. So's you c have a snack afore bed.''

He allowed the teasing smile to break forth. "I never thought you'd offer."

"Mr. Jace, you're a devil, and you'll always be a devil! Now why don't you just scoot on upstairs to Beth? She was fussin' too much to go to sleep tonight. She'll be mighty pleased to see you."

"I'll just do that."

"And maybe you can get Weedy to come home. It ain't right, him livin' at the Red Bull and all."

Callie sighed. Everything was perfect again, except for Weedy.

Jace put his arm around her shoulder. "Don't worry, honey. We'll make things right as rain. Now let's go see my Princess."

He was bursting with impatience as they made their way up the stairs, scarcely waiting for Callie to keep up with him. But when they reached Beth's door, he hesitated. "You go in first," he whispered.

Beth was sitting up in bed, nodding sleepily. Her arm was in a sling, and a large book lay across her lap. She looked up at Callie and pouted. "Where have you been all night? My arm was hurting fierce, and there was no one to brush my hair."

Callie crossed to the bed and stroked the curls back from her sister's forehead. "I went to get you a present."

"Don't need any dad-blamed presents."

"Oh, I think you'll like this one." Callie pointed to the door.

Jace stood there, shaking his head. "Miss Don't says it isn't polite to point. Isn't that the gosh darn truth, Princess?"

"Jace!" squealed Beth, nearly leaping from the bed.

"Hold on there. We don't want that other arm broken." He strode across the room, plunked down on the bed, and grabbed Beth in an enveloping hug.

She giggled and laughed, pounding on his shoulder in glee. "Are you home to stay?"

He hooked his little finger in hers, his eyes grown suddenly solemn. "People who make promises on 'pinky, pinky, bow-bell' aren't allowed to break them. Didn't you know that?"

"I hated you," she said quietly.

He nodded, shamefaced. "I hated me, too." His eyes lit on Horace's bowler hat, resting on her dresser. "You still have that old thing?"

"It looks a dang sight better on me than it ever did on you, I'll be jiggered! You looked like the most monstrous silly critter when you rode into town that day."

He rolled his eyes. "Cheese in crackers," he said, pitching his voice higher. "Did I, now? I thought I looked just splendid!"

"Shucks. Don't give me none of your flapdoodle. Not when my arm is hurting." She twisted her face into a grimace. "I broke it."

"So I heard. I suppose now we'll have to think up 'one-armed Princess' games."

Beth dissolved into laughter and tugged at a lock of hair on his forehead. "I'm *so* glad you're home!" She launched into an excited telling of every adventure he'd missed, every game she'd invented since he'd been gone. Jace interrupted with frequent jokes and sly comments that had her giggling.

Listening to their merry banter, Callie felt her heart swell with love and gratitude. She hadn't seen Beth so happy for nearly a year.

At last Jace stood up and dimmed the light. "Time for you to sleep, Princess. If it's sunny tomorrow, I'll carry you outside and we can make stars." He bent and kissed her, tucked the quilt snugly around her, and reached for Callie's hand. Together they made their way into the corridor, closing Beth's door behind them.

Jace smiled and pulled Callie into his arms. "I'm *home*," he said in wonder.

"Aren't you forgetting someone?"

He gave an unsteady laugh. "I was saving the best for last."

She led him upstairs to the spare room, which had become the nursery as well. She could feel his hand trembling in hers.

and his steps were both eager and tentative. She watched him duck through the door, in a gesture that stirred memories and filled her with bittersweet joy. Not even Big Jim had been that tall.

The nursery was lit by a small lamp that bathed the room in gold. Little Jim's cradle sat under one of the eaves, placed on a small dresser. Jace had to hunch his shoulders to come close. He bent over the sleeping baby, gazing in awe at the tiny form. He stroked the downy black thatch of hair on Little Jim's head, slipped a finger into the softly curled fist. He looked at Callie, his eyes bright.

"You can pick him up," she whispered.

He hesitated, then lifted the little body in his arms and held it against his chest. It looked so tiny, so sheltered in that large embrace. Jace moved slowly to a chair and sat down, murmuring endearments to his child.

Suddenly he bent low, his face crumpling, and began to weep. He rocked the baby, swaying back and forth, as great sobs shook his body.

Callie hurried to him, put her arms around him, held him close to her breast until his weeping subsided. At last he looked up at her through his tears, his eyes shining with wonder and a great, transcendent happiness.

Tenderly, she kissed his tear-stained face, her heart bursting with love and joy. "You have what you always wanted, my dearest," she murmured. "A family."

Chapter Twenty-Nine

Mrs. Llewellyn held out the platter of steaming fried chicken. "Perhaps Mr. Perkins would like more, Callie." She smiled in awkward embarrassment. "That is, Mr. *Greer*."

Callie patted her hand in reassurance. "Don't fret, Margaret. I keep forgetting, too. But Jace insisted on the change. He prefers his mother's name. He used it in Silver Plume, you know. That final estrangement with his ·father before he died . . ." She let the rest of her words die away, leaving Mrs. Llewellyn to imagine the mournful details. It was the lie that she and Jace had agreed upon when he'd returned to Dark Creek.

"But my dear! All that fuss with the marriage license, and your son's birth registration."

She sighed. "I know. It was a bother to change them. But what can a woman do when a man's pride is involved?" She reached for the platter of chicken. "I'll just take this over to him."

Callie crossed the large hall behind the church sanctuary, beaming in satisfaction. The opening sociable was going quite well. The congregation had trooped in from the frosty October twilight, toured the new chapel—admiring the architecture and the decor—then repaired to this room for supper. Everyone seemed to be having a good time, and looking forward to the dance that would follow.

There was certainly enough to eat! The women of the committee had been cooking and baking for days, and the buffet table groaned with food. Callie herself had brought a dozen of Mrs. Ackland's raisin and apple pies.

She saw Ralph Driscoll in the center of the hall, talking to his foreman Carl and the Reverend Maples; she carefully detoured around them. She had no wish to speak to Ralph any more than she had to. Certainly not tonight, when he was basking in the gratitude of the townsfolk. He had made no secret of his financial contributions to the new church, boasting that a man of means had an obligation to his community. Still, they had to live in the same town; she and Jace might as well get used to being civil to him, though she'd had to stop Jace from calling Ralph out when he'd heard what the man had done to Weedy.

Jace sat at a long table with several other men, busily digging into their plates of food. As usual, his arm was curled possessively around his plate. Callie felt a pang of tender sympathy and understanding, seeing the starving little boy in the grown man.

She put down the platter of chicken and gently removed his arm from the table. "The food won't vanish," she said.

He looked disconcerted. "Sorry. Habit, I suppose."

She stroked the side of his face, oblivious of the other diners. "And I won't vanish," she whispered.

He smiled, love shining in his eyes, and pulled her down to the empty chair beside him. "You look beautiful tonight."

She smoothed the skirts of her green silk gown, with its elaborately tucked-up bustle, and smiled back. "Do you like it? It comes from Mr. Greer's dry goods store. He has a wonderful eye for the latest fashion."

"Indeed. It will look splendid on the dance floor."

She jutted her chin. "Not if I don't dance. And I *won't,* Jace. I may have found a lot of friends in Dark Creek, but the thought of making a public exhibition of myself in front of them still gives me the megrims. I'm simply too shy."

He smirked. "That would be a surprise to Netta."

She felt her face burning. "That was different."

"No, it wasn't. I watched Mousekin disappear out the window of the Philadelphia Saloon that day. Don't tell me she's come back again."

"But Jace, my limp," she said with a pout.

"Hell's bells, honey, it's scarcely noticeable anymore. You just keep getting stronger every day." He helped himself to another piece of chicken. "You'll dance," he said with a firm nod.

"And if I refuse?" He was really quite impossible!

He gave her a crafty smile. "If you think it's cold outside, wait till you get into bed tonight. I'll only make love to you *once.* Then you'll be sorry."

"Jace! For heaven's sake." She glanced nervously around the table, wondering if the other diners had overheard his words.

But, despite her embarrassment, she felt her body growing warm at the thought of lying with him. In the month since he'd returned, they had behaved like honeymooners—retiring early at night, and lingering in bed in the mornings for as long as they could. She had never known such bliss. To love totally, and be loved in return.

The house rang with laughter from morning till night. Beth, rapidly recovering from her accident, was a joyful sprite. And Sissy, after a day or two of awkwardness, had seemed to remember the warm intimacy she'd shared with Jace before. And though he had made a wry face and called the little girl fickle, Callie knew that he was secretly pleased.

She fingered the large oval locket hanging at her throat—burnished gold, set with a star of pearls. "Thank you again for my present," she said. She had found it this morning beside her breakfast plate.

He beamed. "I thought you'd like it. It's not every day a woman turns twenty-three."

"I couldn't have wanted anything more for my birthday." Except for one thing, of course. The one thing she couldn't have: Weedy back in the bosom of the family.

Jace had reconciled with him the day after his return, and Weedy had appeared at the store the day after that—sober and eager to begin work. But though Callie had assured him that he and Alice would be welcomed home with open arms, Weedy had refused. He couldn't forget or forgive the terrible things Callie had said about Alice. Moreover, he seemed to be convinced that his ill treatment at Ralph's hands had been Callie's doing, and nothing she could say would change his mind. He had continued to live at the Red Bull with Alice, refusing even to allow Callie to meet her.

Disheartened, Callie had welcomed Jace's suggestion that she stop coming to the store. After all, she had her work with the church, and her plans for a schoolhouse with Dora. And her days were busy and happy, filled with Little Jim. Still, Weedy's absence left a hole in her heart.

She shook off her dark mood. Tonight was for joy, not sadness.

Jace put down his fork and knife and pushed away his plate. "I couldn't eat another mouthful. I reckon I'll go outside for a smoke."

Callie saw Mr. Hepworth coming toward them, poking a bit of food from between his teeth. "Here comes our new sheriff," she said. "He looks well fed. Why don't you go with him?"

They stood up to greet Hepworth as he swaggered to the table. "Howdy, Jace. Mrs. Greer," he said. He grinned and polished his shiny new star with the cuff of his sleeve. The town had grown so much over the summer that the governor of the Colorado Territory had promoted Hepworth to full sheriff.

"I'll be damned, Hepworth," said Jace with a snicker. "If you don't stop strutting like a swellhead, you're going to need a larger hat to go along with that badge."

"That's mighty big talk from a feller who's bein' gabbed bout fer the town's first mayor."

Callie stared at her husband in surprise. "You, Jace?"

He grinned. "The old Greer charm. Driscoll may throw his money around, but there aren't many here who want to call im friend. Not when he keeps to himself and travels in the company of those toughs he's hired."

"You keep runnin' the store the way you have," said Hepworth admiringly, "and you'll soon have as much money as im. Mebbe more."

Callie had to agree with that. It had taken Jace no time at ll to assess the needs of the new arrivals in Dark Creek. With he money he'd made from the sale of his saloon, he had xpanded the stock and was already talking about building a arger store. And the mining towns to the west were discovering hat they didn't have to send all the way to Denver for supplies, f Jace Greer could furnish them.

Jace shook his head. "The town sure has grown since last year. A dozen new stores, our own newspaper, the brickyards .. And now, with the new school that Callie and Dora will be opening . . ." He gave Callie's nose a good-humored tweak. 'Hell, honey, we're getting so citified, you won't miss Boston after a while."

She had stopped missing Boston long ago. Dark Creek was illing with solid citizens, and she found the people more riendly than any she'd known before. Or perhaps she had earned to reach out, to put aside her shyness and welcome riendship when it was offered. She hadn't written to her ladies' circle in months. She didn't miss their shallow sociability.

Most of the congregation had finished supper by now. While he women began to wrap up the food and bring out coffee and pie, the men worked at pushing the tables to one side and ining up the chairs around the room.

Callie spied Dave Culkin standing idly in a corner. "Why don't you get Culkin to help you with the chairs?" she asked ace. "He looks like he has nothing to do."

"It might strain his lungs." Jace frowned. "Besides, every
time I talk to him, he gets his back up."

"He was always pleasant to me," she said in surprise.

"Well, he sure doesn't like *me*. From the first day I came
back to the store. I'm glad I let him go. And Hauptmann was
willing to take him on when I asked."

"Yes. That was good of him." Callie moved away to the
buffet table to help with the rest of the platters.

"May I give you a hand, little lady?"

She turned to see Ralph behind her, smiling warmly. It was
as though he had forgotten what had happened.

She acknowledged him with a stiff nod. "Thank you, no
Mr. Driscoll."

He looked as hurt and bewildered as a little boy. "Why have
you behaved so unkindly to me this past month, Callie? After
all I did to be helpful and neighborly in your time of need?"

"I thank you for that," she said coldly. "And the ladies of
the church certainly are grateful. But my husband and I . . ."

"This has nothing to do with Mr. Greer. I would still welcome
your friendship." He put his hand on her sleeve in a gesture
of tender intimacy. "You gave me certain signs of your
affection in the past. Am I now to be your enemy because of
a misunderstanding?"

Signs of her affection. It shamed her now to recall how she
had wantonly kissed him, allowed him to be her companion
and confidant for months, had even tolerated his disrespectful
talk about Jace. Lonely and frightened, she had clung to him
He could scarcely be blamed now for misreading her senti-
ments. She allowed her stern expression to soften. "What's
done is done," she said. "I should prefer that we both forget
what has happened."

He tightened his grip on her arm. "I still feel a great deal
of affection for you, my dear. I assure you, *I* would never have
abandoned you, had you become my wife. And should Mr.
Greer forget his obligations to you in the future, I want you to
know you may rely upon me."

She felt disloyal to Jace by even allowing this conversation. "Please take you hand from my arm."

He leaned in close, his eyes smoldering. "Callie, my dear . . ."

Jace's voice cut in, sharp and controlled. "I think you're disturbing my wife, sir."

Ralph smoothly removed his hand from Callie's sleeve and gave Jace a tight smile. "I choose to consider Callie a friend. It's up to her to say if I'm disturbing her. I hold her in high esteem. I've always made every effort to do what I could to please her."

"Is that why you beat Weedy?" growled Jace.

"I dealt with the problem as I saw fit, sir. It ill behooves you to be critical of my behavior. In view of the fact that you had absolved yourself of any responsibility to the family," he added with a sneer.

Jace's eyes narrowed and he clenched his fists. "Now, by God, sir . . ."

Callie's heart thumped in alarm. In another moment, they'd be at each other's throats. She wasn't at all sure that Jace wasn't carrying a gun on his person. But Carl was, and he had moved closer at the first angry words between the two men.

Spying Culkin across the room, she thought quickly. She slipped her arm through Jace's and gave him a bright smile. "Didn't you want help with the chairs, honey?" She signaled frantically to Culkin.

He shuffled toward them, glaring at Jace. "Mr. Greer," he grumbled, his voice dark with hostility. "Mr. Driscoll. Ma'am," he added with more warmth.

"Will you help Mr. Greer with the chairs?" She smiled at Driscoll. "Ralph, you can help as well. The musicians will be here soon." She could feel Jace's tense body relaxing beside her, and breathed a sigh of relief.

Ralph seemed equally relieved to avoid a showdown. He exhaled his tightly held breath and managed a thin smile. "I wouldn't think of taking you away from your husband, Mrs. Greer. I can manage the chairs with the assistance of Mr. . . ."

He frowned, as though he were trying to remember the name. "Culkin, isn't it?"

The man nodded. "Yup."

"Aren't you working for Mr. Hauptmann now?"

"Yup. Helping him with this, that, and the other thing."

Jace stiffened in surprise. Callie stared, equally surprised. How peculiar that Culkin should use Ralph's very turn of phrase! As far as she knew, the two men had barely spoken since Culkin had come to town a month ago.

Jace leaned forward. "How are your lungs these days, Culkin?" he asked. His deceptively soft voice held a knife edge.

"Tolerable," wheezed Culkin.

"You've only been here for a few weeks, I understand. Where do you hail from?"

Culkin's eyes darted nervously around the room. "B-back East," he stammered.

"Stop badgering the man!" said Ralph. He jerked his head toward Culkin. "Find something to do."

"No," said Jace, holding Culkin with his burning glance. "You never told me how your lungs were injured."

"Well . . . that is . . . an accident . . ." Culkin looked like a trapped rat.

Callie stared at Jace. This seemed like an absurd, intrusive interrogation. Culkin clearly didn't want to talk about it. She was ready to drag Jace away, when he suddenly reached out and grabbed Culkin by the arm, frowning down at the man's hand.

"Son of a gun!" he exploded. He shook off Callie's arm, grasped Culkin's shirtfront, and ripped it open. He clawed at his undervest, while Culkin struggled weakly, and tore that as well. "You snake!" he roared.

"Jace! For heaven's sake, what's gotten into you?" cried Callie.

Culkin wrenched himself away from Jace's hold and backed up. "What the hell is this?"

"I thought I'd killed you," snarled Jace.

Culkin lunged for Jace, his eyes burning with hatred. "Go o hell and pump thunder." He clutched at Jace's throat, but ace struck him a blow that sent him tumbling to the floor.

The scuffle had brought several men running. "Holy Jumpin' ehoshaphat!" exclaimed Hepworth, galloping toward them. 'What are you doin', Jace?"

Ralph eyed Jace with contempt. "If you intend to disrupt his affair, take your quarrel outside. I see no point in distressing he ladies further."

Callie burned with embarrassment. What had possessed Jace o behave like a savage and spoil the party?

Jace pointed to Culkin, still gasping on the floor. "Take a ook at that man's hand, Sheriff. He's got a zigzag scar. Like he road agent I shot a year ago. Point-blank in the chest. I hink you'll find that my bullet was the cause of his 'lung roubles.' "

Hepworth knelt to Culkin and spread his shirt. Callie could learly see the mark of an old wound—a large, round scar in he middle of the man's chest.

They were now surrounded by grumbling men, muttering larkly about Zeke, the stagedriver, cut down in his prime. Carl idled close to Ralph, his tanned face gone pale.

"By gum," said Ralph in a righteous tone, "the man should hang. Better yet, he ought to be taken out and shot on the pot!"

"Good idea, boss," said Carl, whipping out his pistol and iming it at Culkin on the floor.

Callie screamed. In that moment, Jace leaped forward and truck at Carl's hand. The shot was deflected, only grazing Culkin on the shoulder. Jace swore and wrestled the gun from Carl's hand.

Hepworth scowled. "No call to be wearin' a shootin' iron n here, Carl." He dragged a whimpering Culkin to his feet. 'I reckon I got me a purty good cell fer you. Come on."

"Just a minute," said Jace. "There's still something that's nawing at me." He moved to Culkin and glowered at him.

"Everyone knows you came to town without a dime in you pocket. But that was a mine payroll you stole. And I had fiv thousand dollars on me besides. What happened to all tha money?"

Culkin glared at him. "I shoulda put a bullet through you head that day. Made sure you were good and dead."

"But the money," said Hepworth. "Where'd it go?"

"A feller can spend it."

Jace snorted. "Lying in bed for a year?" He glanced a Ralph, then back at Culkin. "And maybe listening to a ma say 'this, that, and the other' for a year?"

"See here!" said Ralph. "What are you suggesting? I'm a upstanding citizen!"

"And a very rich one," said Jace. "Hepworth, there was string of holdups last year, wasn't there?"

"Too damned many."

"Seems to me, you could take a look at Driscoll's books find out when he made large deposits."

Ralph drew himself up in outrage. "Danged, I'll have m lawyer put a stop to that," he growled. He glared at Jace. "An as for you, I'll sue you for slander. This is nonsense!"

Jace gave a sardonic laugh. "Culkin, it's going to be might lonely for you at the end of that rope, unless you have th money for a good lawyer. And you never saw a cent of wha you took, did you? I reckon your boss won't help you. You' be lucky if they don't break you out of jail and lynch you Didn't he want Carl to kill you just now?"

Culkin turned white and began to tremble. "I ain't gonn hang alone!"

"Shut up, you fool!" barked Ralph.

"I ain't nobody's fool," said Culkin with an angry wheeze "He was always promisin' things would be better. Meantime there's me, holed up in the attic so's no one would get wise Coughin' blood fer months 'cause he don't want no docto And when I'm better, what does he do? Gets me a job in damned store!"

Ralph looked nervously toward the door, but Jace brandished he pistol. "I wouldn't move, Driscoll," he said. "My finger's ust itching to blow your head off." He glared at Culkin. "Who else was in on it?"

"Him." Culkin jerked a thumb in Carl's direction. "And Tom Petty and Koop. But they lit out after the last job."

Hepworth scratched his head. "Wal, I think we got enough o hold 'em till the judge comes to town." He gestured toward several of the men crowded around. "Grab ahold of these varmints. Let's get 'em locked up."

With Jace training the pistol on a crestfallen Ralph, the three men were roughly escorted from the hall.

Callie sank into a chair, limp with exhaustion. The room buzzed with gossip as people exchanged stories, exclaimed in horror, swore they'd always known Driscoll was no good. Dora Watts and Margaret Llewellyn hurried over to Callie, eyes wide with dismay. How could they go on with a festive sociable, when the church's chief benefactor had just been carted off to ail?

"Mercy sakes!" said Mrs. Llewellyn. "Do you suppose all he money he gave the church was *stolen?*"

They quickly gathered up the rest of the committee and the Reverend Maples to decide what was to be done. In the end, hey agreed that the money was already spent anyway, and the church had a new building which ought to be properly cele- brated as they'd planned. After all, other folks had contributed money. Honest money.

Dora signaled the musicians to begin playing, and Margaret went off to supervise the serving of pie and coffee.

Callie sighed. "I think I'll go outside for some fresh air until Jace comes back." Her head was still spinning from the suddenness of Ralph's fall from grace.

The air was cold and crisp, reviving her spirits. It smelled of snow. She hoped it wouldn't snow before next week and ruin the Halloween party she and Beth had planned.

She smiled to herself. Beth would explode with pride, completely "bust her britches," when she found out about Jace's heroics tonight! And, truth to tell, the thought of Jace gave Callie herself a glow of pride. He was a nameless foundling who had made a man of himself with nothing but fierce determination.

She felt blessed to be his wife.

She looked up and down Front Street. It was lively tonight. The saloons and gambling halls rocked with activity, patrons falling out of the doors to stagger down the street, their breaths hanging frosty in the air. But there were unmistakable signs that the town was growing up. The noise seemed less raucous, the patrons came as often from hotels and restaurants as saloons, and several of the wilder variety halls had become Eastern-style theaters, catering to women and families. Callie felt a sense of peace. *Poppy was right. Our future is here, in this vibrant territory.*

She heard the crunch of footsteps on the frozen ruts of the road, echoing above the piano music of the saloons. Jace and the other men were coming back from the jail.

Jace grinned in satisfaction as he strode toward her. "I always knew that Driscoll was no good."

She shivered. She might have married Ralph.

Jace put his arm around her. "Hell's bells, honey. You must be frozen. Why did you come out here?"

"To wait for you."

He waved his arm toward Hepworth and the others. "You folks go on in. I have some unfinished business."

As the men trooped into the church, Jace pulled her into his arms. He kissed her hungrily until she forgot the cold—lost in the wonder of his burning mouth, his comforting arms. He lifted his head and leered. "I think we'll go home early tonight."

"You're feeling very smug, aren't you?" she said with a sniff.

"Why shouldn't I? It's not every day that an old confidence man gets to lock up another one. Especially a scoundrel like Ralph Driscoll."

Though his arms were warm, she shivered again. "I might have been *Mrs.* Ralph Driscoll. I was such a fool."

"Hell, no. You've got more sense than that. You would have seen him clear, long before the wedding."

She still had doubts. "I was ready to marry Horace Perkins, because Poppy wanted it."

He took her by the shoulders and gazed into her eyes. "Not the Horace Perkins *I* met. You would have tossed him out within the week. No matter what your father wanted. Cal, don't you know it yet? You're *strong*. You've got a streak of Big Jim in you, if you'd let it come out. Stop hiding behind Mousekin, like you hid behind your cane."

She wished she had as much faith in herself as he did. "Let's go inside. I can hear the music already."

The dance was in full swing—a lively reel that shook the hall and showed off the colorful, swirling skirts of the ladies. Several of the bystanders clapped Jace on the shoulder as they passed, complimenting him on the capture of the road agents.

Jace steered Callie toward the dessert table. "I'll just have me some pie and coffee. And then, when they play a slow waltz, we'll dance."

She opened her mouth to protest, then sighed and kept still. She dreaded the moment, wondering how she could endure the stares of her neighbors. Surely they would all be watching to see how lame Callie compensated for her limp.

The reel was over. The fiddlers tuned their instruments and swung into a graceful waltz. Jace put down his coffee and held out his arms. Callie swallowed hard, watching the other couples gathering on the dance floor.

The dancers stopped. The music died abruptly. Several people gasped, and a group of women began to whisper excitedly, indicating the door with their fans. Even the Reverend Maples looked distraught, nervously tugging at his collar. Callie followed the direction of their gaze.

Weedy stood in the doorway in his Sunday best, a young girl on his arm. She was extraordinarily pretty, with black hair and dark, soulful eyes. She had a dusky complexion and fine, high cheekbones, a testament to her heritage. She wore a bright red gown, though all the gaudy trimming seemed to have been removed. She looked shy and frightened, and terribly young, clutching Weedy's arm as though she were afraid to let go.

Callie gaped at Jace. "What are they doing here?" she whispered.

"I invited them," he said calmly. "It seemed a fitting birthday present. A good time for you to meet your sister-in-law."

"For heaven's sake, Jace! *Here?* Look at the women's faces. How can you ask respectable folk to mingle with a . . . a woman like that?"

His jaw tightened. "They'll accept Alice if we do. Unless you still think you're better than she is."

She had no more reservations. Whores had given Jace love, had helped to make him the splendid man he was today. "Of course not," she said firmly. "But we can't just let them stand there, humiliated by everyone." She looked expectantly to him, waiting for him to take charge, as he always did. "We *can't.*"

He made no move toward Weedy and Alice. "No, we can't," he said quietly.

She saw the look in his eyes. Trusting, but stubbornly firm in his resolve. She would have to do this alone.

She took a deep breath and moved hesitantly toward Weedy and Alice, feeling her confidence growing with every step. By the time she reached their side, her head was erect and proud, her shoulders set with determination.

She held out her hands to them and led them into the center of the hall, as the dancers fell back in shock. She scanned her neighbors with a slow, deliberate glance.

"What kind of people are you?" she asked, her voice strengthening with indignation. "Have you no Christian charity? Are we celebrating this new church as a tribute to God, or as a testament to our bigotry?" She glared at the Reverend Maples, hanging back in dismay, and wished he had more backbone.

"Mrs. Watts and I will soon be opening the new school," she went on. "Shall we teach your children goodwill and love, or hatred and intolerance?" She pointed a finger at a man who stood in a corner, his face tight with sanctimony. "You there, Mr. Wilkinson. I remember when you were down to the hard-pan, scrabbling to make a strike. Big Jim gave you credit for months, until you found gold. Is this how you treat his kin?"

She glowered at Mr. Llewellyn, who was trying unobtrusively to sneak his wife out the door. "And you, Mr. Llewellyn. My husband has just saved you from a financial loss. I'm sure Mr. Driscoll's bank account has enough to repay what was stolen from the Eureka Mine."

Shamefaced, Llewellyn stopped in his tracks and nervously eyed his wife. She looked as though she were distancing herself from him. "I, for one, think we owe a debt of gratitude to the Greers," she said.

Wilkinson harrumphed loudly and hurried over to the musicians. "Why the Sam Hill did you stop? Play on!"

As the music started up again, Callie exhaled with relief. She smiled gently at Alice, and patted her hand. "Welcome to the family, my dear." She embraced Weedy, overjoyed to see his warm smile.

"I've missed you," he said.

Jace was suddenly beside her, beaming. He bowed to Alice. "May I have this dance, Mrs. Southgate?" Alice blushed and nodded in gratitude.

Her heart bursting, Callie watched them take a turn around the room. Soon the floor was filled with dancing couples. There was scattered applause from the spectators, and calls of encouragement and support. Weedy smiled tearfully at Callie and squeezed her arm.

Then Jace handed Alice off to Weedy and held out his arms to Callie. "Mrs. Greer?"

She melted into his embrace, allowing him to guide her in the steps of the waltz. She was floating on a tide of happiness, barely conscious that she was dancing.

He couldn't seem to stop grinning. "Son of a gun, if you're not pure gold, Cal. Big Jim would have burst his buttons to see what a pip of a daughter he has." The grin deepened. "But I think he always knew that. I sure did."

She had never felt more proud, more conscious of her own worth. "Mousekin was the only one who didn't know, I suppose," she said. Big Jim had called this their "great Western adventure." And surely the past year had been filled with wonders—not least of which was this wondrous man who held her so tightly and smiled at her with love in his eyes.

"I think we'll have to enlarge the house," he said. "Little Jim will need a room of his own, one of these days. Maybe we can build a small cottage next door for Weedy and Alice. I want my family close at hand."

She hesitated, then lifted her head and kissed him tenderly on the mouth. Who cared if everyone was watching? "I think we ought to consider building on several rooms," she murmured. "I'm not sure yet, but I suspect we'll be able to make an announcement by Christmas."

He stopped dead in the middle of the floor, his eyes shining. "Cal, honey," he said in a choked voice.

"Have you ever had a Christmas, Jace?"

He swallowed hard. "No. Not beyond a few presents from the whores. I used to hang around the houses in Philadelphia, freezing my tail off and peeking through windows at the families gathered around their trees. It looked so wonderful."

Her heart ached for the sad little boy. "You'll like our Southgate Christmas. Poppy always wanted it done up brown."

He held her tightly, oblivious of the dancers who swirled around them. "Do you know how much I love you?"

"I think I do," she whispered. "But no more than I love you."

He released her and gave an exuberant shout, throwing his arms wide. "Listen to me, everyone!" he cried. "I want to make this official. Reverend Maples,"—he turned and grinned at the minister—"you married us once as Perkins. Can you do it again as Greer?"

The reverend looked startled. "Well, it's highly improper, of course. But I don't see why not. Now that you've decided to use your other name."

"Good! In that case, I'm inviting everyone in this room to the best damn wedding Dark Creek has ever seen!" He smiled at Callie, his blue eyes twinkling. "Is that all right with you, darlin'?"

She smiled back. "Cheese in crackers, I thought you'd never ask."

He whooped again and pulled her into his arms, kissing her with a passionate fervor that took her breath away. Behind her, Callie could hear the giggles and pleased murmurs of the townsfolk.

Strangely enough, she didn't feel at all shy.

ABOUT THE AUTHOR

Sylvia Halliday has written more than a dozen acclaimed historical romances including *Summer Darkness, Winter Light* and *The Ring,* published by Kensington Books. Writing as Louisa Rawlings she is the author of *Forever Wild,* a finalist for the RWA Golden Medallion for Best Historical Romance, *Promise of Summer,* which received the *Romantic Times* Reviewers Choice Award for Best Historical Romance set in France, and *Wicked Stranger,* which was a finalist for an RWA Rita Award for Best Historical Romance of 1993. Born in Canada, raised in Massachusetts, she now makes her home in New York City. Her mailing address there is P.O. Box 422, Cooper Station, New York, N.Y. 10276.

SPINE TINGLING ROMANCE
FROM STELLA CAMERON!

PURE DELIGHTS   (0-8217-4798-3, $5.99)

SHEER PLEASURES   (0-8217-5093-3, $5.99)

TRUE BLISS   (0-8217-5369-X, $5.99)